Discerning Grace

EMMA LOMBARD

THE WHITE SAILS SERIES
BOOK ONE

ISBN: 978-0-6451058-0-3

This book uses British English spelling conventions.

ACKNOWLEDGMENTS

My deepest thanks to:

My very first readers, the lovely Team Fraser lasses: Beth Kitson, Jo Guscott, Nicole Lloyd, Raylene Williams, Ruth Camejo, and Sherien Vaughan, who deserve sainthoods for persevering through those rough first drafts and for indulging me in endless hours of Book Club feedback; Taya Bessell, whose constructive critique and constant encouragement kept my fires of motivation lit; Lieutenant Commander Grahame Flint of the Royal Navy—a fount of knowledge about historical shipboard life—for patiently enduring the 'romancey bits' while pulling my wayward armchair-admiral-tactics to order (any character delinquencies are entirely my doing); Andrew Noakes and Shel Sweeney for editorial development that compelled me to write a better story; Simon Houska, whose lack of brotherly inhibition lovingly delivered butt-kicking scrutiny of my manuscript during multiple rounds of reading; and last but not least, my four sons: Ethan, Rory, Dale and Travis who have listened to me gush about my plots and characters with a graciousness well beyond teen-tolerance levels.

Come join the crew! Subscribe to my newsletter at
www.EmmaLombardAuthor.com
for fun giveaways and to receive advance notice about future
book releases.

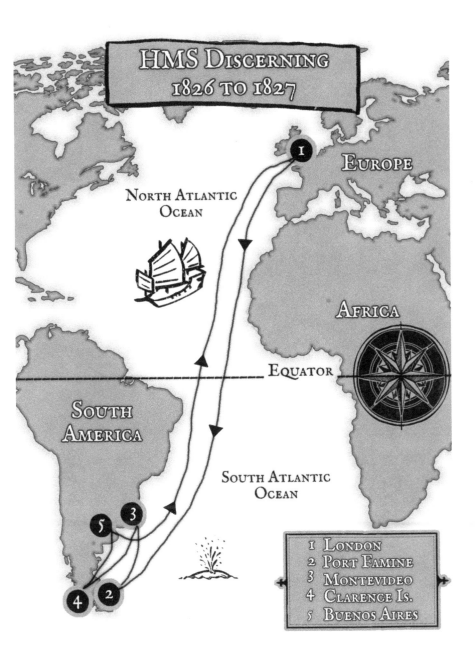

HMS DISCERNING
1826 TO 1827

EUROPE

NORTH ATLANTIC
OCEAN

AFRICA

EQUATOR

SOUTH
AMERICA

SOUTH ATLANTIC
OCEAN

1 LONDON
2 PORT FAMINE
3 MONTEVIDEO
4 CLARENCE IS.
5 BUENOS AIRES

In memory of Kerry Bronwyn Peacock. Life is but a stopping place; you'll never walk alone, my friend.

Chapter One

A deep-throated rumble of laughter drew Grace's eyes across the crowded drawing room and over to Uncle Farfar. Heading over to him, she admired the double row of gold buttons on his blue naval coat glinting in the luminescence of the gilt chandelier above. The crystal beads cast a sprinkling of starlight around the room. The evening had a distinctly tropical aura, with wide-fronded palms and vines spilling from all corners in a waterfall of greenery. Mother's décor was fanciful and faux.

Uncle Farfar beckoned a young man, the single epaulette on his right shoulder announcing that he was a lieutenant in His Majesty's Royal Navy.

"Ah, Fitzwilliam. Just in time," beamed Uncle Farfar, his face flushed with pleasure. Uncle Farfar was actually Admiral Arthur Jameson Baxter, highly decorated for his successful engagement in Admiral Nelson's campaign at the Battle of

Trafalgar. He had lovingly endured the childhood nickname Grace had bestowed upon him when she was eighteen months old and unable to pronounce his name, Uncle Arthur. He had not escaped the deep weathering of a man who had spent his life at sea, and though his face was much rounder these days, he still had a kindness in his eyes.

Centring himself between Grace and the new arrival, Uncle Farfar said, "Lieutenant Seamus Fitzwilliam, may I introduce you to Miss Grace Baxter, my niece and the delight of my life."

Grace smiled politely, admiring the shades of gold shimmering across Fitzwilliam's smoothed-back hair, caught tidily in a black silk ribbon at his graceful nape.

"The pleasure is all mine, Miss Baxter," said Fitzwilliam, formally kissing her hand.

"Lieutenant." Grace took her hand back, fingers curling, and Fitzwilliam clasped his own behind his back.

Uncle Farfar's sharp eyes flicked across the room, and his cordiality shrivelled. "God save us, see who approaches? Lord Silverton."

Lord Silverton appeared closer to a hundred years old, despite him only being in his early fifties. He was also a childless widower of renowned wealth and lineage. His bulging midriff announced no shortage of good food. He had been a mysterious figure on the outskirts of Grace's life since she could remember, but no number of years had lessened her discomfort around him.

"Your servant, madam," drawled Silverton, bowing stiffly.

Grace dipped her head in greeting, lowering her gaze from Silverton's beady eyes to the neatly tied cravat at the base of his bulbous, waggling chin. How could any respectable lady willingly draw herself to the attention of this crusty, timeworn creature?

"Your gown is simply delightful, Miss Baxter," said Silverton. "Reminds me of the gossamer wings of a dragonfly." Silverton's obtrusive stare only blackened Uncle Farfar's mood further. Oblivious, Silverton droned on, "Fascinating creatures! Dragonfly rituals of courtship may appear romantic to those inclined to observe the world through rose-coloured spectacles, but the amazing show of flips and spirals is usually the female trying to escape the boorish behaviour of the males."

"I cannot possibly imagine how *that* feels," Grace muttered, peering impassively around the crowded room. Fitzwilliam's quick, dry cough sounded suspiciously like a laugh, and Grace studied him from the corner of her eye. His face betrayed nothing.

Just then, the butler rang the bell.

Silverton's beady eyes fixed on Grace. "Would you care to dine with me this evening, Miss Baxter?"

Uncle Farfar cleared his throat. "If you don't mind, Silverton, I'd appreciate my niece's company this evening."

Uncle Farfar drew Grace away before Silverton could say anything more and ushered her into the dining room. Fitzwilliam followed two steps behind with his allotted dinner companion, Miss Pettigrew. Her petite hand curled in his elbow, and her coifed black hair barely met his shoulder. Grace had made her acquaintance only once before and realised with a sinking heart that she was in for an evening of little to no conversation with the demure creature, should she be stuck beside her. The stretched table was laid with the snowiest of linen and set with such precision that even the King of England would have been pressed to find fault.

Uncle Farfar waved at the empty chairs. "Would you care to sit between Lieutenant Fitzwilliam and me, Grace dear? You might need to give me a kick under the table if we bore you with too much naval chatter."

Grace sank into her chair. "Nonsense, Uncle. I do so enjoy your tales."

Fitzwilliam waited for Miss Pettigrew to be seated as she

gave him a simpering smile. A wave of relief washed over Grace at not being stuck with Silverton for the evening.

Uncle Farfar clearly had the same thoughts, and he chuckled, "At least you're squirrelled with us, away from that pompous windbag."

Grace peered down the long table, her eyes narrowing as she caught Silverton's eyes, grey as a wolf's pelt, roaming freely across her décolletage. She scratched absentmindedly at the fine lace edging around the low neck of her lavender gown, aware that her unladylike fidgeting would likely irk Father at some point in the evening. But it could not be helped. Lace was so wretchedly itchy.

Fitzwilliam pulled in his chair and nodded at Captain Steven Fincham sitting stiffly opposite him like a squat Napoleonic figure. Dark circles beneath Fincham's bleary, bloodshot eyes gave Grace the impression that he was in poor health, suffering from the crapulous effects of intoxication, or both.

With the soup course over, Grace eyed the line of footmen entering with platters laden with succulent roast lamb. The thin slices were perfectly browned on the outside with just a peek of pink inside. Her stomach grumbled at the rich, buttery scent of the potatoes being served onto her plate. She intended to enjoy every mouthful. At the sound of cutlery pinging on glass, Grace turned her attention to her father, Lord Flint, who rose with his wine glass raised.

"As you know, my dear wife's partiality to dinner parties ensures they happen with alarming regularity." A polite smattering of laughter rippled around the table. "But tonight, we have two guests who deserve our well wishes." Father inclined his bewigged head at Fincham. "Captain Fincham and Lieutenant Fitzwilliam will soon be leaving England's fair shores to expand our great nation's knowledge of the world." His crystal cut glass glimmered in the candlelight. "To a safe and prosperous journey, gentlemen."

"To a safe and prosperous journey," echoed the diners.

Uncle Farfar's grey head peered around Grace at Fitzwilliam. "Where are you off to this time, Lieutenant?"

Relieved to be released from Fincham's melancholy and Miss Pettigrew's muteness, Grace widened her eyes, equally interested to hear his answer.

"Plymouth first, to pick up the rest of the ship's company and fresh supplies, before we sail to Tierra del Fuego," said Fitzwilliam.

"Damned notorious waters off the Horn of South America, eh?" declared Uncle Farfar.

"That's right," interrupted Fincham, his unsteady hand lowering his empty glass to the table. "We're sailing out tomorrow on the *Discerning*. To chart the coasts between Montevideo and Chiloé Island."

"Ah, yes, the hydrographic survey! I recall hearing of it around the Admiralty." Uncle Farfar's eyes blazed. "The Royal Navy has been around those parts for years, but they've few charts to show for it. About time someone had a crack at it." He inclined his head at Fitzwilliam. "Sounds just the kind of adventure a young man like you would relish."

"Indeed, sir," Fitzwilliam agreed.

Grace tucked a chocolate corkscrew of hair that had rebelliously come undone behind her ear. "What a pity you shan't be here for the ball next week, Lieutenant," she said. "Mother will no doubt outdo herself again."

Fitzwilliam was about to reply when Mother's tinkling laughter drew his attention down the other end of the table. Despite numerous suitors declaring that Grace's natural beauty stemmed from her mother, Mother's shrewd eyes and downturned mouth erased all prettiness. Grace glanced back at the handsome naval officer beside her.

"You'll have to pardon me, Miss Baxter," Fitzwilliam said ruefully. "I find society balls to be little more than an exercise in attaching one unwitting party to another, usually for monetary gain."

"Hear, hear!" Fincham banged the table, jangling the silverware. Miss Pettigrew squeaked with fright. Fincham blustered, "The oceans of the world are far less dangerous to navigate as far as I'm concerned."

Grace laughed. "I quite agree, Captain Fincham. Father had me all but married off to Colonel Dunne until he found out he's as poor as a church mouse and about to be shipped off to India." She turned to Fitzwilliam, one brow arching as she whispered from the corner of her mouth, "Dull as a butter knife too."

Clearly amused by her honesty, Fitzwilliam's shoulders jiggled with silent laughter, and he smirked. Grace had never understood how Father threw her at suitors who were highly suitable on paper but wholly unsuitable in person.

Uncle Farfar wiped his lips with his napkin. "Speaking of navigating oceans, when was it you two met again?" His bushy grey brows arched expectantly at Fitzwilliam and Fincham.

Fitzwilliam turned to Fincham, and Grace hoped a little reminiscing might revive the man's spirits. "November 1819, wasn't it, sir?"

Fincham peered over the rim of his glass. "Indeed. I was a lieutenant, and you were but a midshipman. Wasn't it your first voyage around Cape Horn?"

"Yes, sir. We were caught in a gale the devil himself whipped up."

"What an awful experience." Grace smiled with a tinge of sympathy in her voice.

"Not at all," said Fitzwilliam. "Captain Fincham found me quivering under a pile of ropes near the foremast, but instead of chastising me, he lugged me up by the scruff of my skinny neck and forced me to watch the ship and the ocean dance."

Fincham chuckled, but the smile did not reach his rheumy

eyes. "Come now, Fitzwilliam—you were scared witless. Convinced we were going to capsize."

Fitzwilliam pressed a fist to his lips, laughing. Grace dipped her chin, her lips playing with her own amusement.

Fincham offered Fitzwilliam a watery-eyed smile, and shook his head sadly. "It has been a long while since I felt like the reckless young fool I was that day. You were right to be fearful. The sea is a cruel mistress, luring a man in with her sweet songs then breaking his spirit." Fincham rubbed a weary hand across his grey face.

"You gave me a true appreciation and understanding of what it meant to be a navy man that day, sir," said Fitzwilliam.

"Nevertheless." Fincham's chest expanded as he drew in a deep breath. "One more day at sea is one less day to spend on this earth and one day nearer to our eternal home and to my dear Mrs Fincham. I can envisage nothing finer, can you?"

Fitzwilliam's brows tightened. A trill of unease shivered down Grace's neck at Fincham's gloomy words. She was touched to see Fitzwilliam lean forward, lowering his voice. "Perhaps, if you're feeling unwell, Mr Beynon can prescribe you something when we board later this evening, sir?"

"Pah!" Fincham waved dismissively. "That old sawbones already has me drinking his ghastly tea. There's nothing our ship's surgeon can do for me that a fine brandy can't."

With forced buoyancy, Fitzwilliam conceded, "Yes, sir. Nothing revives one's spirits like the clean smell of the open ocean."

As the evening progressed, Grace was keenly aware of Father's growing disapproval from the end of the table. As Uncle Farfar's brother, he was a younger, slimmer version who scowled at Grace when she laughed. Father's ire was also because her fiddling had caused her pins to come loose, releasing even more of her curls. With the meal over, Mother rose to retire to the drawing room, and the party rose with her.

Fitzwilliam turned as Uncle Farfar let out a groan and rubbed his stomach. "It's wretchedly hot in here. I could do with a spot of fresh air," grumbled Uncle Farfar. "Care to join me in the gardens for a cigar, Captain Fincham? Lieutenant Fitzwilliam?" His grey eyes swung to Grace, softening as he offered her his hand. "You're welcome too, my darling Grace. You too, Miss Pettigrew."

Grace, aware that this broke etiquette, flicked a sideways glance at Mother, but she was too enamoured with that lump Silverton to care.

Miss Pettigrew stiffened. "I'd rather not," she said, clearly scandalised. "It would be discourteous to Lady Flint to hurry away so soon."

Grace had no such concern about feigning politeness. She preferred sincerity over the likes of Miss Pettigrew's simpering. "Thank you, Uncle. I'd love to." Grace smiled, placing her hand in Uncle Farfar's palm.

Fincham waved an undulating empty wine glass at a servant. "Not for me, Admiral," he said thickly. "Lord Flint has the most marvellous Duret cognac. Perhaps, Miss Pettigrew, you might like to join me for a drop or two?"

Fitzwilliam hesitated, his eyes fixed on the swaying captain. Glancing between Grace and Uncle Farfar, Fitzwilliam looked set to decline the invitation, but then, turning smartly, he stiffened formally before Fincham. "I think I'll join the admiral, sir." He bowed to his dinner companion. "Enjoy the rest of your evening, Miss Pettigrew."

"Yes, yes." Fincham waved, his shoulders perking back as more wine glugged into his glass. Miss Pettigrew stood beside Fincham, shoulders and mouth curled down.

Uncle Farfar led the way down the veranda steps towards an arbour beneath the boughs of a chestnut tree. In the twilight, oil lanterns cast beams of light among the trees and manicured shrubs, giving the unoccupied arbour a magical glow.

Grace settled on the painted bench, gathering in the silken lavender folds of her gown to make space on either side of her. Fitzwilliam accepted her silent invitation and perched politely.

Uncle Farfar patted down his pockets, growling. "Good God, I'm going mad in my old age. I've left my cigars in the library. Had a drink with my brother in there earlier, before the other guests arrived." His lips pressed together. "Seamus, my boy, I trust you'll take care of my niece while I fetch them?"

"Yes, sir." Fitzwilliam rose automatically and inhaled sharply in likely annoyance. Probably the last thing he had expected this evening was to be left in charge of anyone. "At all costs," added Fitzwilliam.

Uncle Farfar lined the open French doors up in his sights. "Well, let's hope it doesn't come to that. Would be a shame to lose one of His Majesty's finest officers over a scuffle in a garden in Mayfair. Imagine the scandal *that* would cause!"

With her uncle out of earshot, Grace spoke. "At *all* costs?" She tweaked the corner of her mouth up in a mischievous smirk. He surprised her by matching her intense gaze with a widening of his blue eyes. Most men glanced away when she stared so boldly. "Where is it you're venturing to again, Lieutenant? Woolwich first, then on to Plymouth and then Tierra del—Tierra del —" Her cheeks warmed as she stumbled over the name.

"Tierra del Fuego," Fitzwilliam offered helpfully, sinking beside her again.

"Tierra del Fuego, yes. Off the tip of South America."

"Ever been around the Horn?" asked Fitzwilliam with a dip of his head.

"I haven't." She closed her fan and lay it on her lap, genuinely interested. "Is it your first mapping expedition?"

"No, but it is my first in that part of the world. We'll note the physical features of the coastal areas and rivers in the archipelago, and apply our scientific knowledge to predict changes to these bodies over time. For calculating safe navigation routes and determining the economic viability of the coastlines."

Grace shuffled back further on the bench. "How long will the *Discerning* be docked at Plymouth before embarking on her adventure?"

Fitzwilliam hesitated. She knew he had to keep the details to a minimum. She had no authority to know the movements of any naval vessel, but being the only niece of an admiral, her knowledge and interest on such matters was deeper than most.

Recovering, Fitzwilliam said, "Depends on how quickly Captain Fincham fills his crew. Considering his reputation of being a fair man with better-than-average conditions on his ship, I daresay we'll be able to sail within a week."

"I see."

Fitzwilliam shook his head, his tone dry but polite. "Pardon me, Miss Baxter. I must be boring you to tears with all this naval business."

Frowning slightly, she shook her head. "Not at all. It's rather admirable."

"Are you looking forward to the ball next week?" he asked.

She snorted indelicately, and he flicked his gaze at her in surprise.

"*You* might fancy being whirled around the dance floor by would-be suitors who are partial to crushing your toes, Lieutenant." Her voice swelled with humour. "But this isn't the kind of entertainment I favour."

Fitzwilliam's lips twitched. "How providential then that I'm unable to attend. I too am cursed with a toe-crushing affliction."

She scrunched one eye closed. "At least you might have had better conversation to offer than the amorous affairs of dragonflies."

Fitzwilliam chuckled. "I'd probably only bore you with more dry naval talk."

"What entertainment have you to offer now, Lieutenant?" she asked, raising an eyebrow.

"One can't go wrong with literature."

Grace straightened her back. "Oh, indeed. Who's your latest literary interest?"

He cocked his head, scrutinising her. "Dulcinea del Toboso," he replied after a beat.

She paused. "The heroine from *Don Quixote*?"

"Heroine isn't the term one would usually use for Dulcinea," he said. "Perhaps unrequited love interest might be more fitting? Have you read *Don Quixote*?"

Shaking her head, she replied, "I've not. My last governess, Miss Hargraves, wasn't one for sentimental literature."

Fitzwilliam gasped, clearly torn between amusement and indignation at her observation. "Sentimental literature? Miss Baxter, it's one of the greatest novels of all time, replete with philosophy."

"Well then, perhaps you could eliminate this glaring gap in my education?"

"You wish for me to explain *Don Quixote* to you? Now?"

"Well, maybe not word for word." Glancing around the empty arbour, Grace smiled sweetly. "But since I boast no pressing engagements, my ears and undivided attention are all yours, sir."

He nodded and inspected her closely. Grace had laid eyes on plenty of striking men, but there was something magnetic about Lieutenant Fitzwilliam. It was an unfamiliar emotion, one she had never encountered before and not one she was sure she wanted to experience now. She cleared her throat in an attempt to clear her head.

"Her rank must be at least that of a princess," he said, quoting from *Don Quixote*, "since she is my queen and lady, and her beauty superhuman, since all the impossible and fanciful attributes of beauty which the poets apply to their ladies are verified in her."

Grace drew her lips up in a slow smile, and she toyed with the large pearl nestled in the choker around her throat. "I see now why my governess was opposed," she said. "It has far too dreamy a notion for her granite heart." She slid her gaze to his hands, noting the umpteen times he had made her blush this evening. The scar running from the base of his thumb around the back of his wrist was a worthy distraction. Fitzwilliam slipped his cuff lower, and Grace glanced up, frowning. "Does that hurt much?"

"Only in winter or when it's about to storm. But otherwise, no, it doesn't hurt." At the sound of Uncle Farfar's voice, Fitzwilliam snapped his head around and rose automatically.

"Right, cigars fetched and refreshments ordered." Uncle Farfar drew deeply on his cigar, breathing out two curls of smoke through his nostrils like a dragon in a folklore tale.

Grace studied Uncle Farfar's reaction, waiting to see whether he was conscious of his interruption. It suddenly occurred to her that Fitzwilliam was leaving England, and the last thing she wanted was to hold onto a false hope.

Fitzwilliam's jaw muscle twitched under his ear. "With your permission, sir, I'll prepare to take my leave. I should get Captain Fincham back to the *Discerning*."

"Good idea." Uncle Farfar patted him on the shoulder. "Just saw him heading towards the front entrance. Might want to catch him before he pours himself onto the street and causes a spectacle."

Grace took a deep breath. Uncle Farfar was oblivious to the weight of the air between her and Fitzwilliam. It was better—cleaner—this way.

"Thank you for indulging me in a discussion of sentimental literature," she said, wanting nothing more than to flash Fitzwilliam a wide, knowing smile and make *him* blush for a change. Instead, she inclined her head with an air of reluctance. "Goodnight, Lieutenant. Safe travels."

He bowed stiffly. "Thank you, Miss Baxter. Good evening to you."

A knotted frown of disappointment tightened her brow as the intensity of the atmosphere evaporated into the night air.

Chapter Two

Grace winced sympathetically as Uncle Farfar grimaced, stroking his belly in gentle circles and belching discreetly behind his fist. "Damned smoked mussels are disagreeing with me." He belched again. "Come now, poppet. I must take my leave. Let me escort you inside."

"No need," said Grace. "I can see myself to my chamber." He hesitated, but Grace lay her hand on his arm. "Good night, Uncle. See you tomorrow afternoon for our ride?"

"Indeed." He pressed a tobacco-woody-fragranced kiss to her forehead, wrapping her in a memory cocoon of liquorice pomfret cakes, all-enveloping hugs, and chest-rumbling laughter. It sometimes did not seem possible that Uncle Farfar was related to her cold, hard-shelled father. "Good night, my darling."

Grace slunk past the revelry in the drawing room and was passing Father's library when muffled voices reined in her advance.

"Of course. It'll require you take her hand in marriage," said Father.

Grace froze. She peered through the opening, her blood congealing in her heart at the sight of Lord Silverton.

"Your investments in Yorkshire collieries and my investments in steam locomotives create an ideal situation of supply and demand, wouldn't you say, Flint?" intoned Silverton.

Father's jovially replied, "Absolutely, and what better way to seal the deal than make it a family affair?"

"Pity she's not more like her mother," drawled Silverton. "Lady Flint is quite the social butterfly. Though, being so young, I suppose there's time for Miss Baxter to unlearn her wilful ways."

Father chuckled. "Come now, Silverton, by your own accounts about the clubhouse, you relish some spirit in the boudoir."

Grace's blood pooled in her legs, leaving her lightheaded. So, she was merely a pawn in a transaction? She grimaced at Silverton. And to *that* man? Of all the men in England?

Bilious, Grace scurried up the stairs two at a time, her skirts hoicked up high. In her bedchamber, Grace crashed back against her door, panting with horror in the warm candlelight. Her gaze darted to her canopy bed with its ruffles of cream silk, tied to the four posts with velvet tassels. Her lady's maid, Addison, had not yet turned the coverlet back. Grace tugged the tasselled bell cord. Stretching her neck to release some of the tension, she eased over to the fireplace and gripped the warm mantel with both hands, sinking her forehead onto the stone. What was Father thinking? Marrying her off to such an *old* man? Grace had heard the rumour that Silverton's wife of twenty years had curled up and died of misery. It was a wonder the poor woman survived that long. The flames in the fireplace guttered and danced in a scattered formation, matching her current thoughts. Knuckles knocked softly on the door.

"Come in," she called, expecting Addison.

The air in the room changed as the door swung open, and the

flames flickered and flared. At the unexpected sound of the lock engaging with a dull metallic thud, Grace swung on her heel with an admonishment on her lips. "There's no need to loc—" She gasped at the bulbous Lord Silverton.

"Grace, my sweet," he said, looking none too kind. "You retired without bidding me farewell. That's no way to treat your fiancé, now is it?"

Grace stiffened as his stare lingered on her tightly laced corset, and she wished the gown did not perform such a successful illusion of a bosom. Silverton's blatant stare and the discomfort of the constrictive laces further soured her mood.

"How did you know to find me up here?"

"I saw you sneak past the library." Silverton slowly advanced towards her, blocking her path. He swept a pudgy hand over his forehead and slicked back some unruly grey hairs with a smear of perspiration. "Do you make a habit of eavesdropping on private conversations?" His whining voice dripped with condescension.

An uncomfortable heat flared up her cheeks, her anger pounding in her ears. "How dare you enter my bedchamber uninvited!"

"How dare I?" Silverton's granite eyes were bolted to her. "The right is mine, as your betrothed."

"Have you no propriety?" smarted Grace. "You've no right at all. We aren't married."

Silverton shrugged dismissively. "Still, you're promised to me and me alone." He tugged the edges of his waistcoat down. "I wish to further our conversation that ended so abruptly earlier before the dinner party." The spoils of his salivary incontinence stretched like macabre threads in the corners of his mouth.

Grace recoiled. The heat of the fire was uncomfortably warm on the back of her legs. She wanted to take a step back but was deterred by the risk of her skirts catching ablaze. "I'll t-tell Father of your intrusion!"

Silverton smirked coldly. "I don't believe Lord Flint would have any objections, seeing as I'm the one doing him a favour by taking you off his hands."

The swell of horror that had filled her when she overheard news of this betrothal now surged up her throat, leaving an acidic taste in her mouth.

"You're not quite the docile and dutiful daughter Lord Flint desires. He doesn't want you darkening his door anymore." Silverton intertwined his pudgy, pale fingers.

"And you do?" spat Grace. With the instinct of a trapped animal, she slid sideways with her back against the wall.

Silverton reached one hand up to the pillar of the bed's canopy, his skin squeaking on the polished wood as he stepped around the end of the bed, trapping Grace in the corner. "I accept all pretty little playthings, especially ones with a large dowry attached to them." Silverton's deep drawl sent jolts of fear tripping down the vertebrae of Grace's spine.

"Get out this instant!" Her shoulders jammed into the corner of the room, her breathing coming in rapid gasps. "I'll scream."

"And what good will that do with the festivity below?" Silverton inched towards her, blocking any chance of escape. "Besides, the men of wealth and title in this town are particular about avoiding any association with women of loose morals. And your father won't be pleased if you ruin our arrangement."

"My lady's maid will be here at any moment."

"And you'll turn her away."

Grace's eyes flicked to the escape route over her bed, and Silverton smiled like the cat that had got the cream. "Don't look so scared, my sweet. I hoped we might become better acquainted. Sit and talk a little, perhaps?" He patted the silk bedcover.

Warily studying the locked door, Grace swallowed her beating heart. "Just talk?" He offered up a pink palm, but her arms had become deadened weights of lead that hung obstinately by her sides.

"Of course," he crooned. "What do you take me for? An uncivilised brute?" Digging into his waistcoat pocket, Silverton drew out a handkerchief and smeared it across his mouth to obliterate the beads of perspiration on his top lip.

Grace undid the white ribbon around her wrist and laid the ivory-bladed fan on the bedside table with forced nonchalance, hoping he would not notice her trembling hands. "Perhaps we shall be more comfortable in the drawing room downstairs? We could have some sherry."

"We could. Or we could stay here. It's a much more conducive environment for a private conversation."

"This is all most improper of you, my lord." Grace firmed her chin, raising her eyes to meet his in a show of bravado that she did not feel.

"No more improper than your renouncing all pretence of obedience under your Father's roof." Silverton glanced down his nose, his wolfish eyes leering at her chest. He tutted. "Look how you've scored your lovely skin with all that scratching earlier." His pudgy moist finger traced the skin along the lace edge of her gown. Grace's skin crawled like the skitter of a thousand spiders.

"Do not touch me!" She lashed out, her nails scoring his sweaty cheek.

Silverton hissed like an angered cobra as wells of blood sprang up in the ploughed furrows. "Good God!" Rubbing his cheek, blood smeared onto his fingers, and his glare of primal desire morphed into a mask of pain and rage. "I'll teach you never to raise your hand to me." His snarl carried none of the toadying drawl from earlier. "None of those dandies downstairs will want you by the time I'm done!" The violence in him erupted. He smashed his open palm into her mouth, slamming her against the wall.

Grace's eyes bulged in terror, minuscule blood vessels

popping with the strain of trying to breathe under the smothering hand. She could feel his violence shimmering beneath a membrane-thin veil of control. Silverton buried his nose in the hair behind her ear and inhaled deeply. A thin shriek of terror squeezed its way up her throat. Panic and horror added to her strength, but she was no match for Silverton's colossal frame. Grace fixed her eyes on the oil lamp on the bedside table. If only she could reach it, she would brain the wretch.

Jerking her leg up, she smashed her knee into the forked junction of Silverton's trousers. The fleshy mass gave way beneath her kneecap. Silverton's plump lips opened in a silent scream, his red cheeks turning an alarming shade of plum as he crumpled to the carpet. The floorboards reverberated woodenly with the weight of him.

Grace scrambled over the bed, shrieking in panic as her legs tangled in the folds of her skirts. The stitching of her bodice tore as she kicked her legs free and darted towards her bedroom door. Her trembling fingers made hard work of the key, and sucking back sobs, she whipped a look back to see whether Silverton had risen from the far side of the bed. He had not. She tore along the passage, the toe of her silk slipper catching on the torn hem of her dress. Her stays showed through her torn bodice.

Tucking herself onto the landing of the servant's stairwell, she panted, whimpering as a spasm of pain ricocheted across her jaw. A roll of nausea shivered through her as the repulsive memory of Silverton scrabbled up the wall of the inner fortress she was building to block him out.

The hall at the bottom of the servant's stairs was empty, and Grace eyed the coal cellar door, her hands shaking. As a young child, she had always tried to pluck up the courage to explore the cellar, but the fear of her governesses' punishments for ruining her clothes with black dust had been too great a deterrent. Today, fear of another kind pushed her into the coal cellar.

Grace opened the door, entered, and left it ajar just enough to let in some light from the hall. She pressed down the stairs into the dissolving darkness, wrinkling her nose. Coal smelled less aromatic than firewood, like comparing cigar smoke to pipe mixture. The cloying dust stuck in her throat, and she muffled her cough with her hand, wincing as she crushed her injured lips. When she reached the bottom of the stairs, pieces of coal crunched beneath her slippers.

Allowing her eyes to adjust to the inky air around her, she peered up the coal pile at the metal chute leading up to the hatch. She brushed away tears with the back of her hand. Billy always boasted that he could scamper up the coal to thump the metal chute at the top of the pile. It was also a way out of the house without anyone witnessing her leave.

"If Billy can do it, so can I," Grace murmured through swollen lips. She shuffled towards the chute, her skirts stirring a volcanic plume of black soot. She coughed uncontrollably. Tears streamed down her face, clearing the offensive debris from her eyes. She made slow progress up the slithering coalface. The iron chute reached down encouragingly like a rescue ladder against a burning building. At the top of the chute, she clung to the two large metal rings on the cellar doors above her, using the reprieve to catch her breath.

Mrs MacDougall, the cook, screeched at the top of the cellar stairs. "Och! What dolt left the door open?" A sharp wooden thwack plunged the coal cellar into darkness.

With a squeak of frustration and fear, Grace thrust the wooden trapdoors above her open, the metal rings clattering like the bridle of a galloping horse. Gritting her teeth and tasting blood, she hauled herself from the hole and unceremoniously collapsed like a pile of dirty rags onto the cobbled floor of the kitchen courtyard.

She stood and patted her skirts but realised the futility—her gown was as black as a mourning dress. Not waiting to be discovered, she fled towards the stables directly off the kitchen courtyard, which opened onto a narrow service street. The horse stalls and carriage house were on the ground floor, and the servants' quarters were above, where Grace hoped to find Billy.

Mirrored on the opposite side of the mews were the lavish neighbouring terraces' stables and carriage houses. Horses were hitched to parked guest carriages, lining the lane. The stables bustled with activity, guest coachmen congregating for friendly carousing. Distracted by their merrymaking, no one noticed Grace slip up the stairs to the first floor.

Billy Sykes, only a few years older than Grace, had been her only friend and companion throughout her childhood. Billy had always accompanied Grace when his father, the stablemaster, took her on horseback rides in the country. Up in the Yorkshire Dales, the two children had plenty of time and freedom to enjoy their friendship without censorship.

There had been a string of governesses in Grace's life before the hardened Miss Hargraves eventually bunkered down, determined to break Grace's wilfulness. Miss Hargraves abhorred Grace's friendship with Billy, deeming it to be inappropriate for a young lady of such breeding to be roughing around with the stablemaster's son. Grace did not care.

A quickening tug of hope pulled her up the stairs. It was highly likely that Billy would be down in the stables with the others, but she clung to the slim chance that he might be in his quarters.

Grace had viewed Billy's room only once before when Miss Hargraves had taken three days' leave to attend her mother's funeral in Sussex. On this evening, the faint glow of the gas lamps in the lane below shone weakly through the only window. Spotting the silhouette of a candle on the desk beneath the window, she groped for the tinderbox. The head of the match ignited in an explosive flare tinged with green and blue. Lighting the tallow candle's charred wick, she absorbed her surroundings.

Billy's room was smaller than she remembered, and while humbly furnished, it was homely.

It was only then Grace felt safe enough to release a quivering breath of relief. At this unconscious letting down of her guard, her body trembled, the horrors of the evening slithering through every muscle and nerve ending. Drips of wax spattered onto her wrist from the candle, and she quickly placed it back, briskly rubbing the hot globs from her skin. She stumbled over to the neatly made bed and collapsed in a quaking heap.

Shuddering breaths jerked from her body as she wrapped her arms around her torn bodice. A weak keening escaped from deep inside as she lamented the death of her innocence, her childhood, her future. She silenced herself at the heavy stomp of a man's footsteps rumbling through the floorboards.

"Now then, who do we have here?" Billy's deep, rich voice had a hard edge to it. He gasped. "Miss Grace? That you?" He hastened over to the bed and squatted down, his wide-shouldered frame filling her view. He reached out a hand and placed it on her shoulder. "Your lip! You've bled all down your gown!"

"Oh, Billy!" She launched up, throwing herself into the protective circle of his arms. Clinging to his solid neck, she buried her face into the open collar of his shirt. An array of smells surrounded Billy—woodchips, hay, and the sweat of horses, mingled with the fragrance of aromatic herbs and the slightest essence of lye soap. It smelled of familiar safety.

Putting his hands firmly on her shoulders, Billy pushed her back to study her face. "Miss Grace, lass. What's happened? You're filthy! Is that soot? My oath! If I didn't know better, I'd say you'd been down the coal hole."

"I have." Her voice was grave. Her tears spilled.

"Oh, aye? Whatever for?" Billy's voice tightened. He grasped her icy hands—his were as toasty as a bed-warming pan.

Calmed by his presence, Grace swallowed thickly. "You're aware there's a dinner party at Wallace House this evening?"

"Aye. I've just stepped away from the carousing in the carriage house myself. Though I can't imagine how you got into such a state at a dinner party?"

"I retired early." Grace squeezed her eyes shut, the images of the evening dancing behind her eyelids like lantern light projected against the wall as she recounted them to Billy. In the safety of his room, and with his hands clasped tightly around her, Grace blew out a shaky breath. "And that's when I came to find you."

"Good God in Heaven! That bastard!" Billy's voice quavered.

"I must leave. I can't stay and marry that wretched man!" Anger warmed her throat and cheeks.

Billy regarded her with tenderness, his clenched jaw and jittering leg a truer measure of his emotions. "Now, Miss Grace, you're not thinking it through. Where'll you go? The streets of London are no place for a lady to be wandering around on her own."

"I don't want to be a lady!" Her words lost their polish as indignant fresh tears welled.

A rumble of humour rolled from Billy. "You're more lad than lady, what with you scampering up trees and poking toads with sticks and such. That old shrew, Miss Hargraves, has had little success taming your sensibilities, though good Lord she's tried."

Grace's head snapped up. "I'm not returning to the house."

"Is that so? You can't rightly move into the stables." Billy eyed her cautiously. "Are you sore?"

"Mostly my face," she whispered as her fingers feathered her cut lip.

Billy lifted her chin gently with one finger of his long, slim hand. "Allow me to mind you. You know I do well aiding those with ailments. I'll brew you a cup of willow bark tea. It eases pain in horses and men equally. Mind you, I don't offer the horses a cup of tea."

Despite the horrors of the evening, Grace managed to flash her teeth at Billy's attempt at humour. She nodded, gladly accepting his practical, no-fuss approach.

"Hold on a bit." Billy ambled over to the wardrobe and opened the doors. Squatting down, he rummaged in the bottom of the cupboard and rifled through his wooden herb box filled with a variety of cork-stoppered, glass vials and jars, all neatly labelled.

Grace knew he was nearing the end of his indentured apprenticeship at the Worshipful Society of Apothecaries, where he was bound to Master Olgilby. Billy snatched up a glass jar, focussing his attention back on her. "I'll need to pop down to the stove in the tack room to boil it," he said. "It might be a bit of a wait, but I promise, Miss Grace, the willow bark will bring you relief well through the night."

"Billy, don't trouble yourself on my account."

"'Tis no trouble, flower. I wouldn't be doing my duty as an apothecary if I didn't come to the aid of a friend. I can't bear to see you hurting."

As soon as the door shut and she was alone, Grace bolted off the bed. She knew Billy would try to persuade her to go to her parents. She could not stay knowing the lengths to which her father was going to rid her from his house. Her mother was no better, always agreeing with precisely what Father proposed. Even Uncle Farfar could not fix this now.

She winced as the ground flesh of her inner lip throbbed, the stab of pain lending fuel to the fire of her determination. She had to leave London, she decided. But the question was, to where? Anywhere was better than here. The farther the better.

She gritted her teeth, glancing down at her gown. If she were to flee, she would not get far in flouncy tatters. An idea came to mind.

Snatching open the double doors of Billy's wardrobe, Grace eyed the selection of wool breeches, white linen shirts, and frockcoats. She groped through Billy's apothecary box and found the pair of shears he used for herb cutting. Unceremoniously slicing through the remaining laces of her gown, Grace shrugged the bloodied finery to the floor. Her corset's laces received the same treatment—the whalebone stays clattering on the wooden boards. She reached around her back and cut the ribbons that clutched her masses of petticoats in place. Kicking off her slippers, Grace stood in her linen shift and stockings. Her skin rippled with gooseflesh as a fresh draught whistled through the warped window frame, fluttering the thin fabric of her shift. Hoping the bundle of clothes took a decent amount of time to be found, she shoved it deep under Billy's bed.

She pulled on a dark grey pair of breeches and buttoned the front, frowning as they threatened to slip over her hips. She hastily tugged on a billowing shirt and tucked it into her breeches, the extra padding helping to keep them up. Hunting in the bureau's top drawer, Grace found a pair of suspenders and a leather drawstring purse clinking with coin. Fumbling unfamiliarly, she buttoned the suspenders to her breeches and pocketed the purse, silently apologising to Billy for the thievery.

Grace grasped the smaller of the frockcoats, a blue one, and shrugged into it. The sleeves fell below her hands, and she hastily rolled up the cuffs. The coat's skirt should have fallen above her knee, but it was mid-calf length on her short frame. *Can't be helped.* She needed boots to complete her outfit and recalled stumbling over a pile of them in the entrance below.

Grace growled as her wayward, half-pinned curls refused to tuck up under Billy's tweed cap. Exasperated, she returned to the table and gripped the shears. With only the tiniest hesitation, Grace took a handful of her locks and cut them flush with her scalp. She yanked open the bottom drawer of the bureau and dropped her fistful of hair onto the folded linen, the dark tangles a stark contrast to the clean, white sheets. After hacking off the rest of her hair, Grace tried the tweed cap again, smirking as it fitted over her newly shorn scalp.

She caught her reflection in the looking glass on the inside of the open wardrobe door. Her green eyes were wide, pupils unusually large. Her cheeks were mottled with emerging bruises. Blood smeared across her split bottom lip like a macabre rouge. With her oversized clothes, soot-stained face, and swollen, oozing lip, she would have no trouble blending in with the multitude of faceless street urchins begging around London. The shapeless coat hid her femininity.

The urchin in the mirror pressed his lips together in a tight line of determination. Despite the pain of her injuries and the fear of the unknown, she was supremely confident her future would not include being married to Silverton.

Without a moment to spare, Grace fled down the darkened stairwell. She cast her eyes quickly over the pile of boots lying haphazardly after her earlier stumble. She fumbled for the two smallest, hoping they were a matching pair. Padding silently in her stockings, she scurried down the service lane towards the main street.

Behind her, Billy's deep timbre reverberated off the cobblestones. "Right you are, Da. I'll be back shortly."

Grace held her breath as she glanced back, hoping she was in a shadow where the gaslight failed to reach or that her disguise had worked. Either way, Billy did not recognise her. Tossing his head to flick his hair from his face, he focussed on the pot of tea and disappeared into the doorway.

With a stab of panic, Grace realised that this might be the last time she laid eyes on her best friend. Before her courage failed, she sprinted out into the main street, the coins jingling in her pocket.

Chapter Three

When she was far enough away from Wallace House, Grace stopped, panting, and donned the scuffed leather boots. They were a bit big, but she wrapped the laces twice around her ankles, tying them tightly. She had no idea where she was headed and no plans on what to do, but for the first time in her life she was free to make her own choices. She had always imagined independence would be exhilarating, but in truth, it was terrifying. If Father tracked her down before she left London, would he disown her if she still refused to marry Silverton? Would Uncle Farfar keep her? Could she survive being cast out on the streets, penniless?

It was not yet late enough for the bustle of carriages and pedestrians to have abated. Keeping her head tucked low, Grace tightened her coat and stumbled off towards the river. The stiff leather bit into her ankles, and soon her heels throbbed with blisters. The night air was setting in, and Grace's dry mouth demanded she keep an eye out for a drinking establishment along the way. Leaving Mayfair's palatial residences behind her, she neared St James's Park, but the prospect of the unlit common at night was decidedly less appealing than the allure of the green field it was during the day.

The blister on Grace's left foot burst as she hurried down a narrow lane. She limped past an alehouse, well-lit and alive with raucous singing. Peering up, she studied the embossed golden tendrils of leaves and flowers entwined around letters announcing she was outside the Two Chairmen alehouse. Several sailors in blue jackets milled around outside, accosting young patrons stumbling out without a coin left in their pockets, ripe for the picking to recruit onto their ship. Grace's heart sank. She had fended off a similar crowd a few streets back, the sailors pressing in around her with promises of a bright future and wild adventures. One had even slung his arm around Grace's neck, drawing her against him. She had thrust him away, terrified he would feel the shape of her and reveal her secret.

A friendly faced sailor eyed her eagerly. "Oi, laddie! You've the look of a Jack tar! How about signin' up for His Majesty's Royal Navy? Three square meals a day an' good toil to keep you honest."

Grace staggered a few steps away from the sailor who, while friendly enough, was too close. Her laddish appearance in the mirror might have convinced her, but she was not yet sure whether a man would be able to see through her disguise. "Um, n-no, thank you."

Not that easily dissuaded, and with an even wider grin of encouragement, the sailor stepped towards her again, his arms open wide. "Come sail the seven seas! Witness sand so white you'll think it snow."

Grace pressed her back to the wall, her heart pounding as she spotted the alehouse door. The warm aroma of roasted meat curled past her nostrils, and she breathed deeply, swallowing the deliciousness in an attempt to appease her thirsty tongue. She was not sure whether this alehouse offered accommodation, but it was worth a try. At the waft of stale ale and the sweet, fermenting odour of rum, Grace wrinkled her nose and hesitated.

Seeing her hesitation, the sailor tried his luck once more. "Come now. Don't be shy. We don't bite. Shake off those responsibilities and come live the life of a free man."

Grace turned her head sharply in alarm. "No! Thank you!" She whirled round, escaping through the doorway as the sailor's amused chuckle heated the back of her neck.

"Come find me when you're done drownin' your sorrows, lad!"

Grace had never been in an alehouse before. The notion of how incensed her parents would be to find out she had been inside one bolstered her courage to step further into the dimly lit, smoky environs. The alehouse was tiny and cramped, with its tables occupied mostly by men. Some gripped their tankards of beer as though they were anchors securing them to the earth amidst their swirling drunkenness. The few women were in no better condition than the men. A group of red-faced drinkers, arms linked in camaraderie, swayed out of time with one another, belting out a ballad that had the crowd responding with cheers and jeers. Grace slunk up to the counter where the portly publican gawked at her.

He rested both hands on the countertop. "Your mother sent you to fetch your father, has she, lad?"

Grace's ears turned hot at the thrill of being called a lad again. "N-no, sir." She tried not to stare at his balding head over which he had pasted the few remaining strands of his hair. "I'd like some drink, please."

"Ha! Handouts, is it? Begone! Get yourself to the workhouse!"

"I have coin!"

The publican straightened up with interest and rubbed the bulge of his belly. "Ah! That's a different story then. What you after?"

"I ... I don't mind, sir."

"Well, ain't you a bit fancy with your pleases and sirs? Where you from, lad?"

Grace knew she was terrible at lying—betrayed by a furious flush that always bloomed up her neck to the roots of her hair. Tonight, the fine layer of black coal dust neatly hid the lie. "I, uh, I was recently an apothecary's apprentice but I, um ... It wasn't my calling, so I'm moving on." Grace made a mental note to establish a plausible story that would satisfy the curious. "I'm seeking refuge from that sailor out there." The publican scowled at Grace. Had he swallowed her fabrication? She shifted her weight from one heavy boot to the other.

Scrunching his nose, he chuckled, "Indeed, those navy lads are a jolly insistent lot." His attention was drawn to a shout from the table over by the door.

"Hey, Johnny! Gis another bottle of yer good stuff, eh?"

"Hold your horses, Angus! I'm coming!" He cocked his head at Grace. "How 'bout an ale?"

Grace nodded quickly. She had never drunk ale before, but she was thirsty enough to overlook any potential displeasure at trying something new. The publican slid over a pewter tankard with a generous head of froth.

"That'll be a ha'penny." He held out his free hand, maintaining a firm grip on the handle.

Grace reached into her pocket for Billy's purse, her heart jumping into her throat. It was gone! She patted herself down, searching the stained floor. Where was it? Had she dropped it? Oh, Lord, no. That overly familiar sailor! Had he lifted it?

She glanced up at the publican, his scowl obliterating her nerve. Without coin, how was she to find accommodation? Angus, the drunkard by the door, protested the delay of his new bottle of whisky. The publican slid from behind the counter and snatched Grace's ear with a pincered grip that threatened to tear her lobe. She bit back a squeal.

"Out, you little beggar!" He thrust her through the doorway.

Grace's ear throbbed pitifully, and she clasped her hand to her head to check it was still attached. She swivelled her gaze to the high street at the end of the narrow lane. As a black coach clopped past, an idea struck her. A way to the docks!

The blue-jacketed sailor was still outside. He spotted her and grinned, waving familiarly. "Oi, lad, over here! How about you join Lieutenant Wadham and me on the ol' *Discernin'*?" The grinning sailor jerked his head towards his more taciturn companion, and Grace caught the flash of gold on his epaulette. The grinning sailor had no such markings.

Grace stopped, her uncovered ear pricked to a familiar word amongst the sailor's ramblings. Encouraged by her pause, the sailor sauntered over. "Cap'n Fincham's seekin' a new ship's boy right about now, seein' as young George up and offed at the last port. Couldn't find his sea legs, that lad. But you've a sturdy air about you. How old are you?" Without stopping to enable her to reply, he answered for her. "Fourteen or fifteen, I reckon, by your lack of whiskers." The sailor paused to take a deep breath.

"The *Discerning*?" she asked, releasing the grip on her stinging ear to hear better. "The ship setting forth on the mapping expedition to ... to Del Tier— Del Fig— to South America?" Seamus Fitzwilliam's ship! There was considerable risk she would be found out, but the thought of knowing at least one person aboard—albeit from a distance and from behind a mask —would be better than not knowing anyone.

The sailor's two nests of black eyebrows shot up in surprise. "Tierra del Fuego. You've heard of it?" The astonishment in his voice was echoed in the deep furrows of his weather-beaten brow. He could not have been more than in his early twenties, but he had the look of a man ten years his senior. His black hair, tied back with a leather strap, had a tar-coated hat perched jauntily atop.

Grace waggled her head non-committedly.

"What they be calling you, eh?" enquired the sailor.

"Um, B-Billy Sykes," spluttered Grace. She still had not concocted a plausible tale.

"Ha! You don't sound too sure about that, m'lad," laughed the sailor, not unkindly. His dark eyes sparkled in amusement. "Well, Billy, pleased to make your acquaintance." He extended his hand. "Name's Lambert McGilney, but everyone calls me Gilly." His firm handshake ground the bones of her hand. "Ha! Gilly and Billy, we'll make a good team, you and me!" He pumped her hand, frowning at her gasp. "By crumbs! First thing's first, we'll have to teach you how to firm up that handshake. 'Tis as limp as a bloody Frenchie's!" Gilly clapped Grace on the back with a force that drove the breath from her lungs. Clenching her teeth, she hoped her grimace passed for a smile. "You'll also need a bit of a wash. You been hauling coal?"

"Something like that," mumbled Grace, uneasily wiping her palms down her jacket.

"Been scrappin' too by the state of that bottom lip. Fair warnin', Bosun Tidwell don't tolerate scrappin' on the ship, so you'll need to mind yourself."

Grace glanced at the clean-shaven officer nearby but quickly looked away as his eyes narrowed in a scowl of disapproval. "I've *not* been scrapping." Grace jutted her chin out.

"Ooh, with a face like that, you likely asked for it from your ol' man, eh?"

"Perhaps," she lied.

"I'd have thought with that polished tongue, you could've talked your way out of anythin'. What's a toff like you doin' runnin' away?"

"I'm no toff. I am—was—an apothecary's apprentice. Educated under Master Olgilby."

"Never known an apothecary with such upper airs. You're a strange one, that's for sure!" The jolly sailor turned to his superior. "Lieutenant Wadham, sir, this here is Sykes."

Grace stumbled back. "Goodness gracious! N-no, wait. I've not agreed to come."

Lieutenant Wadham's brown hair, short and neatly clipped around his ears, added to the tidiness of his overall appearance. His square jaw tensed momentarily, and two dimples dented his cheeks as he pressed his lips together in consideration. Grace's knees almost knocked together. It was one thing for a publican and a sailor not to notice her fine features, but surely an officer—a gentleman—would? She stared at his single gold epaulette on his right shoulder to avoid the realisation in his eyes.

Gilly jiggled her arm. "Come now, m'lad. 'Tis an honest living with a fair wage."

"A w-wage?" Having lost Billy's few precious coins, Grace had no notion of how to gainfully earn some more. How much did those shoe polishers make? Or the paper sellers? And she still had nowhere to sleep tonight.

Gilly laughed. "You don't expect to sweat for free, do you? By crumbs, you're promisin' to be worthy entertainment with your amusin' ways." He slung his arm across her shoulder.

Goodness, were all sailors so familiar?

"The sea's your escape to freedom and adventure. And the *Discernin*'s the way to it. You can build on the deeds that have happened or put the catastrophes behind you and begin again. 'Tis the way of life, offering a new chance every day."

It was the second time the man had mentioned the ship's name, and Grace's heart leapt into her throat as forcefully as the first time. She stopped pulling against him, and her shoulders sagged.

Sensing her resistance fade, Gilly presented her once more to the lieutenant. "Permission to leave, sir?"

Grace took a deep breath, stretching her spine as tall as it would go.

"Very well, McGilney, convey the recruit to the ship." The officer had a deep voice, with neatly pronounced words.

The shaky breath that escaped Grace's lips came out as a jittery laugh.

"Aye, aye, sir." Gilly hauled Grace away, his arm still crooked around her neck. He quickly led her away on the long walk to the docks.

At the dockyard's brick wall, a guard in a Royal Artillery uniform stepped from the gatehouse. "State your business," he demanded in a no-nonsense tone before noticing the jaunty sailor beside Grace and breaking out in a laddish grin.

"Gunner Scott." Gilly formally knuckled the tip of his hat, the seriousness behind this show of respect negated by the foolish smirk on his face.

"Gilly! Been out picking up new hands? Who's this, then?" Gunner Scott examined Grace curiously from under bushy eyebrows.

"Me new mate, Sykes."

Grace blinked at the lie, but the flickering evening shadows hid her face.

"Billy Sykes, I have the pleasure of introducin' you to Gunner Scott, the lousiest shot in the Royal Artillery, which is why he's relegated to guard duty." Gunner Scott laughed genially at the jibe. Gilly motioned at Grace. "Gunner Scott, Billy here is the *Discernin*'s newest recruit."

Grinning, Scott flicked his head towards the docks. "Haul yourself inside before Captain Fincham has apoplexy for you not being aboard yet." Scott dipped his head towards Gilly. "Mind you, he was in a right state when he came aboard this evening." He made a tipping motion with is hand and gave Gilly an exaggerated wink.

With his signature clap on the gunner's back, Gilly strode through the open gates. Grace hobbled after him through the darkened dockyard while he babbled on with some interesting descriptions of the *Discerning*'s crew.

"The Blighters, them's twin brothers that are joined at the

hip. Benjamin and Jack Blight, two peas in a pod, they are. Not a one of us can tell them apart just for gogglin' them, so we call them the Blighters. They have the reddest hair you ever witnessed. Almost hurts your eyes. And the fact they both insist on bein' fully whiskered don't help matters. The biggest difference is one of them talks and the other don't, else we'd be in a right dither with ourselves."

The night air was decidedly colder on the edge of the Thames. The thick, pervasive haze Grace noticed crossing the bridge now lay in a swirling coat, causing the dockyard buildings to loom out of the mist.

"Now, Bosun Tidwell, he's a regular brick. You'll always know where he is on the ship what with him always tootlin' away on his bosun's call."

"His what?"

"Bosun's call. You know, the whistle what bosuns blow on to pass on the officer's orders. Don't look so troubled, lad. We'll soon show you the ropes. Mind you, don't be caught slackin' or else you'll suffer the bendy end of Bosun Tidwell's cane. He's a fair man, but he don't like idleness."

"I'll remember that." Grace swallowed. She knew all too well the sting of Miss Hargraves' cane across her hands, and she could only imagine how much worse a caning from a ship's bosun would be. Her fingers curled into fists.

"Now, Cap'n Fincham, he isn't a bad one, though he's a bit under the weather at the moment. Bit of a nervy type."

It was late, and Grace was bone weary. She shivered as the chilly night breeze curled up the wide cuffs of her coat sleeves. She stopped in her tracks as the gangplank to a tall ship materialised through the haze.

"Here she is then, the *Discernin'*," beamed Gilly proudly. "Come on, don't dilly-dally. Cap'n Fincham'll want to meet you in the morn, but for tonight, I'll make room for you in the fo'c'sle."

"Where?"

"The fo'c'sle. The sailor's quarters. The purser, sailmaker, and carpenter have filled up most of the fo'c'sle berths with their stores."

"Then where shall I sleep?" Grace's voice quivered with trepidation.

"I'll clear a berth for you tonight. Then tomorrow, you get to swing, m'lad."

"Goodness gracious! Swing? As in hang?" Grace's face turned clammy under its sooty layer.

Gilly roared with laughter and gave Grace one of his customary slaps on the back. Spotting its approach, she leaned away from the impact.

"No, you daft dolt! Swing, as in swing in your hammock. This here's a vessel of the Royal Navy, not the Tower of London."

"I own no hammock."

"Worry not, Billy. Purser Rowlett will issue you with one tomorrow. Along with a blanket."

"Where do you sleep?" Grace did not want to part from her new friend.

"Hmph! You really have no idea about how things work on a ship, do you?" Gilly frowned at her. "Oh well, get 'em young and train 'em up, I say. I'm in the men's mess with the others. Not the officers and warrant officers, mind you, they kip and mess in the gunroom. You, my young friend, have a long slog before you work your way up to sleepin' in the men's mess, let alone the gunroom. You're a bit on the scrawny side, but if you put your back into it and keep your nose clean, you'll get along fine."

Chapter Four

G race hesitated as she stepped onto the gangplank. She peered up, but the thick air engulfed any evidence of the ship's masts. At the top of the gangplank, a sailor scratched at his grey whiskers and greeted Gilly in a gravelly voice. "Mr McGilney."

"Bosun's Mate," Gilly acknowledged. "This here is Billy Sykes. He's the new ship's boy."

"Billy Sykes, may I introduce you to Bosun's Mate Blom, quartermaster of the watch this fine evenin'."

Blom's eyes narrowed as he inspected Grace, waves of hostility rolling off him. She studied him with equal interest in the dim light. Ignoring her, Blom glowered at Gilly, his Dutch accent thick. "That one looks like trouble, Mr McGilney. Might do him some good to kiss the gunner's daughter. Wipe that smirk off his face."

"Good evenin' to you," quipped Gilly, dragging Grace away from Blom and towards the front of the ship.

"What a nasty man," hissed Grace under her breath, pulling

her arm free of Gilly's grip. "He didn't call you Gilly. I gather he's no friend?"

"He isn't normally that grumpy. His piles must be playin' up. Below, my friends call me Gilly, but you must remember to call me Mr McGilney when above."

"Gilly, why would I kiss a stranger's daughter?" Grace whispered.

Gilly tittered. "'Tisn't what it sounds like, lad. It's where you drop your breeches and bend bare arsed over a gun and have the privilege of receivin' six strokes."

Grace grimaced. "That sounds unpleasant."

"It's the navy way, my lad. A proper tannin' of one's rear end never did anyone any harm. I've had my fair share but none I didn't deserve. And truth be known, when 'tis not you layin' over the barrel of a gun as bare as the day you were born, 'tis a fair spectacle to behold. You'll have to jostle with the others to win a better view from up on the riggin'."

"No, I shan't!" Grace squared her shoulders with a show of boldness that did not reflect the tremble inside. Mortified, a prickle of tears welled up behind her eyelids. What she wanted—correction, what she needed—was to lie down, shut her eyes and sleep. Weariness clouded her confidence, and she staggered a couple of steps.

"Steady up, there," laughed Gilly, securing her arm. "Now, on either side of the bow, you'll find the heads. Or privy, as you landlubbers call it." He waved a hand towards two dark cubicles. He stopped before an open hatch. "Here's your berth."

Grace peered into the dark recess. An impossibly steep set of stairs with no handrail led below—more a ladder than stairs. A lantern hung from the side. The cabin below belched out stale air, assaulting Grace with the pong of unwashed bodies, damp wool, and rotten seaweed with an overlay of human excrement.

"Right, down the hatch we go, then," said Gilly, ever cheerful.

Not trusting her trembling, aching limbs, Grace decided on the safer option of climbing down backwards. Gilly braced his hands and feet on the smooth wooden sides and slid down in an efficient swoop. Grace made a mental note to try that next time.

The forecastle cabin was small enough that the glow from the single lantern illuminated the whole room. In the narrowed end of the cabin, the coals of a potbellied stove glowed welcomingly. Along the cabin's walls were two rows of cramped wooden bunks joined head to foot, sixteen in all and crammed with provisions. In the centre of the cabin stood a triangular table, shaped to fit into the ship's narrowing bow. From a line of hammocks hanging like a colony of bats clinging to a cave roof, a cacophony of human noises—grunts, snores, squeaks, mumbles, and thumps—dashed any notion Grace had of a peaceful night's sleep. Gilly nudged her over and moved several sacks of flour to empty a lower shelf.

"That'll be your berth for tonight. Here's Jim Buchanan," he prodding a sleeping form in the nearest canvas sling.

It grunted, and a sleepy voice grumbled, "Leave off, will ye?"

Gilly's whisper was loud in the sleeping cabin. "Ahoy there, Jim. This here is Sykes, a new joiner. Be sure to wake him in the morn and take him through his duties. Then have him assemble with the new joiners on the fo'c'sle at three bells. Don't forget to fetch him to breakfast, all right?"

"Aye, all right, Gilly," mumbled the voice in the dark.

"There's a good lad." Gilly patted the lump in the hammock.

With a final slap on Grace's back, Gilly murmured, "Righto. Sleep well, young Billy."

He climbed out of the hatch, and Grace's bravery sank into her too-big boots. She stared at the wooden berth, contemplating everything that had transpired. If she lay down now, she would be completely committing to her new life as a man. There would be no turning back. If she turned and scampered up the ladder, she would have to go back and face Silverton, not to mention Father. Grace ran her tongue along the salty split of her lip. She shook her head—that was not an option.

Slinking onto the wooden planks, she tentatively removed her boots and peeled back her stockings. The raw blisters had not rubbed so severely as to start bleeding. She rammed her stockings into her boots and shoved them and her cap beneath her bunk. The blanket was scratchy, but it was thick and warm. Cocooning herself, Grace blissfully shut her eyes. Unbelievably, as exhausted as she was, sleep would not come.

The tender skin on the inside of her thighs was chafed raw by Billy's oversized breeches. Grace earnestly prayed for some form of comfort. She was nearly away from London. She knew she must do her best to persuade this lot she was one of them. But how? Stop saying please and thank you? Her grimace slipped into a smirk—learn how to swear? At least she would have food in her belly and a roof over her head.

Her eyes wandered to the planks of the bunk above her. Her new-found bravado slipped into a question of whether this was the wisest move, coming aboard Fitzwilliam's ship? Surely he would recognise her? She resolved to always keep her cap low. Frowning, the memory of the tattered, blood-stained gown she had kicked hastily under Billy's bed loomed in the dark.

Had he found it yet or realised that she had stolen his money? She squeezed her eyes tight. *Lord, forgive me. Oh, Billy, please forgive me.* Grace's eyes shot open in alarm at the image of William Senior, Billy's father, finding her gown. The thought that William might think that Billy had hurt her caused her stomach to spasm in horror, but her whimper was drowned out by the other human noises. She knuckled her eyes to block out the horror. *Oh, goodness, what have I done?*

"Hey, laddie! Wake up."

Grace tensed at the sharp jab in her ribs, renewing the throb of her bruises. She twisted to scowl at the owner of the poking finger.

"Crivens! The front of ye is uglier than the back of ye."

Grace rubbed her eyes, heavy and gritty with sleep and coal dust. One half-open eye dozily made out a halo of spiky hair around a moon face with perpendicular ears, giving the young man the appearance of a monkey.

"Ye'll have to wash yer manky face before breakfast, or Bosun'll be introducing yer bahookie to his Nelly." The heavy Scottish accent further muddled the youngster's words.

"I beg your pardon?" Grace checked her manners, the stuffy cloud of sleep lifting.

"Ye haven't had a look at yer face then, I take it?" The moon-faced man beamed.

"I'm sorry. I don't understand you." Grace shrugged apologetically, swinging her legs over the edge of the berth.

"Och, never mind. If ye bide any longer, ye'll not be getting any breakfast. Come along then. What's yer name again?"

"Gra—Billy Sykes." Grace reached for her boots, wincing at the thought of the leather scraping over her raw heels.

"Och, don't worry about yer boots, Billy. Ye need to feel yer footing about the ship."

Grace gladly tucked the boots back under her berth. Bare and chilly without her hair, she slipped on her cap and rose beside the spiky-haired youth.

"Name's Jim Buchanan." He was taller than her, but despite the shadow of dark fuzz across his top lip, his voice was unbroken. The youth's unfortunate conjoined eyebrows did little to detract from his ape-like countenance.

Grace nodded and rolled her stiff shoulders. The pale light of the dawn shining in through the hatch lessened the shadows in the cabin and illuminated the other occupants rolling and stowing their hammocks. A scuffle behind her snatched Grace's attention to the hatchway where a sailor slid backwards down the stairs, landing with a catlike lightness. With a flourish, the sailor turned to face Grace and Jim as another dropped effortlessly beside him.

Grace stared at the identical beaming faces with their beards and spectacular shock of red hair. Piercing blue eyes peered from beneath the twin thatches of coppery eyebrows.

"Hello, hello. An' who's this, then?"

"It's the new ship's boy," explained Jim. "Billy."

"Ship's boy, eh? Been on the losing end of someone's fists, by the looks of things." The man offered his hand. "Pleased to meet you. This here's my brother, Jack. He doesn't have much to say about things." Catching herself mid-curtsy, Grace shuffled her feet and took the extended hand.

"Pleased to meet you, sir," Grace enunciated neatly.

"Oh ho! Listen to this one's fancy tongue, lads! I'm not *sir* to you, little Jack Horner."

"My name isn't Jack Horner. It's Billy Sykes," corrected Grace.

"Stuck in his thumb and pulled out a plum." Ben recited a line from the familiar rhyme. "Sounds like you've a plum in your mouth." The sailor's lips were hidden behind his flaming bushy beard, but his eyes sparkled warmly. "Benjamin Blight's the name. Ben to my friends. Blight to you above deck. 'Tis only the superiors aboard who are 'sir'. Best remember that if you don't want Bosun tickling your arse with his Nelly."

"I've been informed about the bosun's Nelly," Grace said with a grimace. "Why is it called Nelly anyway?"

"Ha! 'Tis named after his wife. Bosun reckons his cane's not nearly as vicious or as quick to lash out as his wife's barbed tongue." Ben shook his head ruefully at Grace's forlorn face. "You're as low as they come on this ship, little Jack Horner. You'd do well to toe the line and remember your place. Safer for your backside that way. Might want to pull out that plum while you're at it!" He winked.

Three bells clanged above them, making Grace jump.

Jim's eyes widened. "Crivens! We're late to muster! Gilly told me I've to deliver him to the fo'c'sle at three bells." Jim gripped the edge of the ladder. "Come along, Billy. Quick as ye can."

"Ah, yes. Captain Fincham'll want a look at the newcomers. Get along then. We'll be sailing on the turn of the tide at five bells." Ben nodded at Jim and turned to Grace. "You can't go wrong keeping company with this here powder monkey, Jack Horner. Jim's been aboard long enough to tell you what you ought and ought not to be doing." Ben ruffled Jim's hair amicably. Jack Blight grinned and waggled his blazing eyebrows in agreement.

Back up on deck, preparations for getting underway were in full swing. Scurrying along the deck, Jim pointed out Bosun Tidwell, a sour-faced man who was tearing up and down the deck bawling, his threats no doubt audible on the far bank of the Thames. "Put your backs into it, men, or you'll taste my Nelly. Move your lazy arses!"

"Hurry, Billy!" Jim dragged Grace by her sleeve.

A jovial voice called out in an Irish accent from the rigging, "God be with ya, Lieutenant Fitzwilliam!"

"Good morning to you too, O'Malley."

Grace's insides liquified at the sound of the familiar voice. Last night, outside the alehouse and lured in by Gilly's charm, Grace had felt a skewed sense of comfort at the thought of being near Fitzwilliam again. Confronted by the reality of facing him now, she was terrified he would recognise her.

Seamus Fitzwilliam stood against the rail, squinting upwards to acknowledge the sailor who had greeted him. He cast a discerning eye over the activity in the rigging, his face solemn as his eyes flicked over the busy sailors on deck. Fitzwilliam edged around to face her, the crisp white of his waistcoat offsetting the deep blue of his coat and igniting the curiosity in his eyes. Grace ducked her head, yanking the brim of her cap lower.

"Buchanan," Fitzwilliam's familiar voice called out again.

"Aye, sir?"

"Is that late straggler a new joiner?"

"Aye, sir, he is."

"Best be quick about it, Buchanan. Lieutenant Wadham has already mustered the others on the fo'c'sle ready for the captain's inspection."

"Aye, sir. Come along, lad, this way." Jim elbowed Grace.

"One moment!" Fitzwilliam's command glued the soles of Grace's feet to the deck. "What's your name, young man?"

Keeping her face in the shadow of her cap, Grace deepened her voice. "Sykes, sir." Her heart pounded at the base of her throat, choking her words. A silence punctuated the air. Grace risked tilting her head a little higher. Fitzwilliam's gaze was fixed on three sailors attempting to roll a heavy keg up the gangplank. Grace took the opportunity to observe his deep-set eyes framed by neat eyebrows, a darker shade of blond than his hair. His long, straight nose blended seamlessly into a wide mouth, the corners of which had a perpetual upward slant, offering the impression that he was a kind man. He pivoted back to Grace. His stern look was full of authority that had been absent when they had met last night, and she gritted her teeth against him recognising her.

"Welcome aboard, Sykes."

Grace ducked her head, her breath easing slowly through her nostrils. She was immensely pleased he had not seen through her disguise but also chewed the inside of her cheek in disappointment that he had not. "Thank you, sir," Grace mumbled, nodding curtly, and she shuffled after Jim, her shoulders hunched in her oversized coat.

Bosun Tidwell charged past, snapping at Jim, "Before you

head to breakfast, get to the magazine, Buchanan. Help Gunner Ash secure those powder kegs. Not all of us can saunter around like we're on shore leave. Some of us has work to do!"

"Aye, aye," acknowledged Jim. He seized a fistful of Grace's coat. "Be quick about it, Sykes." Jim dragged Grace up to the small, raised deck at the bow where four other men stood stiffly before the captain. Lieutenant Wadham, the officer from outside the alehouse, stood stiffly to the side, his cheeks dimpling with displeasure as Grace hastened to join the others.

Captain Fincham blinked slowly like an owl, squinting against the sharp morning light. His ruffled, thinning hair was peppered with white streaks and plastered limply to his forehead.

"Who the devil is this?" scowled Captain Fincham at Jim.

"Another new joiner, sir. Sykes," said Jim.

"A tardy joiner is more like it," snapped the grey-faced captain.

Checking herself as she almost bobbed in a curtsy again, Grace bowed. "Your servant, sir." Grace hoped that Fincham's overindulgence in wine last night would erase any familiarity of meeting her again this morning.

"Salute, don't bow!" hissed Jim from the side of his mouth. His eyebrows jerked at her head.

Grace wrenched the cap from her near-bald scalp.

"Don't remove yer cap! Salute!" Jim repeated urgently, knuckling his forehead in a motion that Grace valiantly imitated before fumbling to slip on her cap again.

Glancing between the four new men and Grace, Fincham blinked apathetically. "Besides tardiness, what other naval qualities do you possess, Sykes?"

"N-nothing, sir," stammered Grace self-consciously before a wall of curious stares.

"Nothing?"

"My apologies, Captain Fincham. I'm new to navy life," she elaborated, nervously gauging his reaction.

"Good God!" blustered Fincham. "At least this lot have something to show for themselves." He waved towards the three rough-looking youths and an older sailor. "Three experienced gunner's and a carpenter's mate, all essential to a ship." The dishevelled captain studied Grace for a few moments, and she stopped breathing. "You sound polished enough, and once you've had a wash, you won't appear too disagreeable, Sykes. You'll be my new servant. That Mahlon fellow who's been serving me has a displeasing face. Turns my guts to look upon him."

Grace plastered on a respectful look. "Yes, sir. Thank you, sir." She glanced at Jim, the ruck of disbelief in his forehead endorsing her uncanny fortune. The largest of the three gunner's mates huffed through his nose, and Grace averted her eyes from his scathing glower.

Jim nodded warily at Captain Fincham. "Permission to carry on, sir?"

"Of course, Buchanan. Best not dawdle."

"Aye, sir." Jim whirled smartly and scrambled down the ladder.

Captain Fincham clasped a hand over his innards, flapping his free hand towards a small deckhouse on the raised deck at the ship's rear. "Present yourself to Mr McGilney in the charthouse before you begin your duties. You must be added to the ship's book, or Cook Phillips will be inclined to hold back on your rations." With alarming haste, Captain Fincham scrambled towards the ladder. "Dismissed!" he called as an afterthought and scrambled across the deck towards the rear hatch, leaving the newcomers blinking at one another in surprise.

"Right, you heard the captain. To the charthouse," rallied Lieutenant Wadham.

The five new joiners traipsed across the main deck. At the quarterdeck stairs, the large gunner's boy shouldered Grace out of the way to climb up first. "Outta me way, sphincter worm.

Made a fine job of crawling up the captain's arse, didn't you?" The two other boys sniggered. Grace dug her nails into her palms and waited for the three youngsters to go ahead.

In the charthouse, Lambert McGilney was hunched over a large, square table overlaid with charts. The skylight above him spread a veil of light over the page on which he wrote. Gilly motioned to the newcomers. "Over here, let's add you to the ship's book."

He dipped his quill into the inkpot, his fingers already stained from earlier efforts. The slender carpenter's mate went first, introducing himself as Rampersad from the Caribbean, followed by the three unsmiling youths. The brawny lad volunteered his name as Holburton; the other two were Cakebread and da Silva. They turned to leave, and Holburton shouldered Grace again.

"Your turn, maggot," he hissed.

Gilly tapped off the excess ink and grinned up at Grace expectantly. "Ah, Billy Sykes! Any middle names?"

"No."

"Age?" He added her name to a page headed with the date and year.

"Fifteen," she said, repeating his assumption from the night before. It was only a few years off.

"And you've never been on a ship before? Merchant or Royal?"

"N-no." At least she was not lying, which meant she was not blushing. Grace shifted uncomfortably as Gilly's eyes roved over the black muck under her nails.

"Your ol' man have any idea you were plannin' to run off?" Gilly cocked his black eyebrows at her.

"No."

"Good! No caterwaulin' family members to lament your departure from the docks this mornin' then."

"I suppose not." She shrugged, ears burning.

"Name and address of your parents?"

Grace's blood pooled in her feet. "Why is that necessary?"

"So we know where to find you when you scamper off." Gilly looked serious before his quivering lips betrayed him. He burst out laughing. "Relax, young Sykes. 'Tis a standard question for all newcomers. Give us the town or village you're from."

Grace swallowed dryly and gave him the name of an obscure little village she passed through on her summer ventures up north, sending out a little prayer for the forgiveness of her lies.

"Right then! That's that!" Gilly set the quill down.

Grace's throat worked fretfully, and she tried for a smile. Her body ached; a night on the hard bunk had done little to ease her discomfort. Trying hard not to remember her soft bed, she pictured Wallace House coming to life this morning. How long would it take Addison to figure she was gone? Had Billy raised the alarm last night?

"When you're done with breakfast, bring the cap'n some tea to the great cabin. He takes his own special blend of St. John's wort," Gilly elaborated helpfully, nodding in the direction of the door. "Cook Phillips knows how."

Chapter Five

G race found Jim again on the main deck. His black eyebrows rippled across his face like a moving caterpillar. "Give yourself a wee wash in that bucket. Best clear that muck off yer coupon before we head to breakfast." Jim pointed to a bucket near the base of the mast.

"I beg your pardon?"

"Your face. 'Tis covered in soot. Like ye've been climbing chimneys."

Grace splashed handfuls of icy water onto her face, scrubbing between each dousing. She gasped and spluttered as the frigid water took her breath away and numbed her fingertips. Tugging the hem of her shirt from her breeches, she towelled her face, scraping off more soot.

Grace winced as the linen cloth scraped her injured lip. She tested it with her tongue and reckoned the swelling had gone down overnight. Wincing at the dark streaks on her damp shirt, she hid them by tucking the hem back into her oversized breeches. Thankfully, Billy's breeches and coat were dark and hid a multitude of sins.

"Purser Rowlett'll issue you a proper set of clothes later on," explained Jim kindly. "Not for free, mind ye. Nothing's free in the navy." He jabbed her sooty sleeve. "Then you can get that lot washed. Mind where you hang your clothes to dry though. If Bosun catches you employing the rigging as a washing line, he'll as soon lay his Nelly across yer back."

She frowned at him. "Jim, what's a powder monkey? Why did Ben call you such a wretched name earlier?"

"Eh?" Jim swivelled his head towards her, his protruding ears silhouetted against the dawn sky. "Och, he wasn't calling me names. I work the guns. Powder monkey is what they call lads carrying the powder to the cannons. I've been a powder monkey nigh on two years now. Quick as lightning, I am!" Jim nodded at her proudly.

"It sounds awfully dangerous."

"Not if you know what yer doing." Jim hesitated a moment. "We're no frigate. Chance of being blown to smithereens is slim. Before my time, there was this lad who didn't close the top of his powder canister while saluting another ship. A wandering spark blasted him to bits. Captain Fincham wasn't pleased with the mess."

Grace inhaled sharply, trying hard not to show disgust. A boy would not recoil at such a grisly tale. Pressing her grimace into a stiff grin, Grace gave a little shrug. "Still, I'd not care for being called names."

Jim shook his head, laughing. "Best get used to it. Ye've earned yerself the title o' wee Jack Horner."

She chuckled, gleeful at having secured her position as a lad with all the men, even if she did own the lowliest position on the ship. Grace gaped up at the spider's web of ropes and rigging in the masts above her. The flax sails, painted with the pinks of the dawn, were hoisted in tidy folds and stirred gently in the light morning breeze. Despite the early hour, the deck was swarming with activity, heads popping up and down hatchways, bodies scampering nimbly in the rigging.

Grace's heart threatened to pound from her throat as she marvelled at the agility of the sailors. Their bravado swelled with their dangerous endeavours as they balanced along the narrow lengths of the mast's long arms and dropped down to the thin ropes beneath. Grace flinched each time they did it, the ropes all that lay between them and a dizzying, deadly drop. She spotted a new watchman at the gangplank to the shore, glad it was not the hostile Bosun's Mate Blom from the night before. She shivered, the frigid early morning air biting her bare neck.

"There are so many ropes," she said.

"Aye, and you best be learning all their names right quick, like. God help you if ye fumble the wrong rope in a storm. Come along—stop yer dilly-dallying. I hope yer partial to a bit o' burgoo?"

"A bit of what?"

"Well, Cook Phillips calls it burgoo, but it isn't anything more than plain parritch."

"I'm afraid I don't know what either of those dishes entails."

Jim paused, halfway down another hatchway in the middle of the deck. With an amused shake of his head, he dissolved into the dark hole.

It took several moments for Grace's eyes to adjust to the gloom in the mess, and she wrinkled her nose at the rank odour of unwashed men, damp clothing, stale tobacco, and mouldering food. Despite this, she caught a whiff of hot, cooked oats—pleasantly earthy—and burnt coffee. Her stomach grumbled.

Men perched six to a bench, shoulder to shoulder along wooden tables. The air vibrated with the chatter of sailors anticipating their imminent departure. Occasional loud and raucous laughter punctuated the happy rumble, and none of the men even noticed the new, shabbily shorn Grace.

"Sit yerself down beside me." Jim flopped onto a bench, shuffling along until he butted up against the sailor beside him. The sailor gave Jim a cursory glance before returning his attention to another man recounting his last bawdy shore visit to the captivated audience.

"And then she started squealing like a suckling pig, I avow!" An explosion of laughter erupted, several sailors banging their fists on the table in mirth.

Absorbing her new surroundings, Grace noticed the portly cook in the galley at the far end of the mess limping around on his wooden leg. From the galley's bowed beams hung an assortment of sausages and hams, interspersed with low-hanging pots and saucepans. A tall man would have to stoop upon entering the galley or risked being assaulted by cured meats and cooking utensils, but the one-legged cook fitted under the swaying pantry with ease.

Two bowls were slammed before Grace and Jim, steam rising from the piping hot contents, followed by two tin mugs of scalding black liquid. The young boy who served them scampered back to the galley.

"Here you are then, the finest burgoo and Scotch coffee in the land. Thank you, Cook Phillips!" Jim hollered towards the galley. The cook gawked across the noisy mess and caught Jim's eye. Jim raised his tin mug in salute, and Cook Phillips scowled fiercely.

"Cook Phillips isn't so bad if you stay on the right side of him."

"And how do I *get* on his right side?" Grace asked earnestly.

"Why, he's a cook. Ye compliment the man on his delicious meals, even if he serves ye rats' tails and seaweed." The laughter sparkled in Jim's eyes.

"He serves rats' tails and seaweed?" choked Grace.

"You're a funny one! Eat your parritch before it cools. It's a might less appetising then."

In the dim lighting, the contents of Grace's bowl appeared grey and lumpy. Ignoring the ruckus, she scooped up a mouthful of the runny gruel. Bland and salty but hot. She carefully spooned the oats over her injured lip while Jim told her how Phillips had become the cook on the *Discerning*.

Cook Phillips had been an excellent gunner, Jim told her, but after having his leg torn off by a cannonball, he was moved from the thrilling gun deck to the stifling galley.

"You need to watch yerself around him," Jim advised. "Do as he tells you and don't ever criticise the man's food, or ye'll find yourself on the short end of rations. It's better than the stale biscuits serving as wee homes for the weevils and worms." He narrowed one eye. "The trick is to drop your biscuit into a scorching cup o' Scotch coffee to drown out the wee beasties an' then skim them off the top afore taking yer first sip."

The heavy porridge in Grace's stomach churned, and pushing aside her empty bowl, she retched. He laughed as she scowled at him, and digging his elbows into her ribs, he gave her a wink. "Och, I'm only pulling your leg, Billy. Drink up—Lieutenant Fitzwilliam has the ship this mornin', and he doesn't appreciate delay, as you well know."

Grace swigged the blistering liquid from the tin mug, grimacing at the burnt-toast flavour. Realising she could also taste the sweetness of sugar, she took another mouthful before casually remarking, "Lieutenant Fitzwilliam? What kind of a sailor is he?"

"One of the finest. The first lieutenant has an uncanny homing instinct. I swear, you could pit him against an albatross, and I bet you he'd beat the seabird home. 'Tisn't something ye can learn after a year or two at navigation school."

The man opposite them scoffed, and Grace started at his weasel-like face. The scraggly attempts at a beard were scattered in patches across his pock-marked face, and his greasy, slicked-back hair did nothing to soften his features.

Jim waved an introductory hand. "Billy Sykes, meet Mahlon."

Mahlon? Ah, the man whose face displeased the captain. Grace nodded.

Mahlon rolled his tongue across his teeth with a wet suck. "There was that time a year back when we was making slow progress along the coastline. Saw the lieutenant pluck a feather from a chicken Cook Phillips was preparing for the officers' dinner."

Grace blinked in confusion. "And what does a chicken have to do with being a fine sailor?"

The permanent frown in Mahlon's pock-marked forehead deepened. "Well, he tossed the feather into the sea and watched it float off, didn't he?"

Grace raised her shoulders slowly to her ears. "And?"

Mahlon snapped, his fishy odour smacking her from across the table as he growled, "Just from watchin' how that one little feather flew, the lieutenant could warn Cap'n Fincham of the dangerous currents on the leeward side." His tongue sucked noisily again. "Bastard was bang on. Saved us from disaster, he did." The scowling sailor's eyes, as hard and dark as gravel, fixed on Grace, taking the measure of her in the same way Silverton had done across her chamber.

A shiver coursed across her scalp. She indelicately wiped her nose with her sleeve in imitation of Jim and cast her chin up defiantly.

Mahlon's scowl shifted as his mouth fell slack—more a sneer than a grin—revealing a mouth full of decaying teeth. "Back in my day, we had a bosun what kept us boys in line with a regular canin', even if we did nothin' wrong. Bosun Tidwell's a softy by comparison." Stabbing his spoon towards Grace, he said, "Watch yourself, young 'un, or you'll end up strapped to the shrouds covered in a dozen lashes." He gave a phlegmy snort. "Blom's a right mean bastard who'll flay the skin off your back with his cat!"

The talk of flogging quickly eroded Grace's confidence. She folded her arms around her chest, blinking hard to remove the grisly image of tattered flesh from her thoughts. Four bells sounded, and Jim elbowed her urgently in the ribs. "Best get the captain his tea now, Billy." He leaned in, his lips grazing Grace's ear, "And watch yerself around Mad Mahlon."

Giving Mad Mahlon a final scowl of disapproval, Grace walked over to the galley. A large wooden table held half-chopped vegetables, a newly gutted fish, and a jug of fresh milk with a congealing layer of cream. Cook Phillips was massaging the muscle down the thigh of his half leg, his face pinched in pain at each stroke. He was over by the galley stove, a metal monstrosity on a platform of stone slabs. The fire in the stove's belly was invisible, but its intense heat radiated through the cast-iron doors. A chimney disappeared up through the deck above. The sandy-haired cook's boy, who had served her burgoo earlier, was bent dejectedly over a copper pot, stirring what smelled like boiling pork.

The cook struck the boy across the ear. "And let that be a lesson, you lanky streak of piss!" The boy flinched violently at the impact but made no sound of protest. Swallowing anxiously, Grace gave a polite cough.

"Excuse me, please, Cook Phillips, sir."

The round-bellied cook wheeled around and glared at her, ceasing the remedial efforts on his leg. Tufts of thin, white hair hung limply over his broad forehead. A smear of flour coagulated on his sweating brow.

"What you want, boy?" His eyes narrowed. Twisting his hands in his apron, he limped over to Grace with a distinct tapping sound.

Her eyes flicked over the round-tipped wooden stalk

protruding from the bottom of his trousers. The tapping leg moved towards her threateningly.

"After a double dip at the burgoo, are you?" spat the portly man, his red face glowering. "I'll have Bosun on to you as quick as a fiddle, you rapscallion."

"N-no! No, sir," countered Grace, her hands raised. "I'm the captain's new servant. I … I'm after Captain Fincham's tea, please, sir."

"Take your hat off when you speak to me, you disrespectful little shit, before I knock it off your head," Phillips snapped.

The cook's boy glanced fearfully in her direction before flicking his eyes back to his stirring. With a tremulous quail, Grace wrenched the cap from her head. She blinked at Phillips, her lips pressed together miserably. Cook Phillips was no taller than her, but his contemptuous glare shrank Grace into her over-sized coat.

"Wait there!" he barked, turning sharply and limping away. "Christ on the cross, 'tis no wonder the cap'n's got the morbs with all that bloody rat poison he drinks." The cook's boy cast curious glances at Grace as he stirred the pot with a large spoon held in both hands. Cook Phillips poured boiling water into a teapot from the copper kettle sitting on the heated surface.

"Don't stand there gawping, Hicks! Cap'n's tea tray ain't layin' itself," Cook Phillips snarled, his insensitive rasp jolting Grace and Hicks in unison.

Abandoning his stirring, the scrawny boy scrambled franti-cally, the china teacup rattling as he placed it on the saucer. He offered the freshly laid tray to Grace, and she examined the timid eyes staring back at her. They sparked for a moment before sliding away.

Jamming her hat back on, Grace took the tray and smiled graciously. "Thank you kindly, Mr Hicks."

"Back to work, you lazy mongrels!" barked the mean cook, unconsciously rubbing his leg again.

Asking a couple of sailors for directions, Grace navigated her way to the captain's cabin, balancing the tray precariously without spilling too much tea. Gilly was also there, head bowed over a polished writing bureau in the far corner of the cabin. The lantern above him pooled light over the double-paged spread of the book before him. Pouring Fincham his brew, Grace discovered that the pungent curry odour permeating the great cabin was from the herbal tea. The bleary-eyed captain had a cluster of angry, red, weeping ulcers in the corner of his mouth, and he sipped the hot tea judiciously. Five bells rang out.

"Eleven o'clock already?" blustered Fincham, his teacup tipping perilously. He stared dolefully up at Gilly, his face tight.

"Aye, sir. Lieutenant Fitzwilliam was here earlier to report the ship ready to sail, but you were—*indisposed*, sir," said Gilly diplomatically.

The captain sagged. "Ah, Lieutenant Fitzwilliam will see us out to sea, as is his duty." Fincham's hand juddered so hard that the teacup threatened to rattle off the saucer. He slid it safely onto the table. "I simply must lie down again. This London air does me no good. Perhaps I'll be better once we are out on the open ocean, eh?" He attempted a weak smile. "Sykes, pass my regards to Lieutenant Fitzwilliam and give him my apologies." Fincham rolled into his heavily draped berth. With an exasperated shake of his head, Gilly swung around from the writing bureau to face Grace and nodded towards the door.

"Me?" mouthed Grace insistently. She did not mean to be insubordinate, but the prospect of facing Seamus Fitzwilliam again brought about a strong tightening across the back of her shoulders. She had hoped her lowly station would have negated any fraternisation with officers.

Gilly's eyes widened at her silent question. He stepped briskly across the cabin, and firmly gripping her upper arm, unceremoniously pushed her through the door. She yanked it away and glared at him. Glancing back into the cabin, Gilly gently shut the door behind him and leaned in familiarly.

"By crumbs, Billy," he hissed through gritted teeth, more with urgency than anger. "When the cap'n or any superior gives an order, you *must* obey, or you'll be up on charges of insubordination, and there'll be nothin' I can do to spare you the punishment you'll have comin'. Understand?"

"Yes," Grace hissed. Realising he was helping and not scolding, she lowered her chin. The reality of her situation crashed over her like wintery ocean waves. "I'm sorry, Gilly. I'll obey all orders from now on."

Gilly's scowl crumbled as the twinkle reappeared in his eye. He patted her shoulder. "Scamper off then, Billy."

Chapter Six

On the main deck, Seamus coughed and waved away a cloud of steam and coal smoke. A squat tug waited patiently, its paddles churning the foul waters of the Thames. It held position close to the *Discerning*, stemming the tide that promised to take her downriver.

He stood at the rail, his hands clasped behind his back, exuding an undeniable air of authority. From the corner of his eye, he caught Sykes approaching and lowering his tweed cap over his eyes. The new joiner tentatively inched towards him, stopping an arm's length away. The pervading odour of the Thames was not so appalling with a breeze blowing, and Seamus caught the promise of the clean sea air as he stared out over the water.

"What is it, Sykes?"

Sykes stumbled back two steps, blushing fiercely. The boy coughed, in what Seamus assumed was an attempt to try to deepen his unbroken voice. "Captain Fincham passes on his regards and his apologies. He's currently indisposed. Sir." Sykes tacked on the last word hastily. He snatched off the cap and wrung the brown tweed.

Of course he was blasted well indisposed. Probably had half a decanter of brandy for breakfast. In the three years since Fincham's wife had died, Seamus had seen him in various stages of melancholy. Fincham had been at sea when she passed and was wracked with a guilt that was only appeased in the bottom of a brandy glass. Seamus hoped this was not one of those days.

Seamus had a lot of faith riding on Fincham's spirits reviving once they left London. Behind his back, he rolled his stiff wrist, swallowing down his regret for thinking of Fincham in such terms.

Before him, Sykes drew his chin towards his chest and hunched his coat's lapels up around his ears. The youth bit his bottom lip, and Seamus noticed him flinch as his teeth cracked the new scab.

"I understand it's your first day, Sykes, so heed my warning. Bosun will show no quarter if you're out of order." He cleared his throat. "Your standing orders—to be remembered at all times —are to salute a passing officer or warrant officer above deck, not remove your hat. You only do that below. Understood?"

"Yes, sir." He crammed his cap back into place with a petulance that prickled the back of Seamus's neck.

"Have you registered your details with McGilney yet?"

"Yes, sir."

"Did he advise you of your duties?"

"Um, to serve the captain tea?" Sykes's eyes were pinned to the deck.

Seamus coughed dryly, and the youngster peered warily through his lashes. Squeezing his eyes shut in momentary exasperation, Seamus inhaled deeply. His voice rang with an authority that made Sykes flinch. "Bosun Tidwell!"

Nearby, Bosun twisted around, his cane clasped tightly to his side as he stiffened. "Sir?"

"Sykes here needs to be made aware of his duties."

"Aye, aye, sir." The scowling bosun swung his stony eyes to Sykes. "It would be my pleasure, sir."

He approached stiffly, and Sykes looked set to flee.

"Right, Sykes," said Bosun. "I'm placing you in the larboard watch in the afterguard. Every new joiner must learn the workings of the ship. However, your primary concern must always be the captain." He tapped his cane against his leg as he rattled off the orders. "Be attentive, master your vocation, and you might avoid a caning."

Seamus shuffled his feet as he turned back from leaning over the rail to check on the tugboat and caught Sykes scratching his temple. "Don't look so scared, Sykes. You'll be stationed with Buchanan. He'll show you the ropes. He's an upright sort."

Sykes ran his tongue gingerly over the cut on his lip, and Seamus narrowed his eyes. He was surprised McGilney had chosen a lad who clearly was not afraid to scrap.

"Pardon me," Sykes risked a quick look at Bosun's stern face.

"Yes, Sykes?" asked Bosun.

"What's the afterguard?"

Bosun studied him for a moment. "The afterguard is the crew stationed on the quarterdeck." He pointed a gnarled finger to the raised deck at the stern before flicking a thumb in Seamus's direction. "Lieutenant Fitzwilliam here is officer of the watch. He has charge of the ship."

Sykes nodded more confidently, his gaze flipping between his two superiors. "And the larboard watch?"

Bosun readjusted the leather strap of his Nelly on his wrist. "The larboard watch—which includes you and one half of the ship's company—will alternate being on duty with the starboard watch. When on duty, you'll clean the ship, and man the sheets and the helm. Or whatever is demanded of you by a man of senior rank. Is that clear?"

Sykes hesitated, and Seamus arched one brow, bracing for another question. With his shoulder sagging, Sykes replied, "Perfectly, thank you." He did not sound sure. "Sir."

"Yes, *Bosun*," corrected Tidwell. "You'll address warrant officers by their position."

Sykes inhaled tersely. "All right, um, I mean, yes sir, um, Bosun. Aye, aye."

Seamus almost laughed at Sykes's flushing face. The new joiner pressed his swollen lips together, his gaze venturing into the spiderweb of ropes above. "Will I have to climb the rigging?"

Seamus nodded curtly. "That's mostly left to the topmen, but you'll have your fair share of training up there. Can't have a sailor unable to man the sheets, now, can we?"

"No, I suppose not." Sykes's green eyes pooled with worry.

"Right then, back to work," bristled Bosun, his fingers curling around the end of the bamboo stick.

Sykes turned to leave, but Bosun's hissing voice jerked him back around. "Salute your superior, Sykes."

Sykes flapped his hand to his forehead in the untidiest salute Seamus had ever seen. Bosun's eyes narrowed, and he took a long, slow breath as though dampening down his irritation. The corner of Seamus's mouth twitched in amusement as he recalled needing a similar lesson his first time. He adopted a look of earnest interest as Bosun smartly knuckled his forehead.

"*That's* how you salute an officer," Bosun explained to the lad. "Not me, mind you, I'm no officer. Make sure you don't forget, Sykes, or you'll be up for insubordination and will get to meet my Nelly."

Sykes saluted and slunk away, head bowed. There was hope yet for that one. He had an educated enough tongue that spoke of his ability to learn. Sykes snuck a glance over his shoulder at Seamus. He almost wrenched his head off to snatch it back around when he noticed Seamus staring after him. Seamus only hoped the boy's nervous disposition would settle down once they were out to sea.

THAT NIGHT, after Grace had stood hunched beside Jim during the cold, dark hours of the first watch, he showed her how to unroll her newly issued hammock that she had earlier stashed in the netting along the cabin walls, which, he advised her, were called bulkheads. After Grace had made several unsuccessful attempts to climb into the swaying canvas bed, to the amusement of the men, Jack Blight silently lumbered over to her. Holding the hammock open with one hand, he scooped his arm around her waist and, without any decorum, tipped her into the cocoon of canvas.

Grace cried out, and the men laughed. Petrified of rolling out, she gripped the edges of the hammock. When she realised her weight in the centre raised and tightened the sides, she relaxed. Jim threw her a blanket. He slung his right leg up into the hammock next to hers, and gripping the edge of the canvas with his left hand, he hurdled and twisted at the same time, expertly hopping into it. The cook's boy, whose name she learned was Toby, was on the other side.

Toby's bony elbow and Jim's solid knee bumped against her as they wriggled to get comfortable in their canvas beds; the notion of being sandwiched between two men was unnerving. Grace craned her neck up to peek at the row of hammocks strung so near the ceiling—*no, not ceiling, deckhead*—that the sailors could tap the wooden boards above them. The hammocks swung in lazy unison in time with the rhythm of the undulating ship, and with a start of comprehension, Grace realised it was not the hammocks that rocked but the ship itself. The hammock was also more comfortable than the hard, wooden berth. Grace's mind strayed to her soft bed at Wallace House. No! She could not view it with fondness—not anymore. Grace viewed her parents in awe and fear but certainly not with love or respect. Perhaps it was because she was born a girl that they showed no interest in her?

Pushing aside her parents' indifference, and her exhaustion from her first full day aboard the *Discerning*, Grace listened to the lonely bell toll signalling it was past midnight. She melted into dreamless oblivion.

Grace awoke with the bell still clanging in her ears, the few miserable hours of sleep hardly denting her fatigue. The pealing was drowned out by Bosun's Mate's roaring voice reverberating down the hatchway. "Larboard watch, ahoy! Rouse out there, you sleepers. Hey! Out your hammocks or I'll cut you down!" Grace jolted and landed on the deck with a knee-crunching thud. Tears of pain pricked her eyelids as she waited for the throbbing in her knees to settle into a dull ache. Jim nimbly hopped down and lugged her up by her collar. Grace hissed back the pain.

"Quick as ye can, Billy. If ye don't spring from your hammock at double speed, Sorensen'll clobber ye over the head with his rope. Now watch how I roll it." With a speed and deftness achieved only with practice, Jim rolled up his hammock and bedding and tied them together with the ropes. Grace copied him, scowling at the loose and lumpy result.

The new gunner's mate, Holburton, sniggered.

Jim grinned. "Not bad, lad, for yer first try." He snatched her roll and undid the whole lot, but before Grace could be affronted, he handed it back tightly bundled.

Before breakfast, Grace and the rest of the larboard watch scrubbed the decks. With her bruised knees aching on the unyielding wooden planks, she copied Jim, working the pale holystone back and forth, and scraping as much skin from her knuckles as dirt from the deck. Another line of sailors systematically followed the holystoners with brooms, swabs, and buckets to sweep the excess water towards the drain holes—scuppers, Jim called them—and mopped the deck dry.

That afternoon, Ben Blight took her up the rigging. Despite the calm conditions, Grace shuffled only a short distance along the yardarm before she wrapped her arms tightly around the timber trunk and pressed firmly to the wood in terror, her feet wobbling on the unstable rope. With a secure grip of her trousers and a warm chuckle, Ben peeled her off the yardarm and guided her back down. The day passed in a flurry of rope names and naval terms, and by the time Grace collapsed into her hammock, she was fatigued beyond tears.

"Don't worry, lad." Jim winked when he noticed her grimacing at her shredded and blistered palms. "Yer skin'll soon turn to leather. You'll be quicker up the rigging when the ropes don't bite into yer skin so. You're doing a braw job, Billy."

Closing her eyes, Grace was transported back to Wallace House. She was bolting over the furniture in her chamber in a blind panic, only to end up crashing headlong into Silverton no matter which way she turned. Billy's name echoed behind her chamber door, but it was not her voice calling for him. Waking with a mewl of alarm, she flinched away from a persistent pain in her ribs. The hazy fog of sleep lifted, and she recognised Jim's fierce whispers.

"Billy! Billy, wake up. Yer havin' a nasty dream, Billy!" He was hanging over the edge of his hammock, jabbing her in the ribs.

"Ow, all right, I'm awake. Stop that, Jim," she responded groggily. Her head thumped dully, her mouth full of a foul, coppery taste like the time she had sucked on a penny. Nurse Florence had scooped it out of her mouth with a dire warning about the disgusting places people kept pennies.

Jim harrumphed in his usual way and rolled himself back up in his blanket. As Grace lay in the poorly lit cabin, the oppressive sounds and smells of humanity closed in on her—never-ending snores, belches, gassy squeaks, sleep talking, and moans. Her heartbeat, thudding heavily from her nightmare, slowed to a fluttering disquiet that still threatened to crush the breath from her. Her skin puckered at Silverton's lingering touch from her dream.

This was to be her home, her life, for the next few years. A new emotion—regret—flooded through her. It did not feel like any type of home with its strangeness and these coarse men. The corrosive nature of remorse undermined her impulsive decision to join the navy. Though what choice did she have? Silverton had forced her hand—the bastard! Should she surrender to Fitzwilliam? Would he be angry—and offload her in Plymouth? Likely. If so, would she end up married to Lord Silverton after all? Her thoughts came at her with the endless repetition of a Latin conjugation lesson. Besides her best friend, Billy, she yearned for her warm bed the most—and the bell-free liberty to lie in it long enough for the heavy weariness to leave her bones.

She lay staring at the beams of the deckhead above her. Hot tears of misery trickled down her temples, and she scrunched her eyes tightly. A gasping sob erupted from her mouth, and she wadded her musty blanket into her face, biting the rough fibres. Her body convulsed as she muffled her sadness. Despite being surrounded by this seething mass of humanity, Grace had never felt so alone.

Three days later, they docked in Plymouth. The forecastle berths now housed additional crates of fresh vegetables, sacks of flour, salt and oatmeal, casks of vinegar, and two barrels of raisins. A pair of nanny goats were stowed below, bleating unhappily at being rudely dragged down the hatchway.

As their week in Plymouth progressed, Grace set about fulfilling her duties to the indisposed captain, which did not entail anything more than ferrying copious pots of St. John's wort tea and an occasional bowl of broth and biscuits to his cabin. She successfully avoided Fitzwilliam, who was engrossed in the final preparations for their journey.

Joining Jim in the relentless daily chores, she washed dishes, scrubbed decks, pumped the bilges, and buffed brass. Of all the duties she was tasked with, shining the brass adornments was the most satisfying. Together, she and Jim buffed the binnacle housing, the ship's compass, the ship's bell, various scuttles and navigation instruments and even the brass on the cannon. When she was not on watch, she would drop into her hammock in an exhausted stupor until Jim jostled her awake to repeat the same routine.

One day, while shining up the binnacle near the helm with Jim, she learned a great deal more about her rascally Scottish companion. Jim Buchanan was the eldest child in a family of five, he told her, and the son of poor Scottish cotters forcibly displaced from their farm on the Isle of Skye by their aristocratic landowner to make way for sheep farming. Drostan Buchanan vehemently opposed the compulsory emigration of his family; however, with nowhere else to go, and their fares paid by the landlord, they were shipped off to Port Jackson in New Holland. Not wishing to be a burden to his already struggling parents, a then twelve-year-old Jim volunteered to stay behind and join the Royal Navy.

"I live in hope," Jim murmured with an air of optimism, "that one day, by God's grace, I'll sail near enough to Port Jackson to spring overboard and swim to my family. I had no home address to offer the navy, so I haven't a hope in hell of getting any letters to my Maw." His shoulders sagged heavily, and he ducked around the other side of the binnacle but not before Grace noticed his tears.

Moved by Jim's honesty, Grace felt compelled to share. "I didn't proffer a proper address either."

Sniffing loudly, Jim tilted his head back around the binnacle, his black eyebrows dipping. "Eh? What d'ye do that for?"

"Gilly claimed it was so that the navy could track me down if I ever bolted. Therefore, I gave a false address."

"Och, away with ye. He'd have only been chaffing ye."

"He said as much, but I didn't believe him."

Jim shrugged. "Doesn't matter. They wouldn't chase you if you mizzled. The navy retains several months of your pay, so if you take off, 'tisn't any loss to them." Jim quirked one black brow at her. "Do ye not intend sending letters to yer family then?"

Grace tried to stick her chin out defiantly, but it quivered instead. "No, I'll not be sending or receiving any mail from my family in the foreseeable future."

"So, ye write as well as read?" Jim's eyes widened, intrigued.

"Of course!" she flashed back more harshly than she meant.

"Aye, so do I. Only a bit, mind." Jim's lips tightened. "Though, to hear ye speak, it doesn't appear you possess much regard for yer family?"

Grace shrugged and focussed on her shorn-headed reflection, distorted in the curve of the binnacle.

"Hmph." Jim scowled at her. "If you don't intend writing to yer family, do ye at least have a friend to write to?"

Grace blinked guiltily. "I do. My best friend, Bil— William." She wanted nothing more than to reminisce about her friend. "We've been friends since we were all but in clouts." She stopped, sucking her bottom lip against the tears. "He taught me how to ride horses and hunt rabbit."

"Ah, a lad of the land then?" Jim's tongue poked from the corner of his mouth as he buffed a stubborn blemish.

"Yes, I suppose he was—is." She slid behind the binnacle, hiding her misery. She really hoped her leaving had not caused Billy too much trouble.

A squalling flock of seagulls flew overhead, and Grace grimaced at the inevitable mess they would make on the freshly scrubbed deck. At the sight of the birds, the sudden flash of a memory froze her polishing hand, and she steadied herself against the newly buffed brass, her calloused fingers leaving smudges on the gleaming metal.

She had been no more than six or seven when she had found a young bird fallen from its nest in the garden. Back at Wallace House, Mother had marched out of the library where Father sat at his large desk.

"What are you hoarding?" Mother had demanded.

"A little bird. It can't fly." Grace tightened the seal of her bunched fingers against her mother's prying glare. "I'm taking it to Billy in the stables."

Mother glowered at the governess. "How is it my daughter so liberally presumes to set out to the stables? I hope you're not allowing her to mingle with the servants."

"Oh no, your ladyship, never." The governess stiffened.

Father rose from his desk. "What's the commotion out here? Do you not see I'm working?" He towered above Grace, his thin, unfriendly face severe with irritation.

"Your *daughter*"—Mother made it sound like a dirty word —"has brought a wild bird into the house."

Father prised her hands apart, dispassionately eyeing the fledgling. "Have one of the footmen wring its neck."

Grace stuck out her quivering chin. "No."

The young bird released a high-pitched trill of terror as Father's hands twisted violently and dropped its headless, feathered body into Grace's hands followed by its open-beaked head. He snatched his pocket square and smeared the yellow silk with red, glaring at the governess. "Ensure this wilful child learns a hard lesson of obedience. I'll not be told 'no' by anyone in my own house."

Grace glared up at the seagulls, relieved as they flocked towards a shimmering mass of fish in the vast blue distance. The receding trails of her childhood memories sent a chill through her, and she baulked at the sight of the open water. Her audacity was leading her into a dangerous and unpredictable future, but it was still one she would rather face than an equally dangerous and unpredictable future with Silverton. She drew her newly issued, and better fitting, coat closer and shivered in the cutting wind rolling off the harbour.

Chapter Seven

NORTH ATLANTIC OCEAN, 29 MAY 1826

As the days progressed, the monotony that had plagued Grace while they were docked at Plymouth continued without a break. Most challenging was learning the art of holding and cleaning a musket. Captain Fincham insisted all hands, not only the marines, were skilled with muskets and swords. Although they were primarily an exploration vessel, the open ocean's many dangers had the nervy captain insisting on the little bark being well defended. To her absolute surprise and delight, Grace discovered that she had a steady hand and a good aim. After a few weeks of practice, she was as decent a shot as most of the marines.

Grace also adjusted to the company of sailors in the forecastle cabin, particularly the Blighters. The day Ben tidied up her hair, he enlightened her a bit more about life aboard the ship.

"There you go, Jack Horner. You no longer look like the rats have had a feeding frenzy upon your head." In the piece of looking glass Grace held, Ben gave a final flourish of his cut-throat razor, his red mane a sharp contrast to her bald, white scalp. "And you're prepared to enter the dominions of Neptune."

Grace gingerly stroked her smooth head. "Neptune?"

"You've not had the pleasure of crossing the equator before, have you?" His clear blue eyes twinkled with humour.

"No."

"This rite of passage is the greatest honour ever to be bestowed upon a sailor." Ben solemnly tugged on his red beard, ignoring the muffled sniggers.

Ben talked on, revealing to Grace how Toby Hicks's abusive, alcoholic father had placed him as a wager in a game of dice with Cook Phillips one evening in port.

Grace was appalled that such social injustice was even possible. "How could Captain Fincham even sanction such an atrocity?"

Ben shrugged. "To hear the boy tell it, he figured it was an opportunity to scarper from home. With Cook Phillip's persuasion, the lad convinced the captain he was up for the task of cook's boy. Poor lad leapt out of the frying pan into the fire."

While Toby spoke infrequently, Grace took every opportunity thereafter to enquire after him and offer him a kind smile. Consequently, he stopped slinking away from her in terror whenever she approached. He seemed cautiously optimistic about their budding friendship.

As life progressed, Grace was faced with the reality of the brutally unrelenting nature of naval working life. Any spare moments in the day were filled with cleaning and repair. A couple of the young sailors practised their intricate knotting skills, tying, twisting, binding and untying the trails of ropes over and over. Sailmaker Lester was also a master rope rigger who had many a young sailor desperately waiting for him to show them how to create perfect knots.

Some of the men in the forecastle would bring out their keepsakes and share the story behind them. Grace's heart thudded heavily—she must be the only person on board who did not possess one. Craving some intellectual stimulation to disrupt the monotony of the hard labour, Grace boldly asked Gilly if he had any books she could borrow.

"You read? For pleasure?" He sat before a columned ledger, quill stilling, dark eyebrows rising. The hovering quill dripped, and ink splattered across Gilly's neatly formed words.

"I do. Master Olgilby, my apothecary master, insisted on it. To broaden one's mind." Her cheeks barely warmed at the lie. Gilly accepted her explanation with a curt nod and offered her an old copy of *The Times* and his personal copy of Sir Walter Scott's *Rob Roy*.

"I'm done with the broadsheet. Pass it on once you've read it," said Gilly.

That night, Grace rustled the well-read broadsheet flat on the table in the forecastle cabin. Her eyes flicked across the tiny black print of the front-page advertisements, and froze on a small box in the bottom right corner. Oh, dear Lord. No. How was this possible? She checked the date of the publication. The day they had left Plymouth. Scrunching the edges of the paper in a powerful grip to stop her hands shaking, Grace fought for the breath that had been stolen from her. She re-read the advertisement.

£2000 REWARD. Will be paid by Lord Silverton of Clovervale Manor, London, for information resulting in the safe return of his affianced, MISS GRACE ELIZABETH BAXTER, who disappeared at Mayfair, London, May 13, 1826. Description of MISS BAXTER. Age 19 Years. Height 5'2". Green Eyes. Short Curly Brown Hair. May Be Wearing Men's Clothing. Speaks With An Educated Tongue.

The thought that Silverton was after her—hunting her—thickened the recently eaten cheese into a hard lump in her gut. She swallowed deeply to push it back down. Could he not just leave her be? She rose from the bench and side-stepped four sailors crowded on their haunches before the potbellied stove, who were partaking in a rowdy game of craps. Balling the flimsy sheets, she thrust them into the stove. The combustible ball flared brightly, and Grace breathed easier as the blackened curls crumbled to dust, the odour of burning paper overpowered by the dirty scent of burning coal. She glanced around the dim cabin. Several men lounged in their hammocks. Others mended their clothes. A few were already asleep. Running her hand over her shorn scalp, her faith in her newfound disguise wavered. Not many of her berth mates could read, but she wondered which of the officers might have read the advertisement. Fitzwilliam? Fincham? She was no longer in a position to engage in free discourse with the gentlemen who were now her superiors. Besides, she hardly wanted to bring it to their attention if they had no knowledge of it.

Resolving to keep her ears open, and with the evidence gone, Grace curled into her hammock and opened up Gilly's book, escaping with Francis Osbaldistone and the mysterious and powerful Rob Roy on their adventures across the Scottish Highlands.

Most evenings, Toby Hicks retreated unnoticed into the cocoon of his hammock as he had tonight, but when Grace looked up from her book, she spotted him peeping over the canvas edge. With his ears turning bright red, he ducked his sandy head from sight. Within a couple of minutes, he had popped up again, his eyes fixed passionately on the book. Grace flipped the book back to the first page.

"How have I sinn'd," she read aloud, "that this affliction should light so heavy on me? I have no more sons."

Toby melted back, beaming, as Jim jerked his head up.

Harrumphing, he tucked his hands behind his head and lay back. And so began a daily ritual that wove their individual strands of loneliness into a delicately intertwined rope of friendship. Of an evening, the men of the forecastle waited expectantly in their hammocks, ready for Grace's polished diction to take them on daring escapades. Most soon stopped making fun of her prim speech.

Word spread that Grace could read and write, and sailors who could not asked for her assistance in reading letters from home and composing replies. The men pooled together to buy her an inkpot and quill from Purser Rowlett as payment for her services.

"By crumbs!" exclaimed Gilly the first time he saw her writing in the dim lamplight of the men's mess. "You've the penmanship of a scholar! You write better than me!"

"Master Olgilby insisted on a neat hand," laughed Grace uneasily. "You should see my scribbling by the end of the evening when my hand tires!" She discreetly loosened her grip on the quill, resolving to only scratch untidy loops from then on.

After supper one night, at a long table in the men's mess, Grace sat with Toby Hicks, helping him pen a letter home.

Tommy Holburton strolled past with Cakebread and Da Silva just behind him. "Oi, maggot! What's this? A sphincter-worm gathering?" He flicked the back of her skull.

Grace flinched, spraying ink across the page as she whipped her hand up to rub her stinging scalp. She gave Tommy a contemptuous frown, and he sneered at her. Grace gripped the quill hard to stop her hand from shaking as she bowed her head to her writing again.

Without warning, Tommy plopped a pat of bilge grease on top of Grace's head. "Here, have something to grease your pole. Help it slide easier into Hicks."

Grace slapped at the thick glob sliding down her shorn scalp, and her fingers came away black and slimy, stinking of rotten eggs. "How dare you!" she snarled, her skin prickling with fury and disgust.

Toby tipped himself back off the bench, scrambling to escape the thug who made his life a misery too. Grace wished with a startling vehemence that the real Billy was here. He would sort this wretched weasel out in no time. Gulping back her homesickness, she became a wild animal, a snarl clawing up her throat.

"You bloody bastard!" She lunged and swung wildly, her fist connecting with the middle of Tommy's face. Lightning bolts of pain flared down her arm.

The taller youth's head snapped back. He stumbled and tripped over Toby's crouched form, before slamming back into the bulkhead. Tommy's face froze in a mask of shock and blood. He raised his hands to cover his mangled nose. A single tear leaked down his cheek. He glared at Grace over his clawed, quivering fingers and launched himself from the bulkhead.

"I'm no bastard, you mangy maggot!" he roared, his eyes bloodshot with pain and rage. He lifted her by her shirtfront, her legs kicking in the air. The stitching in her collar popped and tore. Blood dribbled into Tommy's mouth as he twisted his lips back in a demonic sneer. Grace windmilled her arms at his bloody face, ineffectively trying to push him off.

A shadow advanced, and Grace closed her eyes against the inevitable blow. She arched and howled as a thick, knotted rope in the hand of Bosun's Mate Sorensen struck her across her back. The pain sliced through her like a cutlass. Tommy dropped her, and she collapsed across the table.

Sorensen, a broad-shouldered man, who had no qualms about assisting Bosun Tidwell with the punishments, hauled her up by her torn collar, his flat face scrunched up inches from her nose. "Oi! What you up to, Sykes? I catch you scrapping again, and it'll be a proper caning for you." He spun around sharply and, disregarding Tommy's bleeding nose, cuffed him around the head with a flat-handed blow that caused the youth's eyes to cross. "You too, Holburton, you lout. With manners like that, I'll wager your mother's skirts only fell to her knees." With a violent roll of his shoulders, Sorensen glared at the two other youngsters behind Tommy. "I know what you three Society bastards get up to when you think I'm not watching. You're the devil's own ankle biters. 'Tis no wonder your mothers sold the lot of yous off." Slapping his knotted rope on the table for effect, Sorensen wandered out of the mess wearing his usual blank, slack-jawed mask, his beady eyes shifting in the hope of spotting any other misbehaviour.

Tommy wiped his nose and glared at the congealing mass of blood and mucus in his palm. With an evil smirk, he wiped his bloody hand down Grace's shirtfront. "Next time, I'll mop the deck with your ugly mug."

"You'll be sorry if you do." Grace tensed her jaw.

"Why's that, maggot?"

"Because you'll not be able to clean into corners properly with my face," she quipped.

Laughter exploded from the sailors at Grace's table as Tommy turned his nose up, limping away. A foot shot out from under the table, and Tommy tripped, his already traumatised nose crunching audibly on the planks. Bounding up from the bench, Ben hauled Tommy roughly to his feet, banging him unconscionably hard on the back.

"Sorry, lad, didn't notice you there," said Ben.

Fresh tears of agony streamed down Tommy's cheeks as he arched away from Ben's tight grip on his shoulder.

"Watch where you're going, Tommy boy," Ben said. "Nasty things happen to those who don't safeguard their step on a ship. Ain't that right, Jacko?" Ben looked at his silent twin brother. Jack clenched his thick fist, and his powerful forearm, hardened by years of hauling sails, bunched tightly. Jack's flared nostrils were enough for the Marine Society boys to twig just who Billy

Sykes's friends were aboard the *Discerning*. Tommy and his henchmen slunk from the mess under a barrage of sniggers.

Grace slumped on the bench, her bloodied hands juddering on the tabletop as she glanced over at Toby seated safely beside Jack. She rolled her shoulders to ease the stinging rope cut on her back and flinched as Ben placed a steady hand on her shoulder.

He withdrew a rag from his pocket and offered it to her. "Here. Clean yourself up. 'Twas beginner's luck you landing that first blow on Tommy's pie hole, Jack Horner." Grace gawked at her shipmate. His bright copper brows were knitted in a troubled frown. "And luck that he lost his balance and fell over Hicks. What followed was an utter dog's breakfast. You flapped at that bastard's ugly mug like a torn topsail." He motioned to his brother. "Me and Jack'll have to teach you how to toughen up and fight—like a man. You too, Hicks. Else the two of you'll continue being trounced by those three oafs." Ben patted her amicably on the shoulder. "Don't worry, lad, you may be small, but you're quick. You need a few of your own moves, and you'll fell those bastards as easily as David felled Goliath."

"How?" Grace firmed up her chin to hold back the tears building in her chest.

"Hop up. I'll show you."

She winced as Ben grasped both her shoulders and turned her away from him.

"Now, if someone grabs you from behind, don't fight to pull away." He grabbed her around the middle and roughly hauled her off the floor.

She instinctively pulled forward, struggling and thrashing her legs, gouging her fingers into the hardened muscle of his forearm locked across her waist like an iron bar. "Put me down! Let me go!"

"No, lad, lean back into me." Ben's voice was filled with the patience of a teacher.

Grace hung limply for a moment then did as she was told, pressing her back into the solid slab of the man behind her. He did not loosen his grip.

"That's it!" encouraged Ben. "It'll shift him off balance, and you'll have the advantage." Ben gripped her forehead with his free hand. "Then you strike back with your head, like this." He guided her head slowly until his nose and lips were pressed into the back of her scalp. His breath was warm on her bare skin, and he seemed unbothered by the stink of the bilge grease. "'Tis hard, and 'tis effective. No matter how big a man is, his soft nose will be no match for your hard skull." He placed her back on the floor. "Now let's try that again."

Grace glanced over her shoulder. "Oh no, Ben. I don't want to hurt you."

"Don't worry, lad. You won't. I'll be ready for you. This move only works when there's the element of surprise." He grinned affably, his white teeth framed by his flaming beard. "Ready?"

"A-all right." Grace turned away and braced herself.

Ben scooped her up again, and quick as lightning, she threw her head back with all her might. It smashed painfully into Ben's collarbone, and Grace cried out, clutching her head.

"Oho! I knew you had it in you!" Ben laughed, dropping her to the floor and ruffling her smooth skull. "Glad I was ready to move out the way."

"That hurt!" scowled Grace, rubbing the lump on her scalp.

"Not half as much as if your opponent brains you with his fist!" Ben gingerly rubbed his collarbone. "You gave it a fair crack there, Jack Horner!" he beamed proudly.

AT EIGHT BELLS ONE NOONTIME, Grace accepted her grog portion from the cheerful Purser, whose economic dispatch ensured the rum would last the journey. Jim and Grace had been separated while polishing the scuttles, and she was now scouring the stifling, noisy mess for her friend. It was not like Jim to be late for the midday meal, but if she did not secure her meal soon, she too would stay hungry until the next one. Cook Phillip's portions were generous enough, but the constant expenditure of energy to keep up with her duties left Grace with a perpetual clawing of hunger. The prospect of missing an entire meal was highly unappealing, though she would rather miss a string of meals aboard the *Discerning* than be forced to watch Silverton dribbling over his breakfast day after day.

She slipped onto a table beside O'Malley. The friendly Irishman nodded in greeting and grinned. "Billy! What's a rapscallion like you been up to today?"

Grace glanced around the table at the other men, recognising a few of them but not yet familiar with all their names. "Sailmaker Lester has been showing me how to repair the ship's rigging." Toby slapped a plate of bread, cheese and salt beef before her and slunk away. Grace slipped the bread into her pocket to give to Jim later. "Oh, and Ben showed me how to drop a man by punching him in the throat." She bit a large chunk of cheese.

"Wise man!" nodded O'Malley, impressed. "Since your attackers will be taller than you, you'll most likely not get a good crack at their face. Throat's the next best spot!"

Grace glanced over at the table nearest the galley where Ben sat nursing his cup of rum, his food ignored. She flushed. "He always tells me to have at him, but I truly hurt him. He didn't block one of my punches in time."

O'Malley barked with laughter. "Christ! Did you drop Ben Blight?"

Grace scowled. "Yes, but it's no laughing matter."

"Don't fret, lad. It'll only be a day or two, and he'll be able to swallow something other than rum or coffee again." O'Malley winked.

Jim flashed into view and nudged her over. She turned to him. "Where've you been? You nearly missed dinner."

Jim sat stiffly, cradling his hands in his lap. "Hmph," he grunted, staring at the lumps of bread, cheese, and meat that Toby had laid before him.

"Aren't you hungry, Jim?" she asked.

"Aye, I could gnaw the arse end of a coo without even stopping to wipe it first." His words were witty, but his voice was strained. Studying him more closely, Grace noticed red-rimmed eyes and grimy smear marks down his cheeks.

"Jim, are you all right?" She widened her eyes with worry, her voice barely a whisper. "Have you been ... weeping?"

Jim flinched, his lips pursed. "Don't be daft, ye great galoot!" Grace recoiled, and Jim lowered his eyes. "Sorry, Billy, truly. It isn't you who I'm crabby with. Ye didn't deserve that. I ken ye mean well."

"Jim! What happened?" She reached under the table to take his hand.

Sucking a hiss through his gritted teeth, Jim started violently, his knees banging the underside of the tabletop. Everyone's plates bounced and clattered. Jim's grog tipped over, the precious contents dribbling onto the floor as he hastily stood and stumbled away from her. A scowl drew his black brows together tightly, and his protruding ears turned an alarming shade of red.

"Christ, man! What did ye do that for?" The confusion in his voice was edged with anger. "Jesus, I took ye for a bit of a softie, but I didn't take ye for a backdoor's man."

Grace froze, open mouthed. "Oh n-no, Jim ... It's not ... I'm not ... I wasn't thinking." Her neck became impossibly hot as the other diners fell silent. A large man at the table beside them rolled his shoulders as if his coat had shrunk and become too tight.

Jim scowled so fiercely that his nose wrinkled, and he levelled a measured eye at her. Grace shook her head and laughed weakly, but her smile drooped as she lowered her eyes from his stony, flat stare. Someone behind her gave a loud hack, and a glob of spittle slapped the floor. Every fibre of her being strained to flee. Run where? She was on a ship. With her chin quivering, she fixed her eyes on Jim's hands. He clutched them gingerly, and she braved glancing back up at him. "Jim! Your hands! What happened?"

Jim studied her for a moment before releasing a slow and wary breath. Cautiously, he settled back down, leaving a deliberate gap between them. He held his hands palm up, and Grace gasped. A criss-cross of raised welts blazed across his hands, some even mottled with blood.

"Nelly's kiss. Missed a bit o' tarnish on a scuttle."

The men muttered darkly, though Grace was sure there was more to their grumbling than sympathy for Jim's hands.

Chapter Eight

SOUTH ATLANTIC OCEAN, 3 JULY 1826

Several weeks later, during the forenoon watch, Grace and Jim were polishing the ship's bell behind the helm when Tidwell's whistle called the hands to assemble. Not part of the predictable drudge of the daily routine, Grace eyed Jim questioningly.

"Och, someone must have earned themselves a caning," he shrugged.

"Oh." Grace's heart plummeted. She had seen a multitude of men caned for various offences ranging from quarrelling and insolence to neglect of duty and disobedience.

"Let's get a shift on before *we* become the entertainment," said Jim.

Grace tucked her cleaning cloth into the waistband of her trousers and trailed after him. Some hands assembled around one of the six-pound cannons near the bow, and others eagerly scampered up the rigging.

"Oi, why you stoppin', maggot? Keep movin'!" Holburton's calloused hand shoved Grace through the pressing mass of bodies, and she found herself at the front of the crowd. She fixed her eyes desperately on Jim as he elbowed his way through.

"Seems we're to enjoy a fine view of the proceedings," Jim said, grimacing.

"I don't want a fine view!" Grace searched for a gap through which they could escape. Tommy hemmed her in, sneering.

"Ye know full well if you're caught not paying attention, ye'll not be too far from a caning of your own. Best you watch, even if it pains you to do so. Besides, it doesn't hurt you as much as it hurts the lad being caned," said Jim.

The assembled crowd parted to allow the offender through, and Grace gasped. Toby Hicks, hands bound, was half-crazed with fear. A sizeable wet patch stained the front of his breeches as he feebly resisted Bosun's Mate Sorensen. Grace dragged her eyes away from Sorensen's rubbery, moist lips and caught Toby's impassioned stare. He whimpered and babbled incoherently. Grace twisted around to leave, but Jim gripped her firmly in place.

"Ship's company!" Fitzwilliam's voice boomed over the seamen's chatter, and Grace squinted up at him on the forecastle deck. He tucked his cocked hat under his arm, and the wind whipped loose strands of his golden hair around his head as wildly as Medusa's serpents. Fincham was nowhere to be seen. He rarely was these days, and Grace knew he would be slumped in his cabin nursing a cup of his special tea or a snifter of brandy or both. A hush settled across the main deck as Fitzwilliam's voice rang out. "The charge is theft of a piece of salt beef and two biscuits. The sentence is a dozen lashes on his bare posterior."

A roar of approval from the men ricocheted up the deck and into the rigging. Toby convulsed, but his captor gripped him firmly. Sorensen pushed the thin boy up to the cannon and yanked on Toby's soiled breeches to expose his puny backside. The men roared with laughter and shouted insults at him.

Behind Grace, Tommy hissed in her ear. "Hey, maggot. It'll be you up there soon enough, waving your throttled shrimp about. Though I imagine Buchanan here's developed quite a taste for shrimp already."

Beside her, Jim stiffened. He did not relinquish his grip on Grace but let off a growl of warning. She glared over her shoulder, but her urge to spit back an insult was cut short by Cook Phillips gloating to Tommy beside him. "This'll teach the ungrateful beggar not to steal food from my galley." Phillips folded his arms in righteous satisfaction, his false leg jutting cumbersomely to the side.

Miserable bastard. Turning back with as much dignity as she could muster, Grace leaned into Jim and whispered in mortification, "What are they doing to him?" All the canings she had witnessed to date had been with Bosun's Nelly, the punishment meted out on the spot.

"He gets to kiss the gunner's daughter," Jim explained in a low voice.

"Why did they remove his breeches?" Grace's eyes flicked frantically between Jim and Toby.

"He's only a lad, so he'll get his flogging across his bare arse. The naval authorities don't want us boys becoming too cocky by taking a man's punishment of a flogging across the shoulders."

"Flogging?" Grace gasped. "Why not a caning?"

"Theft of food aboard a ship leaves rations short for the rest of the men. 'Tisn't a light charge."

"This whole process is barbarous!" Grace smarted, tears of frustration welling up, unable to look away from the macabre scene.

Sorensen bent Toby over the cannon breech, stretching his bound hands down the barrel and securing them with an additional piece of rope. Toby's bare feet and skeletal legs danced agitatedly on the wooden deck, kicking away his breeches as he tried to squirm his way off the cannon, but Sorensen pressed him in place with one hand on his back. The boy's shirt bunched up around his shoulders, and his ribcage jutted out sharply, heaving as he hyperventilated. The vertebrae of his back spiked through his thin skin like a row of knuckles.

"That boy is starving!" Grace whispered fiercely to Jim, her jaw and cheeks blazing in indignation. She glowered up at Fitzwilliam on the forecastle.

He stood with his hands clasped behind his back, his face an impassive mask as he called out to the ship's surgeon beside Toby, "Is the prisoner ready for his punishment, Mr Beynon?"

Beynon wedged a piece of hide between Toby's teeth. "Bite on that for all you're worth, young man." He patted the back of the quivering boy's head in reassurance and nodded at Seamus. "Ready, sir."

"Bosun's Mate, if you please." Fitzwilliam nodded at Sorensen.

Sorensen made a show of untangling the tails of the whip by brushing his thick fingers through the strands as if caressing a woman's hair, his malicious grin curling his lips back from his teeth. Toby whimpered.

"You see, that's the boy's cat. It has but five tails of smooth whipcord as opposed to the nine knotted tails of the men's cat," Jim explained to Grace, his brown eyes mournful.

A high-pitched, inhuman shriek cut through the air as the lash cracked, and Grace jolted, clasping her ears. At the third lash, Toby's body stiffened in a spasm of pain, his rigid legs jutting out from the cannon, his scrawny buttock cheeks clenched in agony as angry blue and purple welts appeared.

Sorensen took his time about it, enjoying the languor of the interval as much as the strike. Bosun Tidwell policed the proceedings, a twisted scar on his face white in contrast to his sunburn. Ship's Surgeon Beynon calmly and officially gauged the boy's reactions. Toby shrieked uncontrollably, the pain clearly still pulsing through his beaten flesh as Sorensen set himself up for the next stroke.

Jim nudged Grace and whispered, "Yer tears won't help the lad. Don't allow Tommy to see yer weakness." Grace roughly knuckled the tears from her cheeks, resolving to be braver. The sight of the helpless boy brought back memories of her helplessness against Silverton.

The men called out to Toby, some in encouragement, others cruelly taunting him and calling him unspeakable names. They were like a pack of wild dogs tormenting a mouse, grinding his gentle spirit into a fine powder with their salty abuse.

With white speckles flashing at the edges of her vision, Grace stepped out of the crowd and stood protectively before Toby's battered backside. She squared up against Sorensen. "Stop it this instant!"

Jim tried to grab her but now stood gawping in silence, as did every other sailor. Sorensen stared at her incredulously, a bark of laughter erupting from his slack jaw. He squeezed his eyes tight and briefly shook his head. The boy's cat hung limply in his hand, the untangled tails swaying with the movement of the ship. Grace jutted her chin out defiantly. She had saved herself from Silverton—she could save Toby too.

Grace glowered at the crowd. "Were the captain well enough to witness this, he'd never sanction the beating of a starving boy," she shouted, flicking her hand towards Toby. "It's no wonder he took extra food. Look at him, he's all ribs and knees. Cook Phillips can't be feeding him properly. This is an abomination!"

Grace wrenched her head around as Fitzwilliam bellowed, "Bosun, seize that man! He's out of order!"

Tidwell snatched Grace by the arm, growling, "Good God, I'll teach you to stick out that insolent chin!" A throbbing, puce vein popped down the side of his thick neck, his eyes agog in astonishment. He glanced up at Fitzwilliam.

"Continue!" Fitzwilliam ordered, nodding at Sorensen.

Grace twisted and writhed, but Tidwell's grip bit into her bone like the teeth of a bear-trap. One consolation was that Sorensen no longer put on a show. He lay the last few lashes across Toby's backside swiftly. Stepping up to the snivelling, snot-covered boy, Sorensen undid the knots of his bindings, and Toby dropped to his hands and knees. Sorensen flicked his head at Jim, who scooped one of Toby's scrawny arms over his shoulder and dragged the near-naked, limping boy through the parting crowd.

Grace's clenched fists shook as she glared up at Fitzwilliam silhouetted against the bright sun. How could she have ever thought he was kind?

"What 'bout this one, Lieutenant?" Tidwell asked, thrusting Grace forward.

"Bring him across the barrel!" ordered Fitzwilliam. "Since he feels so strongly about it, he can share the same fate as Hicks."

Sorensen lunged across the cannon, locking Grace's hands in his. He yanked her forcefully over the iron barrel, winding her in the process. Sorensen crushed her wrists while Bosun Tidwell dropped her trousers.

"I'd expect you to be sporting bollocks the size of cannon-balls after that little lark," laughed Bosun Tidwell savagely, teasing up the edge of her long shirttails with his Nelly. "Give us a look then." The crew roared with laughter.

Grace grunted, her face burning in mortification, and she wriggled furiously, encouraging her shirttails to fall back into place. "You couldn't count *your* balls and reach the same answer twice," she screeched amidst a wave of whistles and jeers.

Fitzwilliam's voice hardened, "Insolence *and* talking out of turn. Double the punishment, Bosun." Sorensen clutched her tighter, grinding the bones of her hands together.

"Bloody hell! Damn you!" The helplessness that had crushed Grace against the wall during Silverton's attack flared into a swirling rage of hatred. "I'll not take this! You bastards!" Spotting Sorensen's clenched hairy paws beneath her face, Grace sank her teeth into the fleshy bulge below his thumb. Her jaw ached as her front teeth connected. Sorensen roared, releasing Grace as though she had combusted. Without his support, she tipped forward, legs splayed with her trousers hooked around her ankles. She tucked her head aside at the last second and catapulted over. The impact slammed the air from her lungs, and she lay on the deck flailing and gasping like a newly caught fish.

"By Christ!" The expletive exploded from Bosun Tidwell. "He's a girl!" The laughter from the men on deck died to an interested murmur, and they shuffled in for a better view.

With the air still locked from her lungs, Grace rolled over onto her hands and knees, wheezing. Tidwell seized her up by her arm, and her shirttails dropped modestly back into place. Coughing, she snatched back her arm. "Get off me!" Wrenching up her trousers, she rammed her shirt into her trouser top and blazed at Tidwell.

"Enough!" roared Fitzwilliam. "Bosun, bring her to the charthouse. McGilney, a word if you please." His dry tone did not invite any argument.

Confusion shimmered across Tidwell's face. Turning and stomping towards the quarterdeck ladder, Grace heard Bosun Tidwell yell out, "Right! Back to work, the lot of youse. You've had enough entertainment for today. This ship ain't goin' to sail herself."

Bosun Tidwell scampered uncertainly over to her, his scowl of disapproval faltering under Grace's venomous glower, and he fell half a step back. At the quarterdeck ladder, Grace turned on him, her polished tone calm. "Thank you, Bosun Tidwell. I can manage from here." The pregnant silence was filled with mutual vitriol, and Grace continued alone.

At Grace's firm knock, Gilly opened the charthouse door, frowning as his dark brown eyes scoured her for clues he had missed when he first met her. His weather-beaten brow crinkled up in a silent invitation, and Grace stepped into the low cabin, relieved to hide from the accusatory stares burning into her back. The charthouse was cool in comparison to the sunny day outside.

The large table was covered with an open map and various brass navigation instruments—remnants of someone's interrupted activity. The skylight above the table spread a natural light on the charts. Outside, the men's muffled voices and the scrape of something sizeable being dragged across the deck signalled the return to duties. Fitzwilliam was standing with his hands clasped behind his back, legs braced apart, elegant neck craned down. Gilly slid around the table, half concealing himself behind Fitzwilliam. Gilly's expression reflected the seriousness of the situation, but his eyes were narrowed with a hint of curiosity.

Fitzwilliam spoke first. "Well, miss, it appears you've successfully fooled a wily crew of sailors into believing you're one of them. No mean task for a young man, let alone a girl pretending to be one."

Grace had spent plenty of time pondering what she would say if she were ever found out. If she told him she had run away, he would believe her a spoiled child and send her back to London. But if she divulged the details of her ordeal, he would think her ruined and discard her at the next port, knowing she would never be accepted back into society. Not knowing which fate was worse, she remained mute.

"Your presence here is causing me to severely reconsider my faith in McGilney's ability to recruit appropriate hands for this ship." The towering lieutenant had a daunting air of authority about him, and Grace covered her vulnerability by bracing her shoulders.

Gilly's eyebrows dipped at Fitzwilliam's words, and his

curiosity transformed into hardened displeasure aimed directly at Grace. Caught between two hard stares, Grace reluctantly settled on Fitzwilliam.

"You catch me in a quandary." Fitzwilliam's blond brows puckered. "Pray, do declare, madam, should McGilney be punished for his poor judgement, or should it be you for your deceit?"

Gilly's nostrils flared, and his boots shuffled uncomfortably as he sucked in a deep breath. Grace raised her chin to Fitzwilliam. "Whatever you decide, Lieutenant, you should consider carrying out the sentence yourself instead of handing it over to another man like a coward."

The breath spluttered from Gilly, and despite only a moment ago prickling at his superior's berating, he took a step towards Grace. "By crumbs, that's enough! Lieutenant Fitzwilliam is an officer, and I remind you to afford him the respect he's due."

Gilly stared as if she was a stranger, and Grace nibbled her top lip with a twinge of trepidation. She considered Lambert McGilney one of her allies aboard the *Discerning*, but she bristled at his condescending tone. She dragged her cap off in exaggerated capitulation.

"You do puzzle me, madam." Fitzwilliam tilted his head, studying her through narrowed blue eyes. "How is it you stand before me looking and smelling like a common scamp, yet your polished speech tells of an excellent education?"

"Puzzles are meant to be solved, are they not, Lieutenant?" Grace had not meant to sound so snobbish, but fear of discovery had her on the defensive.

Fitzwilliam lowered his chin, studying her intently. "Indeed, but one usually requires at least a few pieces to glean an idea of the picture." He inhaled sharply. "What baffles me is that none of your pieces align."

"Perhaps I didn't plan for my pieces to align." Grace met his stare bravely while her insides churned.

Fitzwilliam blinked twice and chuckled without mirth, one golden eyebrow cocked. "Young lady, with a liberal tongue like yours, it was only a matter of time before your true identity was revealed. No boy aboard this ship would survive with such insolence."

Grace was exhausted and ravenous. She was also angry beyond measure at what had been done to Toby. Her tolerance frayed, and she did not care if Fitzwilliam off-loaded her at the next port if she did not keep her mouth shut. Grace drew her shoulders back, elongating her spine. "Tell me then, Lieutenant, how the systematic starvation and mistreatment of the cook's boy escaped your notice, or is he too lowly to be worthy of your attention?" She tried to temper the scorn in her voice, but it was clear from Fitzwilliam's scowl that she had failed.

"You're certainly opinionated, but tell me, did your elaborate education cover the basics of seamanship required on a bark in His Majesty's Royal Navy?"

Grace folded her arms, knowing it was a defensive gesture, but the soured mood in the cabin chilled her, and she needed a veil of protection against her interrogators. Despite feeling unsettled, Grace countered primly, "One doesn't need a formal education to recognise the absence of basic human decency." She was only able to remain standing because of the taut thrum of nerves beneath her skin; a tremor in her knees threatened to send her crashing to the floor.

"By God, girlie, hush your head!" Gilly banged his fist on the table in frustration. Grace could tell he was hurting, and a grip of guilt squeezed her thudding heart.

"Thank you, McGilney, I have the matter in hand," said Fitzwilliam dryly. Gilly flicked a controlled scowl at Seamus, blanching at his dismissal. He cast an even deeper glower towards Grace. Fitzwilliam's tone softened. "Your efforts are appreciated though."

"Yes, sir." Gilly smarted at the dressing down, and Grace averted her eyes to prevent him from further embarrassment.

Fitzwilliam turned politely to Gilly. "McGilney, kindly deliver my dinner to the charthouse. My companion and I have a bit to discuss." He glanced back at Grace. "I trust you'd care for a plate, Miss …?" His blue eyes blinked expectantly. Grace's ears warmed uncomfortably, and she bit her lip again. He coughed delicately. "Please advise Cook Phillips that my *guest* will also be joining me for dinner."

Gilly stood straight, his jaw muscles dancing. "Aye, aye, sir."

"A fine example of naval obedience." Fitzwilliam nodded at Gilly and swivelled his eyes to Grace. "You could do to take note, young lady." The colour returned to Gilly's cheeks at the praise, and he hastily headed out to fulfil his orders.

With slow and measured steps, Fitzwilliam slipped around to Grace's side of the table. The ship was undulating lazily, but at his approach, the floor tipped further, and Grace clutched the edge of the table to steady herself. Her already thumping heart skittered wildly as he seized one of the wooden chairs, lined up out of the way against the bulkhead, and brought it over to her. Grace reached for the chair, recoiling as the sides of their hands brushed.

"Please, allow me." He held the chair out. Grace froze—not a foot separated them. Tempted to duck her head as she always had in his presence, Grace swallowed and jutted her chin out. A shadow of recognition flickered across his face as his gaze evolved from one of scrutiny to one of gentle searching.

"Have we met before?" His wide brow was scrunched in concentration.

With a betraying heat creeping up her throat, Grace lowered her eyes to his top button, her resolve wavering under his inspection.

He hummed softly. "I once met someone who carried such colour in her cheeks." Grace flicked him a guilty look. His pupils instantly dilated, and he sucked in his breath. Pinching her chin none too gently, he tilted her face up, his grip tightening, not enough to hurt, but enough to cause her to gasp.

"Miss Baxter?" Her name shot from his mouth as a wave of confusion and fear crossed his face. At the sound of her name on his lips, her knees finally gave way, and she swayed, dipping dangerously. He reached out to cup her elbow and guided her onto the chair.

"Heavens above, it can't be true!" He swiped at the shimmer of perspiration across his brow.

To Grace's mortification, hot tears betrayed her.

Fitzwilliam stepped beside her. "Miss Baxter, you foolish girl." His voice was tight.

Losing her battle with her resolve, his words unravelled her, and she dropped her face into her hands. With no ability to stop them, gasping, convulsive sobs pulsed from her core, and she poured her distress, fury, and humiliation into her palms.

Grace took comfort as Fitzwilliam stiffly patted her back. With her trembling breaths slowing, her tears eased. Hiccoughing and sniffing loudly, she squeezed her eyes tight. She felt his hardened hand on her shoulder soften, and she chanced a look up at him. His face was as tight and unmoving as a secure knot in a storm. Grace was about to avert her eyes when he dipped his chin, his shoulders sagging. He pinched the bridge of his nose and then opened his eyes. They were no longer a cold steely blue—more like the warm tropical waters in which they sailed. When he spoke, his tone had softened too. "Heavens above. Whatever am I to do now?"

Chapter Nine

Seamus dropped his hand from her shoulder and stepped back, desperately searching for the connection between this creature and the elegant young woman in the gardens back in Mayfair. He recalled her refreshing, bold look—her wide forehead accentuated by her high hairline and her petite, nondescript nose that suited her. She resembled nothing of this grubby, shorn street urchin.

"Miss Baxter," he repeated, shaking his head in wonder. His eyes snapped to the red scar on her lip. He clenched his jaw. "When you arrived … your face. What happened?"

Miss Baxter sucked at the scar on her bottom lip and lowered her gaze. A flurry of scenarios raced through his mind.

"Lieutenant, I … I can't—" Her chin trembled, her words coming out choked. She swallowed loudly.

He sensed her struggle to contain her emotions. Surely, she was relieved to drop the pretence? But what on earth had caused her to create such an elaborate ruse? "Hush now, Miss Baxter."

He straightened his shoulders as the door latch clicked, the leather hinges creaking. "Say no more. All will be well."

McGilney's eyes were fixed on the plates, glasses, and carafe of wine balanced on the tray. Seamus rolled up the map on the table with practised efficiency and stowed the instruments in the bureau. McGilney slid the tray onto the cleared table, and Seamus turned to him. "Thank you, McGilney. Is the captain up yet?"

"No, sir. I took the cap'n his broth while waitin' for Cook Phillips to prepare your tray. Cap'n's ingested enough laudanum to knock down a shire horse, sir." McGilney flicked Miss Baxter a fleeting expression of concern before his face closed over again. "Enjoy your dinner, Bil— Mr, um, beggin' your pardon, miss."

"Oh, Gilly," wailed Miss Baxter thinly.

McGilney bowed to her and spun rigidly towards Seamus for dismissal.

"That'll be all, McGilney," said Seamus.

McGilney's shoulders rounded as he slunk out, slamming the door. Miss Baxter blinked at the solid thump. Her eyes slid to the plates, brimming with roast beef and boiled potatoes covered in rich, thick gravy. Seamus heard her stomach gurgle. Pouring two glasses of claret, he announced, "Dinner is served, madam."

She squirmed, clearly discomforted by the shift in his conduct towards her. "Lieutenant, please don't trouble yourself on my account."

Seamus smiled ruefully as he sat opposite her at the table. "No trouble at all, Miss Baxter."

"Thank you." Her tear-washed eyes shimmered aquamarine as she glanced curiously at his wrist.

"I noticed your scar before, in the gardens at Wallace House." She gave a brave grin, but her swollen nose made a poor effort of it. "What happened?"

He ran his thumb over the smattering of rough, pale hairs

below his wrist, trailing across the scar tissue that curved from the base of his thumb, around the back of his hand, and under his cuff. He smiled politely at her courageous attempt to converse. "A corsair's blade." He reached for his wine, appreciating the slide of the raisin-rich liquid down his gullet.

Seeing Miss Baxter's tar-stained fingers twitch with impatient politeness over her knife and fork, Seamus picked up his own, slicing into a sliver of roast beef. She gobbled her food down twice as quickly as him. Neither of them spoke for a while, Miss Baxter noticeably more interested in food than conversation. Seamus exploited the silence to figure her out, finally breaking the quiet by revealing how he acquired his scar.

He had been a young midshipman under the then Captain Baxter's command. They had been in the Mediterranean and were closing in on a Barbary Corsair. The Royal Navy frigate caught the heavily laden vessel easily enough, but the corsair did not go down without a fight. Seamus, a relatively inexperienced swordsman, cut down two sailors before the pirate slashed the back of Seamus's sword hand with his dagger. With his hand cut to the bone, Seamus believed he was done for as the blood-crazed man bore down on him. Unexpectedly, the corsair dropped like a sack of rocks, and in the chaos of the skirmish, Seamus saw Baxter on the quarterdeck with a smoking pistol aimed into the mêlée. Her uncle had saved his life.

"The ship's surgeon sewed me up with catgut. Said it was fortunate the guard of my cutlass deflected the main blow or else I'd likely have lost my thumb." Seamus waggled the digit in question and picked up his knife again.

"You work a dangerous occupation."

"There's certainly a heightened danger when posted on a frigate," he agreed. "But on a frigate, one sets off expecting conflict. These days, I prefer the more sedate exploits of surveying. That's not to say we won't encounter any trouble along the way, but passing ships are less likely to be interested in a surveyor's vessel than a resource-rich merchant ship."

Her eyes flashed with understanding. Heavens above, he had seen her handle the helm like a seasoned sailor, and she wielded a musket almost as well as Sergeant Baisley. He had known she was a feisty one when they had met, but this? She had proven she could more than adequately hold her own on a ship full of men. But she was still the niece of the man who had saved his life, and it was his duty to protect her.

His stomach roiled uneasily. "You'll be safe with me. No harm—" he halted, and Miss Baxter glanced up from her wine glass as he tightened his mouth in displeasure, his eyes fixed on the scar on her lip. "No *further* harm will befall you. This, I swear."

Seamus cleared the plates away to the sideboard, marvelling at how he felt more at home in the confines of this little charthouse, and in the presence of this young woman, than he felt anywhere else. It was the same sensation he had felt in the gardens, but this time it was not as unwelcome.

Noticing the colour return to her cheeks as she relaxed in her chair, Seamus poured her another goblet of wine. She reached for it, and their fingertips brushed, but Miss Baxter swiftly drew her chapped hand away.

"Miss Baxter, I appreciate the difficulty, but it's imperative you name the man who hurt you. I want justice done so he can never hurt you again."

She squirmed in her seat. "How do you know I didn't fall?"

Seamus's concern deepened. "Must have been quite a tumble." She chewed her lip and lowered her eyes. Leaning forward, he gently probed, "Miss Baxter? *Did* you fall?"

Unable to meet his eyes, she replied meekly, "No." His jaw tightened as she deflected him again. "What makes you presume it was a man?"

"A *woman* did that to you?" The dry cynicism of Seamus's voice forced her eyes to meet his.

"No," she whispered, her breathing becoming jagged as her eyes moistened. She firmed her chin, and he knew she would not weep again. Raising her wine glass, she gulped the remaining contents down.

Seamus poured her some more, wincing empathetically. "Dutch courage, hmm? You can trust me. Anything you divulge will stay between us."

Miss Baxter lowered her hands to her lap. The calming effect of the wine was working with varying degrees of decision marching across her face. Seamus waited, silent and patient.

"After you left the garden," she began, "I retired to my bedchamber." Slowly and hesitatingly, she allowed him entry into her darkest moment, which he endured in revered silence, listening, barely breathing. "Lord Silverton appeared and locked himself in my chamber with me. His pretence was one of conversation, but when he … when he ran his fingers across my décolletage to comment on how I'd scratched my skin, I struck him. My nails caught his cheek, drawing blood." She twirled the near-empty wine glass by the stem. "This sent him into a rage unlike any I've ever seen in a person. He then …" She tipped back the last of the wine, swallowing audibly, and Seamus refilled her glass. "He then threatened to f-force himself upon me. Said that no other suitors would have me. Said it would seal the deal between him and my father. He thought it his right as my fiancé."

Seamus dropped the heavy-bottomed wine carafe on the table with a loud thud, and his fingers whitened around the neck. He took in a slow, deep breath as she continued the whole story of that night and explained how she was lured onto the *Discerning* by a persuasive McGilney. "This tale has been easier for the telling a second time—the first to the real Billy Sykes, of course."

"Ah." Seamus arched his brow questioningly. "You adopted your friend's name?"

"Yes. When Mr McGilney asked my name outside the Two Chairmen, I panicked. Billy's was the first name that came to mind." She sniffed. "Alone in my mind, Silverton looms large, but out here on the open ocean with the safety of distance, his power over me is diminished."

Seamus rubbed his hand across the back of his neck. "I'm sorry, Miss Baxter. For all that transpired." His voice faltered as he took a deep breath and held it.

"B-but you weren't to know what was to happen. None of us did," Miss Baxter reasoned. Seamus exhaled explosively and roughly kneaded his wrist. She eyed him warily.

He was well aware of the rumours of Silverton's sexual peculiarities. Patrons of the gentlemen's establishment, White's, on St James's Street, of which Seamus was a member, often overheard Silverton drunkenly bragging of his conquests, though Seamus had taken his boasting as pure windbaggery.

"I didn't know you'd been promised to him. Heavens above! The admiral! Does he know what happened to you?"

"No," she said mildly. "No one besides you and Billy knows. I fear my impulsive decision to flee meant I gave no thought to what bother my actions will have caused Billy."

"Your mother and father must be out of their minds with worry. I'll not be able to send word to them for months yet."

"Don't write to them, I implore you." Her eyes strained wide. "I didn't come all this way and make all the difficult choices I made to risk being summoned home again by Father."

"Miss Baxter," Seamus admonished lightly, "they are your parents. They'll want to receive word of your welfare."

"Ha!" she barked, folding her arms. "Did my father keep my welfare in mind when he betrothed me to that beast?"

Seamus stared at her for a moment, unblinking. "Fair point, Miss Baxter."

She sagged, and she shut her eyes wearily. "Lieutenant, please excuse me. I'm exhausted. I must go lie down in my hammock."

A breathy half laugh burst from him before he shook his head. "You'll do no such thing. It'd be highly improper of me to allow you to sleep in the fo'c'sle with those men."

"Lieutenant Fitzwilliam, has it escaped your attention that I've been sleeping in the fo'c'sle with those men for nigh on two months?" His exasperation melted as he caught the mischievous grin tweaking the corners of her wine-painted mouth.

"That was before … I didn't realise … A gentlewoman can't possibly …" He snorted. Blast! She had him there. He steepled his fingers before his lips and quirked one eyebrow. "Which begs the question of before, just what do I do now?"

With Captain Fincham still indisposed, Seamus had to determine a solution alone. He had been serious about her not returning to the forecastle cabin. He withdrew her from all duties, as well as musket and sword training, and arranged for the charthouse to be cleared. The large table was to be stowed in the hold, although the wide bookshelf and long bureau remained. Seamus personally oversaw the setting up of a cot with a thin feather mattress, a table with two chairs and a washstand. Folded beside the washbasin was a large square of muslin and his personal silver hand mirror and brush. Not that she possessed any hair to brush.

Miss Baxter sat on the edge of her cot while he inspected the results with a satisfied nod. The charthouse was just over five feet high, and unless he stood directly under the skylight, he had to keep a bent neck so as not to knock himself out on the deckhead beams. However, barefoot, she only stood a smidge above five feet and fitted nicely into the compact space.

"If not exactly cosy, it's vastly less smelly and certainly more private than the fo'c'sle." He stoked the fire in the potbellied stove. "Plenty of natural light." He pointed at the overhead skylight. He glanced out at stern scuttles at the creaming wake. "Good view too." Seamus tapped the leg of the cot with his shoe. "After sleeping scooped up in a rough canvas hammock, I'm sure you'll appreciate the ability to lie flat and stretch out your legs."

"Thank you, Lieutenant." Miss Baxter rose from her cot, shifting her weight from one hip to the other. The small cabin became claustrophobic as his awkwardness grew.

Clearing his throat, he nodded stiffly. "Right, I'll leave you to it. Good day, Miss Baxter." He ducked through the low doorway, deliberating whether he had made the right decision. He could not jolly well allow her to keep a role aboard the ship—the men would not stand for it. Pulling the door shut firmly behind him, Seamus speculated how long it would take his spirited guest to be overcome by boredom.

Chapter Ten

Grace was roused by an insistent hammering on deck and the ringing of the bell. Eight bells. Eight bells! Was it the afternoon watch already?

Jolting upright, she blindly reached for the side of her hammock, coming up short when she grasped the soft, lumpy mattress. Rubbing the sleep from her eyes, she took in her surroundings. Memories flooded back, and finding herself in the safety of her own little cabin, she slumped back onto her pillow. Despite her panic the previous afternoon that Fitzwilliam might reveal her whereabouts to her parents, Grace realised he could not have seen Silverton's advertisement in the broadsheet. He had been thoroughly occupied preparing the *Discerning* for departure—perhaps without a chance to revel in the luxury of reading. She had eliminated Gilly's copy, but how many others still lurked aboard?

Grace recalled the moment Seamus had finished inspecting her newly arranged cabin yesterday. Her senses had filled with the scent of him, the citrusy combination of bergamot and lemon.

She had barely resisted an unsettling urge to step closer and inhale. Instead, she had swallowed the ball of apprehension that had been inconveniently lodged in her throat, rendering her vocal cords useless. Part of her had been relieved by his hasty departure.

The hammering resumed, interrupting her daydream. It was someone pounding on her door. She stood swiftly and snatched it open. Gilly flinched. It was the first time he had stood before her alone since finding out about her deception. A lightness rose in her chest at his familiar face.

"Ahem, beggin' your pardon, madam. Cap'n Fincham requests the pleasure of your company this evenin'." Gilly bowed gracelessly.

The heavy stone thudded in her stomach again. He was there under orders, not of his own volition. Swallowing her disappointment, she rubbed a sleepy eye again. "The captain? Is he awake? Is he well?"

"Indeed he is, madam. The cap'n 'as been up and about for a few hours now. Lieutenant Fitzwilliam has advised him of your … your turn of circumstances. Seems the prospect of entertaining an important gentlewoman has roused Cap'n Fincham's spirits." Gilly was uncharacteristically stiff and proper.

She scoffed gently. "I'm hardly anyone important, Gilly." He stared ahead stoically, awaiting her reply to his message, evidently having not yet forgiven her. Grace straightened and frowned at her dirty clothes, her lips twisting wryly. "I hope Captain Fincham has a forgiving eye." Her quirky smile slid into dismay as Gilly's face hardened. She placed a hand on his arm. "Gilly, you needn't be so guarded around me. I'm the same person."

He yanked his arm away and took a step back, his wounded look full of betrayal. "No, madam, you're not. You had me think you're the son of a coalman. Not the daughter of a lord. By crumbs, you haven't half made a fool of me. The other men'll not let up that I can't tell the difference 'tween a lad and a lady."

"Well, neither could they!" she countered with a flash of anger. "I had you *all* fooled, which was precisely the point." She thrust her hands indignantly onto her hips. "Tell me, Gilly, would you have signed me up if I'd appeared with flowing locks and a lavender ballgown?"

"Course not! Some say I've brought about ill luck bringin' a woman into our folds. Some of 'em won't even speak to me."

"What claptrap!" Her eyes sparked. "I've been aboard since the start. Nothing has happened to us." She studied her friend's consternation and softened her glare into a look of compassion. "Does my being a woman make me less of a friend?"

Gilly's stiff shoulders drooped, and he tempered his frown, wrestling with indecision. A firm resolve fixed itself to his face. "Wait there." He turned abruptly and left.

Grace peered down at the stiff-backed Tommy at the helm, who was clearly ignoring her. She swept her gaze across the vast, curved horizon kissed by the sinking sun. Gilly returned to the quarterdeck with nimble footsteps, clutching a parcel wrapped in brown paper and string. He marched up to Grace and thrust it at her, his voice thick with emotion. "'Twas meant for our Sally, me sister, but you can borrow it. Bought it for her a couple of years back when I went to find her at the orphan's asylum. Our Sally had to go there after Mam died. Da was killed in an accident on the docks before Sally was even born. When she wouldn't see me or accept my gift, I packed it in me trunk, seein' as how I have no one else to leave it with. Thought I might still be able to give it to her someday."

At an unusual loss for words, Grace stared at the package. When she peered up, Gilly was gone. Closing the door behind her, she perched on her bed and tweaked the string bow. Course fibres fell onto her lap, and the brown waxed wrapping unfolded. Grace gasped. On her lap was a carefully folded cotton dress with pale blue-and-white stripes. Grasping the garment by the shoulders, she stood, and it cascaded to the floor. Grace eyed the simple cut with its high curved neck and lined bodice. A common work dress is what Mother would call it, but to Grace, it was gorgeous.

It had long sleeves slightly puffed at the shoulders and ruffled at the wrists. Three bands of dark blue satin wound around the hem of the skirt. She held the bodice against her—it was a close enough fit. A bonnet in matching striped material slid to the floor. Laying the outfit on the cot, Grace picked up the cap. Its ribbons matched those on the dress. She fitted the bonnet over her short hair and tied the satin strands in a large bow under her chin. Inspecting her face in Fitzwilliam's shaving mirror, she noticed it was thinner, her skin darker. Her green eyes shone. Opening her lips in a grimace to examine her teeth, she frowned at a thin, furry layer at her gumline. Picking up the muslin square, she scrubbed her teeth until they squeaked.

"That'll have to do." She nodded pragmatically at her reflection. Removing the bonnet and placing it on the cot beside the dress, Grace discarded her sailor's clothes carelessly and dropped them on the floor. Over at the bureau, she poured cold water into the basin and, using the muslin cloth and the small cube of citrus-fragranced soap Fitzwilliam had provided, thoroughly scrubbed herself. The cloth and the water were the grimy grey of a corpse by the time she had finished.

Grace picked up the dress and undid the row of hooks down the bodice to the waist. She hesitated before stepping into the outfit, peeping shyly at her naked body. Her skin glowed pink from its recent scrubbing. She had always been slim, but the intensity of physical labour had tightened her arms and thighs. A prudish flush splashed her cheeks, and Grace fixed her eyes safely on the new garment. She took a deep breath and stepped into it.

"No shift, no stays, *and* no petticoats. Mother would have a conniption!" She smirked rebelliously as she redid the endless row of hooks over her naked breasts, scandalously liberated by her lack of undergarments. The cotton was luxuriously soft on her scrubbed skin. Grace tied the bonnet on but stopped short as she noticed her lack of footwear. With her only boots stowed in the forecastle, she shrugged dismissively, satisfied that the flowing skirts covered her bare feet well enough. Glancing once more at herself in the hand mirror, she inhaled deeply and yanked open the door.

Grace yipped as she collided with the solid wall of Fitzwilliam. He grunted in surprise, immediately recovering his composure. Her face burned at the fright.

SEAMUS GAWKED at her like a teenage halfwit, wholly unbecoming for an officer of his distinguished bearing. "How did you acquire a dress, Miss Baxter?"

She smiled coyly. "A lady never reveals her secrets, sir."

Recovering, he bowed deeply. "Your most humble servant, madam." He locked eyes with her as she curtsied and looked intently into his face. Seamus remained bowed, and an uncanny wave of déjà vu washed over him of the humour they had first shared in the gardens back at Wallace House.

"Your back will grow crooked." Her eyes sparkled cheekily.

An undignified snigger burst from him, and he shook his head, his face a picture of seriousness as he straightened up. "I'm a sizeable man, yet I find myself wiped mercilessly across the floor by a five-foot maiden."

"Not that any will believe me still a maiden." Miss Baxter's voice quivered, shame colouring her cheeks.

"Miss Baxter." Seamus's tone warned against her self-deprecating thoughts. His gaze softened at the trace of the scar on her lip and the fine lines of her recent sleep crinkling the corners of her green eyes. The wooden hull creaked, and someone dropped a heavy item on the deck behind him.

Seamus blinked hard, and he slid his expressionless mask back into place as he squared his shoulders. He cocked his eyebrow and formally offered her the crook of his arm. "Please, allow me to escort you to supper, Miss Baxter."

Hesitating only briefly, she took his arm. He squeezed her hand against his ribs in an unspoken promise of protection.

Captain Fincham rose as Miss Baxter entered the cabin ahead of Seamus, and Seamus saw her surprise at finding the captain dressed and nursing a goblet of claret. Second Lieutenant Wadham rose from the table, standing erect in his naval dress uniform. Wadham's jaw was square-set, and the dark shadow of his newly shaven face contrasted against the tan of his skin. Seamus flicked Wadham the briefest of glances before turning his eyes back to Miss Baxter and Fincham.

"Miss Baxter, I presume?" Fincham exclaimed, rising and waving a hand theatrically in her direction.

"Good evening, sir" she replied, nodding warily.

Seamus frowned at Fincham's new, simpering demeanour.

Fincham cast his hand in Wadham's direction. "I believe you're already acquainted with Lieutenant Fitzwilliam? Please allow me to introduce you to Second Lieutenant Brian Bartholomew Wadham."

Miss Baxter's eyes narrowed. She swung her gaze towards Seamus, her head tilted with a look that said, *Is he mad?* Before Seamus could respond, she turned to Wadham and nodded. "Yes, we've met." Fincham frowned in confusion, his cheeks pallid and his slate-grey eyes unnaturally glazed. He might be well enough to have risen from his berth, but he was clearly still out of sorts.

Seamus's breath hitched as Wadham's eyes roamed up and down Miss Baxter's dress, his cheeks dimpling in approval. Wadham had been kind enough before when he thought her to be a sailor, but Seamus did not expect this level of scrutiny from him now. The gawk Wadham gave Miss Baxter was the sort usually reserved for human curiosities at a travelling fair—the kind that people paid a shilling to peep behind the curtains for.

Fincham's strained voice pierced the silence, "Please. Sit, my dear."

Seamus and Wadham both advanced to pull out Miss Baxter's chair. Acceding to Seamus's seniority, Wadham tactfully stepped back and lowered himself into the chair beside her. Seamus dropped into the chair on the other side.

A sheen of sweat glistened across Fincham's waxen top lip, and there was still a clump of oozing sores in the corner of his mouth. His arms quivered at the exertion of lugging the heavy dining chair in beneath him, and Seamus spotted a new red rash on his hands.

The table, laid with a crisp, white cloth in Miss Baxter's honour, was set for a three-course meal—a more elaborate affair than the simple supper Seamus was expecting. The captain's finest silver candelabra adorned the table, the five, twinkling beeswax candles and the swinging lanterns lighting the cabin prettily. Seamus poured the wine and handed a goblet to Miss Baxter, his fingertips brushing hers. A jolt shot down the back of his hand, and she flushed, turning deliberately to face Fincham.

"Are you well, Captain?" she asked.

"Yes, quite well. Quite well." Fincham's speech was high pitched and hurried. He flicked his eyes reproachfully in her direction. "You caught us all unawares, Miss Baxter."

"My apologies, Captain. I certainly have no intention of causing you any worry or delay. I beg your understanding. Dire circumstances necessitated my impetuous decision to come aboard your ship."

The Napoleonic man studied her shrewdly. "Quite, quite. Simply put, though, what *am* I to do with you?" Seamus flicked Miss Baxter a quick side look, intrigued to hear how she would answer the same rhetorical question he had asked her. Fincham's shaking hands fiddled with the corner of his napkin.

Seeing Miss Baxter studying her dry, cracked fingers, and licking her lips, Seamus coughed discreetly. "Captain Fincham, if it pleases you, sir, I'll happily assume full responsibility for Miss Baxter. Admiral Baxter saved my life, and I owe—"

"Baxter? Admiral Arthur Baxter? How does he fit into this?" Fincham frowned.

"Why, he's her uncle, sir. I mentioned it earlier." Heavens! The man really was going mad.

Fincham choked, his pasty skin blanching even further as he glared at Miss Baxter. "Good God! It's *you*! From the banquet— in London!" Fincham collapsed back in his chair. "This will end my career! What foolery for a young girl to flee from her social responsibil—"

"Captain!" Seamus's dry voice sliced clean through Fincham's outburst. "A civil tongue please, sir. Miss Baxter has endured far more than a lady of her breeding should be privy to." Christ Almighty! The man's disposition was so unpredictable these days. Whatever was ailing him had completely robbed him of all his faculties, including his blasted humour.

Wadham coughed uncomfortably at Seamus's insubordination, but Seamus ignored him. Fincham bristled upright at being berated by a subordinate, his agitation short-lived as he propped an elbow on the table and sank his forehead wearily into his hand. "If this godforsaken journey isn't the end of me, then this surely will be."

"Rest assured, Captain," placated Seamus, "if it's a matter of cost, I'll cover Miss Baxter's expenses."

"Pah! And what of my reputation and honour?" Fincham bounced in his seat. "I'll forever be branded as the fool who had the niece of the famous Admiral Baxter hiding under his nose in plain sight."

"Sir, I'll personally vouch for your compassion and

generosity with the admiral." Seamus allowed an atmosphere of quiet to settle around him as he calmly regarded the twitchy, sweating man at the head of the table.

"Lieutenant Fitzwilliam, we are *not* on a leisurely cruise on the Serpentine. One can't simply hop off the ship whenever one likes," squeaked Fincham.

Seamus dipped his head. "I'm aware of—"

"These are dangerous waters!" interrupted Fincham. "You know of the sorts of tides and storms we may face. The risk of shipwreck! You expect me to be responsible for Admiral Baxter's niece on such a journey? He'll have me hung, drawn, and quartered!"

"Captain Fincham," Miss Baxter cut in brusquely. "I've lived aboard the *Discerning* long enough to gauge the deplorable conditions. I've known hunger, pumped bilges, and been witness to many canings and even a flogging. Surely my endurance of these trials demonstrates my fortitude? I assure you, sir, I'll not be wilting or expiring on your watch. As a new joiner, I suspect I've already survived the worst your ship has to offer."

Hearing a muted snicker, Seamus flicked a side glance at Wadham and caught the tiny tug of his mouth as he nipped back his mirth. Seamus refocussed on Fincham's puce face.

"You can't surely blame me for your atrocious living conditions and deplorable treatment when it was *you* who snuck aboard *my* ship with such deception!" Fincham barked.

"I blame you for no such thing, sir. I merely point out that I possess the wherewithal to endure passage on your ship." Her voice was firm and steady.

Fincham mopped his sweating brow with his napkin. "And what of the men?"

"What of them, Captain?" she countered. "Due to the close quarters, one has no choice but to become invested in the characters and habits of one's shipmates."

"But you're a *woman*!" The undignified explosion erupted from Fincham.

"How kind of you to notice."

Fincham seemed not to notice her sarcasm, but Wadham's lips quivered on the edge of his wine glass; he was clearly enjoying the spectacle.

"It'll be no surprise if some of the men have a mind to throw you overboard," complained Fincham mulishly.

"The threat of being tossed overboard a second time won't be half as shocking as the first," she said stiffly.

Fincham gawked. "Good God! Who threatened to throw you overboard?"

"Why, King Neptune's wife herself," replied Miss Baxter seriously.

Seamus glowered as Wadham laughed and rammed his fist to his mouth, disguising the sound as a cough. Seamus knew she spoke truthfully. Lieutenant Newlands, in his get-up as Amphitrite, Neptune's queen, had indeed threatened to toss her overboard, as he had every other uninitiated lubber. Seamus had thoroughly enjoyed the spectacle, but now he shifted uncomfortably as realisation slithered across the back of his neck like a cold eel. Christ! He had laughed while Miss Baxter had run the gauntlet, enduring a dousing in seawater and a kick up the backside by the hands. He flinched as Fincham thumped the table.

"Oh, for God's sake, woman!" spluttered Fincham. "I've not the patience for this conversation. You refer, madam, to a sacred seafaring ritual that is, by rights, exclusive to *men*. If, through your own misadventure, you ended up a victim of these circumstances, don't now seek to find sympathy with me."

"I don't seek your sympathy, Captain, I seek passage upon your ship. I'll not impede your explorations, and neither shall I instigate trouble with your men. I'd like to offer my literacy skills to assist Mr McGilney with the ship's books, with your permission, of course."

"Pah! A preposterous notion!" Fincham spat again. "Young lady, you forfeited any opportunity to make demands when you chose to dishonestly portray yourself as a male member of this naval vessel. You're hardly a welcome guest. I'll have a devil's own job keeping the crew turning because of you."

Seamus worried the line of scar tissue on his wrist with his thumb, digesting his sympathetic leanings towards Miss Baxter. He had not sparred verbally with a young woman in such a manner before, certainly not one who held her own against men like she did. Just how far could he push Fincham before he would be hauled up on insubordination charges of his own?

Clearly taking umbrage from Seamus's silent deliberation and Fincham's unsympathetic words, Miss Baxter wrapped her arms around her body. "I hardly had another choice considering"—her voice caught in her throat, and her chin quivered —"my *circumstances.*"

Seamus's heart plunged to his feet. He released a steady breath. "Miss Baxter, I'm sure Captain Fincham didn't mean to cause you discomfort." He rolled his scarred wrist, and the joint clicked as his eyes flicked over to Fincham.

Fincham scoffed and scraped back his chair, and the two officers rose automatically. "My appetite is quite lost. In fact, I'm bilious of the whole affair and grow weary of further discussion." Fincham swayed dangerously and might have fallen had Wadham not caught his elbow. The captain coughed uncomfortably at the contact but did not withdraw his arm; instead, he gazed longingly at the drawn drapes of his berth.

"Perhaps you might like to entertain Miss Baxter another evening, sir?" suggested Seamus.

"Yes, yes. Indeed," quailed Fincham, scowling at them. Wadham released his arm, and Fincham leaned his weight on the table to steady himself.

Seamus clenched his jaw as Wadham's eyes fixed upon Miss Baxter. She shrugged one shoulder—a motion Wadham promptly copied, adding a dimpled smile. Seamus coughed dryly, the sound laden with disapproval, and both Miss Baxter and Wadham's heads snapped around. Seamus gave Wadham a low growl before turning to Fincham. "With your permission, Captain, may I escort Miss Baxter back to her cabin?"

"Yes, yes," blustered Fincham. "Jolly good idea."

Wadham helped Miss Baxter to her feet, and Seamus's spine stiffened. Taking advantage of his grip on her hand, Wadham pressed it to his lips, his brown eyes sparkling, his baritone slow and deep. "Goodnight, Miss Baxter. It was a pleasure to make your acquaintance." She was plainly flattered, blushing and blinking at Wadham and rewarding him with a wide smile.

Seamus escorted Miss Baxter back to her cabin. "I'll have your meal brought to you." He was on the verge of asking if he might join her. No, he could not. Her reputation was already in tatters, and he did not wish to add to her woes by requesting an unchaperoned meal. His courage slipped, and instead he asked, "I wonder, afterwards, if you might like to accompany me on a stroll?" That would be proper enough, in plain sight of the watch on duty.

"A stroll?" She glanced out into the night, the middle of her forehead rucked.

"It'll only be around the deck—if that's not too disagreeable?"

"Not disagreeable at all." Her smile filled Seamus with a satisfaction that curled warmly in his chest like the steam of a newly poured pot of coffee. Not expecting her to agree so readily, the red-blooded man in him preened, while the naval officer stiffened. He was aware of how wholly inappropriate any insinuation of a courtship would appear.

With his own appetite lost, Seamus waited a suitable length of time to allow Miss Baxter to finish her supper before he politely knocked on her door. Together, they made their way outside. Under the full moon in the balmy evening air, Seamus became increasingly aware of her slim shadow as it stretched before his on the deck. He was mesmerised by her strong, roughened fingers smoothing the folds of her skirts.

"I trust you enjoyed your supper, Miss Baxter?"

"Indeed. Cook Phillips outdid himself with that succulent roast chicken. It's quite the luxury, dining alone."

"Before we go any further, Miss Baxter, I must apologise for my boorish behaviour during King Neptune's initiation ceremony. Naturally, had I known it was you, I'd never have allowed them to brush that swill across your mouth."

Miss Baxter's face scrunched. "What *was* that muck?"

"If it was anything like the filth used in my own initiation, I would say it was a mix of chicken manure, pigswill, and tar."

"I must say, it was quite uncanny watching the civilised ranks of the officers come thoroughly undone during the ceremony."

"Indeed. Neither rank nor position nor seniority has any bearing when it comes to being initiated into King Neptune's kingdom." Seamus winced. "I'm sorry you had to endure that."

"On the contrary, Lieutenant, it made me one of the men. That initiation rubbed off the experienced men's rough edge of hostility towards me. Their degree of acceptance evidenced by my being called to man the helm." She tipped her head jauntily, slipping him an amused look from the corner of her eye.

Seamus remembered the moment well. He had been in the charthouse when the ship had begun sheering wildly, turning and dipping out of control. Barrelling from the charthouse to chastise the helmsman, he had pulled up short at the sight of the bald lad wrestling the great wheel. He had even gone as far as to jest with Wadham about the youngster's efforts by asking, "The ship's steering rather heavily, wouldn't you agree, Lieutenant Wadham?"

"She is," Wadham had agreed, his humour undisguised.

Seamus had braced his feet on the heaving deck and, after pulling his cuff over his right wrist, casually clasped his hands behind his back to enjoy the spectacle. "Lieutenant Wadham, I can't imagine Captain Fincham will be too pleased when you send his servant down with two snapped arms. Reckon you'll be needing two men to steer her in this breeze."

He had seen Sykes—Miss Baxter—prickle at his jesting. "I can do it!" she had snapped, and he was impressed how quickly she mastered control of the ship under Blight's instruction.

Now he glanced down at the same wide eyes and shook his head to clear the overlapping memories. She really had fooled the lot of them. It would not do to let his admiration for her achievements as Sykes cloud the reality of her situation. He did not even know whether she would have a home to return to after this, let alone retain her title and place in society. Her circumstances did not square with the ideal he had in mind for a future wife, no matter how appealing he found her company. He was honour-bound to Baxter to ensure the man's niece was well cared for—that was all.

Seamus continued, "I must also apologise for the captain's behaviour earlier this evening. As you're well aware, he hasn't been himself lately."

"Not at all, Lieutenant. I understand how the shock of finding me aboard his ship has aggravated his condition." Seamus caught her attempt at sympathy.

"I'll endeavour to do my best to smooth matters with him." Seamus narrowed his eyes. "However, the captain requires you remain in your quarters unless accompanied by an officer."

Miss Baxter did a double take, frowning. "You're confining me to my cabin? My enjoyment of one solitary meal isn't an expression that I desire such solitude imposed."

Seamus twisted his lips ruefully. "Captain's orders. Please understand, it's for your safety. I promised you protection—and protection you'll receive."

They passed O'Malley at the helm. He eyed them curiously, whipping his gaze forward when Seamus glanced at him, the sailor's fingers guiltily clenching the wheel's wooden grips. Seamus peered around at the other hands on watch. They all appeared unnaturally stiff backed, finding great interest in the empty ocean or fiddling with the already secured knots.

"You're no doubt already aware that it's a lawful requirement for all aboard to follow a captain's orders, madam. Even guests," explained Seamus tactfully. What the devil did he expect? She was hardly the biddable type.

"I understand, but perhaps you can put in a good word for me and persuade the captain to allow me to assist Mr McGilney with his clerical duties? I certainly have no desire to be confined to my cabin all day."

He peered at her for the umpteenth time and resisted the urge to shake his head. She had no notion of the men's shock. Though perhaps theirs paled in comparison to his. "Very well, Miss Baxter. I'll see what I can do. But I make no promises."

"Thank you, Lieutenant. That's all I ask," she said. Up on the quarterdeck, he drew to a halt outside her cabin door. "Thank you for a pleasant evening," she added.

"The pleasure was all mine. Perhaps you might allow me to escort you again after supper tomorrow evening?" The words popped out his mouth before he could stop them. Drat. *Cool your heels, Fitzwilliam!*

She replied with a curtsy and a dip of that pert little chin of hers, her curling lips unable to hide her delight at his question. His heart thumped at the same startling pace as when he stood before a bank of cannons, ready to order the men to fire. He spun away.

Sliding below into the gunroom, he found Wadham slumped at a table nursing a late-night brandy. Lieutenant Sully's deep breathing rattled through the sealed door of one of the officer's cabins. They were little more than tiny holes with a cot and a narrow desk, but each compartment had the luxury of privacy. The sleeping warrant officers swung in their hammocks.

EMMA LOMBARD

"Trouble with the little lady?" Wadham grinned amicably, their earlier ruffled feathers a distant memory. One of the men in the hammocks stirred, thunderously broke wind, and settled back to sleep.

Seamus rubbed his hand across his face. "Little in stature but with a sizeable blasted temperament."

"Indeed," snorted Wadham. "She certainly has no qualms at speaking her mind. Captain Fincham nearly burst with indignation this evening at being challenged so freely—and by a woman, no less!"

"It's a quality I admired upon my first meeting her," confessed Seamus, "but one that won't go down well on a naval vessel full of sailors. I fear her impetuousness may yet land her in hot water."

"Hotter water than nearly being flogged?" Wadham's shoulders shook with silent laughter.

Seamus sighed deeply, eyeing the crystal brandy glass in Wadham's hand. "You pouring? Make mine a double."

Chapter Eleven

For the next week, Grace kept to herself in her cabin, only sneaking off for the luxury of using the captain's head below. Being confined to the cabin was almost as restrictive as a tightly laced corset, and Grace longed for the freedom she had enjoyed when everyone believed her to be Billy. Toby ferried Grace's meals to her cabin, but eventually, boredom set in—there were only so many hours of reading and sleeping to be done in a day.

During the day, she never saw Lieutenant Fitzwilliam while he managed the melancholic captain, oversaw the ship, and prepared to survey their destination, but every evening, he invited Grace to walk with him, enthralling her with an array of topics.

"I don't expect you to understand, Lieutenant, but mine was a stifled existence in my parents' house, especially under the tyrannical thumb of my governess. While I won't diminish the difficulties I experienced in the fo'c'sle, I found it oddly liberating to be my own man, so to speak." He raised his eyebrows at her turn of phrase as she continued, "Women are restricted by what their fathers dictate and then their husbands. We are even restricted by our clothes, with wretched corsets being the worst culprits."

Fitzwilliam coughed dryly before dipping his chin at her. "I can't profess to have any knowledge of corset wearing." His amused gaze grew more serious. "I've always felt a sympathetic leaning towards women for the societal constraints imposed on them, though that might be my mother's influence." His lips twitched again. "She wasn't at all fettered by my father."

"And your father permitted this freedom?"

"He had little choice. Her Scottish stubbornness wouldn't allow any other way."

Grace laughed lightly, and he smiled.

His Adam's apple bobbed as he swallowed. "I'm aware you retain a unique acquaintance with some of the men aboard this vessel, Miss Baxter, but many would rather you not be here. You also comprehend firsthand the likelihood of accident and injury aboard a ship in motion. Only this morning while drilling with the big guns, Cakebread lost his toes. The fool didn't shift his foot in time when the cannon recoiled."

While Cakebread was no friend, Grace's stomach roiled biliously at his grievous injury. She glanced up at Fitzwilliam, her lips pressed together in reluctant acknowledgement, and she playfully knocked her hip against his. "I suppose I should be thankful then that you liberate me from my prison every evening."

"I wish you didn't view it as a prison, Miss Baxter. The captain means well, no matter how unenlightened his views about women may be."

"And what of your views, Lieutenant?"

"I believe women quite capable of forming their own opinions." He paused as Grace drew him to a halt, staring at him. He inclined his head. "Case in point, Miss Baxter."

Grace's eyes widened with interest. "Me?"

"Indeed. You've proven a better hand at writing than some of the officers aboard this ship. Your polished command of the English language puts many a commanding officer or government official I've met to shame—and you're not afraid to use it."

Grace opened her mouth to object, but he cut her off. "The narrowmindedness of the establishment in excluding women from the vote is a mistake, in my opinion."

Grace released a breathy laugh. "Are you truly not opposed to the idea of women being allowed to vote in government elections?"

"I'm not." He flexed his right wrist as he glanced down at her, his smile warm.

Grace sighed. "A generous sentiment, Lieutenant, albeit an improbable dream. But I'm heartened to know there are men in the world like you."

It was a clear and moonless evening, and Grace stared blindly into the night, shivering a little at how small and insignificant she felt in the darkness pressing in on the ship. She breathed in the cool, briny air, tasting salt at the back of her throat. A soft breeze moved the ship at a steady pace, the deck rolling rhythmically under her feet.

"It's so dark without the moon," she observed softly, the splashing water whispering against the hull in the shadows below.

Fitzwilliam halted, casually leaning his elbows on the edge of the gunwales as he followed her gaze into the blackness. "I agree," he nodded. "It's magnificent."

"Magnificent?" she grimaced. "Rather unnerving, if you ask me. You can't determine who or what is lurking in the dark or even recognise where you are."

"Why, yes you can," he grinned, his teeth flashing white. "You simply need to know how to read God's map."

"God's map?" She glanced around, expecting him to unfurl a chart.

He laughed, flourishing his arms in an arc above his head at the expanse of clear sky. "God has delivered us the greatest map of all." He tipped his head back, appreciatively assessing the stars.

Grace scrutinised the lights twinkling in the distance that made her feel even smaller. "How can mere pinpricks of light in the sky disclose this?" She gasped as a luminous shooting star trailed across the sky. "Especially when those specks of light don't even keep still!" She knew sailors navigated by the sky, but she was oblivious to the actual working of this phenomenon.

Fitzwilliam laughed. "Oh, Miss Baxter, there are wonders in this world of which you've no notion yet."

Grace glanced at him, intrigued by the swell of awe in his voice. Catching his eyes flick across her bodice and his lips twitch like he was closely guarding a secret, Grace narrowed her eyes. He coughed guiltily, looking out into the night instead and rubbing his scarred wrist. She leaned towards him, inadvertently pressing her breast against his elbow. He jolted away, laughing uneasily.

"Are you all right, Lieutenant?"

"Yes, yes. Quite all right, thank you." He laughed dryly, eyeing the watch up in the rigging. "I'm determining how to offer you a little insight into astronomical navigation without boring you to tears."

"Hmm." She contemplated the overwhelming expanse of the ether. "Well, stars possess names, do they not? Perhaps you could point out the important ones."

"Indeed," he conceded. "A jolly good place to start. See those four bright stars in the form of a cross?" He drew invisible lines with his fingers between the bright, glowing orbs. "That's the Southern Cross. If you've never been south of the equator before, then this will be the first time you've laid eyes on that magnificent constellation."

"And what of that star on the horizon? It appears to be dipping itself into the sea."

"That's no star. It's another ship but a couple of miles away. She's been there all day."

Grace frowned as Fitzwilliam took another step away from her, and her heart skipped. Blinking away her gritty prickle of disappointment, she devoured the beauty of the night sky sparking to life with his vivid descriptions.

GRACE AWOKE one morning to a severe case of cabin fever. In urgent need of fresh air, she hurriedly stripped off Billy's shirt, which she now wore as a nightshirt, and slipped into her dress and bonnet. Snatching up her coat, she took a deep, fortifying breath to steady the nerves rolling in her stomach, prepared to face not only the curious stares and suspicious glares of the crew but also the wrath of Seamus Fitzwilliam as she stepped unescorted onto the quarterdeck.

The *Discerning* had recently entered the colder and decidedly rougher waters off the tip of South America. The morning was overcast and blustery; dark storm clouds brooded on the horizon. Goosebumps rippled over Grace's flesh as the strong wintery wind needled through the fabric of her dress, and she was thankful for its long sleeves. Ignoring the iciness and glancing out across the main deck, she inhaled deeply, the cold air settling her stomach.

The sails snapped and rippled happily in the unrelenting wind. The ship's bow lifted high on the large, grey swell surrounding them and dipped alarmingly down the other side. As the hull crashed into the swell of the next oncoming wave, a fine white spray of seawater showered across the deck. The men's shouts were whipped away on the wind.

Grace surveyed the ship's lines, a tug of familiarity lifting the corners of her lips as she recognised her friends among the seamen. The red-headed Blight twins furiously worked the stays up the mainmast. Gunner Ash inspected the bindings securing the cannons to the bulwark. Jim Buchanan's dark head vanished down the main hatch. Coming out of the heads, Toby Hicks scurried, mouse-like, past the pock-faced Mad Mahlon who was lashing barrels to the mast with rope.

Mad Mahlon stopped tying and glowered after the timid, skinny boy as he slunk around him in a wide arc before slipping down the main hatch. Mad Mahlon stiffened and swivelled around to leer at Grace. She defiantly raised her chin, ready to stare down his lewd inspection of her when his face recoiled in revulsion, and he spat in disgust.

"Mad Mahlon don't own high opinions of those above his station at the best of times." Gilly's voice startled her from behind, and Grace twisted to face him as he coughed uncomfortably. "But the fact you're a woman has further blackened his mood. He's been a right grumpy sod of late. A few others too." Gilly looked her up and down, nodding in approval as he did every time he observed her in the dress meant for his sister.

"I'm sorry if my presence caused this. I never meant to cause such a ruckus." Grace pressed her lips together tightly. "Lieutenant Fitzwilliam described the absurd superstition that a woman aboard brings bad luck to the ship."

"Might be absurd to you, Miss Baxter, but 'tis a deeply entrenched fear in some of the men, especially the more seasoned shellbacks like Sorensen and Blom. To them, you're a regular curse that needs managin'—if you catch my meanin'."

"Oh, I catch it well enough, Gilly, but I'll not be intimidated by such superstitious twiddle twaddle."

Clearing his throat again, Gilly added, "Speakin' of Lieutenant Fitzwilliam, he's sent me to report we're in for some stormy weather before long. The cap'n wants you in the safety of his cabin." Lightning lashed across the sky, the air heavy with the crisp, clean smell of rain.

"Thank you, Gilly." Grace placed a hand on his arm but dropped it when he flinched. She beamed brightly to hide her disappointment. "And thank you again for the dress."

Gilly shrugged nonchalantly. "It weren't doin' any good sittin' in the bottom of me trunk. For all I know, our Sally might have already outgrown it." His face grew tight. "Besides, who knows when I'll see her next?"

"It's a lovely dress, Gilly." Grace placed her hand on his arm again, and this time, he did not flinch. "Sally would've delighted in it." Gilly's cheeks coloured at the compliment, and Grace shivered as a fine mist of saltwater sprayed across the deck.

"Sorry I don't have a shawl or somethin' warmer for you to wear. The dress is all I had."

"It's all right, Gilly. I'll be fine. I have my old coat," said Grace.

Gilly's impish grin returned, and he chivalrously offered her his arm as the ship lurched.

"Be off with you!" Grace swatted him away, laughing. "I can keep my own footing."

"Bet you're not missing the swabbing?"

She grimaced. "No, though there's a certain satisfaction in bringing tarnished brass to life. And I do miss Sergeant Baisley's drilling."

Gilly regarded her sharply from the corner of his eye, his forehead rumpling. "Enjoyment has nothin' to do with it. You haven't had the pleasure of experiencin' the stink and pestilence of a dirty ship." Grace noted a tone of condescension in his voice. "And as for the drillin', when the time comes, there's not a man who isn't grateful for knowing exactly what he's doin' with his musket."

Craving the warmth of Gilly's friendship, Grace offered him the olive branch of another smile. "I assure you, Gilly, I do intend to be useful. I've never been too good at being a lady of leisure."

Gilly's scowl softened. "You'll have to answer to the lieutenant about that. I'm not sure he'll be—"

Up the mainmast, Ben Blight howled ecstatically, "Land ho! Land on the starboard beam!" A tangible surge of excitement rippled through the *Discerning*. The biting wind and rolling deck did nothing to deter the sailors from dashing over to the gunwales to catch their first glimpse of the Tierra del Fuego archipelago. The chain of islands in the distance was barely visible through the squall of rain heading their way.

Grace marvelled at the sight. "Oh, Gilly! How is it possible for our little ship to survive these rough seas?" She cast her laughing face into the sea spray spuming off the bow. "If anyone had told me that I'd one day visit the places my governesses pointed out to me on maps during my geography lessons, I'd have declared them delusional. Yet here I am!"

Her excitement was contagious, and Gilly's lips turned up. "Come along, Miss Baxter, before you fall too far in love with the sea." With a shake of his head, he escorted her down the quarterdeck stairs. "She hasn't yet shown you the treachery lurking in her bosom. Besides, the lieutenant won't be wantin' you swannin' around the deck in this weather."

"Gilly!" exclaimed Grace in mock indignation. "I don't *swan* about."

Grace savoured how Gilly laughed freely, warming to their atypical friendship. His laughter dribbled away to silence as they arrived at the ladder to the aft hatch. He frowned down at the opening and then back up at Grace, the wild wind whipping strands of his black hair loose from its binding as confusion rippled across his face.

"What is it?" She pushed the flapping bonnet ribbons from her face.

"I've never had to escort a lady down the hatch before. Not sure whether 'tis proper for you to head down first or whether I should, to catch you if you fall." He scratched his cheek in bafflement.

Grace stuck her hands on her hips. "Lambert McGilney, I've been scampering up and down these ladders unescorted without suffering the misfortune of falling even once. I don't intend to start now." With a flourish of skirts, Grace slid neatly into the dark. She waited at the bottom of the ladder, allowing her eyes to adjust to the darkness. Gilly landed with a light thud beside her. The pitching and rolling were just as awful down here. Jim's head popped out of the hatchway of the gunpowder magazine below. Half in and half out of the hatch, he froze.

Grace glanced at Gilly's shadowed face. "Gilly, do you mind? I'd like a word with Jim." Her arm pressed against Gilly's in the confined space, and she felt hesitation hum through him. She gently nudged her elbow against his arm in reassurance and turned to grin at the black-haired Scot. "Hello, Jim."

Jim clambered up, studying her as carefully as Gilly had. His round cheeks bulged as he chuckled. "Ye look bonnie, lass." Grace's face warmed at the unexpected compliment.

"Thank you, Jim. That's kind of you." She inclined her head.

Jim toyed with one of his wildly protruding ears. At first, Grace had thought he had the face of a monkey, but she now viewed his jutting appendages with fondness. "Ye sure have a bold spirit about ye." He cocked his head to one side, grinning affably. "Ye remind me of my maw, except she didn't have as polished a tongue."

"Better not let the others hear you lavishing such compliments, else they'll think you've gone soft in the head." Grace returned his grin and tugged on the lapel of his coat.

"Ha!" Jim slapped his thigh. "Now I know why ye were so keen to take my hand before." His eyes slid to her hand on his collar. "'Tisn't half terrible having a lass rest her hand on ye. But when ye think it's a lad that's being so forward …" He rubbed the back of his neck self-consciously. "Well, lass, I'll no' repeat the thoughts I had towards ye. They're not fit for yer gentle ears."

An unladylike bark of laughter burst from Grace, and she clamped her hand to her mouth. "A bit late to worry about protecting my gentle ears." Her mischievous grin slipped into a sheepish grimace. "Sorry about the confusion with the hand touching."

Jim shrugged nonchalantly, flashing her a smirk of forgiveness.

Grace's smile slipped a little. "Tell me, Jim, how's Toby faring? I caught a glimpse of him earlier."

"Och, he's bearing up. Been a bit heartsore since ye've not been in the fo'c'sle with us. He misses yer stories." Jim's eyes slid away from hers.

Ah ha, Toby was not the only one pining for her storytelling. She blinked earnestly. "I don't see why we can't continue our reading rendezvous in the evenings when you come off watch."

Jim's eyes lit up. "Och, Bil— erm, miss, that'd be grand!"

The enthusiasm in Jim's eyes faded and was replaced with reservation. Grace leaned in. "What is it, Jim?"

"Och, well, 'tis only Toby's a bit worried."

"Rats' tails! Don't tell me he's another who believes me a curse?"

"Crivens, lass, not at all! Not Toby." Jim hesitated a moment, his eyes flicking warily towards Gilly. "But the same cannot be said for Cook Phillips. Toby heard the man mumbling about sorting yer food out 'once and for all'. That doesn't sound like an endearment, d'ye no' agree?"

"Sounds like the rumblings of a grouchy, worn-out man with too much time on his hands," scoffed Grace.

The ship pitched even more violently than before, tipping the deck sharply under their feet. Grace and Jim simultaneously snatched at the ladder, studying one another for a moment before bursting out laughing like two bells tolling together.

"Looks like we're no' likely to be hearing you read your stories any time soon, what with this storm a-brewing." Grace tipped her face to peer out the hatch at the dark clouds. The billowing mass ominously threatened more than a little rain. Angry flashes of lightning jagged across the sky, the drumroll of thunder crashing closer after each strike.

"Since my gender was revealed, some men aboard this vessel have the sudden notion I'm delicate and incapable of caring for myself." Grace bumped Jim playfully with her shoulder and stuck her tongue out at Gilly. "Have I not proven my capabilities in my time aboard the *Discerning*? Alas, I must appease Lieutenant Fitzwilliam just this minute and show him I'm in perfect health."

"Well, I'll no' be mistaking you for a big softie. I've seen ye manage a man's job. Lieutenant Wadham even saw you fit enough to steer the ship." Jim looked her squarely and proudly in the face.

"You're a good friend and a fine man, Jim Buchanan." Grace swallowed an unexpected lump in her throat.

"Och, away with ye now." Jim turned beetroot red. "I should be off, or Gunner Ash'll have my guts for garters if I don't help secure the last of the cannons before the storm hits." With a comical salute, he scampered expertly up the ladder.

Chapter Twelve

"Enter!"

Grace stepped into the great cabin ahead of Gilly. The lanterns swung in slow, sweeping arcs, and the curtain over the captain's berth stood out stiffly at an odd angle, slowly folding back on itself as the ship rolled over the waves. The hull's wood creaked with the effort of hauling the ship's great hulk up and over the mounting waves. Water splashed against the glass of the scuttles in uneven spatters.

Grace scanned the cabin. Seamus Fitzwilliam was poring over a map at the big table. An inkpot and several brass navigational instruments framed the map's edges, which in turn curled around the weighted objects. Pinning a wayward corner of the chart with one hand, Fitzwilliam traced his finger across the sheet, his frown of concentration dissolving as he caught sight of Grace. He was as immaculately dressed as ever, his blond hair tied back with a black ribbon. The whole cabin tipped as the ship rode a swell, and without even looking, Fitzwilliam reached out and stopped the sliding inkpot from toppling.

Captain Fincham was seated to the side of the table, wholly disinterested in the map. He fidgeted, and with a shaking hand, he tipped a slim vial to his mouth, face contorting at the bitter contents.

He caught sight of Grace. "What the devil are you doing here?" he snapped rudely.

Fitzwilliam's head flicked around, and Gilly startled in astonishment. Grace stopped short, equally surprised by the blunt question, as it was Fincham who had summoned her in the first place.

"Ge-rrout of my cabin, wench," Fincham snarled like a rabid dog, rising from his seat.

"Captain Fincham!" barked Fitzwilliam, storming around the table to Grace and curving a protective hand around her elbow. The warmth of his hand radiated through the fabric of her threadbare coat.

Simultaneously spurred to action, Gilly rushed towards Fincham as he swayed and dropped back into his chair with a whimper. Fincham slumped over the table, his head thumping the eastern corner of the map with a dull thud.

Fitzwilliam lowered his face to Grace's, his breath light and tickly on her ear. "I apologise on the captain's behalf, Miss Baxter. He—"

Grace gave an involuntary shiver. His warm breath served to remind her how chilly she was. He frowned as little bumps of cold rippled across her décolletage and up her neck.

"By Neptune's trident! That tattered coat of yours is doing nothing to keep you warm. I'll have Purser Rowlett issue you a new jacket." Fitzwilliam's eyes roamed the curves of Grace's dress, and he pressed his lips. "On second thoughts, I keep my mother's woollen plaid in my trunk. I'll send for it immediately, if you've no objection to warming yourself in a bright red tartan? You might find it infinitely more flattering than a plain jack-tar coat."

"Your mother's plaid?" Grace bit down to prevent her teeth chattering.

"We sailors are a superstitious lot. There isn't a man aboard who doesn't carry a trinket or two for luck." His lips twisted wryly. "Besides, there's great merit in looking one's best. It'll command the respect of those around you. Give you an edge over those who take less care over such matters."

With a gut-swooping lurch, the floor of the cabin tipped, and Grace crashed inelegantly into Fitzwilliam. He hissed sharply, blinking in evident surprise at finding her hanging from the lapels of his jacket. Her bosom pressed against his chest, and the firm flesh of his hip pressed intimately into her. The gust of fiery wind rippling through Grace at their proximity turned to a burning shame as Fitzwilliam clasped her shoulders and moved her an arm's length away, flicking sideways look at Gilly.

"Lieutenant, sir?" Gilly's voice warbled from across the table where Fincham had collapsed. He had a firm grip on the back of the captain's coat to prevent him from rolling off his chair.

With the semi-conscious captain no longer throwing scurrilous slurs in Grace's direction, the gap Fitzwilliam left as he stepped briskly away filled with cold disappointment. Grace frowned as he lifted the captain's floppy head. Fincham lolled and muttered incoherently, his unfocussed eyes crossing into a severe squint.

"Captain Fincham appears to have taken a turn for the worse," Fitzwilliam said. "McGilney, help me lay him down."

Grace stepped aside as the two men folded the groaning captain into his berth.

"Summon the surgeon. Post haste," ordered Fitzwilliam.

"Aye, aye, sir, summon the surgeon," parroted Gilly dutifully.

Fitzwilliam crouched beside Fincham, his hand resting on the ailing man's chest. Grace touched his shoulder, and he peered up at her, his blue eyes glistening with concern.

"What is it that ails him so?" It was a question she had been in no position to ask before but one that had burned for weeks. Fitzwilliam placed his toasty hand over her icy one.

"I'm not altogether certain. His wife ailed with similar symptoms for nearly a year before her illness took her." His voice had turned gravelly.

Grace squeezed his shoulder, the broad muscle responding under her palm.

Fitzwilliam added, "The captain accepts Mr Beynon's ministrations with poor grace, choosing only the treatments he deems necessary."

Grace jumped as the cabin door banged opened, and Beynon and Gilly blustered in, both men dishevelled, windswept and puffing from hurrying. She reluctantly dropped her hand, and Fitzwilliam stepped aside for the surgeon. Gilly helped Beynon lift his heavy medical box onto the table.

Second Lieutenant Wadham materialised at the cabin door, frowning at Fincham in his berth. Dragging his eyes from the bed, he faced Grace, his features softening and dimpling as he bowed. "Miss Baxter."

Fitzwilliam fixed a hard stare on Wadham. "What is it, Wadham?"

Wadham stiffened, his baritone heavy. "We are not making much headway. The *Discerning* is labouring against the violence of the wind."

Grace spotted Fitzwilliam flexing the fingers of his right hand. His wrist cracked. "Steady does it, Lieutenant Wadham. We can't back down at the first little squall we encounter. The miserable weather won't last indefinitely. Keep tacking and keep me informed of our progress."

"Aye, aye." Wadham left as promptly as he had arrived but not before chancing another glimpse at Grace.

Fitzwilliam pivoted stiffly to Gilly, his brow tight with seriousness. "McGilney, I'm acutely mindful that with Miss Baxter no longer acting as the captain's servant, some of the more menial duties have fallen on your shoulders."

"'Tis all right, sir. Don't mind a jot," Gilly replied graciously with a genuine beam.

"Well, in that case," continued Fitzwilliam, "would you please retrieve my mother's plaid from my trunk? It's a red tartan. We don't want Miss Baxter freezing to death, do we?"

"Certainly not, sir." Gilly emphatically shook his head, a smile twitching on his lips before he turned to exit.

Beynon straightened up from examining Fincham and pushed his spectacles back up his nose. "I'm afraid my diagnosis is positive," he said stiffly. "Captain Fincham has been suffering for a while. He has a double infliction of scurvy and the French disease. Both conditions are now in an advanced state, and there's nothing more to be done."

Grace glanced anxiously at Fitzwilliam as he puffed out his chest, drawing himself up to his full height. "I knew he was ailing, but the French disease? That's an unclean disease only afflicting women with loose morals!"

Grace swung her attention to Beynon, who nodded with a regretful air. "Did the captain's wife not also succumb to a similar affliction?" the surgeon asked.

Fitzwilliam stiffened. "I demand you withdraw your sala-cious accusations against the captain's wife this instant."

The surgeon glanced cagily at Grace before taking Fitzwilliam by the elbow and steering him away. His hushed whispers still reached Grace's ears. "Captain Fincham ordered me to secrecy about his ailment. He assured me he never strayed from his marital bed."

Well, one of them had! "Is there anything that can be done?" Grace asked.

Fitzwilliam and Beynon both turned sharply. Beynon blinked slowly and gave Grace a glare that radiated a superiority she had not seen before. He adjusted his eyeglasses. "Laudanum will keep the captain comfortable, though he has already finished the vial I gave him earlier."

"Will laudanum remedy his ailments?" Grace asked.

The surgeon hooked his first two fingers into the fob pocket of his waistcoat and, with his other hand, smoothed down his thick whiskers. "No, madam, but it'll afford the man some peace."

"Mr Beynon, if there's anything else to be done, I should like to try." Grace flicked her eyes at Fitzwilliam, his worried face making her all the more determined to help.

Shrugging, Beynon pursed his lips. "Very well. You need the juice from a freshly pounded raw potato and an onion. Offer him a spoonful at a time or whatever he can tolerate." Beynon picked up his heavy box and headed towards the cabin door. He paused and turned. "If he's able, have him rinse the juices about his gums and throat before swallowing."

When Gilly returned with the shawl, he was sent to fetch the potato and onion from the galley and then dismissed to continue his duties. Grace pounded the two vegetables in a stone mortar. With a teaspoon in hand and the heavy stone mortar nestled on her lap, Grace dribbled the cloudy, earthy-smelling concoction into Fincham's parted lips. She glanced at her shoulder as Fitzwilliam's hand slid over the dazzling, red-checked tartan wrapped snugly around her. Her gaze trailed up his arm until she met his eyes, full of concern.

"I appreciate your efforts, Miss Baxter."

Grace smiled. "I *do* intend to make myself useful." He pulled up a chair beside her, his proximity almost distracting her from her ministrations on Fincham. "You know so much about me, Lieutenant. Perhaps you might like to fill this time and share the story of your family?"

He hesitated, the smile line on his cheek deepening. "If you wish. Though you might find it no more interesting than all that dry naval talk I bored you with when we first met."

"That conversation charted the course of my life," said Grace softly. "I wish you wouldn't always dismiss what you have to say as boring or inconsequential."

He stared at her a beat longer than was comfortable then inclined his neat blond head. "Very well. I'm an only child. My father, Andrew Coulton Fitzwilliam, was a British naval officer too. He was on shore leave in Inverness when he first laid eyes on my mother at church. Glenna Anne Fraser was the only daughter of Thomas Fraser of Abertarff, who vehemently objected to his daughter falling in love with a naval officer."

Grace rolled her eyes coquettishly, her tongue toying with the corner of her mouth in an attempt to suppress her smile. "Those naval officers, they're not *all* bad, you know." She chuckled as he cocked an eyebrow at her. She enquired further, "How did he manage to woo Miss Fraser under her father's watch?"

"With his letters. After three years of courting by correspondence, my father plucked up the courage to ask my Grandda Fraser for my mother's hand in marriage. Fraser eventually conceded, but only after my father assured him of his ability to keep my mother in style."

Grace sighed. "If she truly loved him, I'm sure she would have been happy anywhere." She forced another spoonful of liquid through Fincham's lips. His gums were so swollen he could not fully open his jaw, and the noxious gas of his breath pushed Grace back.

Fincham swallowed convulsively.

Fitzwilliam's gaze drew up from the captain and settled on Grace. "Well, thanks to my father's great aunt, Baroness Morrison, this was easily proved. She died a childless spinster and passed her fortune to her eldest nephew—one Andrew Coulton Fitzwilliam. Her London townhouse, Abertarff House, was my childhood home. My Grandda Fraser had only one other condition."

"Dare I ask?"

"He insisted they be married in the Old High Church in Inverness and the deal be sealed with a traditional handfasting."

"Oh, that's not too disagreeable. I'm sure your father had no objections to that."

As though he had his own objections, Fincham snivelled weakly, shaking his head in feeble protest as he kicked the covers off, his trousers riding up to reveal his swollen legs.

Fitzwilliam gently drew the rumpled trouser legs down. "No, he didn't. He toiled hard to win my mother's love, and for his efforts, she loved him fiercely in return."

With the vegetable juices depleted in the stone well, Grace rose and slid the heavy mortar onto the table. "What a fascinating and romantic tale."

"Indeed. My father was quite the romantic at heart. I don't share his affliction and maintain no such romantic sentiment." Fitzwilliam gripped the two chairs and neatly returned them to their rightful positions with a dry scrape.

"I beg to differ, Lieutenant. Upon our first meeting, you regaled me with the romantic tale of Dulcinea from *Don Quixote*." She smiled demurely. "I declare you do indeed suffer from the same condition. I'm surprised you haven't already found yourself a wife."

"Rightly or wrongly, I've always prioritised my career over my personal life."

Well, she could right that wrong. Emboldened by the heartening satisfaction of her successful ministrations on the captain, Grace took Seamus's long-fingered hand and tugged gently against his warm grip. The lively grin slid from his face as she drew him down, their faces inching together.

The slight flutter of panic in Grace's throat was superseded by a new and strange thumping low in her abdomen. She had experienced it briefly before—the first time he had sat so near to her in the gardens at Wallace House. Her lips met his lightly, the warm, moist caress a physical shock. He tasted slightly salty, and the pulsing in her abdomen quickened. She stood on tiptoes and kissed him harder. Enjoying the little start he gave, she lowered herself back down, her mouth cool after his warmth.

Fitzwilliam drew back from her, pupils dilated, nostrils flaring. His gaze caressed her cheeks and her ears then slid down her throat and moved slowly back up. He stiffened his shoulders and shook his head.

Grace tipped her head. Was that a shake of disapproval at her forwardness, or a shake of marvellous disbelief that she dared to kiss him?

"It's late," he said. "Allow me to escort you to your cabin, Miss Baxter." The dryness of his tone answered her question.

Her heart plunged, and embarrassment crept across her scalp, prickling like a broiling hedgehog. Now he could add promiscuous Jezebel to his growing list of objections to her.

Chapter Thirteen

There had been two weeks of bad weather, and every night, the howling wind had closed in relentlessly around the *Discerning*. As the ship dove into the deep troughs, seawater smashed over the vessel, burying her decks in a foaming frenzy. Seamus had pulsed with frustration as the ship tacked nearly thirty times through the day. Whenever they stole within ten miles of the archipelago, the wind roared with redoubled violence and drove them back.

In the pre-dawn hours of one such night, Seamus found himself being prodded and shaken awake.

"Lieutenant Fitzwilliam, sir!"

Seamus sensed the urgency in the hissed words and came instantly awake. "McGilney? What is it?"

"Mr Beynon requires you in the great cabin, sir! 'Tis the cap'n!" McGilney dashed for the door, his haste to depart overriding etiquette.

Seamus's heart quickened, his mind racing over an assortment of mishaps. Swinging his legs off the edge of his cot, he noticed that while the ship was still rolling, the roaring of the storm had quietened. He scrabbled on the floor in the dark for his shoes. Seamus rushed to the great cabin and smacked the door open.

A scene of hushed determination lay before him, and he almost gagged on the heavy iron tang of blood in the air. In the middle of the table, with his stockinged feet facing the door, lay Captain Fincham. After the darkness above deck, the swinging lanterns illuminated a grim scene. Fincham groaned and mewled, his legs kicking spasmodically as McGilney pressed his shoulders to the table. Beynon laboured with deliberate and determined movements at Fincham's head, his shirt sleeves rolled to the elbow. With sinking dread, Seamus spotted blood on Beynon's hands. Lots of blood.

"I need you up this end, Lieutenant," said Beynon.

Seamus pressed alongside him, and the surgeon thrust a clean wad of fabric into Seamus's hand, guiding it to where his had been only moments before. Seamus gasped. That fleeting second when their hands exchanged places revealed a congealed, pulpy wound on the side of Fincham's head. A whimper erupted from Fincham's distorted, bloody face, and his heels dug into the table as his back arched, and he nearly broke free of McGilney's grasp.

"Christ, man! Hold him still!" said Beynon. McGilney grunted, climbing atop the writhing man to pin him more firmly to the table.

Seamus struggled to mop up the copious quantities of blood leaking from Fincham's head. "What happened?"

Without breaking from his ministrations, Beynon answered through gritted teeth, "He is shot."

The white muslin cloth in Seamus's hand turned an alarming shade of red. He reached for a new one and threw the saturated fabric on the floor with a wet splat. "Christ Al-bloody-mighty!"

After an age of probing, swabbing, and wrapping Fincham's

head, Beynon stood upright and stretched his back with a groan. Fincham had stilled on the table, and Seamus's lips tightened grimly. "Will he live?"

Beynon wiped the blood off his hands with a soiled cloth. "He lives, but for how long, I can't say. The ball remains within his skull, and I boast not the means nor the skill to extract it." The surgeon gave a frustrated huff as he glanced over to the curtained nook. "Help me transfer him to his berth. He'll be more comfortable there." The three men inexpertly manhandled the unconscious captain across the undulating floor and into the tiny berth. Fincham's white muslin crown slowly turned crimson.

Seamus reached up tiredly to rub his face but stopped when he noticed the state of his hands. He spotted a pistol among the wads of discarded bloodied rags and splatters of the captain's blood and brain fluid on the floor. "Why would he do such a thing?"

"He's in a macabre state of melancholy." Beynon adjusted Fincham's limbs into a more comfortable position. He rose stiffly from his knees. Cleaning his bloodied hands with a muslin square doused in alcohol, he sighed deeply. "The captain has obviously sought to free himself from this bitter life. A man only courts death when there are no more sweets to be tasted." He avoided eye contact with Seamus and fussed with his medicine box, returning stoppers to open jars and vials and nestling them back into the velvet-lined drawers.

"But 'tis self-murder, and the Bible says, 'Thou shalt not kill'!" McGilney cried, clearly shaken by the ordeal.

"It's only self-murder if it's found to be so." Seamus lay his hands palm down on the tabletop, fingers splayed like two bloodied starfish. "Quite frankly, Mr Beynon, your irksome talk of unclean disease and McGilney's talk of self-murder undermines this fine man's reputation." His dry tone cautioned the surgeon not to contradict him. He glared at McGilney. "I ask everyone to keep their opinions to themselves. I also appreciate your discretion with this matter. Not a word to anyone."

"Respectfully, sir. How do we explain the shot?" asked McGilney.

"I doubt anyone would've heard it over the noise of last night's storm," said Seamus rising and slinking exhaustedly over to the washstand. "It could've been a heavy item fallen over in the rough weather." Pouring a basin of water, he scrubbed the blood from his hands with a bar of lye soap, his skin burning at the corrosive ingredients as the water sloshed in the bowl. Unable to clean all the dried blood from under his nails, it was a vast improvement nonetheless.

Seamus spotted McGilney searching for a distraction. "Whisky, sir?"

Seamus nodded, and McGilney shuffled over to the bureau to unstopper the crystal decanter of amber liquid. He poured a splash into two glasses and doled them out.

"Pour yourself one too, McGilney. You've earned it." Seamus's stern countenance eased.

The tendrils of the early-morning sun peeked over the horizon—the first Seamus had seen in two weeks—filling the cabin with a rose-gold glow. An ominous silence sank over the three men as they sipped the fortifying whisky. Seamus savoured the smoky, burning sensation on his tongue, appreciating the warm glow it afforded as it slid down his gullet. He swung a sober look towards Beynon. "I'll address the hands and advise them that the captain's malady has worsened and that he has become mortally ill." Strictly speaking, it was the truth, he rationalised, surveying the gory aftermath.

Fincham gurgled alarmingly in his berth. Beynon and McGilney stood quietly by, swaying with exhaustion. The rose hue of the rising sun brightened, and Seamus rubbed a mostly clean hand over his face. Within the half hour, the entire ship's company knew of the captain's plight but were spared the gruesome details. A deep gloom set in—a sharp contrast to Neptune's fun and frivolities only a month before.

Having heard Bosun whistle all-hands on deck, Miss Baxter too had appeared and was leaning beside her cabin door, the red shawl wrapped tightly against the icy breeze. When Seamus finished addressing the men, she inclined her head in invitation, and he plodded over.

Her face was pale and piqued with concern. "Will you come in out of the cold, Lieutenant?"

"Thank you, Miss Baxter."

She shut the door against the bite of the early-morning air, her green eyes filled with worry. "I heard your announcement." The charthouse was toasty, the smoky residue of the potbellied stove mingling with her sweet feminine undertones.

Seamus formally kissed Miss Baxter's warm hand and waited for her to sit before sinking onto a dining chair. "Indeed. Captain Fincham's deterioration is alarming."

"I'd hoped my ministrations would've proven more effective," she said regretfully. Seamus placed his elbows on the table and wadded his hands together in one tight fist that he pressed to his lips. He took a deep breath that quavered traitorously. She leaned forward, placing a hand on his arm. "Lieutenant? Are you all right?"

He peered at her through gritty eyelids. "No, madam, I'm not."

"If it's my being so forward with you—kissing you—I apologise for my audacious behaviour." Her cheeks blazed the same colour as the coals in the stove.

Seamus fixed his eyes on her, his head tilted. "Um, no, madam. That isn't what troubles me. It's I who should apologise. I didn't mean to withdraw so abruptly from your affections. It's only that the display would have been made rather public had someone walked in. The risk of being seen is what unsettled me. Your kiss was— utterly charming."

"Oh." She flushed again. "Well, in that case, please speak what is on your mind. Unburdening oneself is good for lightening the problem."

Seamus swallowed dryly. "Miss Baxter, I must first beg your absolute discretion."

"But of course! You have information that could destroy me. Have I not entrusted you with it?"

"You have indeed." Seamus lowered his arms to the table. "It's not Captain Fincham's malady that has him at death's door. He … he is shot. By his own hand."

All colour drained from Miss Baxter's face, and she grabbed the knot of his hands. "Goodness! How terrible!" Seamus's knuckles clenched tightly beneath her soft palm. "And terrible for you. He's your friend."

"He is. Beynon, McGilney, and I worked through the small hours of the night to save him," said Seamus.

Her eyes darted to the dark residue beneath his nails, and he made to pull away. She tightened her grip. "I'm so sorry you endured such horrors."

The empathy in her soft voice was nearly his undoing, and Seamus swallowed the prickling ball of tears. "Please, Miss Baxter. You can't breathe a word to anyone. I don't wish the captain's reputation ruined. It also won't do the men's morale any good either."

Her grip on his hands loosened, and her thumb gently caressed his scar, sending a shiver up his arm. "I understand, Lieutenant. You have my word. What will happen if he … if he …"

"I'd assume command until such time as the Admiralty appoints a new captain. Though this isn't a responsibility I expected to shoulder just yet."

Miss Baxter crossed the two ends of her shawl tighter around her chest and drew her shoulders back. "Well then, let's pray for Captain Fincham's recovery."

Several days later, Seamus was inspecting the morning watch's efforts while the spray of white horses whipped up by the wind continued to mar the newly scrubbed decks. He stopped, his clasped hands tightening behind his back as a group of four sailors approached him, their expressions openly hostile.

"A word, sir, if you please?" Blom's flat Dutch accent was whipped away on the stiff breeze.

"If you must."

"Well, you see now, the men are talking about how our luck has taken a turn for the worse since Miss Baxter appeared," said Blom. Behind him, Sorensen, Phillips, and Mahlon nodded unanimously.

"It isn't right, sir, having a woman aboard. Every sailor worth his salt knows 'tis bad luck." Cook Phillips bristled, hobbling to keep his balance on the moving deck.

"We've had nothing but storm after storm pushing us back. And now there's the cap'n's health," said Sorensen, running his hand across his lips and sniffing disapprovingly.

"Gentlemen." Seamus tempered his irritation. Flaring at the men would only fuel their displeasure. "I appreciate your concern, but the events of which you speak are quite recent. Miss Baxter has been aboard the *Discerning* since we left Woolwich, and nothing untoward has happened. The foul weather is God's domain, and as for Captain Fincham, well, we've all been witness to his unfortunate decline for some time now. Nothing in these two events indicates Miss Baxter's involvement."

"'Tain't right!" interjected Mahlon, his scarred cheeks lifting like those of a snarling dog. "She has no right being aboard a naval vessel. You need to offload her at the next port. Or else—"

Seamus brought his hands to his sides and drew back his shoulders, raising himself above them all. "I caution you to choose your next words wisely, Mahlon. Threatening an officer or his guest will land you in hotter water than you can imagine. Tread lightly."

Mahlon shut his mouth and flicked a greasy lock of hair from his eyes.

"We're not threatening any harm," placated Blom. "Though Miss Baxter should mind herself 'round those Marine Society boys. With what little mothering they had, there's not much softness about them. I overheard Holburton saying he'll not stand for us becomin' a ship of softies with a woman aboard."

Seamus flared his nostrils. "I can't in good conscience deposit an English gentlewoman on foreign shores, no matter how displeasing the men find her presence."

"Suit yourself then, sir, but don't be surprised if you find half the men scarper at the next chance. They ain't risking their necks to misfortune just for having a skirt about." Blom scratched his grey side-whiskers, peering over his shoulder for the other men's approval. They all grunted in agreement.

"Thank you for bringing me your concerns." Seamus's voice was as stiff as his locked knees. "I'll deliberate on a solution. But for now, kindly resume your duties."

Chapter Fourteen

It had been four days, and Seamus could not believe Captain Fincham was still alive. He surprised Seamus one evening by suddenly asking for a cup of St. John's wort tea. Seamus nearly keeled over in fright, believing that Fincham had died and that it was his ghost who had addressed him. Beynon examined the captain and was baffled at his ability to be conscious and talking with a musket ball in his brain.

Fincham was unable to rise from his berth, and at times, delirium overcame him, but it was his moments of lucidity that surprised Seamus and the surgeon. Fincham's case was unprecedented and of great interest to the medical man. Beynon stayed with him every day, observing and recording him. Miss Baxter avoided Fincham. She no doubt found his unpredictable outbursts unnerving. Seamus could only dream of unshouldering his responsibility as easily.

After more exhausting days battling the windy and unfavourable waters, Seamus woke one morning to a crisp, clear-skied day that gleamed as if scrubbed clean by the storm.

Standing before the chart table, he gingerly coaxed some warmth into his stiff wrist, calculating a landing at Port Famine on the north shore of the Strait of Magellan. By his estimation, with the current favourable sailing conditions, they should be there in another three days. The desolate and rugged terrain had a treacherous history, and Seamus hoped to find the remains of the city of King Phillip, established over two hundred and forty years back by Captain Pedro Sarmiento de Gamboa.

In the name of Spain, over three hundred pioneering settlers had attempted to tame this inhospitable patch of earth. With a great leap of faith, and accompanied by a couple of Franciscan priests with a colossal timber crucifix, the group of men, women, and children found themselves surrounded by hostile, rocky terrain and bitter temperatures. Only three years on and plagued by disease, rodents, freezing temperatures, and disastrous harvests, all but eighteen of the settlers had perished. Seamus was under no illusion about the conditions awaiting them.

He had been exploiting their slow progress by charting the seabed, noting any rocks, shoals, and reefs that would pose a hazard and obstruct a ship's passage. His skilled crew had measured the seabed depth at various points along their journey by lowering lead lines over the ship's side. The lead weight on the end of the rope dragged it to the ocean floor. Flags attached to the cable every fathom enabled McGilney to record accurate depths into his notebook, which Seamus later transferred onto the hydrographic chart—two activities Miss Baxter took a keen interest in observing. Once they had anchored and the survey crew could explore the natural landmarks, these too would be added to the chart. The collation of this information was vital for aiding future navigation of these treacherous straits—and was the whole purpose of their expedition.

Seamus always experienced a curious excitement when the sailors hauled up the rope. The contents of the ocean floor stuck to the wax at the end of the lead line, giving him valuable information about the nature of the seabed below—essential for noting suitable anchoring points. While it was an accurate process, it was labour intensive and time consuming.

After expertly navigating the narrow, rocky channels fraught with racing tides, Seamus's calculations proved correct, and three days later, the *Discerning* prepared to anchor in the Strait of Magellan during the early evening. Standing on the quarterdeck with Miss Baxter, Seamus glanced across to the darkening shadow of land alongside them. Tiny flickering lights speckled the coastline.

"Goodness! Are those campfires?" she enquired.

"Natives," clarified Seamus. "They'll be a wild lot in this part of the world. Won't have had much contact with Europeans. Ships have been passing around the Horn for centuries, but few stop in this barren and inhospitable land."

"Are they dangerous?" she asked, looking more curious than concerned.

"Hard to say. Some tribes are known for their violence, but others scamper off without a trace. Let's hope these are the latter."

The next day was Sunday. The atmosphere on deck was light and carefree as the men enjoyed their half-day off before their onshore exploration began in earnest the following morning. Seamus stepped restlessly onto the deck—it was hours before he was due to escort Miss Baxter on their evening walk. He sidled up to the quarterdeck under the pretence of checking all was in order—when he knew full well it was—so that he could draw nearer to her cabin door in the hope that she might pop her head out. The door remained steadfastly closed. Seamus cocked his head, hoping to catch a sound of her shuffling about inside. He stiffened with the rigidity of a day-old corpse. Voices?

"Please, Jim, how many times must I ask you to call me Grace?"

"'Twouldn't be proper. The lieutenant wouldn't stand for such informality." Buchanan's voice was laced with worry.

"Very well, then I insist on Miss Grace, all right?" She sighed, "Now, what were you saying?"

"You shouldn't be wandering about the ship alone, Miss Grace. 'Tis dangerous," said Buchanan.

"But the storm has passed," she said. "You never worried about me falling overboard before."

"Storm isn't the only danger on the ship," Buchanan added.

"Out with it, Jim! What has you two so rattled this afternoon?" Her question, high pitched and polished, pierced the thin door.

"Well, Miss Grace, me and Toby heard Mad Mahlon and Kendrick blathering at dinner yesterday about you."

"Oh, goodness! What now?" Miss Baxter's voice pitched with exasperation.

"Seems Kendrick's gone right off ye," said Buchanan.

"Kendrick went off me when I declared I'd no longer write his letters for him. He laughed at me the day Tommy Holburton smeared me with grease!" she retorted.

"Aye, well, we heard Mad Mahlon and Kendrick plotting something. Didn't catch it all as they were nattering low and 'twas loud in the mess. But we heard yer name mentioned a couple of times." Buchanan's voice darkened.

"That might explain the rat I found in my cot yesterday after I visited the head," she murmured.

"A rat, ye say? In yer cot? Christ, who'd have the gall to sneak into yer cabin like that?" said Buchanan.

"Clearly someone with too few brains to contemplate the consequences," snipped Miss Baxter.

Hicks's soft voice was tinged with concern. "Or someone with enough ill feeling towards you to take the risk." He implored, "Please inform Lieutenant Fitzwilliam, Miss Grace!

Those wishing you harm will become fearless in their attempts if they think they've got away with it."

"Nonsense! I'll not be intimidated by a dead rat. It's but a foolish schoolboy trick. There isn't a man aboard brave enough to hurt me while I'm under the protection of Lieutenant Fitzwilliam," said Miss Baxter confidently.

She was damned right! Seamus smarted, rapping sharply on the door.

The conversation ended abruptly, replaced by the scrape of a chair and a shuffle. Miss Baxter unlatched the door and gave him a green-eyed blink of surprise. Seamus squashed his cocked hat under his elbow.

"Good afternoon, Miss Baxter." He bowed stiffly.

"Lieutenant Fitzwilliam." She glowed eagerly and tightened the tartan around her shoulders, hunching against the frigid breeze. "You're early." Usually, Seamus relished her wrapped in his mother's shawl, but his blood was up after hearing of more of the men's grievances, and he was in no mood to be complimentary.

"Mind if I join in?" he bit more dryly than intended as he glared over her shoulder. Buchanan and Hicks quailed at the sight of Seamus's murderous glower and sprang up simultaneously, their chairs scraping noisily. Hicks whimpered, and Buchanan stepped protectively before the terrified cook's boy.

Uninvited, Seamus stepped around her, but she stopped his advance with a firm hand on his bicep. "Lieutenant!"

"*What* are you two doing in here?" Seamus demanded, twitching in irritation. Hicks ducked his face from sight behind Buchanan's square shoulders. Buchanan stood taller, and Seamus felt begrudging admiration as the young man prepared to face the consequences. "Miss Baxter, it's wholly inappropriate for the men to seek entertainment in your cabin."

"And where on God's earth do you propose we meet? In the

fo'c'sle? Above, where we can freeze to death?" Anger flashed across her face, and Seamus's own anger tightened.

"No! You shouldn't be meeting with them at all!" he snapped. "Miss Baxter, they are far below your station, and as such, it isn't appropriate for you to fraternise with them on *any* part of this ship." And certainly not out of view of his protective eye. Blom's earlier confession, and the crowd of scowling faces that had accompanied it, had raised Seamus's concern for her safety alarmingly. As had her own revelation only moments ago.

"Rats' tails!" She snorted in contempt, and Seamus flinched, unused to being dismissed so readily. He flicked Buchanan and Hicks another lethal look, and they cowered like cornered rats themselves, their darting eyes searching for an escape path.

Miss Baxter inhaled deeply, nostrils flaring, voice quivering. "Toby, Jim, thank you for an entertaining afternoon. Please excuse me. I wish a private word with the lieutenant."

Seamus staggered in surprise as Miss Baxter blocked him from the two young men with her slim frame. Jabbing her shoulder blade into his chest, she forced him to step back from the door. Astonishing himself, he complied. Seamus determined the exact moment the youngsters gauged the opening, and he clenched his teeth in silent restraint as they scurried past him to freedom.

Buchanan mumbled a quick, "Good afternoon to ye, miss. Sir." Hicks was mute with terror.

She slammed the door and whirled around angrily. "Lieutenant Fitzwilliam!" She spat his name out with venom. "I'll have you know that while you had *no idea* I was even here, those two were among the first of my friends on this godforsaken ship!" Her eyes blazed in a green fury.

Seamus's nostrils flared as he fought to steady his breathing, biting his tongue against a sharp retort. Must she brandish that sword every time? Seeing her fighting back tears, Seamus's anger fizzled as quickly as a flaming arrow shot into the sea.

"Miss Baxter, I beg your understanding." He reached for her shaking hands, squeezing them in his fingers as she bravely stemmed her tears. He was torn between his overwhelming need to enforce ship's etiquette, his knowledge of the disturbingly intimate details of her circumstances, and the even more unsettling knowledge of the men's antagonism towards her. The weight in his chest dropped like a cut anchor as she snatched her hands from his. He tried again, his tone softer. "The men's discontentment grows at having an unchaperoned woman aboard. I, for once, agree with their sentiments."

"I *know*." She rammed her hands on her hips. "I'm bad luck, and they wish to toss me overboard."

Seamus hesitated for a moment before deciding to continue with the truth she needed to hear. "May I be honest with you?" She dropped her arms to her sides, and Seamus reached for her hand again. "There are indeed those who wish to do you harm. Unfortunately, their numbers are too many for me to do much about it without leaving me severely shorthanded. You're a distraction. I can't afford to have the men's heads turned when they've duties to attend to. If this situation isn't remedied soon, some men will leave the ship at the next port. Fine sailors are hard to come by in this part of the world, and losing any number of hands will jeopardise the expedition. The other issue is that we're months from docking at a civilised port. That's a long spell to be mingling with a disgruntled crew."

Her brows knitted uncertainly. "What does this mean? For me?"

"It wouldn't be an issue had you a husband or brother accompanying you. Alas, you don't."

"Does your offer of protection not count?"

"It might have carried more weight had Captain Fincham been more amenable, but you witnessed his response to your discovery. Couple that with the men's displeasure, and I really am caught in a quandary."

"Does that mean our evening walks are out of the question?"

Seamus bowed deeply. "Not at all, Miss Baxter. Would you please do me the honour of allowing me to escort you this evening?" She gave him a shaky smile in return. Feeling mightily pleased with himself, Seamus arched his eyebrows as Miss Baxter placed a hand on his chest, her face painted with a wickedly impish expression.

"I'd be delighted to accompany you, Lieutenant. Though, by your own admission, as a woman of good standing, I simply *can't* step out with you without a suitable escort." Seamus's smile faltered as her mouth twitched mischievously. "Perhaps Lieutenant Wadham might perform this service?" she asked.

Seamus chortled dryly, shaking his head at her sharp sense of humour.

Chapter Fifteen

TIERRA DEL FUEGO, 7 AUGUST 1826

Seamus ordered a skeleton crew to remain aboard the *Discerning* as the rest of the men were rowed across in the two cutters to Port Famine's rocky outcrop. The wind nipped mercilessly at his bare skin, and he noted ruefully that no one had escaped the same rosy, wind-burned cheeks. He chuckled at Miss Baxter's forsaking fashion for warmth. She was bundled up in her newly issued naval jacket, her brown breeches and old boots poking out from under her skirts. She had also wrapped Seamus's plaid like a hood over her short hair before topping it with her bonnet.

Seamus had explained Port Famine's brief and brutal history to Miss Baxter over supper the previous evening. He had also attempted to explain the technical process behind surveying and how he would be using his great theodolite, Gunter's chain and a zenith telescope.

"It sounds complicated and time consuming," she'd said with

a wry twist of her lips. "I hoped you'd explore the island with me."

Seamus's brow knitted. "But I'll be with you, and together we'll explore the lie of the land."

"Our interpretation of exploration differs, Lieutenant. Exploring to me is walking freely and seeking adventure, not pacing out the ground and stopping every few minutes to scribble notes."

"Hmm." Seamus raised one eyebrow, sensing he was heading into a stalemate with this slip of a woman who was far too undaunted by the world for her own good.

"If you'll not share the adventure with me, then I'll invite Jim and Toby. Proper etiquette will prevail, each man account-able to the other."

"Not on my watch, Miss Baxter," Seamus said coolly.

She rolled her eyes at him. "This is the remotest place on earth, with no life around to witness any cavorting. Unless you object to the penguins ogling us?"

He unnarrowed his eyes, and the tip of his tongue played with the corner of his mouth. "A compromise, perchance?"

"I'm all ears." Her eyes flashed in victory.

"What if you spend the morning surveying with me, and I spend the afternoon sightseeing with you?" That was as fair an offer as she would receive from him.

"Very well, Lieutenant. I hope you're up to the task of providing as equally a spirited outing as Jim and Toby would've promised." She scrunched her nose at his low growl.

Now, under Seamus's vigilant watch, the seamen ferried the precious cargo of Miss Baxter and his survey equipment across to the rock-strewn beach. Seamus observed the colony of king penguins jostling in a cacophonous roar on a rocky outcrop, their stark-white fronts and silver-grey backs reminding him of liveried footmen. A few of the penguins stared impassively as they rowed by, unperturbed by the influx of humans on their stony shoreline. A gust of wind swept a choking reek of rotten fish and pungent ammonia across the water, and Seamus grinned as Miss Baxter clasped her hand to her nose.

Seamus studied several of the other islands across the strait. The vegetation in these parts was vividly green, but it was coarse and wild and interspersed with pretty little yellow and white flowers. Botany was not his strong suit. He inhaled a refreshing breath of air which smelled of cold rock, damp earth, and sweet vegetation.

Seamus's survey crew included Wadham, McGilney, and a gang of his strongest men to carry the monstrously heavy equipment, a folding table and two chairs. Caught behind while monitoring the procession, Seamus noted Wadham's fine spirits and watched helplessly as he walked alongside Miss Baxter. Wadham tipped his hat at her, and seeing her beam with pleasure, Seamus hurried to catch up. He was still several steps behind when Miss Baxter giggled at something Wadham said.

"Oh, what sweet air we breathe! Better than London's foul vapours." Wadham's deep voice resonated between the thin trees of the sparse forest.

"Sweet, indeed," she agreed. "Tell me, Lieutenant, are there any dangerous animals about these parts?"

Wadham shook his head. "Not as far as we know. Captain de Gamboa didn't list any dangerous animals in his litany of complaints against this land. The biggest menaces were the vicious winds that froze half his people to death and the ruggedness of the terrain that defied their crop-growing attempts."

"Even so, I don't plan on wandering off anytime soon."

"You stick with me, Miss Baxter." Wadham nodded solemnly and tightened his grip on his scabbard. "I'll see you safe."

"Why thank you, Lieutenant Wadham." She smiled decorously. "I feel safer already."

Wadham's tanned skin darkened, cheeks dimpling with pleasure. "I must admit, your presence here adds a refreshing air."

"Am I such a unique case? Are there no other instances of women aboard ships?"

"Oh yes, many—though none who served in naval crews, to my knowledge. Female passengers are not uncommon, but the captain usually knows of their passage from the outset of the voyage." He chuckled and shook his head. "One tale worth repeating is of the packet, *Princess Royal*. Captain Skinner offered his sister, Mary, passage so she might marry her beau in New York. But halfway across the Atlantic, the bloody Frenchies attacked. Oh, pardon my language, Miss Baxter!"

"It's quite all right, Lieutenant. Nothing I've not heard before."

"Ah, yes. Well, naturally, Miss Skinner attended the wounded, but when she heard that her brother was running short of cloth for the gunpowder bags, she offered up her wedding dress, appreciating that war had to come before love."

"What a handsome tale!"

"Rather like yours, Miss Baxter."

Seamus cleared his throat noisily, and his voice carried an unmistakable authority that caused Wadham's footsteps to falter as he revolved to face him. "Lieutenant Wadham, why don't you scout ahead with McGilney? Ensure the way is clear."

Wadham's face fell, but he inclined his head. "Of course."

Seamus smiled smugly as Wadham sped away to catch up with McGilney. He flicked a glance at Miss Baxter and, a little taken aback by her scowl, fell in silently beside her. He called a halt atop the highest hill that he had seen when they dropped anchor in the bay. He instructed the seamen where to place the equipment and left Wadham to fiddle with the finer settings. Wadham dictated the information to McGilney, who furiously scribbled in a notebook. With Wadham a distance away fussing over the equipment, Seamus settled at the end of the table with his sketchpad and drew the surrounding landmarks.

Tapping his lip in distraction, Seamus discreetly studied Miss

Baxter, who was perched on a large rock studying the spectacular view of the open waterways and multitudes of islands in the archipelago. She glanced back at the survey crew, beaming delightedly at Wadham's wink. Inwardly, Seamus grimaced. If he believed Wadham was even the slightest bit sincere, he might have approved of the match. Becoming an officer's wife would undoubtedly earn her better protection from the men. But he knew she was nothing but a plaything to Wadham—something to alleviate his boredom. Rising from his chair, Seamus shouldered into Wadham's view and instructed him to reposition the equipment on another hillock further away.

After the midday meal, Seamus ordered the survey equipment to be packed up and sent to the beach, where it was to be covered to protect it from the elements and placed under guard. Seamus's fists bunched as Wadham sauntered confidently over to Miss Baxter.

Wadham bowed. "Miss Baxter, may I escort you back to the beach?" His brows rose expectantly, hope glimmering in his brown eyes.

"No, you may not!" snapped Seamus, unfettered jealousy punching the inside of his ribs. The emotion confused him. He had no desirous intentions towards her, did he? Yes, he enjoyed her company—more than most. He had a fine appreciation of her humour. His admiration for her spirit had grown tenfold, even though her presence created an impossible balancing act between his professionalism and affection. But jealousy?

Miss Baxter and Wadham swivelled in unison to stare at him. Seamus glowered menacingly at Wadham who immediately squared his shoulders. At the sound of Miss Baxter's indignant squeak, Seamus twisted around.

"*Pardon me?*" she spat, fisted hands on her hips. "How dare you? What right have you to dictate what I may or not may do?" Her usually measured tone was almost a shriek.

Shit! Seamus blustered, "My apologies, madam. I ... I ...

misspoke." He cleared his throat and swallowed. "I simply meant that you're under *my* protection and are therefore *my* responsibility." He bowed his head, cheeks burning. "I'm sorry if my statement caused you any offence."

Wadham raised a supercilious eyebrow. "Perhaps Miss Baxter might like to choose her escort?"

Seamus's brows furrowed at the challenge, but because of his recent blunder, he hesitated, calculating that any punitive measure he directed at Wadham now would make him appear petty and jealous. Envious tendrils curled around Seamus's lungs. Miss Baxter stepped between them and rested a hand on each of their chests.

"Gentlemen." She flashed them both a captivating glimpse of her teeth, although her cheeks were coloured with annoyance. "I appreciate your offers of an escort. My welfare is perfectly secure surrounded by such courage and loyalty." Seamus's glower deepened, but he attempted to erase it as she widened her eyes at him in warning. "Lieutenant Fitzwilliam, I'm sure Lieutenant Wadham has the purest intention, and I'm flattered he asked." She turned to Wadham with a polite smile. "Lieutenant Wadham, thank you for your kind offer." Wadham's eyes, only a moment ago boring into Seamus's, slid down to hers and softened immeasurably, a smile tightening his lips. "However, Lieutenant Fitzwilliam and I have already made arrangements for this afternoon."

The boyish grin slid off Wadham's face like a chunk of melting iceberg, and a searing thrill of victory surged through Seamus's veins. Eyes averted, Wadham stepped back and bowed.

"Certainly. I'll see the equipment safely back to the beach. Your servant, madam. Good day to you both." He spun around abruptly and stomped down the hill, his back stiff.

Miss Baxter whipped around to Seamus. "Peacock!" she snapped.

"Peacock?"

"Yes, you! With your puffed-out chest, parading before poor Lieutenant Wadham, asserting your seniority. You have been doing it all morning! That poor man." Her green eyes flashed.

Seamus's eyebrow twitched irritably, and his right wrist cracked as he rotated it. "That *poor man* is simply seeking distraction from the monotony of ship life. He isn't as invested in your welfare as—" Seamus bit off his confession.

"As *you*?" she snipped.

Seamus clasped his fingers before him to still the shake of his hands. "I apologise, Miss Baxter. I didn't mean to be so bombastic." He stared at her in another stalemate. Seamus took a deep breath, and as his shoulders slumped, the anger in his blood faded. He untwined his fingers and let his arms drop loosely to his sides.

"It's all right, Lieutenant." She placed her hand on his forearm, and he felt the tremble in her too. "I know you're honour bound to my uncle to keep me safe and that you mean well." She peered up through her lashes. "Though you're *the most* stubborn human I've ever known. When you decide something, little can be done to sway you." Her words tripped lightly from between her smiling lips.

"I'm the embodiment of a navy career man, madam. I know no other way." He softened the dry edge to his voice as he lifted his brow in mock seriousness. "Since you've an objection to the authority I hold over the men, I humbly relinquish my authority over you." He bowed theatrically and waved his cocked hat to one side. "I'm yours to command for the afternoon, Miss Baxter."

Her eyes narrowed, but her lips curled. "Be careful what you wish for." She grasped his hand. "This way."

Seamus glanced over his shoulder at the retreating line of men making their way back to the beach, their progress slow and methodical under the weight of all the brass equipment. A delicious thrill of impropriety twirled in his chest as he allowed himself to be dragged away by a determined Miss Baxter.

Inland, they discovered the ruins of the original church built by the first settlers. Although the church had lost its roof, its sturdy stone walls remained. It was a physical reminder of the hardship endured here, like a scar upon the earth. Inside the church, a large bush flourished in the shelter of the stone walls. No evidence remained of the wooden cross hauled in by the settlers.

Walking a short distance from the church, they found a graveyard housing an uncomfortably high number of inhabitants —a warning to other visitors.

An unpleasant wind had arisen, and Seamus suggested sheltering in the ruins of the church. He whipped out a hip flask containing his favourite Duret cognac and offered it to Miss Baxter.

"My, my, Lieutenant Fitzwilliam, plying me with liquor?" Her eyes glinted mischievously as she delicately sipped from the flask. "Hmm, it is still an acquired taste." She wrinkled her nose.

"It's sacrilegious to be drinking cognac from a hip flask." He took a swig and hummed as the fruity warmth of the liquid left a sweet burn down his throat, reminding him of roasted peach cooked over an open flame. As Seamus took another sip, Miss Baxter snapped off the stalk of a small plant at her feet. She held the delicate, white, star-like flower to her pert nose, and her eyes widened in delight.

"Ooh! It smells like cocoa." She offered it to Seamus to smell, and he leaned in, locking eyes with her as he sniffed.

He tenderly took the leafy stem from her and, nudging aside her hooded shawl, tucked the chocolate-smelling flower behind her ear. He traced a line around the soft lobe and along her jaw to the pulsing artery in her throat. Bringing his fingertip slowly to her lips, he brushed her scar lightly. His frown at the thin, red weal deepened as he curled his fingers in regret. "I'm sorry.

Being so near to you and not being able to touch you is driving me to distraction." Seamus took another step toward her but hesitated as the proud and proper officer in him wrestled with his inherent maleness.

Miss Baxter inched closer and, reaching up and grasping his face, drew his unresisting mouth to hers. He groaned. Her mouth and chin were soft, her cheek warm against his icy nose. She gasped against his lips as his hands reached down the hollow of her back and explored the curve of her behind. Even through her thick breeches and skirts, his palms moulded to the shape of her. Magnificent! Cupping her buttocks, he drew her hips to meet his. He pulled back, soaking up the pink flush of her smooth cheeks.

She placed her palms on his chest and gently pushed him back. She slid her hands down his arms, and her hand stopped on his scarred wrist, her thumb tracing the weal of knotted tissue.

"I appreciate your scar," she whispered. "It shows me that even though someone hurt you once, you healed. And the pain stopped."

His mind flared to Silverton—the bastard! Seamus turned his palm upwards, and she slid her fingers through his. "Oh, Miss Baxter," he uttered softly, "you too will heal." He shook his head sorrowfully. "I'd gladly take your experience and make it my own."

"I'd not wish that upon you."

Seamus huffed through his nose. "While you're safe enough when you're around me, were I your husband, it would be my name that would protect you when I wasn't." Christ! What was he saying? The words had slipped out before he could weigh up how she might interpret them. Though, they were true enough.

"Husband?" She lifted her head in surprise, drawing her fingers back. "*My* husband?"

He stared fiercely and protectively at her. "Indeed! Not only for the sake of propriety but because"—Seamus snorted again

—"I admire you far too much to allow your reputation to be sullied."

"You *admire* me?" said Miss Baxter slowly, and he caught the slide of disappointment in her voice.

"Yes. Admiration is but *one* of the reasons."

"You need not be so obliged."

"Miss Baxter! Would that we had a priest, I'd wed you on the spot to assure you of my protection!" He curled his fist and rotated his wrist until it clicked, hoping that had not come out too pretentious. He did not want her to believe he had a double set of standards—his wish for women's freedom to vote but not giving her a choice in husband. Damn and blast the situation!

"And what if I didn't want to be wed to you? Would you still force my hand?"

"Of course not."

"Would you still have me, ruined reputation and all?"

Seamus's heart somersaulted in his chest. Would he indeed? Could he risk his own standing? His thoughts divided like a shoal of fish panicked by an approaching shark. "Your uncle saved my life. Were it not for him, I'd not be here with you now. Call me sentimental, but is that not destiny?"

"Is your debt to my uncle so great that you'd gamble me being your wife?"

"Would you like to be my wife?"

"I hadn't given it any thought until now."

"Is the idea so disagreeable?"

"Well, you're certainly an improvement on any of the suitors Father had lined up for me. But no, it's not an unpleasant notion." She hesitated. "Except it's a rather *permanent* one. Would you chance it merely for my interim safeguard?"

"As with all my decisions, madam, it's not done by half measure. From where I presently stand, the benefits outweigh the risks—for us both." At least he hoped they did. "We're both well educated. We've the shared bond of Admiral Baxter. Our minds meet on common ground more often than not."

"And what of the times when we don't agree? We've had our fair share of those already."

"I find those who are too agreeable to be a bore. And you, Miss Baxter, are certainly no bore."

"If this is your attempt at a proposal, Lieutenant, then perhaps you might like to call me Grace?"

"A poor attempt." The back of his neck warmed. "Had I a remedy to fulfil a proposal, I might call it one. But until I can determine a solution, I hope you'll bear with me. When I do ask you to marry me, I want to be in a position where I can make it a reality."

Grace grinned. "Your persuasion won't leave much room for refusal, will it?"

"We are not always blessed with abundant choices in life. We must make do with what we are given." He dashed a hand across his mouth, suddenly bashful.

"Then it's fortunate that my only option is so favourable." She squeezed his fingers, and a flood of hope pumped warmly through his limbs.

Chapter Sixteen

G race settled into a new routine over the next few days. She joined the survey crew, and on days when the weather was too wet and blustery, she stayed aboard the *Discerning*, reading or resting up from her long days in the field with Seamus. Grace enviously eyed the men's musketry improve under Sergeant Baisley's supervision, and her fingers itched to curl around the trigger and squeeze off one of her shots that almost always found the target. When she suggested that she might join the men in their musket training, Seamus shut the notion down without negotiation.

Grace discovered that, while there was little time for a leisurely exploration of the island, she was kept sufficiently occupied by Lieutenant Wadham's explanations of surveying by day and Seamus's lessons in celestial navigation by night. With Captain Fincham indisposed and in no position to object, Seamus also permitted Grace to help Gilly with his clerical duties.

Gilly showed her how to draw up the watch and assign parts of the crew to duties during specific times between the ship's bells. She also recorded the station bills—the official lists of duties and posts assigned to the hands. Working closely with Purser Rowlett, each week she updated the muster book with details of everyone aboard. The lists of men in the muster book were then used as the basis for paying wages and distributing food and other rations. Grace was surprised to learn that the crew could request extra clothing, bedding or tobacco, which was deducted from their wages.

Despite there now being two of them at this job, they were perpetually bent over the ship's books, recording illness, miscon-duct, punishments, and a description of each man's conduct. As if this were not a mammoth enough task, Grace was astounded to discover that as captain's clerk, Gilly was required to make two extra copies each of the muster book and logbook to be sent to the Admiralty back in London. And while Seamus was profusely apologetic that she could not explore the island more freely, he was equally stubborn in his refusal to be distracted from his commitment to surveying.

One morning, while observing the men loading the cutters for the umpteenth time, Grace decided to broach the subject again with Seamus. He stepped up to the bulwark, hunched under the pack containing his notebooks and his precious brass compasses, dividers, and callipers—vital tools of the trade he never went ashore without.

"Good morning, Lieutenant Fitzwilliam." She offered a dazzling smile, and Seamus did a double take, his eyes narrowing suspiciously.

"You're up early, Miss Baxter." He surveyed the crew's preparations. "Will you be joining us?"

"I'd appreciate a lift to shore, if you please, Lieutenant, but I'll not be joining you on the survey."

"Miss Baxter, I've no time for riddles." His confusion crumpled into a frown. "We must exploit this fine weather and set off right away." Seamus gave another order to two passing men, and he twisted tetchily back to Grace. "What is it you're after?"

"I'd like to further explore the island out past the little church," she blurted, sticking out her chin. "Alone. If you permit me to carry a musket, I'll not be in any danger." Seamus became immobile, and it was like staring at a marble bust.

"Absolutely *not*, madam. Since our previous discussion on the matter, my answer remains the same."

"Please, Lieutenant! Your exploration has not uncovered any dangers."

"Mother Nature always has tricks up her sleeve, Miss Baxter. You could plummet off a cliff or stumble into a crevice. How would we know where to find you if harm befell you? And what if you encounter the natives without an adequate escort?"

"I understand your concern for my safety, Lieutenant, but I'm going out of my mind with the repetition of it all. Perhaps you might permit Jim and Toby to escort me? They can carry me home if I break a leg."

"We've also had *this* discussion before," Seamus snorted. Closing his eyes briefly, he groaned, and hope pulsated in Grace. "Very well," he said, and Grace's jolt of disbelief flittered into a smug grin. Frowning at this, he added quickly, "But only if McGilney accompanies you too. Our venture ashore today is more about scouting for supplies than surveying. I don't require McGilney's scribing skills. He can make himself useful by keeping a close eye on you and those two rapscallions."

"Do you really mean it?"

"Regretfully, I do." He wrung his scarred wrist with his other hand. "The protection of three muskets should keep you out of trouble. I don't want you wandering off willy-nilly. You may only venture as far as is charted."

"Oh, Seamus, thank you!" exclaimed Grace, gripping his arm. Sensing him bristle as a passing Blom glowered at her familiarity, Grace released him. "May I have a musket of my own?" she asked.

"No."

Seamus ordered Gilly to round up Jim and Toby. He also ensured that Holburton, Cakebread and Da Silva accompanied him, and Grace appreciated that he was trying to keep them away from her. On the beach, she bid Seamus farewell and ignored Holburton's glare burning a hole in her back. The four of them clambered over the rocks, examining the teeming life in the rock pools and skirting around the deafening, reeking colony of penguins. They headed inland, crossing grassy plains and exploring the edges of coniferous forests. Eventually, they arrived at the church ruins, and Gilly suggested they shelter from the stiff breeze inside while they ate.

Grace had packed a picnic. Out of her carry bag, she plucked a bottle of red wine, a hunk of salt beef, and a wheel of sorry-looking cheese. Freshly baked biscuits made up for the meagre meal.

"This countryside reminds me of the Highlands back home," said Jim wistfully, munching on a biscuit. "'Tis a cold, hard place to live in too, but the Highlands' saving grace is it isn't at the arse end of the world as this place is."

"By crumbs, Buchanan!" reprimanded Gilly sharply. "There's a lady present. Mind your tongue, m'lad."

"Och, aye. Forgot, sorry," replied Jim bashfully.

"Gilly, please!" said Grace. "My initiation in the fo'c'sle exposed me to every foul word known to man. One little slip is hardly likely to offend me."

Gilly huffed through his nose. "I know, but you know what the lieutenant's like. He's tryin' real hard to forget that ever happened to you. And he's makin' sure the rest of us do our hardest to forget too."

"The lieutenant is rather set in his ways," Grace declared.

"Aye, 'tis the naval man in him," agreed Jim, chewing on a

slice of beef Grace had cut. "Though he only wants to keep ye safe until he deposits ye aboard a ship that'll ferry ye home."

"Oh, I have no intention of returning home." Grace lay back on the grass, tucking her hands behind her head.

Toby giggled. "I'll wager he'll ask for your hand in marriage. Like Frank did with Diana in *Rob Roy*." Three heads swung around in astonishment. The usually mute Toby immediately cast his eyes to the grass, his fuller cheeks splashed with colour from a day in the fresh air. Grace smirked in satisfaction—the lecture Seamus had served Cook Phillips about starving the cook's boy had paid off.

"*Rob Roy*? The novel, *Rob Roy*?" said Gilly. "And what would you know 'bout the amorous affairs of Frank and Diana, young Toby?"

Toby blinked guiltily. "Only what I heard read to me by Miss Grace."

After a beat, Gilly burst out laughing. "Well, I never! We have here a right romantic soul." He slapped Toby's back. "And we thought you were only good for makin' burgoo."

Grace sat up. "Lieutenant Fitzwilliam has already declared his intention to marry me." She dusted grass seeds off her hands as three jaws dropped. "Said he wished a priest were available to marry us right away." She reached for the last biscuit.

"By crumbs! Did he now?" Gilly's weathered forehead creased. "The notion's not half bad. 'Twould certainly put you in better standing with the men."

"Well, we shan't be dashing off to church anytime soon," said Grace. "They're a bit thin on the ground around here."

Jim's eyebrows shot up. "Back home, you don't need a priest to be married if ye are handfast."

"Handfast?" Fascinated, Grace sipped her wine.

"Aye, where ye stand witness before your kin and your friends and swear yer vows to one another while binding your hands in union. 'Tis your promise to one another."

"But surely it can't be a true marriage if a priest doesn't sanctify it?" Grace frowned.

"On the Isle of Skye, a priest isn't always available. Generations of Scots folk have been married by handfasting alone, my Maw and Da included." Toby and Gilly listened with interest as Grace popped the last bit of biscuit in her mouth and chewed contemplatively. Jim continued, "A couple need only express their desire to be joined as one for it to be considered so, to be legal, ye ken."

Gilly grimaced uncertainly. "You might find Lieutenant Fitzwilliam has a few objections to such a sacrilegious affair. He's a by-the-book kind of man."

"That may be so," countered Grace, squinting craftily, "but his mother *was* Scottish, and his parents *did* add a handfasting ceremony to their wedding."

THAT NIGHT, after the evening meal, Seamus stood beside Grace at the quarterdeck railing. He had with him two glasses of port. He glanced fondly at her within the new and intimate proximity they shared, admiring the way her full lips curled when he regaled her with a funny story. He loved how she could not hide much from him on her elegant face. Grace took the proffered glass and tentatively sipped the port, her lips beaming in genuine pleasure.

"Oh, it's sweet." The pink tip of her tongue darted over her lips. "A light plum taste. Certainly preferable to whisky or brandy."

"To what shall we toast?" Seamus beamed.

"The future."

"To *our* future." He pressed her hand tenderly to his lips.

"And how do you propose *our* future might look, Lieutenant Fitzwilliam?" She stared boldly at him with those bewitching green eyes of hers. Her hair had grown out a bit, and while it was still closely shorn, it showed signs of those rebellious chocolate curls he had admired when he first met her.

"Well, for one, it'll start with you walking down the aisle towards me, as radiant as …" He pursed his lips for a moment.

"As?" prompted Grace.

"Give me a moment. I don't want to spoil the image of you with an over-used cliché."

"Does it matter, Lieutenant, for is love not blind?" Her look of sincerity lasted only seconds before she giggled.

"I see what you did there, Miss Baxter. Your proficiency as a wordsmith outshines even your beauty."

"Beauty is only skin deep, is it not?"

Seamus dipped his chin in surrender. "I give up! I'll refrain from attempting to flatter you with flowery words."

"What of the truth? Perchance I might find your sincerity even more enchanting than your flattery." Her eyes crinkled with a smile, and she stared at him, unblinking.

Seamus glanced around and, determining that the nearest sailor was out of earshot, firmly clutched her hand hidden in the folds of her skirt. "Oh, that we could find a priest!" He could not hide the impatience in his voice.

"Actually, Seamus, I've an idea." Grace squeezed his fingers, clearly tickled at his daring display of affection.

Seamus lifted his brows expectantly. "I'm all ears, Grace. I find your ideas to be rather singular and enlightening." Reluctantly releasing her fingers, he tucked her hand in the crook of his elbow and took a sip of his port.

"Your parents were married in Scotland, were they not?"

The glass paused against his lips, and he slowly lowered it. "What on earth do my parents have to do with your idea?"

Grace fiddled with the fabric of his coat sleeve and looked to be losing her nerve. She took a deep breath. "Were they not handfasted?"

"Yes. My grandfather insisted on it. My father didn't hold much merit in the old ceremony, but he went along with it anyway, knowing it was significant to my mother. That and the fact that the stubborn old codger wouldn't have sanctioned him stepping from the church with a wife if he hadn't gone through with the handfasting." His lips twitched, recalling his father narrating the story. "Why do you ask, Dulcinea?"

"What if *we* were handfasted? Would you consider us married? Truly married?"

Seamus stared incredulously, his eyes darting from her face, out into the night and back again. "Heavens above!" The words gushed from him. "You … you … *magnificent creature!*" He yanked her to his chest with such force that she shrieked. Seamus scanned the decks for any eavesdroppers, glad for the anonymity of the night. Composing himself, he took a reluctant step back. "Apologies for my rambunctiousness, but if handfasting was good enough for my parents, then it's certainly good enough for me!" His voice was low and passionate. "I see no reason to wait."

Exhilaration radiated from Grace's upturned face. "Mrs Seamus Alexander Fitzwilliam," she tested. "I fancy the sound of that."

"Oh, my Dulcinea, what I wouldn't do to kiss you now," he whispered hoarsely. "If I don't deposit you back in your cabin now, I can't promise to be able to restrain myself." With a secret smile, Seamus traced his finger across his lips.

Chapter Seventeen

PORT FAMINE, *23 AUGUST 1826*

Grace woke the next morning, lazily eavesdropping on the creaks and moans of the ship that had become as familiar to her as breathing. The ship's bells chimed, and footsteps and muffled voices signalled the change of the watch. Stretching luxuriously on the padded mattress, she wiggled her toes from beneath the warm blanket and quickly tucked them back under. She really should add more wood to the potbellied stove, but she wanted to stay cocooned in her warmth a moment longer. The frosty air cleared her sleepy mind, and with a yelp, she bounded out of bed and hurried to get dressed.

There was a knock at her door. Expecting Toby with her breakfast, she unlatched the lock. "Lieutenant Fitzwilliam! To what do I owe the pleasure?"

Seamus bowed. "Miss Baxter. My visit isn't a pleasant one. Might I come in?" Seamus wore his mask of impassivity, but his eyes were troubled. As soon as the door closed, he blurted out, "Captain Fincham is dead."

Grace uttered a cry of despair and threw her arms around him, pressing him tightly to her. He folded into her, and she felt the tremor of grief coursing through him. "I'm sorry, my love," she comforted. "What happens now?"

"As captain of the ship, it wouldn't be uncommon to bury Fincham at sea. But ... but he ..." Seamus's voice tightened, and he swallowed hard. "But he was afraid of the sea in the end. I believe he'd prefer to be buried on land."

"He wouldn't be alone if we buried him ashore." Grace caressed him with her gentle gaze. "I've no doubt the cemetery is hallowed ground. The Franciscan priests would've seen to that. And the view is spectacular from up there."

Seamus nodded wordlessly at Grace and sniffed. She kissed him tenderly on the lips, and his hands slid behind her head, drawing her in. His kiss intensified until he was crushing her lips against her teeth, his tongue probing deeply and desperately, his stubble scraping her chin.

Pulling back with a gasp, remorse flooded his features. "I'm sorry!" He dropped his arms. "I'm not thinking clearly!"

With her lips smarting and her chin burning, she shook her head gently. "It's all right." She brushed the side of his head. "Everything will be all right." Grace thought she caught a quiver in his chin, but when she checked again, his jaw was firm.

"I must go," he announced gruffly, pressing her palm to his cheek before turning his head to kiss it. "There's much to be done." Pivoting neatly, he ducked through the low doorway.

Grace knew that as the senior lieutenant aboard, Seamus's duty was to assume command of the *Discerning*. His first official task was to issue instructions for Captain Fincham's burial. Carpenter James was ordered to make a coffin. While a crew of seamen rowed to the shore to dig a grave, Ship's Surgeon Beynon prepared Captain Fincham's body. Sailmaker Lester created a shroud from a sail while Purser Rowlett oversaw the transport of the rum keg that would be served at the wake on the pebbled beach afterwards. Seamus was making this concession since it was a Sunday and the men already had the afternoon off. The load of survey equipment was also hauled ashore, ready for surveying this piece of the coast in days to come.

Appreciating Seamus's need to keep busy, Grace looked on approvingly as he and Gilly set off with the hunting party in search of ducks to be plucked and roasted. With his musket slung over his shoulder, a grinning Gilly reckoned that duck life on the island was abundant and, from his earlier hunting expedition, found them easy to hunt as they had no fear of muskets or humans.

Grace helped Toby and Jim gather wood for Cook Phillips, who was unbalanced by the pain in his half leg after slipping on the rocky ground. The disgruntled cook screamed infuriated insults at Toby while remaining on the beach with his piles of kindling, preparing several large fires on the shore in anticipation of roasting the ducks. Having ventured a little deeper into a thicket than intended, Grace turned at the sound of a snapping twig behind her.

The three Society boys created a shoulder-to-shoulder wall. Holburton had a musket resting casually over his shoulder, and Da Silva leaned ominously on his shovel. Cakebread wobbled on his crutch, his bandaged, toeless foot resting lightly on the ground.

"Good morning." Grace swallowed deeply, her eyes flicking over their shoulders. She could hear the men on the beach, but the thicket hid her from view.

"Reckon we could make it a *good* one," smirked Tommy. "You know, Miss Maggot, 'tain't safe for a lady to wander off on her own in the wilderness. Never know what wild creature might take you."

"I'm quite capable of taking care of myself. As you well

know. Or would you care for a reminder?" Grace dropped the bundle of sticks, keeping hold of the thickest branch and squaring up against him. "You'll not touch me again, in *any* manner."

Tommy snorted, sneering in disgust. "Wouldn't want to go diving in that soggy cockle cave of yours for all the Kings jewels. 'Specially since McGilney found you on the streets. God knows *where* you've been."

"I'll bet the only services of Cupid you're acquainted with are the ones you *paid for*!" Grace taunted.

Tommy's ears flared against her insult, and he swung the musket from his shoulder, aiming it at her. "We've a musket and a shovel. 'Tis enough to make sure you'd never be found. Folks'll think you've simply wandered off—got lost. Made yourself maggot food."

"I'll lay you out with this stick before you've half a chance of priming your weapon." Not to mention the gunshot would have the entire crew running in this direction—dolt!

Grace took another step forward, and Cakebread hopped back. Tommy's head snapped around, and he glared venomously at the young man. Cakebread flushed and flicked his eyes warily towards Grace. "C-come on, Tommy. We're s'posed to be digging firepits. Cook Phillips is in a right mood today. Don't want him holding back our share of roast duck just 'cause we didn't help him dig his pits."

"Yes, *Tommy*, run along, like the obedient little sailor that you are," glowered Grace, gripping her stake with two hands and angling it back ready to take a swing.

Tommy scoffed and shifted the musket over his shoulder again. "Watch yourself, Miss Maggot. You're as useful aboard the *Discerning* as a wet blanket and just as easy to chuck o'erboard on a moonless night."

"Plug your mouth, you puddle of wax! I'll not be threatened by you or anyone else!" snarled Grace, swinging the stick like a broadsword. "I might not be able to take all three of you down, but I can certainly manage two. So, which of you fleas will it be, hmm?"

She whipped around at a loutish bellow from the edge of the brush. Toby Hicks launched at Tommy, hooking his arm around his thick neck and tumbling him to the ground. Toby and Tommy rolled around in an uncoordinated scuffle, fists thudding on flesh exploded into muted grunts as they found their marks. Tommy flipped Toby onto his back, his meaty fits pummelling Toby's face into a bloody mess.

"Stop it!" shrieked Grace. "Get off him!" In her periphery, Da Silva raised the shovel, and Grace swung the branch with all her might. It connected with his chest, the impact juddering through her hands. The shovel clanged on the compact earth, and roaring with pain, Da Silva clutched his arms across his body and thudded onto his backside. Jim burst from the bush and landed a solid blow to the side of Cakebread's head. Folding like a piece of paper, Cakebread collapsed in the dirt, his crutch sprawling.

Grace raised her stick again, feet braced as Bosun Tidwell stormed into the clearing with Nelly gripped firmly in hand. Slashing his way past Cakebread and Da Silva like a farmer scything wheat, Bosun loomed over Tommy and Toby, his cane whistling through the air and cutting across Tommy's back. With a snarl of pain, Tommy wrestled Toby for the protected position below. Toby and Tommy clung to one another, rolling each other over while Tidwell's cane lashed out viciously. Finally conceding defeat against Nelly, the two fighters split apart.

"Right, you yellow-bellied landlubbers!" yelled Bosun Tidwell, swishing his cane around threateningly. The scar on his face puckered into a sneer. "Who else wants a kiss from Nelly?" He caught sight of Grace, his eyes widening in alarm. "Jesus! Miss Baxter? Are you hurt?"

Grace steadied her breathing, swallowing dryly. "No."

Bosun glared at the crowd of bleeding dishevelled men. "Who started it?"

Toby stepped forward, swiping the bloody mucous coursing freely from his nose with his arm. He pointed a shaky finger at Tommy. "He did. I heard him threatening to harm Miss Grace."

"Did not!" spat Holburton, spraying blood droplets from his split lip.

Bosun's brow crumpled, and he fixed Grace with a firm glare. "Is it true? Was Holburton set to harm you?"

Grace trailed her eyes over the three Society boys, biting back a smirk as they shuffled uncomfortably. She knew their fate lay in her hands, and she felt a surge of power at holding them to ransom. Had Toby and Jim not intervened, she was sure she would have managed the Society boys on her own. Ben Blight had taught her how to stand her ground well enough. A tiny ember of disappointment flickered out that she had not had the chance. Giving them over to Bosun now was too easy. As the excitement of the fight cooled in her muscles, she leaned on her stick for support. "But a misunderstanding, Bosun."

Bosun twisted his lips and shook his head. "After that little lark, I'm recommending the lot of 'em for punishment."

"Please don't." Grace turned up the charm in her smile. "I'm *sure* you can make allowances for the men's heightened emotions today?" She tipped her head and set her face sympathetically. "It's never easy losing a crewmate, let alone the captain."

Scowling, Bosun growled. "Right you are. The lot of you— back to work!" Beckoning his head towards the beach, he said, "Best head back to the open beach, Miss Baxter. 'Tis a much safer bet.'"

"Yes, of course." Grace smiled. "I'll just gather this last load of wood for Cook Phillips. We all need to do our bit if we're to enjoy the treat of roast duck tonight."

Bosun grunted, slapping his Nelly across his palms, and

sauntered off towards another group of voices hidden by the shrubbery.

Hearing a whimper behind her, Grace turned and froze as the tatty bandages around the Cakebread's toeless foot bloomed crimson with fresh blood.

"My foot!" whimpered Cakebread, his cheeks colourless. "'Tis bleedin' again!" Grace's gut clenched with guilt, her teeth worrying her bottom lip. She wanted the Society boys put in their place. Not dead.

"Jesus wept! Hush your snivelling!" scolded Tommy, his glare gangrenous.

Da Silva dropped to his haunches to inspect his friend's foot. Tommy peered down his swollen, bloody nose. By the red swelling around his eye, Grace was thrilled that Toby had landed a decent punch or two. Da Silva hissed, "Mr Beynon said we had to get him to sickbay quick smart if this happened again."

Grace stopped chewing her lip. "Better get a move on then, before your friend bleeds to death." She raised her chin at Holburton.

Tommy snorted and, with Da Silva's help, roughly hauled Cakebread up in a two-man hold. Cakebread cried out again, gripping their necks with an urgency that implied he did not trust them not to drop him.

As the Society boys disappeared through the brush, Grace leaned heavily on the stick that had served her so well. She took several gulps of the fresh air to steady her thrashing heart before she swooped down to pick up her discarded firewood. Toby scuttled to her side to help. When she rose, she stopped short at the sight of Jim's black brow, rucked into one hairy line.

"Why d'ye let them off?" he asked, his tone unimpressed. "'Twas a fine chance to have them dealt with properly, once and for all."

"Where's the satisfaction in that?" She grinned. "I'm not

about to let anyone else fight my battles. Especially not with Tommy Holburton!"

"Crivens, lass! Yer truly asking for it. Ye've trouble aplenty already without fuelling Holburton's vengeance."

"He started it—from the very first day of muster." Grace firmed her chin. "Go on then. What's stopping *you* telling Lieutenant Fitzwilliam what just happened?"

Jim rubbed his hand across the back of his neck. "That's no' fair, and ye know it."

Of course she knew it. It was a code of honour among the men of the lower decks not to snitch to the uppers. Aware that it was an unfair position to put Jim in, she bumped him with her shoulder. "Besides, with you two at my back, I've nothing to worry about, do I?"

By mid-afternoon, the preparations were complete, and Grace and the hands of the *Discerning* found themselves gathered around the freshly dug grave in the rocky cemetery. The air was uncharacteristically calm and crisp. Without the biting wind, the mourners soaked up the weak warmth of the sun. If the sky remained cloudless, they were in for another bitter night.

Toby and Jim stood protectively behind Grace. Holburton's hostility was no longer a muted undertone. Firming her chin against the venomous glares across the coffin, Grace sidled closer to Gilly and looped her arm through his. Lieutenant Wadham stared enviously at Gilly but slid his eyes away when he caught Grace watching him.

Seamus, pristine in his dress uniform, conducted the funeral with stoic self-control, delivering Grace an inkling of what it had meant for this steadfast officer to drop his guard in her arms. He had not been afraid or ashamed to show her his vulnerability, and standing at the graveside, a warmth swelled in her chest as that bull-headed but honourable man took another piece of her heart.

The tears pouring down her cheeks were not in mourning for Captain Fincham as she hardly knew the man—they were for

Seamus. Clearly hurting behind his official façade, she knew he would not permit himself to weep before the men, so she cried for him. A hum of activity brought her back to the desolate graveyard. As the coffin was lowered into the ground, Seamus began to sing "Amazing Grace," and the men joined in with a surprisingly decent harmony—Grace's alto was high and sweet among the bullfrogs.

Chapter Eighteen

The next morning, Seamus was roused by a familiar
"Sail ho!" Scrambling to dress, he rushed from his
cabin and opened the binnacle housing near the helm
in which he kept a spare spyglass. He went to stand beside Lieutenant Wadham, whose own glass was already trained on a
distant ship. Fitting his eye to one end of the brass tube, Seamus
swept the other end across the water until he fixed upon a two-
masted brigantine with a black hull. The penguin chorus ashore
carried loudly in the cold morning air.

"Visitors, Wadham?" Seamus enquired casually.

"They show no colours."

Steadying the glass, Seamus stared at the passing ship for a
while longer, his instincts prickling uncertainly. He lowered his
telescope, his wrist aching in the icy breeze.

"Who is she?" Wadham gave Seamus a doubtful flick of his
eyes.

"Hard to tell."

"She shows no intention of anchoring." Wadham squinted across the expanse of water.

Seamus trained his telescope on the shore, surveying the scene the passing ship would be observing just as clearly as he was. A handful of his men, guarding the canvas-covered survey equipment, stamped their feet against the early cold, hands tucked deep in pockets. Smouldering grey pits were the only remnants of the massive bonfires from the night before. Brave seagulls strutted fearlessly past the men, pecking at morsels from the previous night's feast.

"Should we hail them?" asked Wadham, his breath curling white. "Find out who they are? It's a little unusual for a small ship flying no flag to be in this desolate part of the world."

Seamus swung his spyglass towards the receding vessel working her way through the scattered maze of islands in the archipelago. "They look harmless enough. And they're leaving."

"Lieutenant Fitzwilliam." The seriousness in Wadham's tone did little to ease the weight of recent events pressing on Seamus's shoulders. "I must ask of your intentions."

"Intentions?" Towards Miss Baxter? Seamus lowered the glass and drew his brow tight.

"Will you not take us to Montevideo now that we are without a captain?"

"My priority right now is to return this ship to order and continue our surveying." Seamus waved the spyglass at the shore.

"I'm not sure you're the right man for the job, Fitzwilliam." Wadham shuffled his feet, facing Seamus square on.

Seamus clasped the spyglass behind his back, his spine rigid. "Might I ask why not?"

"I believe your judgement to be compromised by Miss Baxter's presence."

And there it was. She was never far from Wadham's mind, was she? "As the senior officer, my duty is to take command of the ship," said Seamus. "Though, pray tell, what would you do in my position?"

"Miss Baxter must be returned to England—to the bosom of her family. A naval vessel is no place for a woman."

Seamus narrowed his eyes. "Don't tell me you're one of those who believes a woman aboard to be ill luck? I took you for a liberally educated man. Am I so sorely mistaken?"

"That's not what I mean, and you know it. You took her under your protection to unburden Captain Fincham of the responsibility so that he could continue with his orders. How do you now propose to do both?"

"I've broad enough shoulders to bear the weight of both. In fact, I intend to marry Miss Baxter today."

"Today?" Wadham drew his shoulders up. "But how?"

"Up at the church ruins. I intend to have Buchanan officiate a handfasting, since he's the only Scot aboard who's likely to have knowledge of such affairs." By rights, Wadham as the most senior lieutenant should undertake the task, but Seamus determined it was grossly unfair to ask his rival. He was not *that* callous.

"Good God, Fitzwilliam! That's an audacious plan, if ever I've heard of one."

"It's my only option under the circumstances. You must be aware of the men's displeasure."

"I am, but are you sure that marrying Miss Baxter will remedy this?"

"It'll offer her a protection she doesn't currently have—as an officer's wife. Naturally, I'd rather see her safely back to England, but I can't leave her exposed to danger in the meantime."

"So you're marrying her out of a chivalrous sense of duty?" Wadham pinched his lips unhappily.

"I would if the circumstances demanded it—as they do." Seamus peered around at Wadham, his mouth softening with a self-conscious smile. "But no, I also have a deep and abiding affection for Miss Baxter."

Wadham coughed uncomfortably, turning his gaze out across the open bay. "Does she know?"

"Yes. We've discussed it. The handfasting was actually her idea, though she won't be expecting it today. I thought I might surprise her." Seamus drew shoulder to shoulder with him at the gunwale. "If you so genuinely care for Miss Baxter, I'd appreciate it if you were to keep the men's opinions of her from further souring. Can I entrust you to ensure the officers and marines are properly attired for the occasion? The ceremony will be rudimentary at best, but there's no reason for us to do away with civility altogether."

Wadham turned stiffly. "In that case, I'll see to clearing out the church ruins." Thrusting his open hand at Seamus, he said, "I also offer you my congratulations. Clearly, the best man won." His fingers were colder than Seamus's.

While Wadham made to shore, Seamus inspected the ship after the morning watch. He also wished to keep an eye on that brigantine—make sure she was definitely not up to any mischief. After breakfast, once Seamus was sure the passing ship had gone, he ordered Bosun Tidwell to call the men to order.

"With the untimely death of Captain Fincham, I, Seamus Alexander Fitzwilliam, do hereby assume command of HMS *Discerning* until such time as I'm instructed otherwise by the lords of the Admiralty."

Several heads nodded in approval, and statements of affirmation buzzed through the crowd. Seamus knew the men craved the authority that he had already demonstrated during Captain Fincham's illness. He strove to be one of those men other men sought to follow, the type of man who gave other men their own sense of purpose and belonging, a man whose men thrived under his leadership.

"I also invite every man here to be present at the old church

ruins at the sound of bells at eleven o'clock to witness my
nuptials to Miss Baxter." As a prudent reminder, the bell aboard
the *Discerning* sounded once, signifying the time to be half-past
eight in the morning. The sailors shifted, their curious murmurs
punctuated by a few stroppy coughs. "Carry on." The chatter of
the men rose as they turned to leave.

Seamus glanced at their departing backs. "McGilney,
Buchanan, wait up if you please."

BREAKING the icy layer in the water jug on the washstand, Grace
dampened a cloth and gave her face a quick wipe over, gasping
at the cold, and then rubbed her teeth until they squeaked. She
was just finishing tying the laces of her boots when a knock
sounded. The tartan shawl was twirled around the puffed shoulders of her dress, cloaking her in earthy woollen tones. Cook
Phillip's hot oatmeal would be most welcome this frosty morning. She drew the door open.

"Gilly!"

Gilly winked cheekily, his eyes roving down her skirts. "May
I have one of your ribbons?" He pulled his knife from his belt,
his black brows arching.

"You're cutting Sally's dress?" spluttered Grace, her
surprised words dissipating in a misty bloom.

"Borrowin' the trimmin', more like it."

"Whatever for?"

"'Tis a surprise." He knelt, the sharp tip of his knife worrying
the stitching of the ribbon, taking extra care not to nick the
cotton. With a ribbon freed of its binding, Gilly rose and tucked
it into his pocket.

"Stay put," he grinned. "I'll be back to fetch you soon."

Just before midday, Grace and Gilly were waiting outside the
roofless church. He still had not told her of the surprise, and

Grace's cheeks now stung with the cold. A respectable crowd of sailors milled around, all eyeing her curiously and all clearly knowing the secret she was not privy to. She searched for Seamus and Jim down the path of trampled vegetation leading to the little church. A flock of green parakeets screeched in the nearby trees.

"Miss Grace." Jim's voice startled her from behind. He stood in the darkened doorway of the church ruins. He had wet his hair and attempted to comb it neatly, and an obviously borrowed dark blue coat hung too large on him. His cheeks were uncharacteristically clean and pink with exhilaration, but his round face was earnest as he beckoned to her. "Lieutenant Fitzwilliam would like to see ye now."

"See me? Where?" Grace peered around the overgrown churchyard.

"Inside." Jim tossed his head back towards the arched doorway, his black eyebrows jiggling. Wordlessly, Grace went inside. Gilly tailed behind obligingly, but Jim stopped him at the door. "'Tisn't us the lieutenant wants to see, Gilly. Only Miss Grace."

Gilly cast an eye around the glen that was slowly filling with men. "I'll be right outside if you have a need of me, Miss Grace." He bowed chivalrously.

"Thank you, Gilly," she beamed. Grace stared at the transformation inside the church. The large bush had been dug out, the scar of discoloured dirt in the middle of the floor the only sign of its existence. All other weeds and vegetation had been cleared too, and the air smelled of damp, freshly tilled soil. Mild sunlight filtered through the canopy of trees above the roofless church, the pale rays shining upon Seamus as she glided towards him. Despite the little church having no roof or windows, it exuded a promising aura.

Seamus stood upon the spot where the altar would have once been. "Dulcinea," he murmured as she tucked herself into the fold of his embrace. With his warm lips brushing hers, he undid the ribbon of her bonnet, the bow unfolding slowly. He peeled it back with tenderness as if he was unwrapping tissue paper from a gift, and stepped back to admire her uncovered hair. He gently caressed her curls, enticing the hairs on Grace's arms to attention.

"What is the meaning of this, Seamus?"

"I have something for you." Seamus reached around for something on the floor behind him. When he stood again, he was clutching a floral wreath. It was an exquisite mix of the island's wildflowers bound with long green stems. The tiny white flower clusters stood out against the rich greenery, the stems of the flowers twisted and plaited into a circular green vine. Grace inhaled the sweet chocolaty fragrance as he placed the wreath lightly on her bare head.

"I promise to deliver all that your heart desires—if it's within my power to do so." His eyes drifted from the wreath to her face, the smile line around his mouth and left eye deepening. "Are you ready to become Mrs Seamus Fitzwilliam?"

"Pardon? Now?"

"If you wish?" A ball of laughter vibrated through him, and he bowed his head.

Grace lifted her chin jauntily. "How?" She had not expected him to act so quickly upon her idea. Was he truly that impatient to be with her? Or was the men's displeasure towards her more severe than she had imagined? Goodness! It was happening so fast.

"It's all organised. You need only give me the word."

Grace glanced up at his expectant face. Why did he have to be so pleasant upon the eye? She pondered her prospects. As a naval wife, she could at least remain at sea. Becoming another man's wife would certainly take Silverton out of the running. Her solitary knowledge of Silverton's reward for her return tipped her decision. "Well—yes—of course! It's all so sudden. Such a surprise."

"A good one, I hope?"

"Um—" A band of guilt tightened her jawline. Marrying Seamus would serve her purpose well, but she was uneasy with her deception. Then again, he was marrying her out of a sense of duty to Uncle Farfar, was he not? She supposed they both had their reasons. Grace nodded firmly. "Yes! Yes, it's a good surprise." Grace glanced around the empty church. "Will the others be joining us?"

"In a minute. I've one more gift for you, first." Unable to hide his delight, Seamus reached with one hand into the side pocket of his jacket. He held out a gold brooch with two intertwined hearts. "My grandmother's Luckenbooth brooch. My grandfather gave it to her on their wedding day. It passed down to my mother, and she, in turn, passed it down to me." He studied it for a moment before handing it to Grace.

Grace's eyebrows knitted into a frown. "Is this another of your lucky keepsakes?" The twinkle in his eyes confirmed his answer. She shook her head. "I can't take it from you, Seamus. I know how essential these trinkets are to a sailor."

Obviously unperturbed, he brightened. "I've kept it safe with me all these years, and I now gift it to you on our wedding day. I plan to keep you just as safe and as near, so it won't be going far." Seamus fixed the intricately woven golden hearts onto her plaid, pinning the edges of the shawl together like a cloak. "With God as my witness, I've never been more ready to make you Mrs Seamus Alexander Fitzwilliam."

In the roofless stone church, the witnesses gathered, and even the pungent reek of the unwashed seamen crammed into close confines was not enough to dampen Grace's spirits. Gilly, Jim, and O'Malley were grinning madly. Ship's Surgeon Beynon and Master Chapman were chatting amicably and sending approving nods in her direction. Even Bosun Tidwell's scowl was less severe this morning. Grace scanned the sea of faces, spotting Toby and Travis Hopwood standing near the two, solid, red-headed towers of the Blighters, all four beaming proudly at her. Sergeant Baisley and his red-coated marines flanked the rear of the crowd near the doorway. Wadham regarded Seamus coolly, but even he could not hold back a smile when he looked at Grace. Grace was not surprised that none of the Society boys nor Blom, Sorensen, Webb or Kendrick were present.

She swivelled back as Seamus addressed his men. "Thank you for coming this morning." He took a deep breath before dropping his hands behind his back. "Every man here today joined the navy for their own reasons. Some of you sought to escape difficulties, some wanted a fresh start, and some were seeking adventure. With those adventures comes the excitement of the unknown and unexpected turns. Captain Fincham's death and my elevation to commander of the *Discerning* is one of those unexpected turns." Grace bowed her head at Seamus's mention of his late friend. Seamus then cleared his throat, securing Grace's undivided attention. "Miss Baxter's discovery is another." He drew her closer and tucked her hand protectively into the crook of his elbow. "The good Lord knows I'd have her on the first ship back to England, but He likes to try us, and He has not, thus far, presented this opportunity. Consequently, it is my duty, obligation, and"—he looked at Grace, his dry expression softening—"*honour*, to ensure Miss Baxter's safety and to protect her fine reputation. Therefore, she has done *me* the greatest privilege of agreeing to become my wife."

In the corner of Grace's eye, Wadham shuffled. The previous silence was filled with deep, curious rumblings, and Seamus smiled at her. As though suddenly remembering his crew, he gave a little cough and turned to the men who immediately fell silent again.

"In the absence of a priest, we'll be married today by my mother's Celtic tradition of handfasting on the hallowed ground of this church, and before God and you as our witnesses. I expect each of you to show the soon-to-be Mrs Fitzwilliam the respect she deserves as the wife of the commander of the *Discerning*." Drawing himself up to his full height, he explored the sea of faces.

Grace also cast a quick look out at the crowd. Their mood was considerably lightened.

"Without further ado, let's begin." Seamus squeezed her hand in the crook of his arm. "Buchanan, if you please."

Grace swung her head in surprise as Jim stepped from the crowd. Her friend strutted forward proudly, squirming in delight at the honour of being called out by Seamus. He took his place in front of them as a minister would do.

"Lieutenant Seamus Alexander Fitzwilliam. Miss Grace Elizabeth Baxter." Jim nodded towards them. Grace, dazed by Jim's role as officiator, glanced uncertainly at Seamus. Seamus was studying Jim through narrowed eyes but his scowl of authority, usually reserved for subordinates, had softened. Undaunted, Jim gave Grace a quick wink and a grin before his mask of reverence fell into place once again. Turning to face the solemn young man, Grace dropped her hand from Seamus's arm.

"Today ye shall be handfast as a vow to one another of yer commitment to be wed. Afore these, yer friends, and as God as yer witness, ye will pledge yerselves to one another." Jim's voice appeared deeper, and it rang out clearly across the little church.

"Yer hands, if ye please." Jim reached for their hands and clasped them together, weaving Grace's blue ribbon around them. "Repeat these vows together after me—"

Red blurred in the corner of her eye as a uniformed marine burst through the doorway. Spotting Sergeant Baisley, the lanky marine shouldered his way through the mumbling crowd, his carelessness lighting a wick of alarm in Grace's belly. The man had an extreme urgency about him. Stopping smartly before Sergeant Baisley, the man bent low, his back stiff. Baisley's eyes widened in his waxen face, his wheat-coloured head rotating towards Seamus. Shuffling around the crowd, Baisley stepped up to Seamus.

"Explain yourself, man," urged Seamus. "What's so important you feel it necessary to interrupt my nuptials?"

"'Tis the local inhabitants, sir. They've stolen a cutter."

Seamus swivelled to fully face Baisley. "What of the guards protecting the survey equipment?" frowned Seamus.

"They were distracted by another group of natives advancing from inland, sir. I suspect this was but a ruse to steer their attention away from the cutter."

"Clearly not the sort of natives who scamper off without a trace." Grace twisted her lips wryly at Seamus. Baisley's eyes flicked in her direction.

"Apparently not, Miss Baxter," nodded Baisley grimly. Despite his interruption, he blundered on. "The previous settlers of Port Famine reported no trouble with the locals, sir. This is unexpected, is it not?"

Seamus growled in agreement.

Grace eyed the lines of armed marines ordering themselves near the door. "What are you planning, Sergeant?"

"We'll be retrieving His Majesty's property." Baisley turned his square jaw towards Seamus. "With your permission, sir."

"Surely you shan't shoot unarmed men?" she asked.

"Oh, they'll be armed, don't doubt that, Miss Baxter," explained Baisley. "But with our muskets against their bows and spears, it won't take long to retrieve the cutter. Not once we show them the might of the Royal Marines." Baisley puffed out his chest. Seamus dismissed him with a wave, and Grace watched him scurry towards his waiting marines.

"Seamus." Grace's cheeks flared. "Surely you can't condone this potential bloodshed over a simple boat?"

Seamus's tone was dry and even. "No one is talking of bloodshed. I'll endeavour to exercise my powers of persuasion to encourage the locals to return our boat."

"You're leaving too? Now?" Grace could not control the pitch in her voice, her eyes darting to his hand unwinding the blue ribbon.

"I'm sorry, Miss Baxter. Duty calls," he said, pocketing the satin strand.

"It's just a boat," she grumbled.

"No, madam, it's an essential piece of equipment necessary for our continued exploration." He cradled her elbow, his voice softening as he beckoned to Gilly. "McGilney will escort you back to the ship and safeguard you."

"Is that necessary?" objected Grace.

"I promised you protection, and protection you'll have." Seamus intensified his glare.

Grace sensed he was in no mood to indulge a debate, but she could not help one final dig. "Which you promised to remedy by making me your wife, did you not?" Her heart lurched as she petulantly stuck out her chin, staring at the varying degrees of guilt and frustration marching across his face.

"Yes! But not right now. Please understand. The quicker we lay chase, the quicker I can get back to the business of making you my wife." His grip tightened on her arm. "Until I establish that the locals are not hostile, I'd prefer you to remain under guard."

Clenching her molars, she pressed a tight smile to her lips. "Of course, Lieutenant. I understand. Duty first." *God, King, and Country before me*! Grace knew she was unjustly targeting her disappointment at him, but it did not feel any less wretched.

Chapter Nineteen

O n the pebbled beach, Seamus swung his gaze over the empty ocean, the memory of the mysterious, dark-hulled vessel prickling the nape of his neck with unease. This first encounter with the locals was not helping his restlessness. He glanced at the scene unfolding before him. The gunner's boys darted around madly, helping Gunner Ash offload the other cutter of the necessary shot and gunpowder to equip the marines and sailors. Even Cakebread, with his heavily bound, toeless foot, hobbled around on one crutch in a state of painful readiness. Holburton relieved his limping friend of a heavy bag of shot and hurried it over to the cutters.

Beside Seamus, Baisley's twittering continued, his rambling a sure sign of his nervous excitement. "Failing persuasion, there's always bribery. Some cultures marvel at intricacies such as glass beads, copper, and bits of mirror. Perhaps these natives will be no different?"

"Perhaps not, Sergeant, but until we pull this chaos into

order, there'll be no opportunity for bribery. See to your men, won't you?"

"Yes, sir!"

It was late afternoon when Seamus ordered Lieutenant Sully and Sergeant Baisley to lead the ranks of red-coated musketeers across the grassland. Three crews of armed sailors, headed by Seamus, Lieutenant Wadham and Bosun Tidwell, took three other rowboats and manoeuvred them along the shoreline. Another contingent of armed sailors, under the watchful eye of Master Chapman, stood guard on the beach. Seamus had also ordered the skeleton crew aboard the *Discerning* to arm themselves.

The following late afternoon was clear skied, the weakening sun attempting to brighten up the foreshore's desolate rocks that Seamus was earnestly scanning. The excellent weather revealed the two masts and sails of another brigantine across the bay, her colours announcing her as an American merchant. The vessel approached head-on before dropping anchor. She bowed and curvetted like an excitable stallion reined in by its rider, and the bright copper plating along her hull flashed in the sunlight.

The master of the American merchantman hailed Seamus. "Ahoy!"

Seamus stood balanced in the bow of the cutter. "Hulloa! What ship is that, pray?"

The dark-haired American grabbed at his cocked hat as the wind tried to whip it off his head. "The *Carolina* from Philadelphia bound to San Diego. Captain Penman speaking. Where are you from?"

Seamus's deep voice boomed across the swell. "HMS *Discerning* from Plymouth. Lieutenant Fitzwilliam, commander of HMS *Discerning*. Are you perchance passing Valparaíso?"

"We are." Penman clamped his hat with his elbow. "We'll be restocking there."

"May I press you to pass on a packet to Admiral Otway of

the fleet flagship *Ganges*? She's stationed there—British Admiralty headquarters."

"Indeed, you may. Your men are welcome aboard too."

"A most generous offer, sir, but we must press on. I require only a moment of your time, if you please."

"Please come aboard, Lieutenant Fitzwilliam."

The cutter was lashed to the *Carolina*, and Seamus climbed up the netting dropped down by the hands. Captain Penman was a small, clean-shaven man with a head full of childish curls. His rich brown eyes were warm and welcoming. Two women stepped onto the deck. The older one smiled politely, and the younger one's eyes widened with interest.

"May I introduce my wife and daughter?" Penman beamed at the two women. "My lovelies, this is Lieutenant Fitzwilliam."

"Your servant." Seamus bowed before fixing his eyes back on Penman.

"Tell me, Lieutenant, what business sees you scouring the shore so minutely?" asked Penman.

"The locals have stolen one of my cutters."

"Goodness! What an inconvenience!" said Mrs Penman, drawing her silk shawl tighter around her shoulders.

"Indeed, madam. It's an aggravating delay to our exploration duties."

Miss Penman's crop of curly hair was held with a red silk ribbon which matched her dress. Her eyes twinkled excitedly. "Papa, did we not witness fires upon the shore yesterday evening?"

Her rich and intoxicating floral perfume was a welcome change to the tar, stale sweat, and sulphur that usually filled a ship. Seamus turned towards her, interested by this tidbit of information. Flattered by his attention, Miss Penman's neck flushed, and she giggled. Her mother gave her a flinty-eyed stare of disapproval, and the young lady composed herself.

"Indeed, we did," confirmed Penman. "Less than a day's sail

back. It'll take you longer by cutter, naturally, but the tides about here are regular and not strong."

"Most fortuitous information, Captain Penman. Thank you." Seamus glanced towards the charthouse. "Might I beg the use of your paper and ink?"

"Of course," agreed Penman amiably. "This way."

Walking beside Penman, Seamus said, "Our meeting like this is most fortunate. You see, Captain Fincham died a few days ago. I'd not banked on getting news of his death to the Admiralty so quickly."

"Terrible business," winced Penman. "Might I ask what happened?"

"Alas, he had been plagued by a malady for many a year. It caught him swiftly at the end."

"Ah, though when a seaman's time is up, what better way to go than into the bosom of the ocean, hmm?"

Seamus licked the salty spray from his lips and pressed them into a thin smile. "Unfortunately, Captain Fincham's illness caused him to distrust the sea in the end. I thought it best to bury him ashore."

While writing the letter to Admiral Otway, Seamus told Penman of all that had transpired since they had left London, neatly omitting Grace's discovery. He did not want news of her presence aboard the *Discerning* reaching London before he had a chance to explain. Plus, there was the matter of his promise not to tell Grace's parents of her whereabouts. He would not give that bastard Silverton a chance to discover her location—not until Seamus had the opportunity to deal with the man himself.

After another two full days of rowing along the rocky shoreline, Seamus spotted, at the edge of the brush, a dishevelled conglomeration of huts made of stakes, dry sticks, and leather. This had to be the camp Penman had mentioned. Though structurally sound, the simple huts were plainly those of nomadic inhabitants, quickly and easily erected or dismantled.

"To shore, if you please," ordered Seamus, and the Blight twins expertly manoeuvred them to the rocky shoreline. A tribe of mostly women and children milled around the huts.

"They're clearly not trying to avoid being seen," said O'Malley. "Not with those smoky fires."

"Perhaps not, but ready your weapons nonetheless," said Seamus in a low voice, glancing back at their cutters wedged above the waterline under Jack Blight's guard. As Seamus approached the huts, an ancient man with white body paint challenged his arrival, chattering hurriedly and waving a stick that was more a walking aid than a weapon.

"By the looks of him, he must be the shaman," Seamus said from the corner of his mouth. He smiled and bowed to the wizened man before him. Despite the shaman's apparent status, the women and children also crowded around the sailors, curious and interested in communicating with them. Seamus peered around at his men who were enduring the pokes and tugs on their clothing good-naturedly. Ben Blight's fiery beard attracted the most attention.

Seamus kept his voice light. "They seem a peaceful lot, but keep your heads up. There's a distinct lack of male adults about —they're likely out testing the merits of the stolen cutter—but they can't be far."

Seamus attempted to gesture his intentions, which only resulted in fits of giggles from the women and children. Inhaling a deep breath of restraint, Seamus squatted down and, picking up a stick, sketched the cutter in the sand. The hum of the tribespeople's conversation rose excitedly as they nodded and pointed at the drawing.

"Seems they recognise the cutter, sir." Blight nodded at Seamus.

"Seems so, Blight," agreed Seamus, relieved. "Now to get them to understand the notion of returning it to us." He pointed at the picture and then at himself. "This is *my* boat." The tribespeople found this amusing, and one of the women pointed at the drawing and then at herself, repeating something in her own language and causing the rest of the group to erupt into laughter.

"By Neptune's trident! We'll be here all day at this rate." Seamus pointed at a youth in the crowd who was cloaked in a thick fur. "You! You'll be coming with us. Seize him." The tribespeople's chuckling turned to cries of protest. Seamus held up his hand in an attempt to quiet them and, through the charades, communicated, "*He* is coming with *me*," He pointed at the sketch of the rowboat. "Until you return my boat."

The tallest woman of the group, clearly the young man's mother, stepped from the crowd to snatch her son's arm, her protestations furious and threatening.

Seamus knew he needed to take control of the situation before it grew out of hand. "O'Malley, fire your musket in the air. We need to show these people that stealing His Majesty's property is no game," he said grimly.

O'Malley primed his weapon, drawing some curious looks until the catastrophic explosion of gunfire shattered the air. Seamus was relieved when the villagers fled into the tree line, squealing in terror. It was preferable to them turning and taking up arms. Seamus knew it would not have been a fair fight. The youth pulled against his captors in a panic to follow the others.

"Hold him fast!" Seamus ordered. He scanned the tree line and the ocean's horizon for the umpteenth time. "To the cutters, gentlemen. Make haste. That shot will no doubt have alerted the tribesmen to our presence. I'd rather they come to us on our terms aboard the *Discerning* and not by way of ambush in their familiar surroundings."

Seamus studied the wide-eyed youth as he was escorted into one of the cutters. Seamus had seen men respond to terror in different ways during his career. Some fled without fighting; others, determining that the odds of fighting were against them, simply gave up; and then there were those who fought to the death, despite being severely outmanned or out-strengthened. Seamus was relieved that his captive did not put up a fight and that the others hiding in the trees offered no further challenge either, confirming Seamus's initial assumption that they were not a warring tribe. He wished for the negotiations to be over sooner rather than later.

Chapter Twenty

PORT FAMINE, 30 AUGUST 1826

our days had passed since the search party left, and
Grace was waiting impatiently for Seamus's return. It
was early morning, and the air was charged with static
electricity from the unrelenting lightning flashes outside. The
clamour of the hard rain pummelling the deck had eased,
replaced by the tackle pitter-pattering against the masts like a
symphony of dripping taps. Grace dozed in the grey, early-
morning light. The cabin was toasty from the glow of the newly
stoked potbellied stove that she had darted out of bed to
replenish earlier. Her eyes shot open at a shout from outside.

"Vessel approaching!"

He's back! Bolting up, Grace hurried to get dressed. Her
heart leapt at the thump of footsteps outside her door. She swung
the cabin door open and admitted a decidedly bedraggled Lieutenant Fitzwilliam. A damp, frigid blast of cold air followed him
in. He shrugged out of his oilskin and slung it over the back of

one of the dining chairs. Grace stepped before him, and his cold lips urgently found hers.

"Icicled rats' tails! You're wet and freezing," she giggled.

"Heavens above, Dulcinea! It's good to see you." He pressed his chilly kisses against her neck.

She gasped. "You're shivering!"

"Hmm, then perhaps you should warm me up." He drew his mouth back to hers, his stubble scratching her slightly.

Grace drew back and studied him. Despite his uncharacteristic dishevelment, he looked magnificent. Good Lord, he was striking! The long, dripping strands of his fair hair were darker when wet. His regrowth was visible, and he had two patches on his cheeks where his whiskers did not grow. He would be one of those men who never managed a bushy face full of hair— the blend of blond and gold hues rendering it less discernible.

She swept the soggy hair from his face and gently placed her hand on his cold, stubbly cheek. "Not before you tell me if you found the boat."

"Not precisely." He kissed her hand, his voice muffled against her palm.

"What does that mean?"

"Well, we did come across an American merchantman. Captain Penman was on his way from Philadelphia to San Diego. This fortuitously allowed me to send word to Admiral Otway, advising him of Captain Fincham's demise."

"Admiral Otway?"

"Commander-in-chief of the fleet flagship *Ganges*, the Admiralty's headquarters at Valparaíso in Chile. We'll no doubt, in time, be advised of our new orders and of who our new captain will be."

"And the stolen boat?"

"We searched the coastline in the cutters with limited success. We encountered the indigenous people, but the language was a bit of a barrier. Between hand gestures and pictures drawn in the sand, I believe I adequately conveyed a request to return our boat."

"And?"

"They refused. So, I took a hostage."

Grace yanked her hand back. "Why on earth would you do such a thing?" Splashes of heat burned high on her cheeks.

"I don't expect you to understand, Miss Baxter," Seamus said dryly. He walked across to the potbellied stove and vigorously rubbed his hands over the warmth.

"By your own declaration, Seamus, my intelligence is equally matched to yours. Will you not afford me the decency of an explanation? Or do you presume my female sensibilities incapable of comprehending such lunacy?"

He peered over his shoulder, one damp eyebrow arched. "Madam, any decision I make has to be in the interests of this expedition's continued success."

"Oh, don't use that official twaddle on me! Have I not the right to voice my opinions in the privacy of our cabin?" Glaring at one another with mutual stubbornness, Seamus surprised Grace by turning to face her, throwing his head back and laughing heartily.

"I don't see what you find so amusing," she piped.

"Come here, *wife-to-be*." Stepping over to her, he hooked his arm around her, drawing her against him. Grace only half-heartedly resisted. She jolted at the iciness of him, her anger suitably deflected as his hand curved around her back.

"Don't even consider it, Lieutenant." She flashed him a look of defiance, but her lips twitched. "Not until you explain *why* you've taken a prisoner." Grace placed her hands flat on the damp lapels of his coat and frowned into his face. His hands stilled.

"Hostage, not prisoner," clarified Seamus. "I don't intend to keep him tied up and locked away. He'll remain aboard as my guest, under guard, and I'll return him to his people once my boat is returned to me." He resumed his gentle stroking.

"And if your boat isn't returned?"

Seamus hesitated again, his eyebrows drawing together. "Let's cross that bridge when we come to it." He traced the outline of her jaw with his icy finger.

"Where's he now?"

"I invited my guest to share my cabin."

"Well then." Grace squirmed out of his arms. "We simply can't leave your guest waiting."

Seamus rolled his eyes humorously as she hurriedly added an extra pair of trousers beneath her dress and wrapped herself in her shawl. They headed below where two armed marines stood sentry outside the great cabin. Private Doyle and Private Burgess straightened up smartly, saluting. Knocking politely, Seamus entered and Grace followed. She recoiled at the odour of wood smoke, untanned leather, and urine. The inhabitant had been squatting calmly in the corner until he spotted them. He rose silently, and Grace jolted at the sight of the youth's nakedness. His fur lay at his feet.

He had a wide forehead and an unsmiling mouth. His bronzed complexion complemented his jet-black, dead-straight hair which had been hacked untidily into a short cut below his ears. He was barefoot and wore an anklet made of seashells. The young man's almost black eyes assessed Grace with fear.

"By Neptune's trident, man!" exploded Seamus at the naked local. "Make yourself decent. There's a gentlewoman present." Seamus stepped before Grace to block her view.

Grace peeped over Seamus's shoulder at the man as his eyes darted at the open doorway behind them. She rested a gentle hand on Seamus's arm and addressed his back. "I doubt he comprehends, Seamus. I'm honoured you strive to protect my modesty, but perhaps adopt a gentler tone?" Grace averted her eyes from the naked youth as she sidled over to the linen trunk and pulled out a blanket. "He's but a youngster. His lack of attire is the least of his worries. Look at him! He's half out of his mind with terror." Holding the blanket before her as a screen, she handed it to the young man, who took it warily and cloaked himself in it. Grace smiled and nodded.

Seamus drew her protectively behind him again. "Nonetheless, I'm not comfortable with you laying eyes on his naked form."

Amused that he should worry so much about her so-called delicate sensibilities after sharing close quarters with the other sailors in the forecastle, Grace rolled her eyes and stared at the floor. "Surely you were aware of the state of his attire already?"

She saw him flex his stiff wrist in annoyance. "He was wrapped in his fur during his transport here. Christ, he'll catch his death of cold disrobing in this weather." He coughed dryly. "He must be properly attired before joining us for breakfast." Grace studied the cabin, sniffing surreptitiously, her nose wrinkling as she spotted a large, damp stain on the bulkhead near the door and an equally large stain on the floor. Seamus had spotted it too, and gave a low growl of disapproval. "Then, the next order of business will be to instruct him on the proper use of the heads." Seamus opened the cabin door, his head jerking towards the sentries. "Private Doyle, Private Burgess, escort our guest to Purser Rowlett and have him procure suitable attire," he ordered. "And when you're done with that, escort him to the heads and ensure he garners the concept of proper ablutions."

Doyle licked his lips nervously. Burgess straightened his back and replied, "Yes, sir."

"Once he's decent, escort him to the gunroom for breakfast."

"Yes, sir."

Seamus beckoned for the hostage to follow the two marines. The Fuegian hesitated, shrinking back against the bulkhead. Grace smiled at him again. "It's all right. Are you hungry?" She imitated eating. The youngster's eyes flicked at the two marines waiting behind Seamus. Grace beckoned. "Come. It'll be all right."

Sweeping his fur cloak off the floor and fitting it over the ships blanket, the Fuegian stepped past Grace with light-footed trepidation. Closing the door, Seamus sagged, unmistakably relieved that the man's nakedness was no longer able to offend her eyes.

"Poor thing. He's scared half to death. Why did you have to take a boy?" asked Grace, settling on a dining chair.

Seamus peeled off his damp coat. "He was the eldest male in the group," he said, slinging on a dry coat. "The other men were likely away hunting or fishing—or frolicking in our stolen cutter."

Ironing out her frown, Grace studied his long, nimble fingers as they combed his hair and tied it neatly and tightly against his elegant nape then worked the razor to shave himself over the bowl on the dressing table. She was fascinated by his routine to efficiently groom himself back into his usual immaculate state and thrilled that he allowed her to share this intimacy.

Freshly turned out, he offered his arm. "Miss Baxter, would you do me the honour of escorting me on my rounds before breakfast?"

"The honour is all mine."

Up on deck, the weather was bleak and blustery. The rain spat but not heavily enough to deter Grace from accompanying Seamus as he inspected the crew's morning duties. Although this was principally now Wadham's duty, Grace knew Seamus still felt a pull of responsibility towards the smooth operation of his ship. From the quarterdeck, she inspected the morning watch wash the decks with saltwater and scrub the planks with holystone. Spotting Jim rub the brass on one of the cannons stirred a nostalgic twinge. She missed the daily, animated conversations with her Scots friend, she missed the carefree friendship she once had with him, and she missed the beam of his eager face as she read aloud.

Sergeant Baisley, returned only this morning from his unsuccessful overland trek with Lieutenant Sully, had some of the men running through drills and cutlass practice upon the forecastle deck. The pinging and slicing of metal on metal rang out in the fresh morning air as men parried in pairs.

"The men need to keep their reflexes sharp and strengthen those sword arms," explained Seamus. "Especially now we've crossed paths with locals."

Grace was ready to comment that perhaps the Fuegians would not be a threat had he not taken one of their people captive, but not wishing to quarrel with him this morning, she bit her tongue.

Seamus spotted Bosun Tidwell. "Bosun!"

"Sir," Tidwell saluted. "Mornin', Miss Baxter." He bowed stiffly.

"Bosun," she smiled back brightly, delighting in his awkwardness.

"My guest used the bulkhead in my cabin as a substitute for the heads. Have it scrubbed, Bosun." Seamus cast a professional eye into the rigging and over the activities on deck. Grace noted his nod of satisfaction that all was in order.

"Aye, aye, sir," nodded Bosun.

Seamus escorted Grace to the gunroom where the newly attired guest sat uneasily at the long table. Grace smiled at Wadham and Sully sitting opposite the Fuegian, who warily eyed the two privates guarding the gunroom door. Grace empathised with the young man. She knew how intimidating a room full of naval officers could be on a good day, let alone as complete strangers of a different culture.

Grace sat on Seamus's right as he settled at the head of the table. She turned as Toby carried in the silver serving trays and slid them onto the credenza. Seamus waved to the Fuegian as

Toby slunk over, bearing thick fillets of fried fish on a serving platter.

"Guests first, Hicks," said Seamus.

Leaning over to serve the Fuegian, Toby reared back as the man reached for a fillet with his bare hands. A fillet slipped to the floor with a wet splat.

"Good God, man!" yelled Lieutenant Wadham. "Let the boy serve you!" He glared onerously at the Fuegian, who shrank back in his chair.

Grace winced at Toby quailing in panic near the credenza, his shaking hands almost causing more fish to jiggle off the platter. He glanced wide-eyed between Seamus on his right and the doorway on his left, clearly calculating his chances of escape. He and the Fuegian both.

"Lieutenant Wadham, a little patience. He's obviously unfamiliar with our customs," Grace used an upbeat tone to ease both quaking youngsters.

"It's all right, Lieutenant Wadham," said Seamus calmly, smiling at the Fuegian. "Hicks, will you please serve me some fish and eggs to demonstrate to my guest how our meals are served?" Toby scurried over to Seamus and, with quaking hands, dished up some fish before fetching the serving bowl of scrambled egg.

"And now Miss Baxter, please." Seamus nodded. Grace studied the Fuegian's mistrustful fascination at their peculiar meal ritual, and by the time Toby came around to him again, he allowed himself to be served. The Fuegian scooped the scrambled egg up with his chapped fingers and sniffed it cautiously. Finding it not too offensive, he shovelled it into his mouth.

Wadham and Sully bristled, coughing in embarrassed indignation. The Fuegian stopped eating and glanced around the table at the disapproving stares. Smiling kindly, Grace picked up her knife and fork, cut a sliver of fish, and scooped a little egg on top. She delicately popped the fork into her mouth and pulled it back out, clean of food. Clearly confused by the peculiar dining process, the Fuegian dropped his hands to his lap and lowered his eyes to his plate.

Seamus proceeded to consume his breakfast while addressing the table enthusiastically. "It'll require patience and time, but I don't see why our guest can't be trained to become useful as an interpreter, do you? Think how useful it will be to foster relations between his people and ours."

"Lieutenant Fitzwilliam," interjected Grace. "Is it not your intention to return this man in exchange for the stolen cutter?" An uncomfortable hush filled the room, the officers' eyes averted from Seamus and focussed on their meals. The only sound was the clinking of metal utensils on crockery. Unruffled by the awkward atmosphere, Grace continued, "What's this talk of training him as an interpreter?"

Lieutenant Wadham half coughed and half choked on his mouthful, his brown eyes watering at the strain. Aloof at the head of the table, Seamus's eyes roamed over the diners before fixing on Grace.

"Miss Baxter," Seamus said dryly, his voice hardening in authority. "While I appreciate your opinion on many matters, the employment or disposal of this hostage is my decision entirely. If I deem it necessary to master relations with his people in order to establish a friendly disposition towards Englishmen, then it'll be done." He laid his knife and fork down on the edge of his plate and frowned at her. "I don't expect you to question or countermand my authority, madam. I do not suffer insubordination in my men, and I'll certainly not suffer it in you."

Grace's cheeks blazed at her dressing down in front of the officers. Her chin quivered, and she felt like a scolded child. Slowly placing her knife and fork over her unfinished meal, Grace wiped her lips with her napkin and placed it beside her plate. Standing, she glowered as chairs scraped back in unison. The newcomer remained seated, his eyes darting about.

"Gentlemen, please excuse me. I require a little fresh air." Without waiting for a reply, Grace rammed her chair into place, and snatched up her tartan shawl draped over the backrest.

She stormed to her cabin, and slamming the door with a satisfying crack, threw her shawl on the cot with a shriek. Bleeding rat's tails! How dare he humiliate her so!

A short while later there was a loud knock. Grace wrenched the door open and took a step back in astonishment at Seamus's thunderous face. She had not expected him to abandon his breakfast engagement so soon.

"May I come in?" he asked formally.

Grace stepped back silently, her hand gripping the door handle tightly to steady the tremor in her arm. She closed the door behind him and whirled on him like a dueller, hoping to fire off the first word before he did.

"How dare you dress me down like that in public!" The heat of her anger sizzled away any potential tears of upset.

"How dare I?" Seamus's face, bowed because of the low deckhead, morphed from a swirling thunderstorm to a solid chunk of ice. "I dare because I am the *commanding officer* aboard this ship, madam."

"Yes, but you are also my fiancé," she hissed through gritted teeth. "Goodness, I was all but set to become your *wife*!"

"A position that does not grant you immunity against insubordination," he added stubbornly.

Grace wanted to shriek and shake him by the shoulders. "I thought by my considering to marry you that things would be different."

Confusion flitted in his dangerous blue eyes. "Different to what?"

"I escaped my father's domination and a life of oppression under Silverton. Had I known that my expression of interest in marrying you would negate my views, I'd never blasted well have aired it."

Seamus stepped into the middle of the cabin, under the skylight, and straightened out his neck. His blond hair reflected gold and ash in the sunlight. "As with most things in life, there is a time and place for everything, Grace. Countermanding my authority in front of my men is *not* the time for you to air your opinion. You should know this from the time you served."

Grace gasped at his rigid nerve. Blood pumped in her temples, and she squeezed the ache throbbing in her skull. "I was *not* countermanding your authority, Seamus. You lied to me! You said you were simply holding that man hostage until his people returned the boat."

"It's no lie if I hadn't determined it at the time of our conversation. Besides, there's no telling how long it will take his people to comply. We may as well make use of the man while he's here."

"I don't believe that for one second. You've known exactly what you wanted to do with him the minute you took him."

"So, now you presume to know my mind?" Seamus's eyes narrowed coldly.

"Yes! No!" Grace shrieked in frustration at his turning the conversation in a different direction. "I thought I knew your mind, but I was clearly mistaken. I can endure many things, Seamus, but lying isn't one of them. Why didn't you trust me with the truth?"

"I didn't lie, Grace." He braced his hands on the back of a dining chair, leaning towards her.

Grace jabbed a finger at him, figuring that if he would not listen to his words, then he may pay more heed to her actions. "You told *me* one thing, and then told *your men* another. What do you call *that*? And then you had the audacity to make me look like the fool for asking a clarifying question."

Seamus raked his fingers across his forehead, scrunching his eyes. He was definitely frustrated, but a small flame of hope surged in Grace as he hesitated. He blew out an exasperated puff through his cheeks. "I'm sorry if I've given you cause to mistrust me. My instruction to you at breakfast was meant as a gentle reminder of how things work aboard this ship."

Grace gasped, her teeth snapping together as she slammed her mouth shut. He had to be jesting! "*Gentle*? You insulted me!" She mimicked Seamus's dry words, "I do not suffer insubordination in my men, and I'll certainly not suffer it in you."

Seamus reared back, clenching his fists at his side. Grace had never seen his face contort with such a mixture of hurt and anger before. "I'll not stand here and be ridiculed by you—fiancée or not."

"Ha! There's no chance of me remaining your bloody fiancée now! I'd never have agreed to consider it if I'd known you'd become as controlling as my father the instant my agreement was given."

Seamus snapped upright, his blue eyes sharpening as though fixed on an enemy target. "As commander of this Royal Naval vessel, I don't require your, or anyone else's, approval or permission to make my decisions."

Ha! He had made that perfectly clear. She thrust her hands on her hips, the prickle of sweat in her armpits cooled by the motion. "I don't know what I was thinking agreeing to marry a man I hardly know. You did a devilishly marvellous job of flying false colours. Good thing for me it's not too bloody late to change my mind!"

Seamus squeezed his right wrist so hard that his hand turned red. He flashed his fingers in and out in annoyance. "Clearly, nothing I say now will dissuade you from your poor estimation of me." His face pinched, his lips pressing into a thin white line. "And God forbid I *dare* try change your mind. Good day, madam." Seamus spun on his heel and disappeared through the low doorway.

The cabin closed in on Grace, crushing her ability to breathe. "Bleeding stinking rats' tails! That bloody, bloody man!" Bolting outside, she inhaled deep breaths of the damp morning air to steady her anger. Dropping to the main deck, she paced the planks in an attempt to walk off her boiling rage. She caught sight of Gilly as she stormed past the main hatch.

"Miss Grace? You all right?" His forehead wrinkled in concern.

Whipping around to face him with tears brimming, she snapped, "No! I'm not all right! That insufferably uncompromising man will drive me to hurl myself overboard." Alarmed by her threat, Gilly cradled her elbow securely as though to prevent her from following through.

A cutter had returned from shore with fresh hunting supplies. The men offloaded a selection of ducks and a strange creature that looked part camel, part horse but with a long neck. Its tan fur appeared crinkled and soft. Other sailors rolled empty water barrels towards the gunwale, lowering them onto the rowboat. Seeing her opportunity for escape, Grace snatched her elbow back, whirling towards Gilly.

"Take me ashore, please, Gilly." She roughly wiped the tears away with the back of her hand. "I cannot stay aboard this ship a minute longer."

Gilly rubbed his hand across the back of his head. "Where'll you go? 'Tisn't safe with them natives runnin' about."

"They hardly seem the violent type. If they were, they would've put up a fight when Fitzwilliam took one of their own."

"Please, Miss Grace, you're not thinking this through."

"Precisely! I need some space to clear my head. I need to go for a walk."

"Hmm, not sure 'bout that. Lieutenant Fitzwilliam won't like it."

"To hell with him!" Grace buzzed euphorically at the release of emotion and rammed her hands on her hips. "He's too busy playing tutor and emissary to notice." Grace whirled around on the spot and trudged over to where the cutter was being reloaded.

Alarmed, Gilly called after her, "We must have the lieutenant's permission to leave the ship."

Stiff backed, Grace waggled a pointed finger above her head. "Good point, Mr McGilney. Toddle off, seek your permission."

Gilly paused and swore under his breath as Grace stepped around the pile of dead creatures and leaned over the gunwale to peer at the bobbing cutter below. The men stepped back as she swung her skirts over the rail and clambered down the netting. She silently cursed her long hem and bulky boots that doubled the difficulty of the task, but sheer grit and determination had her manage the descent to the waterline.

"Wait up!" Gilly scampered over to the rail, growling in despair as she dropped into the bobbing rowboat. Tommy Holburton, Da Silva, and Cakebread gripped the three sets of oars, staring aghast.

"Good morning, gentlemen," said Grace primly, positioning herself on the rear bench. "To shore, if you please."

The three pimpled youths looked uncertain, and Grace gritted her teeth. "I swear by my grandmother's cross-stitch, if you don't take me to shore this instant, I'll send a hoard of rats to piss in your coffee!"

Their heads jerked up simultaneously as Gilly shouted down, "Belay that order!"

"Holburton." Grace's voice was icy. "As the commander's wife-to-be, I order you to ferry me ashore unless, of course, you wish my fiancé to hear how you assailed me—on *two* occasions."

Tommy scowled murderously, but Cakebread and Da Silva eyed each other apprehensively. Da Silva nudged Tommy in the ribs and hissed, "He'll hang you if he finds out you laid your hands on her and that you threatened to off her."

Cakebread added, with matched urgency, "Ain't an order from the commander's missus as good as from hisself?"

"Your friends are right, Tommy boy," jeered Grace unkindly, her frayed nerves adding malice to her voice. She waved a pointing finger upwards, "And with all these witnesses, if anything should befall me ashore, Lieutenant Fitzwilliam will know *exactly* who to blame."

Uncertainty flicked over Tommy's face as he peered up at the row of spectators. Grace scoffed internally at his stupidity. His ignorance was her gain.

Clearly unhappy with his limited options, Tommy snorted and muttered mulishly, "Righto, suit yourself. We was already headin' that way to fill the water barrels." He reached for his oars, and the other two followed suit.

Gilly dropped heavily from the netting, thudding beside Cakebread, who yelled in alarm as the narrow cutter lurched and tipped dangerously to one side.

"Hold up!" Gilly's face was colourless except for two flushed rounds on his cheeks. "I'm comin' with."

Chapter Twenty-One

W hen they beached, Grace did not wait for Gilly.
She launched herself over the side of the rowboat
and gasped as she landed in icy, knee-deep water,
her boots instantly filling. She marched determinedly from the
shallows and across the beach, and her drenched skirts dragged
around her legs as she headed in the direction of the church
ruins. Behind her, smooth pebbles crunched as the Society boys
rolled the empty water barrels up the beach. Gilly's squelching
footsteps caught up with her.

"Please slow down, Miss Grace."

"Please keep up, Gilly," she snapped, more sharply than she
meant. The same steely determination that had settled in her gut
in Billy's room, after Silverton's attack, returned. The same
wretched determination that caused her to run away and start the
whole disaster that was now her life in the first place. Gilly had
found her in her darkest hour then and had scooped her into the
folds of her new life—and here he was again.

Gilly increased his pace to keep up with Grace's ferocious

strides. Slowly, her rage subsided. Puffing breathlessly, she settled into a comfortable pace. Realising that in her anger she had mistreated Gilly, she turned to him.

"I'm sorry for how I spoke to you," she said. "I apologise that you bore the brunt of my anger meant for Lieutenant Fitzwilliam."

"By crumbs, he'll flay me alive for this?" Despite the dire prediction, Gilly tilted his head forgivingly, his cheeky grin returning.

"No, he shan't." She took his arm reassuringly. "I'll make sure of it."

Gilly cocked a black eyebrow at her and hummed sceptically. "We'll see about that." He gave a one-shouldered shrug. "May as well make the most of my last day on earth."

"Oh, Gilly!" A coil of doubt unfurled in the back of her skull, sending a shiver of uncertainty down her spine. How much trouble would he be in? At worst, a flogging for dereliction of duty and desertion. At best, peeling potatoes in the galley or picking oakum. Squaring her shoulders, she resolved to allow no harm to befall her friend.

"I understand though. 'Tis a little testin'," Gilly said compassionately, "livin' for so long in confined lodgings with others, fiancé or not. You've seen how the men scuffle in frustration, especially when they have a bit of grog in them." The usual chatty Gilly returned, and Grace plodded silently as he prattled on about the men's minor disputes and quarrels. The conversation then took another turn, and Gilly described the hunt with Seamus before Captain Fincham's funeral.

"'Tis a good thing the ducks on this island make decent eatin'. D'you see the creature they were heftin' aboard earlier, the half-sized camel one? We found a herd of them the other day! Didn't know if they were dangerous or not, so we were a bit wary about approachin' them. Lieutenant Fitzwilliam sent me ahead with a musket, so as the crowd of us didn't bear down and scare them off. The creatures weren't the least bit frightened. I even walked up real close to one, but you know what that cheeky beggar did? He spat at me! A great big slimy face full of spittle is what I got as thanks."

Grace could not prevent the laughter from bubbling up. "What did you do?"

"Well, I rightly should have shot him, but I was too gobs-macked at bein' spat at. Then he flicked his tail at me and saun-tered off to join his mates." Grace threw her head back and howled again. "I copped a right ribbin' from the men, I avow. But I proudly lay claim to bein' the first adventurer from the *Discernin'* what discovered those animals. Right brazen crea-tures but harmless enough and easy to approach and hunt."

They entered the clearing of the church. Grace stopped at the memories cascading over her in a waterfall of emotions. She certainly could not complain that the new life she had chosen for herself was boring.

Gilly scanned the thickets in front and behind them. He stopped, squinting back over the bay. "By crumbs! There's another ship out there. Look! Behind that island. You can see the top of her masts."

Grace shielded her eyes with her hand, focussing in the direction of Gilly's scowl. He was right. Just the tips of two masts were visible from this vantage point. "She doesn't appear to be moving," said Grace. She squeaked as Gilly snatched her hand, dragging her down to her haunches. "Gilly! What's the meaning of this?"

"Hush! Look!" He aimed an ink-stained finger at the trodden path of vegetation the *Discerning*'s crew had made from the beach up to the church. Nearly a dozen men, armed with muskets, were tramping purposefully towards the church, led by a thickset, bald man dressed smartly in a fine-cut, black waist-coat and matching breeches.

"Who are they?" whispered Grace, gripping Gilly's sleeve.

Rat's tails! An icy suspicion dripped down her spine. It was not possible, was it? Surely not? What captain in their right mind sailed halfway across the world to claim a prize of two thousand pounds? Had Silverton increased the reward?

"Don't know, but they don't look the sort to be headin' up here to pray. Cripes! We need to hide. Come!" Gilly grabbed Grace's hand, pulling her behind the church and sprinting through the brush to the low cliffs in the distance.

"Where are we going?" Grace panted.

"Trust me! I know a place to hide," puffed Gilly. Grace twisted back briefly, scanning the empty church clearing. "C'mon, Miss Grace! Hurry! Before they come around the church and see us."

Fear spurted through Grace's veins, and her boots drummed quickly and lightly as she sped up. At the cliffs, Gilly burst through the curtain of foliage and hauled Grace in beside him. They both collapsed on the cave's mossy carpet, gasping and heaving. Grace rose to her knees and peered through the dense greenery. She caught glimpses of dark clothing passing through the salt-bleached brush, and the sun glinted off the sweaty patina of the leader's bald head as the crowd of men circled the church several times. They then broke off into twos and fanned out from the church, clearly in search of something.

"Do you think they saw us?" quailed Grace as Gilly knelt beside her and surveyed their pursuers.

"Don't think so. Else they'd be headin' over here, quick march." He sank back onto his bottom, his arms drawn around his knees, his bowed back heaving as he caught his breath.

"How did you know of this place?" wheezed Grace, settling beside him.

"Found it the other day when we were out huntin'."

"Jolly good thing you did," nodded Grace. "Or we'd be in a bit of strife right now."

Gilly frowned. "Wonder if that's those same lot what passed us without colours the other day?"

"We'll be fine," said Grace with an optimism she did not feel. "They won't find us here." She twisted her lips ruefully. What was she doing keeping her secret from Gilly? Swallowing deeply, she confessed, "I think I know who they are."

Gilly's black nests shot up. "Eh? How're you acquainted with a lot like that?"

Grace pressed her hands to her temples and squeezed her pounding headache. Running her hands down her face, she turned to Gilly. "There's a reward on my head."

Gilly chuckled, "Is there now? And which bank did you rob?"

"I'm serious, Gilly. There's another out there who believes me to be his fiancée. A Lord Silverton. I was fleeing my betrothal to him the night you found me."

Gilly's face fell. "By crumbs! I had no idea! Does Lieutenant Fitzwilliam know?"

Grace hesitated, pressing her lips together before replying, "He knows I was fleeing from Lord Silverton. But I don't believe he knows about the reward—at least, he's not mentioned it to me. I only know myself because I read about it in that old broadsheet you gave me to read."

Gilly scrubbed his fingers through his hair, messing it. "Jesus! And you didn't think to tell him? Tell *anyone*?"

"I figured I was safe enough disguised at sea." Grace shrugged. "Lieutenant Fitzwilliam promised to keep my secret and not write to my parents."

"Ha! And here I was thinkin' it was just him bein' all chivalrous."

"Do you think I'll be in trouble with the lieutenant for dashing off like this?"

"Aw, Miss Grace, everyone knows the lieutenant's as unbendin' as a rock—'cept when it comes to you." Gilly quirked a dark brow. "If you don't mind me askin', what had you so riled?"

In hushed tones, Grace explained the events from breakfast and their heated argument afterwards. The interior of the cave slowly darkened as the advent of storm clouds did battle with the sun.

"The way I see it, Miss Grace, is the lieutenant's assumed a big responsibility becomin' commander of the *Discernin'*. The hydrographic office of the Admiralty has tasked the *Discernin'* with surveyin' the archipelago round these parts. And now I know he's doubled that responsibility by keepin' you under his wing—for jolly good reason—the man has a lot on his plate."

"I understand all that," sighed Grace. "But sometimes he treats me like I'm a simpering fool. And the way he spoke to me was inexcusable."

"Well, now you see, Miss Grace, the commander has to keep a tight ship. He can't be seen to be soft, even towards you, especially before his men." Gilly peered through the vegetation again as the thunder rumbled. "Looks like the heavens are about to open."

"A little rainwater doesn't scare me. Besides, my boots and skirts are already soaked."

Gilly huffed. "I wish you'd have let me help you off the boat. What'll the lieutenant think when he finds out you jumped in the sea, and I did nothin' to assist?"

"I'll explain it to him." She smiled at her friend's injured chivalry. "He does listen to me—sometimes." Grace took a deep breath and released it in a sigh.

"How about you try speak to him in private like, you know, not before the other officers or the men? 'Tis obvious to every man aboard that he only has eyes for you. Love makes a man do foolish things, especially when he's tryin' to protect his lady's honour. But in the lieutenant's case, he also has to keep the men from turnin' mutinous on him. He clearly plans to avoid that by

offerin' to marry you, but I'd watch my back if I were you."
Gilly glanced sideways at her.

"I know you're right," conceded Grace, tilting her head.
"I've never been very good at keeping my temper in check."

Gilly's weather-beaten face crinkled in pleasure. "By crumbs,
you're a good sort, temper and all!"

"I'm glad you think so, Gilly. I'm well aware that there are
still some aboard who would rather I wasn't there." She rose to
peek through the veil of shrubbery again. "It's getting rather dark
with the storm coming. I don't see those men anymore." She
glanced over her shoulder as Gilly scrutinised the outside world
too. "Do you think it is safe to go out?"

"Reckon it's been long enough," agreed Gilly, rubbing the
back of his neck. "They should be gone by now." He paused.
"You must tell Lieutenant Fitzwilliam they're after you. Give the
man a fightin' chance to protect you."

"I fear all that'll do is make him restrict my freedom even
further. I wish he'd just let me carry a pistol. Give *me* a fighting
chance to protect myself!"

"Perhaps if you explain what you've seen here today, he
might change his mind? I'll put in a good word for you, eh?
C'mon, let's go."

Gilly led the way, his head twisting about like an owl scanning for prey. He rounded a dense bush ahead of Grace, and the
air erupted in an agonised scream as he was catapulted face-first
into the grass. He twisted onto his back, and Grace plunged to
his side, horrified by the arrow sticking out from his thigh. Gilly
clasped his leg near to where the shaft jutted cruelly from his
flesh, blood seeping through his breeches. Through clenched
teeth, he panted and grunted. With his face a sallow mask and
beads of sweat breaking out across his top lip, Gilly fixed his
stare over Grace's shoulder. Turning, she screamed in fright and
collapsed backward, bumping Gilly's injured leg as she fell. He
hissed in agony.

A surreal sight stood before Grace, a figure painted completely white, empty bow still pointed at them. Five other tribesmen emerged silently from behind the pale, salty bush like ghosts, all covered in intricate patterns. Beneath the paint, the men were naked. One wore a shell necklace. Grace stared at the five nocked bows as the man with the shell necklace yelled unintelligibly at her. She bravely shielded her injured friend as one of the other men lowered his bow and toddled over to them. Gilly struggled upright, grimacing, and he pushed Grace as far behind him as possible.

"Halt there!" Gilly yelled, holding his bloodied hand up to a tall man with a pattern of dots on his face. Without breaking his stride, the man roughly grasped Grace's arm and yanked her to her feet. Gilly hung on to her other arm and tried to drag her back down. A brief tug of war ensued between the two men until the spotted man reached back and struck a stunning blow to Gilly's face.

"No!" Grace screamed as her friend's eyes rolled back in his head, his nose bursting in a spurt of blood. Gilly sagged momentarily and lost his grip on her arm, but then he shook his head and blinked hard. He fixed his eyes murderously on the spotted man.

"Unhand her!" Gilly roared fiercely, his grimace laced with pain. Without any warning, the fully painted man shouldered his bow, seized the shaft of the arrow and yanked it out. The arrow tore chunks of muscle and shreds of skin and cloth from Gilly's leg. His screaming jarred through Grace's brain into her teeth, her jaw grinding in horror.

The spotted man gripped her more tightly and hurled a string of abuse back at Gilly, gesturing wildly. Gilly rolled on the ground, clutching his ruined leg.

"G-Gilly," Grace's voice trembled. "Gilly!" she called louder. "He wants you to stand."

With tears teeming unchecked down his cheeks, Gilly

clenched his teeth and flipped over onto his hands and knees, fixing his injured leg out straight. He paused, panting. With a mighty roar, he pushed himself off the ground with his hands and one good knee and stood, hobbling precariously on one leg.

Grace wrenched her arm away from her captor and rushed to aid him, slinging his arm over her shoulder and supporting him. Her escape did not perturb the shell-necklaced man, and he gestured at both of them to follow him. The five other men looped behind Grace and Gilly, their arrows still nocked threateningly. Grace strained as Gilly leaned heavily on her, and they hobbled after the shell-necklaced man, who was heading towards a thickly forested area past the cliffs.

The journey was slow and arduous, and both Gilly and Grace were huffing and sweating with exertion, despite the rapidly cooling afternoon air. Gilly occasionally groaned aloud when a stumble caused him to jolt his leg. Blood poured freely down his breeches, and the fabric was soon saturated and clinging wetly to the contours of his limb. As the party reached the edge of the forest, the sky began to spit. The shell-necklaced leader continued into the darkened trees, his bare backside waggling as he confidently wended his way through the maze of trunks.

Grace was nearly collapsing with exhaustion when the leader halted in a natural clearing, the grey and ashy remnants of an earlier fire at its centre. The rain fell more heavily now, and the open clearing offered no protection from the deluge. Unperturbed by their paintwork streaming in rivulets down their bodies, the men gestured for Gilly and Grace to sit. Gilly needed no second invitation and collapsed onto the ground with a groan. Grace cradled his head in her lap.

"Oh, Gilly, I'm so sorry! I'm so sorry I forced you out here. I'm so sorry you're hurt. Please forgive me."

Gilly glanced up at her, his lips twisting in an attempt to grin past his chattering teeth. "N-now, M-Miss Grace. We'll have n-none of that." He fumbled in his pocket, drawing out a well-used handkerchief. "B-bind my leg, will you? B-efore I b-bleed to death."

Grace's fingers trembled violently as she struggled to knot the fabric around Gilly's thigh. "I'm such a stubborn fool for insisting we leave the *Discerning*!"

"You didn't f-force me to come." Gilly crossed his arms tightly across his chest against the sleeting drizzle.

"I did! You were duty bound to come, but I paid no heed to the consequences. I'll inform Lieutenant Fitzwilliam of the truth of it. Plead clemency on your behalf."

"'T-tis all right, M-Miss Grace. I knew what I was d-doin'."

"It's not all right that you lie here injured because of me." Her tears cut warm paths down her freezing cheeks.

Gilly shivered again and groaned.

"Oh, Gilly, what must I do?"

"B-by crumbs! 'Tis c-cold enough to freeze the tail off a brass m-monkey. P'haps you c-could lie beside me? K-keep me warm?" Gilly's lips were bright blue in the white of his face.

"Yes, of course!" Grace shuffled alongside Gilly and wrapped herself around him, taking care not to bump his injured leg. Fool! Fleeing without her shawl! What had she been thinking? Ignoring the cold, she tentatively rested her head on his shoulder.

The six men crouched on their haunches in a huddle, oblivious to the icy rain pelting their bare backs. They were deep in conversation, their weapons laid on the ground within reach.

"What do you suppose they mean to do with us?" asked Grace.

"D-don't rightly know. T-trade us for their man, I s'pose."

"I declared it a terrible idea to keep him hostage, but the lieutenant wouldn't hear it. Stubborn bloody man!"

"H-he didn't mean n-no harm by it. W-wanted to study him is all."

"Then he'll jolly well be able to study a fiancée in full fury!"

flared Grace. She gnawed her bottom lip. "Do you suppose he'll search for us?"

"W-without a d-doubt. That m-man would sail to the edge of the earth f-for you and p-probably leap off it too if he thought he'd f-find you there." Gilly coughed in the cold air, and he moaned loudly as his leg tensed. The six men glanced around casually before resuming their chatter.

"If they mean to keep us out here all night, we'll surely freeze to death!" Grace made to rise, but Gilly grabbed her arm.

"Where you off to, Miss Grace?"

"I'll see if I can reason with them. See if we can't purchase our freedom."

"There's no tellin' how this lot see reason. I'd rather you didn't, Miss Grace. I'm in no position to aid you if they turn." Grace eyed Gilly's bloodied bandage and slumped down again. "Huddle closer, Miss Grace. 'Tis already b-better. And s-save your breath. 'Tis w-warmer that way." Grace wriggled closer and closed her eyes, imagining that the clammy press of fabric between them was warmer.

Jolted awake from her icy doze, Grace shrieked as a furry and putrid-smelling creature careered into them. She thrashed at the smothering weight, and Gilly roared awake. Grace's fingers grabbed a clump of thick fur, and the stinking pelt flew aside. Panting in terror, she glared at the two captors scurrying away, chuckling.

"It's a fur." Grace gagged at the stench of rotting meat permeating the cloak beside her. Gilly gasped, steadying his breathing.

"S'pose that means we're stayin' the night, then? Least it's stopped rainin'."

With their paint washed off and their faces glowing warmly in the light of a newly lit fire, the gathered men amicably shared the roasted meat of a skewered carcass. With no invitation to edge closer to the fire or share the meal, Grace tightened her arm around Gilly's chest, settling herself in for a long, uncomfortable night. She ignored her grizzling stomach as Gilly's breathing deepened into shallow snores.

The early-morning sun stayed hidden behind the gloomy grey clouds. When Grace awoke, she studied the men who had resumed their huddled debate. The tone of their voices were different this morning.

"Mornin', Miss Grace," Gilly whispered.

"Good morning, Gilly. What's happening?"

"Don't know but they sure aren't chucklin' anymore."

"How's your leg?"

"Feels like someone's tried hackin' it off with a rusty axe." He reached for her hand under the furs. "Thank you for keepin' me warm. I wouldn't have made it through the night without you." A lump formed in Grace's throat, her unspoken words solidifying as she squeezed his fingers. Gilly coughed softly. "I don't s'pose you could help me up to that tree over there? Gotta see a man about a dog."

"Do you think we are allowed up?"

"Won't know unless we try, will we?"

What on earth it would take for this man to lose his sense of humour? "Yes, of course." Grace drew the warm fur aside, wrinkling her nose. Seeing Grace and Gilly stand up, the six men jabbered at one another before two strode over and snatched Gilly from Grace. She shrieked, scrabbling at Gilly's coat, the shoulder seam ripping as he was torn from her grasp.

"Gilly! Oh, Lord, Gilly! Release him, you bastards!"

Gilly snarled, his head thrown back. Gasping, he glared at the two men gripping his arms. "I only need a piss!"

He tried to motion his intentions, but with his arms clamped tightly, the men mistook his struggles. Their voices rose in alarm, and a third man thundered over from the fire, an arrow nocked tightly against his bowstring. Before Grace could yell out a warning, he loosed it, and it sank deep into Gilly's chest. He jerked in a macabre dance of agony, his primal snarl shredding the air.

"Gilly!" she shrieked, her voice cracking. "No! No! Stop it, you fiends!" Tears of helplessness and fury coursed down Grace's cheeks as she screeched, "Wretched monsters! I vouched for you! Demanded my fiancé free your kin!"

Unable to bear weight on his injured leg, Gilly slumped in his captor's hands, and his long, black hair fell around his face, hiding his terror and agony. A dark stain spread slowly across the front of his breeches, and his shoulders jerked.

With a rush of hatred and rage, Grace rose and stumbled clumsily over the slick grass towards him. She tripped on the saturated hem of her dress and fell heavily. Floundering on her hands and knees, she stilled the instant the sharp edge of a blade was pressed against her throat. From her captor's ominous squint, Grace knew that one slip on her part would result in her wearing a bloody smile across her neck. Her eyes flicked despairingly over to Gilly. Sobbing in horror, she slowly sank back on her haunches and bowed into a heap of wretchedness.

The rain started up again, and without Gilly or the pelt for warmth, Grace's teeth began to chatter, her body convulsing. The rain poured steadily, the thunder booming while the leaves and branches were whipped into a frenzy. Grace had an unrestricted view as the men dropped Gilly in a heap.

Grace wailed, but as horrifying as it was, she was unable to tear her eyes away from her friend. Whimpering his name, she curled beside him as his life force slowly leaked from him. For one horrifying moment, Grace believed him dead. She convulsed with relief when a wet gurgle bubbled from him.

Suddenly, gunshots mingled with the thunder, loud and insistent, and approaching from all directions; the yellow blaze of musket flashes danced alongside the blue darts of lightning. Gilly lay silently on his back, but a discord of loud English voices reverberated around the forest.

From her prone position on the grass, Grace squinted as one, then two, then three of the tribesmen plunged to the ground with crimson blossoms erupting on their chests. With her eyes fixed on Gilly's pale face, Grace barely noticed the hard-soled foot-steps. Iron fingers yanked at her shoulders, and Grace screeched like a banshee and lashed out, scratching, hitting, biting, and kicking. "I don't care if I die! I don't care if you kill me!"

She lashed out weakly, her ribs creaking as she tried to escape the arms that were squeezed about her chest. Gulping in a lungful of air, she inhaled the familiar lemon and musk scent, a golden raw aroma. *Seamus!* He clasped her against him, rocking her and murmuring her name. Slowly, she rose from the fog of terror, clinging to his name as if it were a lighted beacon. "Seamus?"

"Oh, thank Christ!" Seamus tipped her head back, wiping the rain from her forehead. "Oh, Grace, I thought I'd lost you!" His voice splintered, and he kissed her face all over.

Grace whipped her head around wildly. "Gilly! Help Gilly!"

"Shh-shh-shh," comforted Seamus. "I'm here now, come to fetch you home." He scooped her in his arms and lifted her as though she weighed nothing at all. Grace caught a glimpse of four sailors close around Gilly. She struggled in Seamus's arms, but he held her fast.

"Put me down," she squalled, her fists raining down ineffec-tual blows against the bunched muscles of his chest and shoul-der. "I must go to him. Please!" At her impassioned plea, Seamus hesitated. "He protected me, Seamus. He tried to save me. Please, allow me to tend him." Seamus lowered her feet to the ground and, keeping a firm grasp of her, steered her back towards the macabre figure on the forest floor. The sight of her wounded friend caused the bile to rise in the back of Grace's throat, but she swallowed it back. The Blight twins were working swiftly to re-bind Gilly's leg that had begun bleeding again. Grace butted between them, her knees buckling into the mud beside Gilly. Tenderly, she stroked his black brows and his cheek.

"Oh, my brave, brave Gilly," she murmured, her breath hitching as he opened his eyes and gazed at her. Goodness! How was he still alive? Averting her eyes from the arrow sticking out of him, she snapped her head towards Seamus. "Give me your cravat—your shirt—anything that can stop the bleeding."

Seamus peeled off his cravat, but Grace caught his shake of remorse as he fixed his eyes on the arrow in Gilly's chest. Grace wadded the white fabric around the stem of the arrow to hide the gruesome injury.

Offering Gilly her bravest and brightest smile, she said, "We make a good team, you and I. Remember?" Her forced bravado was not enough to stop her tears, but the rain hid them from Gilly as he glanced up at her, his face soft with recognition.

"G-Gilly and B-Billy." He gave a shaky smile, his voice wavering. Blanching, he gasped, "D-don't leave me, M-Miss Grace. I'm scared."

"Oh, Gilly!" Grace took his hand and held it gently. Leaning over, she shielded his upturned face from the rain, wincing as her shoulder bumped the arrow jutting from his chest. "I'm right here, Gilly. I'm not going anywhere." Her throat was in knots.

"B-by crumbs, I'm f-freezing," he whimpered, his jaw chattering. His body shivered, causing the jutting arrow to jiggle gruesomely in his tortured flesh, and he groaned loudly.

"You'll be warm soon enough." She soothed his hair back from his agony-furrowed forehead. "Cook Phillips can whip you up a pot of hot chocolate."

Gilly's smile was more of an agonised grimace. "Talk to me, Miss Grace. Tell me somthin', anythin'." His wide brown eyes bore a hole straight through her heart, stretching and tearing it in grief and panic.

"Um ..." Fumbling for a topic while stroking his forehead, Grace stiffened. "Sally! Your sister, Sally."

Gilly's sad little laugh emerged as a cough, and he moaned. "Jesus Christ! The pain!"

Desperate to distract him, Grace kept burbling on. "I promise you, Gilly, if I ever return to London, I'll find Sally and declare what a kind and brave and funny brother she has." She gently cupped his cheek. "I'll describe how much you love her and affirm that you never stopped thinking of her." Grace's emotional conviction caused fresh tears to brim in her eyes, and she blinked them away rapidly.

"The d-dress ..." Gilly gargled, his mouth contorting in a macabre smile, revealing crimson teeth. Averting her gaze from the bubbling rouge of death on his lips, Grace locked eyes with him. "I'll have your dress cleaned and mended to be like new. Sally will look like a princess. I *promise* you this."

Panic fluttered in her chest as Gilly rolled his eyes towards the clouded sky. The rain no longer patted the back of her head, and Gilly's unfocussed eyes no longer recognised her. Grace swallowed a convulsive sob as he took another unexpected gasp.

"I want to see her, our Sal." Gilly's brown eyes widened and softened. "Beau'iful. She's so beau'iful."

Grace hiccoughed and leaned down to whisper in Gilly's ear, "It's all right, Gilly. You'll see your Sally soon enough. We'll get you back to London—I promise. Please, hold on!"

Gilly breathed out a deep sigh that puffed gently against her ear. He twitched once more, stilling peacefully as the grip of his fingers slackened. Grace's resolve to wrestle back her sadness shattered, and hard, burning weeping erupted from her soul.

Seamus squeezed her shoulder, and at his touch, her bones liquified, and she collapsed in a heap beside the lifeless body of her friend. Grace was barely aware as Seamus scooped her up, cradling her as gently as a newborn as he carried her back to the *Discerning*.

Chapter Twenty-Two

T he three Society boys were huddled in irons where Seamus had ordered they be cuffed to the ring-bolt in the deck. Holburton scowled defiantly while Cakebread and Da Silva hung their heads in abject terror.

Seamus stepped into the charthouse to see how Grace was faring and to escape the mutinous stares of his men. Peaky and dishevelled, she was awake and propped up against the pillows on her narrow cot. Seamus settled on a chair beside her, running a finger tenderly down her pale cheek. "Are you well, Grace?"

Grace clamped her bottom lip with her teeth, her puffy, red-rimmed eyes pooling with tears. She shook her head. Seamus took her hand. It felt so tiny and cold.

Withdrawing her hand, Grace grasped her head in both hands. "Goodness, Seamus. I can't still my thoughts!" She sucked in a juddering breath, squeezing her eyes shut. "The remorse is crushing! I can barely breathe. I keep envisaging Sergeant Baisley snapping the arrow in Gilly's chest. The marines carrying him back to the beach." Her bloodshot eyes sprung open. "Oh Lord, I can't bear the idea of leaving Gilly in that desolate graveyard!"

Seamus leaned forward, scooping her into his arms and kissing her damp temple. "I know, my heart." Seamus gripped her tighter as she buried her face in his shoulder, clinging to him as powerful, silent sobs wracked her whole frame. He kissed her again, his newly shaven skin dampened by her tears.

"Do you still have that … that *man* aboard? Your *hostage*," she hissed.

Seamus slid his steely mask into place, but when he spoke, his voice was gentle. "Grace, that youngster wasn't the perpetrator of that ghastly event." He shuffled to the edge of his chair.

"No!" she spat venomously. "But it was his people who perpetrated it."

"Which wouldn't have happened had you not impetuously fled without my permission," said Seamus, struggling to keep his tone reasonable.

"Which wouldn't have happened if *you* hadn't treated me like a child!" An angry blush race up Grace's neck and populated her cheeks. "I warned you it was a bad idea taking him in the first instance."

Seamus's shoulders slumped. "How was I to know his people were not interested in exchanging him for the stolen boat?"

"Damn that bloody boat! You should have put him ashore regardless. It was inhumane of you to steal him from his community in the first place." Grace's voice was shrill, but furious tears brimmed in her eyes.

"I've put him ashore," he said woodenly.

Grace swiped her eyes with the back of her hand. "Pardon?"

"I put him ashore after we found you. He'll no doubt have made it back to his family by now." Unable to infuse any warmth into his voice, Seamus stared flatly at her. Had she any notion of the trouble she had caused him? How his heart had almost torn in two when he discovered her missing.

"Say what you're thinking!" Grace sniffed loudly. "That it is *my* fault. That my recklessness killed Gilly."

Seamus inclined his head. "You forced my hand to risk the lives of my men to come and find you. McGilney died protecting *you*." Seamus glared a moment longer and then lowered his eyes in a ceasefire. This would not do. They would just end up in a circular argument again, and Seamus desperately wanted to avoid that.

"Ha!" snarled Grace. "It's *your* fault too." She threw the accusation at him as a choking sob exploded from her. "How were those men to know you'd not harmed their man?" She angrily wiped her nose with the back of her hand. "Were it not for you and your wretched, high-minded anthropological pursuits, I'd not now be drowning in the guilt of my friend's death."

The muscles in Seamus's neck tightened testily. Christ Almighty! As much as it galled him, he knew he had to take responsibility for this—as commander of this ship, as her fiancé. The anger slowly left his quivering frame. "You're correct." He cupped her face, his thumb wiping more tears off her cheek. "As your fiancé, I should have protected you and delivered you a stern enough warning to prevent you from venturing into harm's way. I assume full responsibility for what has happened."

"A stern warning wouldn't have helped. I don't need to be treated as a child if I'm to be your wife!"

His shoulders slumped dejectedly. "Please, don't hate me for this, Grace. I do view you as my intellectual equal, but whether you care to admit it or not, your smaller physicality is a weakness that can be exploited by other men. I can't help but worry about you." He was relieved to see his impassioned whisper cut through her veil of anger.

Fatigue and grief melted away the resentment on her face, and she pressed back into her pillow. "I'm shattered. I haven't energy for another argument."

Seamus wearily ran a hand across his face, his fingers tracing the bags of exhaustion beneath his eyes. "Very well, I'll let you rest. Though, you should know that I'm charging Holburton, Cakebread, and Da Silva with negligence. Their sentence will be a dozen lashes each."

Grace's head jerked on the pillow. "Oh, please don't! Has there not been enough violence and bloodshed?"

Seamus made an enquiring noise in his throat and scratched the back of his head where his ribbon was coming loose.

Grace took a deep breath. "They only did as I ordered. Can you not show leniency? Offer them a pardon?"

Seamus rucked his forehead. "Not without looking weak, I can't."

"Seamus, I've lived with those men. Most are good men. Admittedly, Tommy Holburton is nasty enough to kick a kitten just because he can."

A hot scratch of unease raked down Seamus's nape. "God help him if he *ever* laid a hand on you. I'll hang the bastard twice."

Grace sniffed. "If you were to hang every man on this ship who has ever flicked me, pinched me, kicked me, punched me, whipped me, or spat on me, you'd have no hands left." Seamus bunched his fists on his knees, his knuckles whitening. Grace attempted a weak smile. "It's all right, Seamus. I learnt to defend myself. Even broke Tommy Holburton's nose once."

This piece of information did not have the desired humorous effect on Seamus, and he snarled, jolting to his feet. He cracked his head on the low deckhead and spat out half an oath before catching himself. Taking several deep breaths to steady himself, he waited for the splitting pain in his skull to abate beneath his rubbing fingers. He was equally to blame for her mistreatment. Had he not laughed and encouraged her to be kicked, fed muck, and dunked in a trough of water at her initiation?

Grace shuffled upright against the padding of pillows. "Seamus, this ship is ruled with cruelty extended through Tidwell's cane and Sorensen's knotted rope."

"Order and discipline *must* be maintained," Seamus said tersely.

Grace tilted her head, and Seamus's heart lurched at the depth of sadness in her green eyes. "And yet the men still step out of line," she said softly.

The fatigue that had rounded his shoulders shattered like a roller crashing into the ship's bow and scattering in a fine mist. Seamus tightened his jaw, and to his own surprise, he leaned down and placed his cocked hat on her head. If only sharing responsibility was as easy as sharing his hat. "Go ahead, Miss Baxter. I'm all ears. What do you propose?"

Her eyes widened before she set her jaw in decision, though her voice was level and reasoned. "Before joining the Navy, all those boys knew was poverty, hardship, and brutality. They know no different." Seamus stared at Grace without blinking, so she elaborated, "They are unused to kind words."

"So, you're proposing I unshackle them and make them a hot cup of tea?" Seamus instantly regretted his tone.

"Sarcasm doesn't suit you, Lieutenant. You're a better man than that." The hat slipped over Grace's brow, and she pulled it off slowly, settling it in her lap.

Seamus worked the tension in his jaw, grinding his molars. "Leniency will lead to mutiny," he said.

Grace tucked a curl behind her ear, keeping her tone light in an obvious attempt to ease him into her way of thinking. He already knew that a hot head was no way to win her over, so he listened intently. "Won't a flogging teach them and the others to rebel against you and revile me even further?" she added.

Seamus stiffened, his back as flat and rigid as the planks on deck. "I didn't choose this career for the approval of my men."

"Perhaps not. But tell me, Seamus, until you knew pain, did you truly appreciate your health? Until you knew failure, were you able to appreciate accomplishment? Until you worked for something, could you honestly take pride in owning it?" Seamus remained silent but softened his gaze. Grace continued, "Allow those Society boys to earn your respect. Make them work for it rather than trying to beat it into them. If their hard life has not taught them anything up until now, maybe a lesson of compassion just might?"

Seamus rolled his neck in thought. Was she right? Was there another way to handle this situation—a better way?

"Please," she implored, her voice dropping to a whisper. "I couldn't bear any more violence right now."

Gently taking back his hat, he said, "Very well. Let's try it your way." He pulled her bedcovers up under her chin, and Grace wriggled down, her puffy, bloodshot eyes drooping wearily. He kissed her warm forehead. "Sleep well, Dulcinea."

As Seamus made his way down to the main deck, he pondered all the ways this could go. If it went wrong, he would be strapped to the bilge pump before nightfall. Stopping before the prisoners, Seamus clenched his hands behind his back, barking, "Unshackle these men."

The three youths shuffled restlessly as Seamus stared impassively at them. They all lowered their eyes to the deck, but unlike Cakebread's and Da Silva's faces of terrified misery, Holburton's jaw clenched angrily. The rest of the men gathered around with a brewing atmosphere of curiosity and contempt.

"I'm aware of the current discord among you. God knows I've heard enough mutinous whispers to hang most of you." The crowd wavered in an uneasy jostling of feet. He glared at the three youngsters. "Gentlemen." Seamus's respectful greeting had the guilty culprits glance up in surprise. "You're Royal Navy men, are you not? And, as such, are you not bound by the honour and code of the sea?" Three confused faces looked shiftily at one another. "I've a great responsibility to *all* men aboard my ship. Therefore, I'm making an example of you."

Holburton's grey eyes hardened, and Cakebread whimpered. Da Silva blinked hastily at his feet to hide his moist eyes.

"You're all in the starboard gun crew?" asked Seamus.

Holburton's voice rang out clearly, "Aye, sir."

"I can't afford to have all three of you languishing in the sickbay recovering from a flogging. It would leave Gunner Ash short on hands and leave us in a predicament should we need our guns." Holburton's eyes narrowed in suspicion. Cakebread swallowed painfully. Da Silva still stared at the deck. "Therefore, I'd like each of you to come up with a suitable punishment. One that fits your crime but doesn't render you useless on my ship."

The three heads swivelled, waiting for one of the others to speak first. From their apparent unease, it was clear none of them had expected this. Seamus waited. Holburton coughed awkwardly. "Well, sir, I suppose we could scrub the hold for a month?" Seamus nodded at the suggestion and then fixed his eyes on Da Silva.

The lean young man swallowed audibly. "I, um … We, um … We could pump the bilges for a month after that, sir."

The panic on Cakebread's face was that of a rabbit cornered by a cobra. "Y-you c-could separate the th-three of us, I s-suppose, sir. P-put us on d-different watches."

Da Silva gasped, and Holburton hissed from the corner of his mouth, "What'd you say that for?" Cakebread shrank under the glares of his two companions.

Seamus leaned forward on the balls of his feet. "Thank you for your suggestions." He remained uncannily still, his authority demanding the silence that fell over the deck as he rubbed his thumb and forefinger together in contemplation. "You'll spend two weeks pumping the bilges and a week scrubbing the hold." Three pairs of eyebrows shot up in surprise. "As for separating you, I don't believe this to be prudent. Gunner Ash assures me that despite all your failings, you make an excellent team on the guns and that you three can prepare and fire your gun a good ten seconds faster than any other gun team. I'll need men of your calibre when the time comes."

The three Marine Society boys froze before him, immobilised in disbelief.

Seamus nodded. "Very well. Though, I warn you, don't take my leniency for weakness." Seamus's voice was full of power that invited no second chances. His ominous glower turned Holburton's ears crimson. "Bosun reported your scrap on the beach. You ever lay a finger on *any* person aboard my ship again, and I'll keelhaul you myself and hang what's left of you from the yardarm by your testicles."

Holburton blanched, his eyes darting to his companions as he swallowed deeply.

Chapter Twenty-Three

MONTEVIDEO, 12 SEPTEMBER 1826

Grace woke with a jolt, the back of her neck damp on the pillow, her chemise plastered in the valley between her breasts, her throat raw from shouting. The world no longer rocked.

"Dulcinea." Seamus's voice was like a tipple of smooth port, as was his cool hand sweeping her hair from her damp forehead. "Shh-shh-shh, you're dreaming again." He sat on a chair beside her, his elbows on his knees, his body straining toward her as he squeezed her hand. "My heart," he whispered hoarsely. "I'm here."

Grace sank slowly into the feathery pillow and stared at the swathes of the canopy above her. Under different circumstances, she might have appreciated the pretty bedchamber. The logs stacked beside the fireplace gave off a sweet aroma, while the burning hickory logs smelled mildly of baking ham. There was no doubt that Lord Ponsonby, the British representative here in Montevideo, had a lavish residence.

"Oh, Seamus!" Reeling from the nightmare, Grace's eyes scanned the room, its newness unsettling. A violent flash of Gilly's body writhing in agony against his captors slashed across her thoughts like a sickle hacking through grass. The tear in her heart wrenched open, and she wanted to wail at the pain of it. *My poor Gilly! What have I done?* Recollections bounced around Grace's mind: Ship's Surgeon Beynon's examination of her in her berth, Toby's doleful grey eyes as he took away untouched trays of food, the pardoning of the Society boys, Seamus's bent head at his writing bureau, perhaps writing, possibly sleeping, probably praying.

Seamus's gentle voice interrupted her unsettled mind. "Are you hungry?" His blue eyes pierced her aching soul.

"Not particularly."

"Still, I'd like you to try." Seamus rose, fetched a tray from the table beneath the window and laid it on her lap. An aroma of bacon, onion, celery, and potato wafted up from the bone-china bowl. Grace tasted it as Seamus scrutinised every bite, knowing he would wait until she had devoured the lot. Everything tasted like nothing these days. He had been so insistent about making her eat since Gilly—*No! Don't think about it!* Her stomach clenched, and for a moment, she could not swallow her mouthful of stew. Gritting her teeth, she forced it down.

"I hope our detour to Montevideo won't delay the expedition?" said Grace, her eyes burning from too much crying.

"We were due to restock anyway. I don't want you worrying about the expedition." He took her hand in his and kissed her knuckles in a gesture that should have made her feel better. It did not.

Grace knew he meant his words to comfort her, but they added another stone of guilt to her bucket of misery. The bucket would not bear too many more stones before the bottom fell out —Gilly's death the heaviest of all.

"How long until departure?"

"As soon as we're restocked." Seamus studied her, looking hopeful at her tentative interest in the world again.

"I trust that's going well?" she asked as a distraction from eating any more stew.

"It is. Though I've not yet received word from Admiral Otway advising of our new captain. But in the meantime, Purser Rowlett is overseeing the resupply of the *Discerning* with dried goods. He has procured hay for the livestock and also replenished our wine and rum supplies. The two nanny goats are being sired as we speak. Bosun Tidwell has seen to the repairs and maintenance to ensure the ship is fit to continue."

"Sounds as though all is in hand." She pushed aside her uneaten stew. "I'd like to get up today. Take a stroll in Lord Ponsonby's tropical gardens. I do so enjoy how different they are to the manicured grounds back at Wallace House." She plastered an unnaturally bright grin to her face.

Grace, leaning comfortably on Seamus's arm and feeling better for the fresh air, was completing a second circuit around the tall palms when a man, almost as tall as Seamus, strutted across the lawn. His smooth-shaven cheeks were kissed golden by the subtropical sun, and his short, jet-black hair was slicked back.

"Is that Lord Ponsonby?" Grace eyed the approaching man. "He cuts quite the figure."

"Indeed. He's quite the ladies' man."

"It's not hard to see how they might fall for his charms. He's rather striking."

Seamus arched one brow comically. "Has my wonderful fiancée fallen under the charismatic Lord Ponsonby's spell?"

"No, she has not." Grace bumped her hip against his. "Her hands are full enough with her dashing headstrong officer."

Seamus leaned in, whispering, "Apparently, Lord Ponsonby landed himself in a spot of hot water with the wife of a key government official back in London, promptly earning himself a free voyage here to South America."

Grace appreciated his attempts to humour her with this little piece of gossip. "What does his lordship do in exile?" she asked, glancing sideways. Her heart skipped a beat at his strong jawline above the neatly tied cravat. He looked relaxed and happy, and she pressed her shoulder into his arm.

Pressing back gently, he elaborated, "His charms don't only extend to the ladies. He's an excellent diplomat and negotiator between men too. He has fostered the creation of a buffer state between Spanish-ruled Argentina and the Empire of Brazil. He single-handedly persuaded both sides to allow Uruguay to serve as a military-free buffer zone between them. The result is the newly independent country of Uruguay, where we presently find ourselves. And naturally, British commerce in the region benefits from this peaceful brokerage too."

Seamus's words trailed off as Ponsonby's wide smile displayed an impressive row of neat white teeth, accentuating his square-set jaw and deep dimples. He dipped his head at Seamus, who nodded back.

"Lord Ponsonby, may I introduce my fiancée, Miss Grace Baxter."

Ponsonby took Grace's hand. "*Enchanté*, Miss Baxter." His voice was a rich, resonant timbre. "Fitzwilliam neglected to report his fiancée's beauty. You're a most glamorous creature." He kissed her hand.

Realising Lord Ponsonby was flirting shamelessly with her, Grace blushed and flicked Seamus a sideways look. He was laughing at her. She flushed even more furiously and curtsied. "Thank you for your kind and gracious hospitality, my lord."

Ponsonby's dimples deepened. "My, my! Such refinement.

Wasted on this scoundrel!" He lightly flicked Seamus's shoulder and winked.

"You keep a delightful home," Grace added conversationally to steer Ponsonby's attention away from her.

"My home is at your complete disposal, Miss Baxter. Please stay as long as you need." The genuine concern in his eyes warmed her as he tutted, "Ghastly business with the natives."

"Indeed it was, my lord," agreed Grace tightly.

"Never you mind. We'll secure you passage home to England." Ponsonby puffed up. "Might be a few months, though, since the docking of British vessels in this part of the world is regrettably infrequent."

"England?" A cold dread settled in Grace's gut.

"Indeed, madam. Though there's no need to concern yourself with the delay. You're a most welcome guest." His brilliant smile faded at her grim face.

"England?" she repeated, glaring at Seamus with a heat that would melt an iceberg.

Seamus sucked in a deep breath, his eyes carefully avoiding hers. "Indeed. I've commenced negotiations with Lord Ponsonby to see you safely back."

Grace stiffened with horror, sharing her scowl equally between Seamus and Ponsonby.

Withering under her sharp glare, Ponsonby coughed in confusion. "Do pardon me, I see my groom has readied my carriage. I was just on my way out. Heading west to conduct business with Emiliano Perez and his daughter Sofia. He's a filthy rich cattle rancher, and if I don't attentively lavish kisses on his daughter's hand, he's likely to string me up in the street. Between you and me, I'd rather kiss one of his cows." His attempt to lighten the mood failed. Coughing awkwardly, he bowed and strutted towards the lanky footman who was holding the carriage door open.

"How dare you think of sending me back!" Grace squeaked in indignance.

Seamus held his hand up. "I understand your reluctance to return to your parents, but what of your uncle?"

"You presume to make decisions about my future without even conferring with me. You're being just like Father again!" Her eyes flashed as she poked her chin at him. "I may be as angry as a boiled cat right now, but it doesn't mean I want to be separated from you."

"And I don't wish to be separated from you either," he placated.

Grace's anger subsided as he lowered his chin in regret.

"Unfortunately, neither of us has a choice in the matter," he said. "Regulations don't allow women to be carried to sea without orders from a superior officer or from the Lords Commissioners of the Admiralty." The official tone of his voice evaporated. "Unless the new captain has no objection to your coming with us, we won't own the luxury of time to wait for packets to be sent back and forth to the Admiralty. We'll need to sail without delay."

The remaining heat of Grace's ire drained completely, and she placed her hands upon his chest. "Seamus, until I met you, my life had no purpose, no love. The life my parents have mapped out for me is a bleak existence." She reached down for his hand, absently stroking his scar. "With you, I'm free. I'm whole."

With nostrils flaring, Seamus took a deep breath. "Even if the new captain permits you to sail with us, I've already expressed my discomfort at not being able to keep you safe at sea."

Grace swallowed thickly. "You're right. It's dangerous. This, I know too well." Flashes of Gilly's lifeless body crumpled in a bloodied heap speckled her vision, and she blinked rapidly to rid herself of the images. "Perhaps, had I carried a musket, I could have saved Gilly?"

Seamus pressed his lips together. "It goes against every fibre of my being to keep you in a position where you need to arm yourself for your own protection. It galls me to imagine you—*a gentlewoman*—armed!"

Grace arched her eyebrows at him. "I can outshoot most men aboard the *Discerning*."

Seamus rolled his right wrist, the old injury clicking beneath Grace's fingers. "There's more to protecting yourself than firing a musket. It's wholly impractical to fire a pistol or a musket in some circumstances. Close-quarter combat requires skill with a blade."

"Sergeant Baisley instructed me with the bayonet too." Seeing Seamus's look of horror, Grace bit back mention of Ben Blight's knife lessons. Peering up at the face of the man who was swiftly stealing her heart, Grace tiredly conceded, "Perhaps you're right. At least back in London, I'll not lead anyone else to their death." She had meant that as a criticism of herself, but she caught the flood of remorse in Seamus's eyes before they flicked to his feet.

Wanting to draw him from his regret, she added, "God only knows I don't need any more enemies out here." Grace widened her eyes, the memories of the past burning through her fog of grief like the summer sun. "Oh, Seamus, with everything that has passed, I've forgotten to tell you about the men—armed men—by the church."

"Christ, Dulcinea! What men?" Grace slumped under his harsh tone. Immediately contrite, he cupped her damp cheek in his palm. "Sorry. I didn't mean to snap. I'm on edge with all that has happened." His hand caressed up and down her arm. "Tell me of them, these men."

"They all carried muskets and dressed in European clothing. Gilly—" Grace's voice faltered on the name, and she licked her dry lips. "Gilly and I saw the tops of two masts behind that island to the west."

"Did you see her colours?" Seamus massaged his wrist.

"No."

"She must be that brigantine we observed a little while back. The one with no colours."

"Yes, Gilly thought the same."

"By Neptune's trident! Why the devil are they following us?"

Turning away neatly to hide her face, Grace retook his arm with the pretence of walking on. She knew the reason well enough. Aware that the time had come to tell him, she inhaled a long, cooling breath. "Lord Silverton has a reward out for my return."

Seamus wrenched her to a halt. "Christ Almighty! How do you know?"

Grace chewed the inside of her cheek. "I read it in a broadsheet Gilly gave me."

"Heavens above! Those men could be any number of miscreants. Prize hunters aren't picky with their crew or their methods."

Grace frowned, her eyes squinting against the bright sunshine as she looked up at him and said, "Surely no ship is foolish enough to attack a British vessel?" A worm of worry bore its way into her brain.

Seamus stared at the fountained palm-heads above, his gaze fixed on nothing for an overlong moment as though he were weighing the odds. Looking down at her, he cleared his throat. "One would hope not. But we are venturing into remote waters with very little chance of rescue should we not withstand an attack."

"There's no danger in you failing at that, is there?"

Seamus kissed her hand. "Don't trouble yourself about this, my heart. The ship is my responsibility."

Grace loathed the thought of leaving Seamus, but she had already caused him enough disruption. Was she prepared to invite an attack on the *Discerning*? No. It was only fair to take Lord Ponsonby up on his offer and let Seamus continue his journey unhindered. Resolving to let him go, frosted despair coated her heart with a brittle layer of ice that, should it crack, would shatter her very existence into a thousand ice chips.

Chapter Twenty-Four

S eamus pulled his coat tighter against the late-night air as
he strode, head bowed in thought, through the dusty
streets of Montevideo. He had not intended his inspection of the *Discerning* to keep him so long. The flavour of
patrons filling the streets had changed from busy shoppers and
traders to drunken sailors and prostitutes.

Sidestepping a suspicious puddle, Seamus pulled the lapels
of his coat higher around his neck. Rounding a corner, he hurried
past a squat, whitewashed building with a flat roof that boasted
the name *Almacén El Hacha*. Lord Ponsonby had warned him
about this particular drinking establishment. He said that if he
lost any of his hands, this would likely be where they would be,
drowning their sorrows with the potent *uvita*, a sweet, wine-
based drink that was all too easy to consume in large quantities.

A commotion spilled out onto the street—a surge of tottering
patrons tangled in a knot of boots and fists. Foreign sailors and
locals were all equally embroiled in the mess, including a few
half-dressed women. Some brandished earthen jugs as weapons,

and a wave of objection rose as a metal rod swung above the crowd before being lost in the tumble of humanity. Seamus crossed to the other side of the street but his feet stuttered to a halt at Wadham's dark head towering in the middle of the mêlée. A meaty fist caught Wadham on the jaw and he staggered back, propelled to the edge of the crowd. Another black-haired man pounded Wadham's assailant, grinning like a fool at Wadham.

"Christ, Wadham! What are you playing at?" Seamus snapped.

At Seamus's sharp tone, Wadham blinked in inebriated surprise and staggered towards him. "Fitzwilliam?"

"What on God's earth are you doing brawling like a commoner? You're an officer in the Royal Navy, for Christ's sake!"

Wadham tottered a couple of steps to the side, and Seamus gripped his arm. "Was just looking for a bit of company," he slurred. "You got something warm to stick your cock into. 'Twas only fair I found myself the same."

"Watch your tongue, Wadham! That's my fiancée to whom you refer."

"Don't I know it," pouted Wadham. "I bloody tried my damnedest, but she only had eyes for you. It was her honour I was defending back there."

The black-haired man who had fought alongside Wadham shuffled up, slapping him on the back with unsettling familiarity, his accent an indiscernible blend of English dialects. "Oi, Lieutenant! Not leavin' without me, are ya?"

Wadham's frown dissolved into a chuckle. "Not at all, my good man!" He turned to Seamus, swaying. "Found us a new topman! This is Tibbot."

Seamus inspected the man. He certainly had the build of a sailor—broad shoulders, narrow waist, corded and calloused hands. He had a strong jawline and an open face. Knowing he could not be overly fussy with his choice of crew in this part of the world, Seamus nodded curtly. "Good to have you aboard, Tibbot."

"Thank you, sir!"

"I trust you can find your way to the *Discerning*?" Seamus noted the man's clear eyes—he certainly had not indulged himself to the degree Wadham had.

"Yes, sir. Seen her at the docks."

"Very good. Make yourself known to Purser Rowlett in the morning. He'll sort you out."

"Yes, sir. Thank you, sir." Tibbot eyed the crowd of brawlers that had begun to break up, and he slunk, long limbed, around the corner.

Seamus, not taking Wadham's earlier slight against Grace to heart, steered the drunken lieutenant back towards the docks. "Come on, Wadham. Let's get you home." From the corner of his eye, he noticed Wadham gingerly rubbing his jaw. "What was all that commotion about?" asked Seamus.

"I was minding my own business, working hard to convince young Tibbot back there to come aboard the *Discerning* when some ugly Irish bastard began waving a bag of coin about, asking if anyone knew of a Miss Baxter's whereabouts. Figured there couldn't be too many Miss Baxters in this part of the world and took him to mean your fiancée. Tibbot told me the Irishman's one of several private merchants chasing a reward offered by a Lord Silverton for his fiancée's return to London."

Seamus wrenched Wadham round. Christ! Silverton was like a wolf on the spoor of an injured deer. Seamus knew him to be ruthless in commerce, but this was personal. Did his absurd need for power in the business world bleed into his personal affairs too?

"Ow! No need to take my arm off!" Wadham shrugged his arm back belligerently.

"What else did he say?"

"The Irishman accused her of being caught in some scandal

with a stable hand back in London." Wadham laughed coldly. "I told the Irishman he was too late—that she'd already agreed to marry you!"

"By Neptune's forked trident, man! Did the drink loosen your tongue *and* your common sense?"

Wadham ran an uncoordinated hand across his face, and shrugged. "Didn't see the harm. Told him he'd lost out on the reward since you're returning her to London anyway."

"This matter is my private affair. I don't appreciate your spilling details of it to every ruffian in town." Seamus squeezed his eyes. "What else did you learn?"

Wadham flapped his hand dismissively. "Doesn't surprise me his lordship wants her back to warm his bed—she's a rare beauty, that's for sure."

"Lieutenant Wadham! Refer to my fiancée in such a salacious manner again, and I'll be forced to defend her honour. I've let it pass twice now because it is the drink talking, but I'll not let it pass a third."

"Ha! That's if you live to see the day. That Silverton fellow sounds like a right mean bastard—lives on both sides of the law, if you catch my meaning? There's no telling what he'll do when he finds out you've stolen his fiancée."

"And who the devil shared that licentious piece of gossip?"

"My new man Tibbot, of course! He's been around the world and back a couple of times. Knows a great deal." Wadham winked with drunken exaggeration.

"You'll surely regret your familiarity with him by the sober light of day," bristled Seamus. "I don't expect this fraternisation to continue aboard my ship."

"Rest assured, I said nothing discourteous about Miss Baxter. In fact, when I demanded the Irishman cease his scurrilous remarks about her, the bastard hit me in the face. Tibbot came to my aid, and that's when you showed up."

Seamus drew to a halt at the dock. "Wadham, I urge you to

EMMA LOMBARD

head aboard and sleep off your stupor. When you awake, I expect your civility to return to its fullest. Should I find that you've revealed any of this evening's conversation, I can assure you that Admiral Otway will hear of your appalling lack of discretion when it comes to protecting a British subject—and a gentle-woman to boot—in a foreign land."

Recognising Wadham's comprehension slowly dawn, Seamus turned smartly, his urge to check on Grace overriding any further desire to berate his colleague.

Thank Christ she was safe under Lord Ponsonby's roof for now. Some of his men would not have hesitated twice to hand her over for a reward. But how could he possibly leave her now? Without Seamus there to safeguard her, God only knew what might happen to her. It was not a risk he was willing to take. He must write to Admiral Baxter, he decided—to assure him that Grace was under his protection and let him know he would personally deliver her back to London once the expedition was complete. He would have a devil of a job ahead persuading her to come with him when he had only just got her to see sense in returning to London. Pushing back his twinge of guilt at keeping his first secret from her, he made up his mind to protect her from this news that Silverton's prize hunters were so close. He saw how his name still affected her, even after all this time.

For the next couple of days, Seamus insisted Grace remain at the grand house to regain her strength. She was safe enough within the protected walls of Ponsonby's residence. Seamus knew she was happy to spend her days reading in the shade of the wide black-and-white tiled veranda. Ponsonby's library selection was impressive. Seamus attended to business around town during the day, but in the evenings, with Ponsonby away at the cattle ranch, he ate supper with Grace in her room by the light of the candelabra.

As on most evenings, a loud rap on the door announced the arrival of supper. A plump servant entered, her round face shining. She was in a plain brown housedress with a white apron tied at the front, but Seamus admired the bright yellow wrap swathed around her head.

"*Hola, Capitán* Fitzwilliam." The motherly figure had a faintly sweet, herbal smell about her, and she nodded politely at Grace as she slid a tray with two bowls of stew onto the table by the window. Seamus looked balefully at yet another bowlful of Luiza's stew, brought with alarming regularity. The monotony of food aboard the ship was one thing, but here on land, where the choice was plentiful, Seamus had hoped for a change of diet. Though he could not complain too much—Luiza's stew was wholesome, filling and delectable. He thanked her in Spanish, and the woman departed.

Grace mopped up the gravy in the bottom of her empty bowl with a chunk of white bread—a habit no doubt learned in the mess. Seamus chuckled, and she glanced up. Her cheek bulged with a large chunk of the crispy crust as she chewed industriously, licking at a crumb on her lower lip.

"It's good to see your appetite returned, Dulcinea." Seamus dragged his eyes up from her labouring jaw, his head cocked. "I have news."

"Mhm?" Grace said, the wedge of crust crunching audibly.

"Admiral Otway can't be faulted for his expedience. I received a packet from him today."

Grace took a large swill of wine. "And?"

"The *Discerning* has a new captain," he said dryly, gauging Grace's eyes narrowing at his secretive tone.

"Anyone I know?" She had tried for a casual air, but Seamus's heart thumped in his chest. She put her hand over his. "Wait!" she said.

He bit back his reply, allowing her to continue.

"I don't want you to say it out aloud," she said. "I'm afraid it'll mean the end of our time together."

Seamus could not keep the twitch from his lips, "It is I!"

Her chest swelled as she held her breath a beat longer. Then it exploded from her. "Do you jest, sir?"

Seamus saw her recognise the excited flush creeping up his neck as he spoke the truth.

"Oh, Seamus! That is, that is—*wonderful*!" she gushed.

Despite his best efforts to maintain his aplomb, Seamus grinned boyishly. "It's marvellous, Dulcinea!"

"You're surprised?"

"I thought for sure the admiral would've appointed McKell, his man aboard the *Ganges*. Christ knows McKell is in line for a promotion before me."

"Do you not keep stressing how pressed for time the expedition is? Perhaps this is how Admiral Otway will ensure the *Discerning* gets underway post haste."

"Perhaps, but it is still an unexpected honour."

"Surely it is merited?"

"Unbeknown to me, Captain Penman of the *Carolina* gave Admiral Otway his own account of the events that I shared with him. Captain Penman told the admiral about the state of affairs aboard the *Discerning* before Captain Fincham died. The admiral was impressed to hear how I turned the whole sorry mess into a productive affair. I'm to keep Captain Fincham's original orders and continue the hydrographic survey down the eastern coast of Patagonia on the Atlantic Ocean and up the western coast on the Pacific." He shook his head in disbelief.

Grace tried for a smile, but her quivering chin won out. "Congratulations, Seamus. Though, my heart is still heavy since your good tidings mean we shall be parting ways soon."

Seamus laid down his spoon and wiped his lips, giving Grace a fixed look that had her put her bread back on the side plate and turn her attention on him. "I've been giving it some thought. I'd like you to come with me," he said.

"I beg your pardon?" Sparks of hope and clouds of confusion

drifted across her face. "But what of the danger? Your declaration that you can't keep me safe?"

"I accept what you said about your abilities with a musket and bayonet, and while I don't ever intend leaving you in a position where you'll need to employ either, I acknowledge that you're skilled enough to defend yourself."

"What of the men? Of their disapproval of me?"

Seamus propped his elbows on the table, his fingers steepled before his lips. "Those with the greatest objection to your presence have resigned their positions. We've lost Kendrick, Webb, and Blom, plus half a dozen marines. What with also losing Captain Fincham and McGilney, we are now rather shorthanded. However, Lieutenant Wadham has secured the services of at least one other able seaman." *Even if it were under dubious circumstances.* Seamus reached for her hand across the table. "Additionally, you're the finest clerk with which I've had the pleasure of serving. And with the loss of McGilney, God knows I'm sorely in need of your assistance right now."

"Oh, Seamus. I don't know what to say. I've readied myself to return to London, even though the thought of leaving you is all but tearing me in two."

"I feel the same, Grace. I apologise for wrenching you in all directions, but I truly need your assistance with the *Discerning*'s logs."

"Very well, then." Grace offered him an olive branch. "I'll endeavour to advise you of my whereabouts from now on. I promise never to leave the ship without your permission."

Seamus stared contemplatively out of the window, noting the purple colours of twilight and the first sprinkling of stars in the sky. Turning back to Grace, he furrowed his forehead earnestly. "And I'll endeavour to educate you of the lie of the land and any potential hazards to allow you to make more informed decisions."

Seamus was extending her a privilege beyond measure—not

dictating what she could or could not do but empowering her to make her own decisions. He only hoped it was not the biggest mistake of his life. He shut his eyes briefly before opening them again. By Neptune's trident, he wished he knew what he was doing.

"Seamus, I apologise for undermining your authority before your officers. Gilly—" Her voice cracked. She swallowed and tried again. "Gilly explained the danger this poses for you."

Seamus leaned in. "And I apologise for my boorish behaviour. As a naval man, my life revolves around hierarchy and control, which are integral for maintaining a tight ship, but perhaps"—he brushed a finger across his lips—"it's not the most conducive approach to being a husband." His raised an eyebrow. "Particularly not *your* husband."

"I still have more to learn about becoming a captain's wife myself."

"Speaking of becoming my wife, I enquired at the cathedral about us being married, but the *padre* wouldn't sanction marrying Anglicans."

"What of our handfasting?"

"A fanciful notion, that while wildly romantic, will not ultimately stand up to legal scrutiny. I want to see it done properly and give Silverton no doubt that you are *my* wife. I also wouldn't wish the legitimacy of any firstborn child of mine to come under question." He grinned, and his heart swelled at the striking cut of her mouth as she smiled back. "I've sailed with many fine men, Dulcinea, but never have I met anyone like you."

"Does this mean I may continue with musket training?" She cocked her head. "Sergeant Baisley says I'm a natural."

Seamus chuckled. "I'll wager you are, Miss Baxter. I'll wager you are." He sighed. "Very well. I'll have a word with the sergeant, but know that a guard will still be stationed at your door whenever I'm ashore." Seamus set his face with absolute certainty, thrilled to see a glimmer of hope bring life to her eyes again. Everything was going to be all right.

The next two days were filled with hasty preparations for their departure. Grace's first job was to officially record her position as captain's clerk in the ship's book. At Seamus's request, she registered her name as G.E. Baxter to prevent unwarranted scrutiny of her gender or relation to the captain by anyone examining the books. Seamus thrilled Grace by promoting Buchanan to clerk's assistant, positioning him perfectly for her to further his education by offering him daily reading and writing lessons. Hicks was promoted as the officers' new steward, and Wadham and Sully progressed in seniority too, with Master's Mate Newlands named Acting Lieutenant.

Seamus knew he was cutting it fine with the number of hands aboard, but of the crew that remained, he had absolute faith in their abilities and dedication to his expedition.

Chapter Twenty-Five

ANCHORED OFF CLARENCE ISLAND, TIERRA DEL
FUEGO ARCHIPELAGO, 27 FEBRUARY 1827

Grace was alone in her berth and unable to sleep. Seamus and the survey crew had once again gone ashore with the burdensome survey equipment. This pattern had been their way of life since they had left Montevideo four months ago, slowly winding their way down the east coast of the long continent to the tip and around the multiple islands of the archipelago.

Eight bells signalled the start of the middle watch. It was midnight, and footsteps shuffled outside her door as the guard changed. Grace stared restlessly into the gloom, blue and yellow lightning illuminating the brewing storm. Except for the rumble of thunder, the rare night-time silence of the anchored ship was disconcerting.

Something solid landed on the deck above. At the muffled, thudding footsteps, Grace shook her head dispassionately. A scuffle? How easily the men still fell for one another's goading. She sighed, wriggling uncomfortably, her feather mattress lumpy and unyielding.

Now, a whoosh of moist air cut her reminiscing short as her cabin door was thrust open, and what seemed like an entire ship's company poured in. Grace bolted up in alarm. Holburton, holding a lantern before him, led Tibbot and two other men into the cabin. Grace stared defiantly against the bright light, heart thumping wildly.

"Holburton!" Grace glared fiercely at the thick-set sailor. Her eyes flicked to the man beside him, and she gasped. Good Lord in Heaven! It was the bald man from the church!

The fourth man stepped around Holburton, revealing a wrinkled, scowling forehead with three livid scars disappearing beneath a maroon headscarf. He wore a surprisingly smart, grey, hip-length jacket, ornately embroidered. A sword scabbard hung from his left hip, a blunderbuss holster on his right. A burgundy sash, matching the headscarf, was tied around his waist. The smoke from his sweet, spicy cigar wafted Grace's way.

"What is this?" she demanded, her voice a dry croak.

Holburton deposited the lantern on the table, and in one smooth motion, dragged Grace off the foot of her cot, thrusting her at the bald man. Before she could cry out, the bald man's large hand muffled her protestation. Grace kicked out, bruising her toes against several hard shins.

"Ya'd best be holdin' her tight, or I'll gut ya where ya stand," said the smartly dressed man, his voice a gravelly, smoke-damaged rasp. The red tip of a cigar glowed before his face.

Grace snuffled furiously through her nostrils. She leaned back into the hands that held her and kicked both legs forward with the ferocity of a bucking horse.

"My, my," jeered the intruder, jumping back. "Is that the way ya greet all your guests?"

Grace's eyes darted to Holburton beside her, her eyes widening. Bloody, bloody hell! The turncoat! And Tibbot? Wadham had trusted him. Her eyes snapped back to the cigar-waving intruder before her.

"Miss Baxter, I take it? You're no easy lass to track down. Been tailing you these past months, just making sure ya were the one I wanted. Course, your man Holburton here was kind enough to confirm." The Irish inflection in his voice did little to soften the sneering grin illuminated by a flash of lightning.

Grace wrenched her head back, sinking her teeth into the bald man's iron fingers, the familiar flavours of tar and manure bringing back a flash of her initiation.

He hissed in her ear and jerked his hand free. "Jaysus, the little bitch bit me!"

"Ha!" the cigar man's laugh rasped like sandpaper. "I was warned to expect a vixen, and I see she's not afraid to use her teeth."

"Who are you?" snarled Grace before the bald man flicked a filthy rag around her head, gagging her tightly. Coarse rope fibres bit into her wrists as rough hands bound them before her.

"Name's O'Reilly." He waved his needle-pointed sword in casual little circles towards the bald man. "The mad bastard ya just bit is Jonas. Yer already acquainted with my other man—that whore's melt, Tibbot."

Grace glowered at Tibbot with the blistering heat of the desert sun.

"Come along now, Miss Baxter, without a song an' a dance, if ya please." Stepping up to Grace, O'Reilly placed the tip of his sword under Grace's chin and pressed it into her soft flesh. She tipped her head as far back as it would go, hissing through her nose as the point punctured her skin. O'Reilly drew on his cigar and exhaled the eddying smoke into Grace's face. "That's of course if ya'd prefer I didn't slit yer throat?" He gave a malicious grin that exposed his dingy grey teeth.

Wide eyed, Grace coughed behind her gag as she shook her head minutely. O'Reilly dropped his sword. The puncture wound stung, and a warm trickle leaked down Grace's neck. O'Reilly drew his face nearer to hers. She recoiled at the reek of rancid meat and stale tobacco. "You won't be wakin' the rest of the hands now, will ya?" his tone warned. "'Cause I'll kill every last one of 'em." He narrowed his eerily pale green eyes, one of them with an odd brown fleck doubling the size of his pupil. "And I'll cut yer bleedin' heart out and gorge on it before yer pretty little eyes if ya make me work that hard." He paused. "We share an understandin'?"

Grace nodded in horror, her heartbeat pounding in her ears.

"Let's go!" O'Reilly flicked his head at his men.

Shivering in the frigid cabin, Grace awkwardly snatched her red tartan shawl draped over the chairback, not wishing to make the same mistake as before. Tibbot tugged her arm, dragging her towards the cabin door.

Grace was hauled onto the main deck where the crumpled body of one of the *Discerning*'s crew lay face down. The ragged ends of the scarf tied around Travis Hopwood's middle were congealing in a black pool of blood. Grace's eyes flicked up to the darkened, empty rigging and along the deck to the bow. Where were the rest of the watch? Goodness gracious, were they all dead? One of the Blighters' broad-shouldered forms loomed out of the dark, orange hair indistinguishable in the low light. He stopped in an instant. Frowning, he opened his mouth in mute protest as he reached for his dagger.

"Oh ho! Not on my watch," murmured O'Reilly past his cigar, lunging at Jack Blight with his needle-point. Jack hissed, curling around the blade like a sunflower closing up for the evening. The whites of his bulging eyes shone in the blue lightning flashes. Grace thrust her shawl against her mouth, the thick tartan and tight gag muting her scream of horror. O'Reilly lowered Jack to the deck, almost gently, and drew his thin blade effortlessly from Jack's chest.

Grace briefly considered running, but the certainty that O'Reilly would use his sword on the rest of the crew reduced her legs to jelly. Tibbot brusquely threw her over his shoulder like a sack of turnips. Grace's stomach dropped as he released her to grip the flimsy rope ladder with both hands. It was incentive enough for her not to struggle, lose her balance, and plunge off his broad shoulder into the icy water below—a fatal move with her mouth gagged and hands bound.

Grace curled miserably in the bottom of the wooden skiff, tucking her freezing bare feet under the hem of her shift as large, icy drops of rain plopped down from the heavy clouds. Her shawl, clutched fiercely to her chest, offered little warmth as Holburton dropped onto the planks beside her. Stinking, wretched bastard! He was not going to get away with this!

The shadowed form of the *Discerning* shrank as they rowed around the far side of a neighbouring island. The heavily laden skiff bobbed about like a cork as the waves of the open water splashed over the low edge. The rain fell steadier. Saturated and shivering, Grace's teeth champed painfully against the gag as the bulky hull of another ship shaped the gloom.

After being hastily hauled aboard and ushered below to a surprisingly luxurious cabin, Grace's gag was removed. She stood trembling and dripping water onto an expensive-looking Persian rug.

A double berth lay between two square, wood-framed windows. The entire interior was painted black, which offset the rich burgundy of the heavy velvet drapes around the lavish bedstead. The garish gold trim of the curtains matched the golden silk pillows on the bed. Large oil paintings of the Irish countryside hung about. The result was a bizarrely decorated but cosy interior.

Everyone bar O'Reilly and Jonas left the cabin. Wiggling the numb fingers of her still bound hands, Grace glared at the griz-zly, bearded Jonas guarding the door, his meaty arms folded across his chest. His bald dome glistened in the lantern light, and his deep-set eyes narrowed guardedly as O'Reilly sauntered over to Grace.

O'Reilly's beady eyes scoured Grace's soaked nightshift, stopping on the glint of the intertwined-heart brooch on her bunched shawl. Grace flicked the edge of her shawl over, and O'Reilly pulled his cigar from his mouth, slicking his tongue over his furry teeth.

"Now then." He breathed his sour fumes over her. "If I untie yer hands, yer goin' to promise to be a good lass, aren't ya?"

Grace's chin jutted out defiantly. "Depends! I don't make promises to filthy beasts who kidnap me in the middle of the night and slaughter my friends." Grace's eyes narrowed. "I hope Captain Fitzwilliam gives you the same treatment you gave poor Jack. That man was mute! He couldn't have raised the alarm even if he wanted to." Waves of fury rolled off Grace. "When Fitzwilliam finds you, he'll have your guts for garters. If you think I'll be a compliant prisoner, you're greatly mistaken."

Jonas scoffed near the door, and O'Reilly's scarred forehead rucked as he gave a loud, husky laugh. "By Jaysus! Brave little thing, aren't ya?" He regarded Grace with something akin to admiration. "So, I'll be freein' ya now." O'Reilly unsheathed his knife. "After which, and dependin' on the way ya behave, ye'll be welcomed as a guest aboard my *Annabelle*. Misbehave an' ye'll experience the pleasure of bein' tied to the bilge pump 'til we reach our destination. 'Tis a hellhole down there, enough to try even the hardest man, let alone a scrap like yerself. 'Tis your choice entirely, *mo chara*."

Grace knew only too well from experience how awful it was in the bilge. It had been her most detested duty aboard the *Discerning*. The reek of excrement and dry rot had caused her to vomit the first time, and she had no desire to be tied up down there for God knew how long. Especially not with the luxury of this cabin on offer.

Peering through the halo of smoke, Grace bristled, displeased with her lack of options. "Very well. I understand."

With a quick flick of the knife, the knotted rope fell away. Clamping her shawl under one arm, Grace rubbed her wrists, encouraging blood into her numb fingers.

"This is where ye'll be sleepin'." O'Reilly waved a casual hand around the cabin. Grace eyed the comfy-looking berth.

"Ha!" O'Reilly laughed huskily, his eyes flinty and humourless. "Not there, *mo chara*. That's where I'll be restin' my pretty little head. You'll be sleepin' over there, where I can keep my eye on ya." Grace glanced at the thin mattress against the bulkhead upon which were a neatly folded padded quilt and a pillow.

"There's a fair few hours yet before dawn, so ya best settle yourself. This'll be yer home for a while."

"Where are we headed?" Grace sounded bolder than she felt.

"You leave the navigatin' to me, darlin'," dismissed O'Reilly. "Best be getting' out those drippin' clothes before ya catch yer death of cold."

"What would you care?" snapped Grace, the fire in her belly flaring.

"Can't have ya dyin' on me, Miss Baxter." O'Reilly pulled on his cigar again. "You're worth a pretty penny." He exhaled a puff of smoke, pointed his cigar at her.

"Captain Fitzwilliam will not pay you. He'll kill you!"

"Oho! You're a spirited one!" O'Reilly laughed callously, tucking the cigar back into his cheek. "'Tisn't the grand captain who'll be payin' us." He paused for dramatic effect. "'Tis your fiancé's reward I'm chasing."

"Silverton?" Grace glared at O'Reilly, her tone smarting. "That pompous lump of lard has no claim over me." The room tilted, and Grace swayed precariously.

"Hold up there, darlin', don't ya be fallin' over." O'Reilly flicked his head at Jonas, and Grace fell into the chair that was thrust behind her. "Can't be handin' over damaged goods, now, can we?" O'Reilly shook his head. "Go on, rid yerself of those wet clothes."

She flicked her eyes down to her sodden shift and snapped her chin up. "And *what* do I change into? You gave me no chance to pack before *kidnapping* me."

O'Reilly gripped her face, his fingers like iron claws. He snatched the cigar from his mouth, his nose almost meeting hers. "You mind yer fancy tongue with me, darlin'." O'Reilly's grip made Grace's teeth ache. "Keep up that cheek, an' Silverton might even thank me for cuttin' it out. Save him from a lifetime of havin' to listen to yer forked tongue wagglin'." O'Reilly thrust her face aside. "Now get back there and get changed."

Grace shivered. The prospect of dry clothes was not a bad one. Rising with as much dignity as she could muster on her wobbly legs, she slunk behind an ornate black folding screen in the corner that was decorated with detailed scenes of a Chinese palace and its gardens. A clean shirt and pair of trousers hung on the back of the screen.

Once dressed, she removed her wedding brooch from the wet and stinking woollen shawl and, ruffling up the hem of the long shirt, pinned it to the inside. Tucking in the hem, she ran her hand down her side, comforted by the little metal hearts pressing against her hip.

Grace stepped out from behind the screen, and O'Reilly gave a cursory nod towards the mattress. "Down ya go. Sleep." He stubbed his cigar butt in an ashtray on the bedside table.

Fatigue and fear had Grace comply without objection. Lying on the thin pad, she turned to face the bulkhead and settled her cheek on the pillow, snatching the quilt over her head. The rush of the evening wore off, and her heart thumped fearfully. Seamus would have no idea who had her or where to begin searching.

When Grace awoke, the rain from the night before had

abated. She scoured the dim cabin, relieved to find it empty. The large double bed was neatly made. With little else to do, Grace folded her quilt and placed it at the end of her mattress. Tiptoeing towards the door, she pressed her ear to the wood, listening to the usual sounds of a ship—the creak of the masts, the familiar, high-pitched singing of the ropes as a sail was brought in, the metallic clanging of pulleys and clews, and sailor's voices. Tentatively, she tried the latch. Locked.

She headed over to the two large windows, both ajar, and cautiously pushed the right-hand pane. Her heart soared as it swung open, the hole easily big enough for her to climb through. She poked her head out, and the strong wind whipped her curls into a frenzy. Her heart plummeted at the drop to the churning grey water of the wake below.

Grace oriented herself at the stern, in the great cabin like that of the *Discerning*, except this one was lavish by comparison. She scanned the horizon, eyeing the shadowed shoreline on the pink hoizon. The drop wouldn't kill her, but the icy water surely would. Sagging in disappointment, she pulled the window to. Circling the cabin, she looked for something with which to arm herself. Not even a bloody quill knife! Resigning herself to a long wait, she sat at the dining table.

Soon, the lock rattled, and the door swung open, letting in a damp gust of wind and the silhouette of O'Reilly—broad in his oilskin. Grace caught a glimpse of the world outside and realised the cabin made up the quarterdeck of a large two-masted brigantine. O'Reilly swaggered into the cabin, with a covered plate and a bottle of ale tucked into his elbow.

"*Dia dhuit ar maidin*," O'Reilly rasped. Grace glowered at his arrogant tone.

"And the pox on you too," Grace replied sarcastically. O'Reilly halted, his scowl blistering enough to melt the flesh off Grace's bones. His scarred face contorted, and he erupted into a barking laugh. He unceremoniously banged the covered plate and bottle down on the table. The top plate jolted off, revealing a surprisingly pretty arrangement of food.

"Jaysus, Mary, and Joseph!" O'Reilly gasped, laughing. "Let the devil break me bones if Silverton doesn't realise what he's gettin' with you." O'Reilly loomed over Grace, his oilskin dripping as the grin slithered from his weathered face. "'Tis not polite when you're offered a civil good-mornin' and ya fling back a curse."

Grace shot to her feet, hovering near the table. "There's nothing *civil* about this situation."

"Behave yourself, darlin', unless ya care to dance on the tip of my sword?"

"Oh, I think not!" Grace drew her shoulders back. "Without me, there's no merchandise. And no merchandise means no payment. Silverton may be many things, but he's no fool, and neither am I."

"Eat up," O'Reilly ordered gruffly. "The piss pot's under the bed." He spun towards the open door. Grace glimpsed the usual flurry of sailors, some scampering up wet netting, a couple carrying ropes and bits of rigging across the deck. The cabin was plunged into dimness again as O'Reilly slammed the door and locked it behind him.

Grace prodded the food on her plate, astounded to recognise chunks of chicken as well as flakes of fish. A hard-boiled egg had been shelled and cut in two. She prodded the vegetables— pickled cabbage, pickled cucumber, and black olives nestled inside raw onion rings. The outer edge of the plate was decorated with thin slices of orange as well as chunks of a yellow, soft-fleshed fruit Grace had never seen before. She poked the new fruit and tentatively licked her finger, a delicious sweetness teasing her grumbling stomach. Despite her dire circumstances, she was thrilled by the delectable fare, which put the standard British Navy rations of bread, beef, and an occasional dollop of butter and cheese to shame.

Gilly's words echoed in her mind. *You can build on the deeds that have happened or put the catastrophes behind you and begin again. 'Tis the way of life, offering a new chance every day.* She stuffed the food into her mouth, contemplating what chances of escape lay ahead of her.

Chapter Twenty-Six

Seamus spotted the *Discerning* as he scrambled around the headland, his thrashing heart skipping a beat at the sight of his dark-hulled ship anchored peacefully in the bay. By Neptune's forked trident! Why had they fired the cannons? Nothing appeared amiss.

Hearing the shots in the icy middle of the night, he had cursed at having to leave his relatively warm and dry tent.

The entrancing lure of one particular person aboard the *Discerning* quickened his steps across the gravelly terrain. It was a windless and sunny day, the first in nearly a week. Until the cannons had echoed in the distance last night, his heart had been joyful and light at the successful expedition, despite the unending rain. Even Buchanan had surprised Seamus by his eagerness to learn about surveying and his ability to retain it all.

On the *Discerning*, tiny figures scurried about, and a cutter was lowered into the water. Seamus strained to pick out Grace's willowy figure amongst the scampering men, but the distance was too great. His eyes watered against the white flashing sparkles of the new morning sun glinting off the ocean. Traipsing through the final stretch of long grass, Seamus and the cutter reached the beach simultaneously. He frowned as Wadham splashed hastily in the shallows. Christ! The man looked as though his mother had died. He restlessly scanned the bay again. Wadham's grim-set face set Seamus's heart pounding.

"Sir!" Wadham made no preamble. "Miss Baxter has been kidnapped."

Fear chilled Seamus's blood. "What? When?"

Wadham's square jaw mashed. "Last night, sir. Just before we fired the cannon." He clawed his fingers through his short, brown hair.

Seamus snarled, snatching the lieutenant's lapel. "Who was it?" Fury vibrated from him like shockwaves from an epicentre. "Tell me, man! Did you see?"

"No, sir. It was in the small hours of the morning, during the torrential downpour. It's likely they hid behind one of the islands and rowed up under cover of dark." Seamus dipped his chin, tightening his uncompromising glower. Wadham cringed. "They killed Jack Blight and Travis Hopwood on the middle watch."

Seamus barely flinched at the mention of his murdered crew. "Was it natives?"

"Unlikely, sir, as it was done neatly with a blade."

Of course it was! Silverton's lot! Despite his engulfing panic, Seamus took several deep breaths and focussed on slowing his thrashing heart. Seamus released Wadham's collar with an apologetic grimace.

"In which direction did they head?"

"Not sure, sir."

"Any witnesses?"

"No, sir. But the new man, Tibbot, is missing. Along with Holburton."

"Christ! I knew Holburton disapproved of her presence, but

to go so far as to have a hand in her abduction? And Tibbot was *your* man!"

Wadham swallowed deeply. "They were both on guard outside the great cabin at the time, sir."

"Damn and blast!" Seamus's brown leather boots crunched across the pebbles, and Wadham scurried to keep up with him. "Prepare to lay chase," ordered Seamus.

"Yes, sir."

"If it's the Irishman who has her, he'll be heading back to London to deliver her to that bastard Silverton. I'll wager it was he who followed us without colours. I believe we have the advantage over that tub with our faster ship—it shouldn't be too hard to catch him. He's only half a day ahead."

Seamus curled his fists tightly, his nails cutting into his palms as his imagination dove into its deepest recesses at some of the horrors Grace could be facing. He had known he could not keep her safe out here, and now she was trapped aboard a ship of strange men, heading back towards a lion's den.

Before dawn the next morning, Seamus rose, unable to sleep. With his hands clamped about a steaming pot of coffee, he scoured the horizon, coloured pink in the sunrise. He glanced up at the *Discerning*'s straining sails. Ordinarily, he would be pleased to see the canvas up and full, but the pain thumping behind his eyes soured his mood.

"Sail ho, fine on the starboard bow!" Blight bellowed from the topmast. With his heart bounding, Seamus slammed his pot on the binnacle housing, sloshing warm coffee over his fingers, and snatched up his spyglass. His thumping heart surged at the prick of sails specked against the colours of the new day. The two-masted brigantine was dead ahead in this wider section of the strait.

Wadham arrived beside him, his spyglass also trained on the fleeing ship, the tension in him humming like the taut stays above. "Is that her, sir?"

"By every instinct I own, I believe so." Seamus's calm words contradicted the iron fist of worry that had been threatening to choke the breath from him since he first learned of Grace's disappearance. "We've got the bastard now."

The *Discerning* ploughed on faithfully all day as they continued the chase, changing course when the brigantine changed hers, easing through the narrower channels. By late afternoon, Seamus checked their progress against the other vessel, exhilarated by how much they had gained. Rolling his neck back to ease the crick of tension, Seamus ordered, "Have the ship cleared for action and beat to quarters."

"Aye, aye, sir," said Bosun, bellowing the repeated orders.

The marine drummer beat out a drum roll that sent a thrill of anticipation down Seamus's arms. It also spurred the men to stow away all unnecessary items and load and ready the guns. Seamus studied the dark-hulled ship. With the archipelago's islands impeding her path, she had no choice but to veer towards the *Discerning*. He glanced at Wadham whose cheeks dimpled as he pressed his lips in satisfaction at his own calculations. Seamus spoke in a low and steady voice. "At this pace, she should be in range of our bow chaser long enough to land some fair shots, wouldn't you agree, Wadham?"

"Yes, sir. The guns are well served. It's only a matter of whether we catch her before nightfall."

Seamus climbed the forecastle deck, frowning at the orb of the sun brushing the flat water of the horizon. The gun crew around the bow chaser worked with practised precision. Bending low over the gun, Seamus sighted the Irishman's ship through the chase port. They were nearly within range.

Standing up and stepping back from the gun, he studied the two remaining Society boys setting out the powder charges and rolling the balls across the deck to select the roundest shot. He caught Cakebread's eye. "Here's your chance to show me I was right in my decision about you, Cakebread. I was sorely mistaken about Holburton. Don't twice make a fool of me." What choice did he have but to trust the lad? Holburton breaking his bonds with these two was not something Seamus had anticipated. They were as thick as blasted thieves. At least under Gunner Ash's scrutiny, Seamus trusted no foul play would be allowed.

"Yes, sir." Cakebread stiffened importantly.

"As soon as they're in range, I need this gun to take out their rigging. Can I rely on you to do this?"

"Yes, sir!" The youngster redoubled his efforts.

Ash bellowed out the well-rehearsed sequence of orders to the gun team. "Charge in." Cakebread loaded the cartridge and cloth wad. "Ram her home!" Da Silva drove the wooden rammer down the muzzle. "Shot your gun!" Buchanan loaded a round shot into the barrel, followed by another wad. "Ram her home!" Da Silva stepped forward with the rammer again. Ash leaned in, pushing a long, wire spike down the touch hole to pierce the flannel cartridge, calling out, "Home!" He immediately ordered, "Run out."

Seamus smirked in satisfaction as Cakebread, Da Silva, and Buchanan heaved on the tackles, trundling the cannon forward until it thumped to rest in the chase port. Ash primed the touch hole with a quill of fine gunpowder and pulled the hammer back to half cock. Gunner Ash was right, mused Seamus; they were a good team, even without Holburton.

Seamus glanced across the stretch of water. He did not need his telescope to observe the antlike figures lined up on the other ship, studying them in return. Silently cursing the fading light, he fixed his gaze on the *Discerning*'s canvas. It could be worse, he reasoned. Had the wind changed direction, requiring a change of sails, they would have been too shorthanded to match the expedience of the brigantine's larger crew. With Gunner Ash waiting expectantly, Seamus peered through the chase port again, elated by the perfectly framed brigantine. By Neptune's trident! The bastard was in range. This was it! It was now or never. He knew there was a risk of the ball missing its target of the masts, endangering Grace, but by all calculable odds, the probability was small—and worth it. He turned to the gun captain, "Gunner Ash, engage the enemy."

"Aye, aye, sir. Stand clear," shouted Ash, fully cocking the hammer and raising his hand to signal the gun ready.

"Fire!" bellowed Seamus.

Ash yanked on the trigger line, and the gun whumped, bursting backwards and snapping to a stop against the breech rope as it expelled a puff of pungent smoke. The ball splashed just behind the Irishman's ship.

"That was short and to the right," said Seamus calmly, quelling his disappointment. With this poor light, there would not be many more chances. "Again, please, Gunner Ash." He clasped his hands tightly behind his back, his grip on his old injured wrist tight enough to keep him discomforted and alert.

The second shot splashed harmlessly. "Again!" ordered Seamus tersely.

Instead of a splash following the third explosion, wood cracked and creaked like a felled tree fighting against its butchered splintering trunk. Blinking away the astringent cloud of gunpowder smoked, his heart surged. Heavens above! It was done! The geometric silhouette of the sails was skewed by the main yard angled awkwardly into the sky.

"You did it, lads. Grand shooting!" Ash roared above the cacophonous cheers.

As the last tip of the sun dipped below the horizon, Wadham stepped up beside Seamus. "It's almost too dark to see her," said Wadham, the flat tone of his voice dousing Seamus's excitement like a bucket of water on a bonfire. Wadham continued, "Destroying one yardarm isn't enough. Their crew will be swarming up the rigging to affect immediate repairs. God knows they've enough hands to do so."

"Damn them to hell!" Seamus called a halt to his gun crew's frantic efforts. Cakebread, Da Silva, and Buchanan breathed heavily, the others milling limply in defeat. Despite his crew's best labours, the crippled ship dissolved into the night.

Seamus stood watch all night, his eyes fixed to the darkness for a careless flame that would show him they were still in pursuit, his ears pricked to the sound of repairs. The black shaggy creature of his nightmares dragged him back through a flood of panic and a dreadful surging surety of impending doom. The prospect of facing a life without Grace was far more terrifying than he believed possible. Having convinced himself he was marrying her out of loyalty to Admiral Baxter, he had entirely disowned his true feelings towards her. With her, he had purpose beyond a career. She was the only woman who had set him thinking about a family, about future generations.

In the early grey of the morning, Seamus's eyes burned hot and prickly from lack of sleep. The tightness in Seamus's chest squeezed into a stabbing pain at the back of his throat. He tried to cough loose the restriction, but it would not budge. What a fool for pitting himself against his original instincts—his inability to keep Grace safe.

Wadham stepped shoulder-to-shoulder with him, his own glass scouring the ship in the distance. "Morning, sir."

"Morning." Seamus rubbed his eyes. He sensed Wadham's restraint from commenting on the obvious and drew back his shoulders. "We've lost a little ground in the night, but I'm confident we'll catch her again," said Seamus.

The muscle in Wadham's jaw twitched. "She could have hidden behind one of the many islands or inlets, waiting for us to pass. She might also have chanced doubling back in the dark. Finding her now is akin to a moving needle in a watery haystack."

"I'm well aware of the tactics at her disposal, Wadham," Seamus's temper flared, fuelled by the sleepless night and an extraordinary amount of worry that he was unaccustomed to bearing. He raked his hand across his stubbled chin and softened his voice. "It's fortunate that this time, we have the advantage of a full day of light ahead of us."

Wadham swept his spyglass away from the Irishman's ship and panned across the nearby shoreline. "By God!" He tensed so stiffly that Seamus sensed the strain vibrating from him.

Almost at the same instant, Blight yelled out from the yardarm, "Ship off the larboard bow!"

Seamus ran an ice-numbed hand over his tousled hair to bring it to order. Heavens above! What now? He lifted his glass. A schooner, with her short foremast and taller mainmast, listed heavily on a sandbar exposed by the low tide. She looked as if she had been stripped, and the skeleton of a newly formed boat leaned on the rocky shore. Men, clad in heavy skin coats, hopped and waved like little crickets. Christ! There were at least two dozen survivors. This was all he needed now.

Wadham lowered his glass, his face tight and white in the frigid morning air. "They're hailing us. Permission to change course and render assistance, sir?"

"She's a sealer," declared Seamus, snapping the telescope shut and wincing at the ache in his wrist. He peered up at the sails, puffed to capacity in the strong wind, and quailed at the prospect of losing their good pace. He glanced towards the Irishman's ship, scowling. "We can ill afford the delay."

Wadham fixed him with a look of incredulity. "Surely to God, you can't in all good conscience pass by men in distress, sir? By the state of them and by virtue of the half-built boat they've attempted, they've already been here a considerable time."

"You needn't point out the obvious, Wadham. I have eyes." The tension in Seamus's shoulders bunched tightly, shooting a headache straight into the base of his skull. Was he not to be granted a reprieve? Every delay took Grace further from him and straight into the hands of that monster. But, if he left those sealers behind, what little remained of the crew's faith in him would become none. No man would stand behind a captain who lacked the morality to put the lives of many over the life of one. Momentarily resenting Wadham for his calm logic, Seamus took a slow, deep breath. "Very well. Make to shore."

Seamus stepped off the *Discerning*'s cutter to a raucous round of applause and cheers, the shipwrecked sailors giddy with relief. While his hands endured vigorous backslapping and never-ending handshakes of thanks, Seamus made a beeline for the ship's master. He was a slim and wiry Scotsman whose dour face belied any happiness at meeting his rescuer. The tip of the man's nose was frostbitten, and his dull, grey eyes glared ungratefully at Seamus.

"Burns is the name. Master of *Prince of Schwarzburg*." He held out a hand and gave Seamus's a quick, bone-crushing shake. "Ye've arrived in time to stave off this mutinous lot. Ran into pack ice and was then blown ashore by a williwaw. We didn't stand a chance."

"Not to worry, Captain Burns. We can accommodate you and your men aboard the *Discerning*. Though, I do ask you to make haste in gathering your belongings as I'd like to keep the advantage of these fair winds. A pressing matter awaits me." He scoured the horizon, staring miserably at the shrinking brigantine as she slid behind a distant island. By Neptune's trident! Wadham's watery haystack prediction had just become his living nightmare.

That evening, the sour Scotsman sat at Seamus's table and heartily attacked the large, roast leg of rhea—the ostrich-like bird roaming wild on the local shores. "Hmm," he hummed appreciatively. "Tastes of young beef. Ye've a decent cook."

"I'm sorry we couldn't transport your furs," said Seamus, spearing a gravy-laden chunk of meat and slicing it neatly. "You'll no doubt return to retrieve your cargo?"

"Aye, if thieving bastards don't get to it first," the hard-faced Scotsman grunted. He squinted at Seamus. "What trouble sees ye racing about these parts?"

Seamus hesitated, arching his scarred wrist back to ease the tightness. His dislike of the man caused him to pause before divulging his sensitive news. "My fiancée was recently kidnapped from my ship."

"Yer fiancée?" The man's wiry eyebrows shot up. "What man in his right mind drags a woman to this godforsaken frozen hellhole?"

Laying down his knife and fork, Seamus stiffened and gulped his wine silently.

Too full of his own self-importance to notice Seamus's discomfort, Burns bemoaned, "I'll declare one thing, ma ship was tight, staunch, and strong when we left London. And sufficiently manned. Not a man alive can say ma ship's company didn't do their utmost to preserve our sealer."

"Captain Burns, I'm not the one to whom you need to plead accountability." Seamus placed his empty glass on the table and stood to signal the end of their conversation. "I'm sure the British consulate in Buenos Aires will be eager to hear your account. Your extreme adventure must have you exhausted. I hope you find your accommodation in my charthouse adequate." Seamus smiled dismissively, and Burns left, muttering unintelligibly in Gaelic.

Two weeks of fair weather and steady winds had them back in Buenos Aires in record time. The hands of the sealing schooner disgorged onto the dock. Seamus barely received a grunt of goodbye from Burns before the miserable man disappeared into the crowd, leaving Seamus simmering with rage and impatience at the missed opportunity to hunt down the Irishman.

Beside him near the gangplank, Wadham grunted. "You'd think he'd offer a word of thanks for his safe deliverance."

Seamus pressed his lips tightly. "Some folk wouldn't know good fortune if it struck them in the head."

"What now, sir? How long until we depart for the archipelago?"

Seamus hesitated. He had not anticipated rescuing a ship-wrecked crew, but the fortune of depositing them back to civilisation meant he was partway back to London himself. Had he not caught the Irishman within a couple of days after his attack, he would have had to press on with his surveying orders with no chance of chasing after Grace unless he wanted to risk a court martial and a firing squad.

"I'm continuing on to London."

Wadham twisted sharply, his baritone deep with disapproval. "What of our orders, sir? We've no authority to return to London."

"There's no *we* about this, Wadham. *I'm* returning to London."

"But, sir! We'll be hanged for piracy. I can't allow you to steal a Royal Navy ship to go chasing after your bride-to-be on a whim."

Seamus snapped upright. "A whim? Christ, Wadham, I'd have expected some understanding, from *you* of all people."

Tugging his ear uneasily, Wadham said, "I understand she's your intended, sir, and that you want her with you. But is she not better off being returned to London?"

"No, she's bloody not!" exploded Seamus. "And I wasn't planning on stealing the blasted ship!"

Wadham flinched at the severity of Seamus's reaction.

Seamus wadded his fist against his mouth and screwed his eyes closed. He knew he was being unfair. Wadham had no notion about the depth of Silverton's obsession with Grace. Should he chance sharing the details with him? If he was about to abandon a fellow officer, he supposed he at least owed him an explanation.

Seamus opened his eyes. "Apologies for my outburst, Wadham. This situation leaves me no choice but to share a delicate matter with you. I'd appreciate you keeping it to yourself."

He waited for Wadham to nod warily.

"It's not safe for her to return to London," said Seamus. "Particularly not to the man who attacked her and prompted her to flee London in the first place."

"Lord Silverton?" frowned Wadham.

"Yes. They were betrothed, and he assumed it his right to take a heavy hand to her. His perverted way of controlling her."

"Jesus! I had no idea." Wadham blanched.

"And so you understand my urgency to reach her?"

"I understand your *personal* quandary, sir. But what of your orders?"

"I'm resigning my commission. It's the only way to earn enough freedom to return to London immediately. I'll find passage aboard any ship heading back."

"Good God man, you'd sacrifice your career for a woman? You've only just been made captain. What of your duty to the men? To the mission?"

A sour ball of regret squeezed its way up Seamus's throat. "Regrettable to say the least, but a burden I'm prepared to bear for Miss Baxter's sake. I owe Admiral Baxter a debt for my life. While it's not his life I am attempting to save here, it would be remiss of me to niggle over details when the life of his beloved niece is at stake."

Wadham stepped up to the gunwale, gripping the wooden railing, knuckles white. "I can't make up my mind whether you're a bloody fool or a bloody hero, Fitzwilliam!"

Seamus let Wadham's slip of formality slide. It was not that long ago that they were equals, and Seamus had valued his opinions then, just as he did now. "I suppose, only time will tell," said Seamus. He pivoted neatly and headed below to write his letter of resignation.

Chapter Twenty-Seven

NORTH ATLANTIC OCEAN, 29 MARCH 1827

Miss *Baaaxter* ... *Miss Baaaxter!* The voice grew louder and more urgent through the haze of sleep. *Miss Baxter!*

The call of Grace's name was accompanied by a brutal shake that jolted her awake. Sleep blurred her vision, and she blinked rapidly, revealing O'Reilly's dimmed face. The sky outside carried a tinge of pink, the sun not yet awake.

Grace threw her hands up. "Get away from me, you harbinger of evil!"

"Oh, the devil mend ya." O'Reilly clamped Grace's mouth with his calloused hand. "Hush ya gob, woman."

Grace's panic pounded in her chest. O'Reilly's predatory face froze with the cunningness of a leopard laying eyes on its prey, and he angled his head to listen. All around, shouts of alarm and frantic thumping feet rolled in like thunder. Snarls and screeches clashed with the unmistakable clinking of metal on metal. Grace bolted upright, her senses snapping awake. They were being boarded. Seamus! He had not fired upon them this time, and she rejoiced that his tactic of stealth had been rewarded. As terrifying as it was to have balls blasted at the ship, she had almost yelled out in victory when the *Discerning*'s ball had splintered the yardarm.

"*Allāhu Akbar!*"

"God damn it all to hell, they've boarded." O'Reilly's explosion thrust Grace into her mattress. "Stay put! Lock the door behind me."

"What's happening?" Grace winced as zinging metal ended in a bowel-loosening scream, and she shot to her feet. Her flame of hope that threatened to splutter out in disappointment flared again in alarm.

"Fecking Ottoman corsairs! May the devil swallow 'em sideways." O'Reilly raced to the far side of the berth to retrieve his sword. "They've been pursuing us since yesterday, but the bastards have caught us."

"How's that possible? The United States put an end to the Barbary states a few years back." Grace frowned in concentration, urgently recalling Gilly's naval history lessons. The bulkhead behind her vibrated as something weighty crashed on the deck above.

"We're sidlin' past the Barbary Coast. Must be a few fleas left takin' their chance!" O'Reilly slung the scabbard mounting strap over his head and across his shoulder. "Heathens want me men." He tightened the leather sword belt around his waist, the metal buckle biting into his soft belly. "We're not flyin' any colours to deter 'em." O'Reilly shouldered roughly past Grace, grabbing his boots.

Grace made a strangled noise. "Then raise the British ensign!"

"And miss the merriment? I think not, *mo chara*." O'Reilly

flashed her a discoloured grin before bolting through the door, needle-point drawn.

If Gilly's stories were to be believed, she would suffer a worse fate with the Ottoman corsairs than with O'Reilly. Long-gowned men swarmed like white ants over the rails of the *Annabelle*. Grace slammed the door, her heart pounding against her ribs, the hairs on her neck prickling like pins with the terror of it all. Snapping the lock, she yanked out the key, ramming it into the pocket of her trousers.

Grace wedged the back of a dining chair under the latch. Disregarding O'Reilly's potential ire, she rummaged through his drawers, looking for something she could use as a weapon. She grabbed a pair of chunky silver shoe buckles. Tossing open the lid of the small box beside her makeshift bed, Grace snatched up several of her clean monthly rags that O'Reilly had ungraciously dumped on her pillow after she had asked him for them. Knotting the rags together and tying them through the heavy buckles, Grace whirled her makeshift weapon above her head like a lasso. It might not be as effective as a metal ball-and-chain flail, but it was better than nothing.

Sinking onto the ornate bed, Grace glued her eyes to the locked door, expecting it to splinter open at any moment. She swung her head, following the warring men in their grisly dance from one side of the deck to the other. Behind her, a bloodcurdling yell launched her to her feet. Spinning violently, Grace braced her feet apart and swung her improvised weapon back. She jerked as a plummeting body smashed into the protruding corner of the part-open window. In a blink, the black-bearded face contorted as it connected with the wooden frame and tumbled in a fold of white robes, splashing solidly into the water below.

Time passed with infinitesimal sluggishness, but eventually, the noises changed from snarls and yells to groans and chokes until an eerie silence descended. Footsteps thumped across the deck towards the cabin door. Grace squeaked in terror as the brass latch rattled and the wood panels vibrated under a pounding fist. She sagged with relief at O'Reilly's hoarse voice.

"Open the door, Miss Baxter!"

Dropping her makeshift weapon on the dining table, Grace pulled the chair aside and took the warm key from her pocket. With trembling fingers, she slid the key into the lock and hesitated. "I'll let you in on one condition, Mr O'Reilly."

"Don't you *mister* me, lass! Open the door!"

"On one condition."

"Agh, the pox on ya! I'm in no mood to negotiate. Open this door, or I'll open yer belly and watch yer gizzards slither out."

"No, you'll not. I'm worth nothing to you dead!" Grace pressed her forehead to the wood, venturing bravely, "I wish to be granted time on deck. I'm done being confined like a songbird. I'm sure Lord Silverton never meant for me to die of boredom."

There were several beats of silence, and Grace took a cautionary step back from the door, expecting O'Reilly to kick it in. Footsteps shuffled outside. "Jaysus wept, yer a bloody mulish one, aren't ya? Fine. One hour a day, right after the midday meal," barked O'Reilly. "Now open this bloomin' door!"

Grace flicked the key, recoiling in horror at the sight of O'Reilly's shirtfront saturated in a sticky, dark crimson. A trail of red was splattered across his sullen, disfigured face. Noticing Grace's horror, he wiped the back of his sleeve across his mouth, crudely applying a bloodied rouge to his lips. Beneath the congealing blood, he was dangerously pale, and the crudely tied dressing on his upper arm was bright red with fresh blood. He swayed momentarily and clutched the wooden doorframe.

Staggering in, he knocked Grace aside, growling, "On yer bed. I haven't time for ya right now."

"I protest at you always rudely ordering me around," she declared.

O'Reilly reared like a cobra ready to strike. "Shut your gob, ya yammerin' strumpet!" He caught sight of the homemade flail on the table and growled again—whether in appreciation of her ingenuity or in disapproval, Grace did not know. Just as suddenly, the fight left him, and he sighed wearily. "You've got yourself your daily sojourn. If you don't leave me be, you'll lose it before it begins." He collapsed in a bloody, boneless heap on his berth. "Take off me boots." O'Reilly's words were muffled.

"I'm your prisoner, not your servant," retorted Grace.

"If you make me get off this bed, I swear by all the holy saints, I'll take yer own bloody flail to ya."

O'Reilly might not gut her, but Grace did not trust that he would not beat her. She hastened over and unclasped the buckles on his blood-soaked boots. Tugging hard, she dropped them to the floor in disgust and wiped her shaking, bloody hands on a muslin cloth beside the washbasin. Swivelling at the sound of gentle, rasping snores, Grace stared at O'Reilly's prone figure lying half on and half off the bed.

Catching sight of the open door, she stepped out into the warmth of the early morning sun. A solid hand reached for her shoulder. Whirling in terror, Grace blocked the hand with a vicious back-blow worthy of Ben Blight's praise. She yelped but braced, ready for a further assault. The hand hanging limply from the quarterdeck above was the bloodied hand of a dead man. Grace stared hypnotically at his death mask. Beneath the skewed turban shone black hair the same colour as his chest-length beard. His plump, purpled lips were agape with the gasp of his last breath, and Grace's skin crawled at his sightless brown eyes fixed on her. At the sound of a fleshy squelch and a gasp of pain, Grace spun just as Tibbot drew his sword from the chest of one of the few enemies still aboard. Glued to the deck with distress, Grace witnessed the *Annabelle*'s crew systematically slaughter every surviving invader without quarter, unceremoniously tossing the butchered corpses overboard. A renewed waft of blood and excrement assailed Grace's nostrils, and her stomach heaved in objection. She flicked her eyes back to Holburton as he gleefully surveyed the cleared deck. He caught sight of Grace and fixed his hawk-like eyes on her. Her heart skipped a beat. Traitorous bastard.

Grace climbed up to the quarterdeck, avoiding the dead man sprawled on the planks. Shivers careened over her scalp. Rat's tails! She was not alone. A lanky fellow, with features that reminded Grace of a mournful street dog, slithered alongside her, glowering at the chaos below. His clothes were little more than rags.

"What do you want?" Her chin quivered as her liver threatened to leap up her throat. "Leave me, or I'll scream."

The man lowered his eyes, stammering in an Irish voice as rich as warm treacle. "Hush, Miss. You don't want to do that."

"Why not?" Grace stepped back.

"Your friend Holburton won't need a second invitation to stick you like this lot." He waved a bony hand at the carnage below. "Don't know what you did to rile him up so, but he's set to do you in the first chance he gets."

"What's it to you? Why warn me?"

"I'm like you. Brought aboard O'Reilly's ship against my will. Even though this godforsaken tub is all I've known as a home since Tibbot peeled me off the streets of Dublin as an orphan, I can't say I view it with much fondness." He raised his gaze hesitantly.

"Why do you care if Holburton kills me?"

"I've been the underdog my whole life. Learned how to stand up for myself the hard way." He waved his left hand in the air, his disfigured fingers waggling stiffly. "If there's one thing I abhor more than anything, 'tis an unfair fight."

"Who are you?"

"I'm Darcy."

Grace eyed the neatly tied red kerchief around his neck. "My name is Grace Fitzwilliam. Captain Seamus Fitzwilliam of the *Discerning* is my fiancée."

Darcy's brow rumpled, his voice heavy with regret. "I know."

"He'll come looking for me!" Grace raised her chin.

"I know," he repeated. "He fair near got us last time."

"What do you want, Mr Darcy?"

Lifting the edge of his shirt, he drew out a knife tucked into the top of his breeches. Grace yelped, slamming her backside against the bulwark to escape being stabbed.

"Hush!" Darcy ducked his head and swivelled his eyes below, checking if they had been heard. Frowning, he rotated the knife and offered it hilt first. "'Tis for you."

Placing her hand on her heart to steady it, Grace studied the neat knife made of bone with strips of leather around a handle that would fit comfortably into her palm. It was crude compared to the honed metal blade that blacksmiths produced, but the bone blade had been sharpened into a thin edge.

"That Holburton's a nasty one." He waved the knife at her. "Take this. Give yourself a fighting chance if it comes to it."

Grace regarded the young Irishman. Her face was damp with perspiration. Surely if he meant to harm her, he would have stabbed her outright? She already knew this crew had no qualms about impaling innocents. "Why should I trust you? If they're so bad, why haven't you escaped yourself?"

"O'Reilly has eyes and ears in most ports. I know too much of their dealings for them to let me go peacefully."

Grace's eyes flicked down to the blade. One nudge and she could end him. A glimmer of regret drew the centre of Darcy's forehead up, and his eyes flicked to the blade aimed at his unprotected belly. He gave her a look that said he would not stop her if she wished to stick him with it. Grace briefly wondered whether he actually wanted her to. Being a captive aboard this ship was hard enough while favoured by O'Reilly. She could not imagine the hardship this good Samaritan might endure if he crossed O'Reilly.

"But why help me?" Grace stayed light on her toes in readiness to launch out of his reach.

"I recognised a fire in you the night O'Reilly took you. You showed no fear. Reminded me of my sister. She had the same liveliness about her." One corner of his mouth drew up. The commotion on the main deck shuffled nearer, and Darcy thrust the leather handle into her palm. "Flaming heck! Just hide it!" Turning abruptly, he reached down for the sprawling dead man and tipped him overboard with a resounding splash. Without giving Grace another look, he dropped to the main deck.

Grace was in turmoil. Who was this stranger aboard this heaving cesspool of evil? This crew had had no qualms about murdering Travis Hopwood or Jack Blight, but they had not hurt her—yet. She was sure O'Reilly's wrath played a large deterrent in this, but Holburton was not familiar with or afraid of her captor. Darcy's urgent whispers of caution sat like soured milk in her stomach. Having Darcy's knife renewed her hope for escape. Even though all she had stabbed up until now was a sack of hay, she was willing to give human flesh a go. Holburton better watch himself.

O'REILLY AWOKE at midday and struggled up groggily from the big double bed, peering at Grace eating her meal with as much curiosity as a shark eyeing a clump of seaweed.

"Thank you for your concession earlier, Mr O'Reilly." Grace attempted a conciliatory tone in the hope that she might negotiate some more terms in her favour.

"I told ya, don't *mister* me," he snarled. "O'Reilly's fine."

"Jonas fetched you some food, for when you awoke." Grace pointed to a large plate on the dining table overflowing with a selection of delicious morsels. Grace's plate and cup were already empty. She frowned at the dried, bloody scales flaking from O'Reilly's face and hands as he reached for a cigar from the wooden box on the bedside table. Ignoring her, he struck a match. He exhaled slowly, and the cloud of fragrant smoke filtered lazily out of the open window. He spotted Grace eyeing him.

"If 'tis idle chit-chat you're after, ye can save yer breath."

Grace averted her eyes down. Spotting her own shirt, no longer white, she pressed a tight smile. "*Captain* O'Reilly, I was hoping to procure another pair of breeches and a shirt. So that I might launder these ones."

"If it'll shut yer blatherin', there's some in that bottom drawer." O'Reilly nodded towards the chest of drawers. "Though I suppose ya know that already since ya rifled through there yesterday." He took another drag of his cigar. "And then I'll thank ya to still yer tongue and let me sup in peace."

Grace bristled at the scolding, but she inclined her head stiffly at O'Reilly's offer. She fetched the tan trousers and white, soft-brushed cotton shirt from the drawers and slunk behind the privacy screen. Transferring her brooch to the inside of the clean shirt, she patted it against her hip. Oh, Seamus! Where was he?

Slipping from behind the screen, Grace lurched to a halt. O'Reilly stood naked by his dressing table, furiously scrubbing himself with a foaming loofah sponge lathered with eye-watering, acerbic lye soap. For propriety's sake, Grace wanted to peel her eyes away from the naked man, but she was inexplicably drawn to his battle-weary back with its tapestry of healed scar tissue. A nasty purple slash twisted from his armpit to his hip. That cut must have near sliced him in half! O'Reilly edged around, and Grace sucked in a horrified breath. His thick-waisted stomach was flamed with stretchmarks, as were his flat, drooping breasts.

"Bloody rats' tails! You're … you're … *a woman?*" Grace's

teeth snapped together in an astonished grimace. "But your clothes ... this ship ... you're a pirate!"

"Course I'm a bloody woman," growled O'Reilly, "but I'm no pirate. I prefer *shrewd negotiator*. Procurer of goods, if ya will. An' I'm not opposed to a spot of mercenary labours here or there. Anyone not prepared to do business my way has the pleasure of being introduced to me needle."

Soap bubbles, tinged pink, dribbled into the blood-tinged tub of water in which O'Reilly stood. Grace gasped at the flap of skin hanging open on her upper arm, the yellow globules of fat visible under the skin. Blood trickled down her arm, painting over the gaudy red and blue anchors, ships, and goddesses of liberty tattooed into her skin. Unperturbed, O'Reilly continued her savage scrubbing with the loofah.

Grace looked away, legs wobbling as she slumped at the dining table. A peculiar grunting and hissing replaced the splashing sounds of O'Reilly's cleansing ritual. Unable to contain her curiosity, Grace swivelled her eyes around and instantly wished she had not. O'Reilly was tugging at a hooked needle threaded with a long piece of gut, unskilfully sewing the sliced skin together. Grace swung her head back around, dizzy from the repugnant sight.

A light ruffling and swishing accompanied O'Reilly's efforts at dressing. The wooden chair scraped the floorboards, and a scrubbed, respectable-looking, and surprisingly pleasant-smelling O'Reilly sprawled beside her, seizing the plate of food. Grace scrutinised her. The face was still scarred and ugly, the eyes were still green and lethal, the clothes were still a man's. Nothing about her was even remotely feminine.

Grace initially avoided leaving the cabin despite O'Reilly's permission. The horrors of the blood-slicked deck haunted her. And now that she knew Holburton still had it in for her, she had to guard her step. Eventually succumbing to her stifling cabin fever, Grace bravely stepped out. She was relieved to find that the days of scrubbing she had heard had yielded thoroughly cleaned decks. Not brave enough to venture around the main deck, Grace climbed to the high ground of the quarterdeck.

The *Annabelle* pitched heavily in the swell, and Grace folded her arms in protection against the fierce wind. She was surprised to find them anchored off the coast of an isolated island. The narrow beach had a strip of white sand beneath a towering, crumbly cliff face. The rain-laden sky was tinged with hints of yellows and pinks, cut by a flash of zigzagging lightning. Large crashing breakers rolled onto the narrow beach where a little wooden boat had left drag marks in the sand.

Hard thumping of boots ascended the quarterdeck stairs, and Jonas's domed head popped up. Grace tensed, unsure whether to return to the empty cabin or stay and enjoy the freshness of the impending storm and deal with Jonas's inane chit-chat. At least it was not Holburton. The bald sailor had been nothing but polite to Grace, but she was not fooled. She had seen him hunting her back at the church ruins. She braced as Jonas shuffled over.

"Mornin', miss." He stood at a respectable distance, taking in the vista of the island.

"Good morning."

"They picked a rare mornin' to fetch fresh water."

Grace bristled. "Hmph. Is that where O'Reilly disappeared to at dawn? What's the master of the vessel doing fetching water like a deckhand?"

"Let's just say she's unaccustomed to permanent company in her cabin. You've quite the knack for settin' her teeth on edge," said Jonas smugly. "'Tis best for us all she clears her head. Her son's the man to help her do that."

"Her *son*?" Grace's head snapped towards the bald man. "Who's her son?"

Jonas's lips curled in a warped sneer. "Why, Tibbot, of course. I'm pretty fond of the wee bugger myself."

"Tibbot!" Grace spluttered. "So … so … if he's O'Reilly's son and … and … you … then … is O'Reilly your *wife*?"

Jonas barked a hostile laugh. "And here's me thinking you were a bright one. You don't need to be married to plough a field and sow your seed, you know? But indeed, she's me wife. Married me to spite her da. 'Twas a long while back now. We're all three O'Reillys, so Tibbot and me are called by our given names." The fabric of Grace's trousers pressed around the outline of her thighs in a powerful gust, and Jonas eyed her lewdly.

"Don't size me up like you do your dock whores! What will *Mrs* O'Reilly have to say about *Mr* O'Reilly lusting after her prisoner?" At Grace's threat, Jonas clenched his fists.

"I'd caution you to silence your tongue on that matter, girlie," he growled. "O'Reilly would gut me on the spot and" — he wavered— "she wouldn't hesitate to finish you off too, reward or no reward." The flash of fear in Jonas's eyes left no doubt in Grace's mind that his prophecy held a ring of truth.

Chapter Twenty-Eight

After weeks of boredom, Grace awoke one morning, immediately aware that the *Annabelle* was no longer undulating over the oceanic swells. She caught the sound of civilisation: a horse's whinny and metal-shod hooves clopping along cobblestones, the bawl of a fishmonger selling his wares, and the gentle *phut-phut* of a tugboat. London! Who could forget the stink of the Thames? Her heart flopped in dread, and panic slithered down her arms and tingled in her fingers. *Silverton.*

O'Reilly kept her locked in the cabin for the day, and Grace was as alert as a cat in a granary when the cabin door slammed open. O'Reilly's boots clomped across the floorboards.

"Rise and shine, Miss Baxter." O'Reilly's gravelled voice was like fingernails scraping a blackboard. Frantically processing her options and pressing her elbow against the hidden knife at her hip, Grace made no effort to move from her cross-legged position on her mattress. She could not stab O'Reilly now. Not with all her men around. O'Reilly threw a paper-bound package on the mattress beside her. "Put that on. Need to have you half presentable."

Grace hesitated, and O'Reilly kicked her. The blow caught her brooch, stabbing it into her flesh. Grace shrieked, and her leg shot out in a reflexive spasm of pain.

"Pah!" spat O'Reilly. "Barely scraped ya. If ya don't get up, I'll show ya what a proper kickin' feels like. Now hop to!"

Rubbing her stinging thigh, Grace stood and exaggerated her hobbling. Perhaps O'Reilly would not rush her if she believed her injured. It would give her time to think.

Unwrapping the paper, Grace frowned at the pale, yellow gown and dainty lace headpiece. Ducking behind the screen, Grace wriggled into the rustling folds of the ill-fitting dress and skewered the lace atop her head with the pins without decorum. It smelled of stale sweat and old ale. Jonas likely procured it from one of his dock whores, she thought ungratefully. She was in the middle of her courses, so she looped a fresh rag onto her makeshift girdle that she had fashioned from a strip of canvas. She buried the soiled rag beneath the discarded trousers on the floor, not caring who might have to clear it up later.

Stepping from behind the screen, Grace pinched her lips and stuck her chin out at O'Reilly's scarred face that had turned to granite. "Oh, what I wouldn't do to wedge me fist through that insolent smirk of yours, darlin'."

O'Reilly pressed a meaty fist into Grace's cheek, her simmering anger vibrating beneath her knuckles. She leaned in closer, their noses nearly touching, and Grace twisted her head aside.

"Come along, Miss Baxter. I'm sure yer fiancé is dyin' to get his hands on you."

Grace clutched her mouldy-smelling tartan shawl around her shoulders. Flanked by O'Reilly and Jonas, Grace was whisked towards a nondescript hackney carriage waiting at the end of a rotting jetty. This part of the river had not been used for some time and was disconcertingly devoid of life. She glanced back at the *Annabelle*, her heart swooping at Darcy standing stiffly on the forecastle with his hands behind his back. His black hair was sleeked back, his hooded eyes expressionless. Beside him, Holburton unfolded his arms and waggled the fingers of one hand in her direction in a dismissive wave. The Society bastard could not have looked more pleased with himself. Grace wanted to wave farewell to Darcy, but she was afraid it would bring him to Holburton's attention. Darcy had risked his life to arm her. She could not betray his kindness now. O'Reilly would surely kill him, not to mention the mischief Holburton might cause.

She squeaked as Jonas hoisted her into the carriage where an enormous man filled one of the benches. Grace whirled around as the carriage door slammed without O'Reilly or Jonas joining her inside.

"No more lip from you now, darlin'," warned O'Reilly. "Watson here's not half as forgivin' as meself."

"What are you doing? Where am I going?" Despite her resentment of the O'Reillys, Grace was at least accustomed to their unpleasantness. With them, she knew her limits. She eyed the colossal man before her who smelled of sausage and ale.

"'Twas a pleasure doin' business with ya, Miss Baxter. Hope to see ya again someday," rasped O'Reilly through the open window. O'Reilly lifted a cautionary eyebrow at the giant man, her scarred forehead rucking. "This one's a cheek about her. You'll keep a close eye on the package if you're wanting to deliver her in one piece."

The solemn man in the carriage squinted at Grace before scoffing to O'Reilly, "Little slip like that don't stand a chance against me." He tossed a bulging burlap sack of coins through the window, and Jonas staggered as he caught it. "Compliments o' his lordship."

O'Reilly banged the carriage door to signal the driver, her rasping laughter ringing out after the departing carriage. Grace sank back on the rear bench, eyeing the hulking man opposite her warily. As she pressed her elbow to her hip, the bone knife hooked in the top of her girdle offered a glimmer of comfort. Grace peered forlornly out of the window as the inhabitants of London carried on with their daily lives.

At one point, the lumbering man's head drooped in a doze. Seeing her chance, Grace threw herself at the door, not caring how much it would hurt to barrel from the moving carriage. The handle jammed. Stinking bloody seaweed! The stranger snarled, his fingers spiking into Grace's arm as he threw her back into her seat. His other fist punched deeply into her solar plexus. Pain exploded in her belly like a show of fireworks, the burning embers blasting into her lungs and sucking the air from them. Grace gagged and coughed.

Watson drew his knife with equal speed and jabbed the point against her neck. "Try that again, and I'll take your ear," he growled. Grace shuddered as she managed to sip in a wheeze of air.

The metallic clatter of hooves on the cobbles eventually morphed into a heavy stomping on the packed earth of a narrow country lane. Densely wooded thickets fragmented out into open fields clumped with freshly ploughed ruts. At the sight of this increasing isolation, Grace hugged her bruised middle to steady her churning innards. The further they were from town, the further she was from rescue.

The steady beat of hooves slowed, and Grace's heart sped up, her armpits prickling with sweat. The carriage was swallowed by the black wrought-iron mouth of a pair of gates, guarded by two beady-eyed gargoyles and a high, stone-columned wall. Etched into the sandstone blocks and blackened from the weather was the surprisingly pleasant-sounding *Clovervale Manor*. The smartly dressed gatekeeper, standing stiffly near the gatehouse's white wooden door, glared after the carriage with the same suspicious scowl as the two gargoyles.

The hair on the back of Grace's neck rose as they swept up the winding, tree-lined driveway. She imagined that the carriage wheels crunching on the gravel sounded a lot like one of the hunched gargoyles chomping on dry bones. The front of the mansion shone the sickly yellow of a bilious sailor just before he vomited.

Grace's courage juddered to a halt as she peered up at the looming, three-storey mansion, rigid with the uniformity of its matching rectangular windows and French doors. No downpipes. Ben might have taught her how to be sure footed up a ship's rigging, but even he would not chance those narrow windowsills. A premonitory shiver pricked the back of her neck as a large shadow fluttered across one of the French doors on the lower floor.

A footman, butler, and maid waited at the bottom of the beige stone steps. Where was Silverton? The knot in Grace's chest tightened. If the wigged footman sensed the tremble in her hand, his professionalism forbade him from showing it. The borrowed slippers on her feet were unbearably heavy as she lifted them to walk towards the yawning mouth of the dragon's lair.

In unison, the butler bowed, and the maid curtsied. The butler straightened up formally in his black suit, his eyes darting over Grace's shoulder to the giant in the carriage. The tightening of the butler's lips was as infinitesimal as his nod. Behind Grace, the carriage door slammed shut and immediately drew away. The butler's unsmiling mouth curved down at the corners, his voice nasal through his squashed nose that looked similar to a boxer's.

"Welcome to Clovervale Manor, Miss Baxter. I'm Dickson, the butler." He turned to the dark-haired woman beside him. "Your lady's maid, Lloyd."

The maid wore a blue cotton dress with a high, round neck

and standing collar. A white mob cap covered a tight bun that tweaked the corners of her eyes upwards.

"Welcome, milady." The adolescent girl was stunning, her hazel eyes warm and welcoming. Grace fleetingly acknowledged the servants.

"Lloyd will show you to your room, milady, so you might freshen up before you acquaint yourself with his lordship," offered Dickson.

At the mention of Silverton, Grace's breath caught in her throat, and her cheeks flamed. Lloyd noticed her reaction. "You must be awfully anxious to be with his lordship again, milady?" The bubbly maid's eyes crinkled as she beamed sweetly.

Grace frowned bitterly. "I wager you're new here?"

Lloyd's smile faltered. "Y-yes, milady. I started last week."

"I can tell. Your naivety in believing Lord Silverton is anything other than a kindly employer is as plain as the nose on your face."

"P-pardon, milady?" Lloyd stumbled after Grace.

"Never mind. Just show me to my room." Grace was exhausted, and right now, she relished some privacy.

"Yes, milady." Flushing at Grace's dismissive manner, Lloyd took the lead up the sweeping staircase, chattering the whole way up. At the landing, Grace followed her down the right wing. The stale waft of an unused room greeted Grace. Two olive-green armchairs faced a grey-and-white marble mantel beneath which a fire blazed. She noticed a fire poker. She eyed the metal rod, mentally estimating its weight as Sergeant Baisley had taught her to do with a sword. Grace gave the ornately carved bedstead a calculating gaze. The sheets! She could shred and fashion them into a rope. Thank you, Sailmaker Lester! She studied the tall rectangular windows, thrilled they were big enough to climb through.

"H-his lordship has arranged several gowns for you, milady." Lloyd timidly waved at the dressing room. "There are day dresses and riding dresses, should you choose to venture out," she explained a little more confidently. "There's a riding cape and a pelisse. Oh, and—"

"My goodness, you're quite the chatterbox," interrupted Grace, plonking herself in the chaise longue that overlooked the gardens. Unwrapping her mouldering shawl, Grace held it out. "See my shawl is washed."

The maid tentatively took the foul garment, and Grace resolved to soften her attitude towards her. She seemed sweet enough. If she could not make her own way out of here, having an ally might be prudent. Smiling, Grace said, "I've suffered quite an ordeal, Lloyd, but this is no excuse for my poor behaviour. I apologise." The young maid fumbled with the shawl, almost dropping it, her mouth popping open. She had clearly never had an apology from a mistress before, mused Grace.

"N-no, milady, I apologise if my prattling upset you." Lloyd curtsied, her eyes darting respectfully to the carpet.

"My troubles aren't of your doing," placated Grace. "How long did you say you've worked here, Lloyd?"

"But a few days, milady," offered Lloyd cautiously. "I shouldn't be so glad under the circumstances, but I was greatly in need of this job. My father left my mother a few months back, and it's been up to me and my older sister to feed the young ones." Lloyd wrung the dirty shawl.

"What circumstances?"

"Of how this position became available." Lloyd stared wide eyed. "Oh, you'll not have heard of the tragedy."

Grace shook her head. "Please, enlighten me."

"His lordship's previous maidservant was my second cousin, Jenny Parks. She was a right beauty. Anyways, she was attacked and murdered on the way to her parents' house on her afternoon off." Lloyd's voice hitched, and she swallowed deeply.

Grace winced. "Oh, Lloyd, what a terrible tale. I'm truly sorry about your cousin."

Lloyd leaned in with the air of a conspirator. "Rumour has it his lordship was enjoying a busy social season when he heard Jenny was to become engaged, but as her duties increased, his lordship demanded she stay longer without any days off. He was right partial to our Jen. Mind you, she said his lordship's generosity always made up for his attention. Her beau disapproved—I seen Jenny's bruises with me own eyes. Apparently, he turned up here one day, legless with drink, demanding a conversation with his lordship. Made all sorts of scurrilous remarks about his lordship keeping Jenny toiling until indecent hours of the night and blaming his lordship for inappropriately handling his intended."

Lloyd straightened. "Course, Dickson thumped him soundly and booted him from the property. He might look all proper in his tails, might Dickson, but he was a smuggler once. His lordship saved him from being nicked and sent to Newgate. Been in his lordship's employ nigh on ten years now. His lordship's never short of a good tipple of French brandy—if you catch me meaning." Lloyd winked.

"Goodness, you do know a lot considering you're so new."

"Heard it mostly from Jenny. She were here over three years. Anyway, 'tweren't two days after Dickson threw out her beau that poor Jenny was beaten to death and shoved into a hedgerow."

Drawn in by the macabre story, Grace's brows rose. "Did her beau do it?"

"'Tis the likely tale. He was one of those fellers who raged with jealousy when his woman didn't lavish all her attention on him. And he was notorious for not being able to hold his drink."

"What happened to him?"

"Drank himself into a stupor one night and fell into the

Thames. They trawled him out a few days later after the fish finished feasting on him."

Grace shuffled uncomfortably in her seat. "Why would a man who loved a woman enough to propose to her suddenly start hitting her?"

"There's no telling with fellers," said Lloyd. "There's those who think a woman becomes his property once he's put his mark on her."

With her heart thumping, Grace feigned nonchalance. "Has his lordship ever asked *you* to stay behind?"

"Not yet, milady. I daresay I'll comply, knowing how generous his lordship is with those he favours."

"You're a sweet girl, Lloyd. I feel it only prudent to ask if you're aware of Lord Silverton's ... *propensities*?"

Lloyd's eyes flicked to the carpet again. "Jenny said it wasn't so bad if she played along with it." She glanced pointedly at Grace. "Besides, 'tis like I said before, I need the money."

"So, you're willing to sell your soul to the devil for a bit of silver?" Grace's voice dipped in disappointment.

Lloyd's fair cheeks flushed. "Well, some of us have mouths to feed."

Grace pressed a tight smile to her lips. "Speaking of mouths to feed, might I trouble you for some tea, please? A little fruit cake wouldn't go amiss either."

"Yes, milady." Lloyd bobbed. The maid's skirts swished, and the door latch clicked. Restless, Grace rose and leaned her head against the smoothly painted window frame, peering down miserably at the immaculate lawns and peculiar animal topiaries. An ominous dread in her gut set like a lump of cold burgoo. Church bells chiming in the distance taunted her with the knowledge that there were people out there but none near enough to call on. If she could only get past the front gate, it would be easy to flag down a passer-by on the road.

Crockery rattled, followed by a tentative knock. Grace strode to the door, wrenching it open. "What are you doing?" she snapped, her cheeks combusting as she glared up at Silverton's bulbous face. She swallowed, her mouth as dry as the dirt road outside. Lord, give her strength! No—she could do this! She was no longer the little mouse he had trapped before.

"I live here," Silverton quipped superciliously.

Grace pursed her lips smugly at the permanent red score marks down his cheek, a reminder of her last encounter with him. He would earn himself a scratch of her knife next time. Grace's eyes flashed. "My, my, how far the great Lord Silverton has fallen, bringing me tea like a common servant."

Silverton harrumphed, pushing her back with the edge of the tea tray. "I see your little adventure on the high seas did nothing to smooth your sharp tongue, young lady."

The empty teacup tipped off the saucer, knocking over the milk before plummeting to the floor. Silverton's raging indignation darkened into a puce mask of fury. He slammed the tea tray on the polished top of the Pembroke table. The porcelain sugar bowl crashed into the silver teapot. Scalding tea spurted across the back of Silverton's hand. Hissing in pain, he flicked his pudgy hand furiously, and a malevolence filled the room that sucked the air from Grace's lungs.

Her knees almost buckled at the indescribable madness in his face. She rushed towards the door, but Silverton, one step ahead, slammed it shut with a loud crack. Fumbling behind his gargantuan frame, the lock clunked into place, and Silverton waved the key at her.

"Hmm," he purred tauntingly, "this is tantalisingly familiar."

Grace's blood throbbed in her temples, and she lunged for the key with the snarl of a trapped badger, ineffectually straining to snatch it as she bounced against his distended belly.

Silverton lashed out with his plate-sized hand and slapped her across the side of the head. A loud ringing exploded in Grace's ears, and she was flung sideways across the room. She crashed heavily against a spindle-legged side table between the two armchairs, the fragile wood splintering as the table collapsed under her weight. Her hip caught the edge of the broken tabletop, the wood biting into her flesh and bruising her hip bone. Her right palm scraped along the patterned carpet, and the friction burn ignited her skin. She sucked some air back into her lungs.

Silverton snatched a fistful of her hair and grunted with exertion as he yanked her to her feet. Grace's eyes watered in agony. Clenching her teeth, she swung furiously at him, her wadded fist catching him awkwardly on the pudgy rolls of his multiple chins.

He chuckled reprovingly. "That's no way to thank me for saving your sorry hide, now, is it?"

"You *bastard*!" screamed Grace, swinging again. He snatched her wrist, and Grace screeched, "Let go!" She kicked his shins, bruising her toes through her soft slippers. She felt the bone knife slip from the top of her girdle and tensed as it spun across the floorboards like a well-struck croquet ball, sliding under the chest of drawers. Twisting to free herself from his iron-fisted grip, she snarled, "I'd rather die before I let you have me!"

"Tut, tut, my sweet," admonished Silverton, his eyes flashing dangerously. "Stop fussing."

Grace jerked her leg up hard, but Silverton twisted at the last second. Her kneecap crashed into his thigh, and while the blow was hard enough to bruise him, it was not enough to debilitate him like the kick to his privates had done last time. "Bleeding bloody rats' tails!" Grace shrieked in frustration, and Silverton sniggered.

"Is that the best you can do, Miss Baxter?"

Incensed, Grace drew his hands towards her gnashing teeth. Silverton yanked her off her feet, and she reeled through the air in a disorientating spin, landing painfully on her knees. He was so strong! Silverton twisted her arm so far back that she thought her shoulder might pop; the pain was excruciating. She tried to adjust her position to lessen the pressure, but she was pinned tight, her cheek crushed into the carpet. The solid mass of Silverton's arm compressed the back of her neck, digging her chin deep into her chest. She couldn't breathe! He pressed his weight further, and Grace's knees splayed involuntarily. She gurgled in protest, her free hand weakly hitting his wobbly flesh. He was going to crush her!

Silverton drew his arm off her neck, and Grace coughed and gagged, painfully sucking in a wheezing trail of air. The force on her twisted arm kept her pressed into the floor, and her lace headpiece flopped over her face. Silverton's finger brushed the thin fabric aside, leisurely caressing her cheek and chin. Grace flinched, not wanting him to feel her tears. Unpinning the headpiece and letting it slide to the carpet, Silverton's fingers then trailed along her body and over the curve of her hip.

Never let 'em pin you in a defenceless position. Ben Blight's cautionary words ran through Grace's head, and she snarled again in frustration. Her eyes flicked to the bone knife lying abandoned beneath the chest of drawers.

Silverton groped down her thigh and found the edge of her gown. Fondling his way up her leg, his sweaty palm mauled the bare flesh of her inner thigh. Grace convulsed, her mouth filling with bile.

"No!" Suffocating with rage and shame, she desperately wanted to fight him, but he had her pinned.

"Try stop me," panted Silverton. His swollen fingers thrust between her legs, but he jolted violently away. With a ghastly cry, he whipped his pudgy hand out from under her skirt, glaring at his bloodied sausage fingers in horror. "God damned cursed woman!" he exploded, releasing her.

Grace pitched forward, catching herself on her burned palm to prevent her face from smashing into the carpet. Lying on her side, gasping and weeping, Grace spied the fallen teacup, its handle snapped off.

Silverton was on his knees, the bulge of him pressing

DISCERNING GRACE

grotesquely through the front of his high-waisted breeches. "You should have warned me you were unclean." He wiped his hand on her skirts, leaving four snaking trails of blood across the pale fabric.

"You whoremonger!" Grace conjured one of the better insults learned aboard the *Discerning*. Snatching up the teacup, she hurled it at his head. Her aim was off, and it bounced harmlessly off the side of his puffy, pink neck.

Silverton lunged, crushing her to the floor, his hands braced either side of her head. "You foul-mouthed bitch!" He licked a grey globule of dried saliva from the corner of his mouth as his blubbery lips stretched into a demented grin. "By God, you might just spice up this marriage, after all." With a grunt, Silverton hauled Grace to her feet, and she hobbled, favouring her uninjured hip as she tried to pull away from him.

"Even the most pious of nuns must endure a period of testing to determine her calling to a life inside cloistered walls," Silverton panted, gripping her wrists. He slicked his tongue into the sweaty corner of his mouth. "You need a dose of contemplative ministry to pray for your blackened heart and to accept your vocation as my wife. A spell in the coal cellar should do the trick." Silverton's giant hand smothered Grace's shriek of protest. Wedging her against his fleshy hip, he hauled her off the floor and strode down the stairs to the ground floor.

Grace shuddered at the chill on her skin as Silverton thrust her from the warmth of the house into the begrimed depths of the coal cellar. The musty air smelled of rotten potatoes. He dropped her roughly, and her injured palm slapped on the dusty floor, stinging like a fistful of wasps.

Silhouetted by the light coming from the open door above, Silverton huffed breathlessly. "Since I'm feeling generous, I deliver you fair warning. I keep eyes and ears everywhere. My staff's loyalty is handsomely rewarded. Try leaving my property, and I'll know about it. My servants' complicity leaves no room for doubt, and I expect the same obedience from you." He thundered up the wooden steps and slammed the door shut.

Hearing the scrape of heavy furniture butt against the door, the rush of the fight drained from Grace, and she slumped, her injuries throbbing painfully. Blind in the dark, Grace nestled her face in her arms, sobbing until her eyes swelled shut.

Chapter Twenty-Nine

I n the entrance hall of Clovervale Manor, Seamus hovered restlessly, the floor beneath him still undulating as it always did when he first stepped off the ship. He clasped his hands behind his back, his casual air conflicting with the coal of rage smouldering behind his breastbone. Casting his gaze up the broad staircase, he viewed the diminutive maid buff the ebony banister until her reflection shone in it.

She was adept at avoiding his eye. Despite her best efforts to avert her face, Seamus could not miss her swollen, purpled cheek that almost closed her eye. He walked up a couple of the steps but stopped when the maid turned sharply and stumbled backwards, plonking down heavily on her bottom.

"I beg your pardon. I didn't mean to startle you." Seamus did not wish to scare her away. "That's quite an injury you're sporting. Are you all right?" Was that Lord Silverton's handiwork?

A tremulous squeak escaped the maid as she grasped the banister to pull herself to her feet. "Begging yours, sir. Must get on with me polishing."

"Of course. I don't mean to impede your duties. Tell me, is there a mistress about this house?" Seamus dropped one step lower, hoping to lessen his threat to her.

The maid's already peaky face paled at the sound of light footsteps in the hallway, and she gripped her rag with trembling fingers, her eyes darting to her feet.

The butler approached stiffly, the corners of his mouth turned down. "His lordship will see you now, sir," the butler announced, casting a baleful glare at the maid. In a flurry of skirts and dusting rags, the maid slunk down the stairs. She slid silently past Seamus and the butler, leaving a pleasant odour of furniture wax in her wake.

Seamus followed the smartly dressed butler down the passage and swept past him into the library. Silverton lumbered to his feet, pulling down the front of his waistcoat that had crept up the bulge of his stomach. His pudgy hand slicked his grey hair back off his forehead, and Seamus's gut clenched at the image of those fat-knuckled fingers fumbling with Grace's décolletage. He swallowed back his disgust.

"Captain Fitzwilliam, please come in. Sit, sit," Silverton coaxed, waving a casual hand at the plush-cushioned chair opposite his desk. "May I offer you some tea? Or something stronger, perhaps?"

Seamus drew to a halt, rigid and to attention. "I don't want tea. I want answers."

Silverton glanced over Seamus's shoulder at the butler and minutely shook his head. The door latch clicked closed.

"Do you have her?" blurted Seamus, not in the mood to exchange pleasantries.

"To whom do you refer?" Silverton dripped. Dropping heavily into the chair, his weight tested the integrity of the groaning wooden joints.

"Playing an ignoramus doesn't suit you, Silverton. You know

310

full well I mean *my fiancée*." Seamus felt his ears warm, but he deliberately kept an even tone.

Silverton chuckled coldly. "Miss Baxter, you mean? Captain Fitzwilliam, last I heard, you professed to have her securely under your protection."

"How did you come by this information?" A hot and cold trill rippled down Seamus's arms to his fingertips.

"That foppish fool, Admiral Baxter, produced the letter you wrote from Montevideo, alerting him to the fact that you had his niece in safekeeping."

"Christ Almighty! That letter named you as the perpetrator in Miss Baxter's attack. How is it you stand before me? You should be rotting in Newgate."

"There isn't a man in this town that doesn't have his price. It wasn't as expensive an exercise as I'd envisaged, intercepting all mail to Lord Flint and Admiral Baxter. I presumed Miss Baxter would try to contact her family at some time. What I never expected was for such a detailed accounting of our little rendezvous. Naturally, I fashioned your letter in a way for it to appear travel worn, with just enough of the corner of the packet torn, and smudged to eliminate my name from the slanderous incrimination."

"Do you deny the accusations?" Seamus wrestled with his self-control, the urge to launch himself at the vile creature before him fiercer than anything he had ever felt in his life.

"What matters is what the court believes." Silverton dug his finger down the front of his cravat, twisting it irritably. "Baxter was the only one who believed the boy's tale that I was the guilty party. He wanted the boy's trial postponed until he received confirmation from Miss Baxter in person. Except your letter provided the perfect evidence that she had indeed been attacked, and her bloodied dress in the boy's room sealed his fate."

"You're a contemptible creature, Silverton, pinning your foul deeds on an innocent boy."

Ignoring the jibe, Silverton dipped his chin, adding a fourth roll to his neck. "Don't tell me you've lost her."

"Don't pretend as though you didn't have a hand in her abduction."

"I can't be held accountable for the methods employed by those responding to the generous reward I offered for her safe return. Why would I risk my neck and reputation sending someone to deliberately attack a British vessel? Any man of half-decent social standing knows that's tantamount to ruination. Not to mention the explaining one would have to do to the Admiralty."

"Perhaps for the same deluded reason you purport to claim my fiancée as your own. If I find you had any hand in her abduction or if any harm befalls her, I'll hold you personally accountable."

"Contrary to what you believe, I care for Miss Baxter." Silverton had the audacity to cast a droopy-eyed look, but the man's feigned innocence did not fool Seamus.

"Rubbish! She's but a chit to you. Nothing but a chattel worth a pretty penny! Except she isn't yours—she's *my fiancée*."

"Is she? *Really*?" Silverton wrinkled his nose facetiously.

"Of course she is! We've a mutual promise. Unlike your one-sided bamboozlement."

Silverton hummed with exaggerated contemplation. "Can't *imagine* the staunch Anglican folk of London society approving of that little lark. Two ill-matched pariahs equalled by your shared disgrace. You must know you'll lose face with your naval counterparts for your heroic efforts?"

"I don't care a fig what London society thinks!" Seamus's eyes bore into Silverton's.

"I doubt the Admiralty would have taken too kindly to you living in sin with a woman aboard your vessel, especially without approved orders."

Heavens above! Was there anything the man did not know of

his affairs? Seamus's mind scrambled to make the connections. Of course! Tibbot. The *Discerning*'s men would have told him everything. He would not dignify Silverton with an explanation that he and Grace had not been living in sin, instead steering the conversation away from her. "Is the Irishman in your employ?"

"What Irishman?" feigned Silverton. "Don't you have bigger problems to concern yourself with, Captain? Such as explaining your sudden appearance in London? Surely the Admiralty wasn't expecting you back quite so soon?"

"Shut your mouth before I shut it for you, Silverton!" Seamus prided himself on maintaining an aura of calm in heated situations, but that was when his life and reputation were on the line and not his fiancée's. He did not owe this bastard any explanation.

"You might have had the authority aboard your ship to issue such orders, Captain Fitzwilliam, but this is *my* house, and I'll not stand for it. Leave now before I have my butler forcibly remove you from my property."

Seamus's jaw muscle twitched, and he narrowed his eyes. "Your day of reckoning will come, Silverton. Mark my words."

Chapter Thirty

Day after day, Grace had stared into the perpetual dark, the sound of her breath loud in the enclosed space, the air tasting heavy and earthy. In the unnerving quiet of her isolation, she had craved Lloyd's brief daily whisperings more than she hungered after the extra tidbits of food or clean rags the maid brought. She yearned for the roll of a ship under her feet and the crackly salt residue of sea spray on her cheeks. She missed the clang of the ship's bell, the hum of voices, and the thud of footsteps on deck reminding her she was not alone. But, most of all, she ached for Seamus. Imagining him returning to the *Discerning* to find her gone, realising a prize hunter had finally caught up with her. His despair at failing to disable the brigantine. Grace wept in the dark for his panic and anguish. She lost track of the days.

Grace stood at the scrape of Lloyd's shoes tiptoeing into the bowels of the house, and her ears perked up as she laid down the new plate and pot with a dry scratch. She struggled to open her eyes against the piercing lantern light.

"Here, milady. Brought you an apple along with your bread. Though don't let his lordship know. You'll have to eat it core and all."

The stench of Grace's waste bucket clogged the stagnant air, and Grace squinted one eye open, spotting Lloyd's black eye and split lip.

"Oh, Lloyd! Your face! Did Silverton do that to you?"

"'Tis nothing, milady." Lloyd's eyes flicked nervously to the closed door above.

"Come now, Lloyd. Surely now you see you must flee this monster?"

"I … I can't." The young maid's chin quivered, and tears filled her eyes. "He'll kill me."

"No, he shan't," assured Grace. "You'll be safe with me. But I need your help to escape."

"N-no, milady. I daren't risk it."

"Lloyd, please get me out of here! Leave the door unlocked. I'll sneak out."

"Can't do that, milady. His lordship has made clear what he'll do to me if I aid you in any way. Besides, Dickson's up there now, guarding the door. 'Tis him who pulls the kitchen dresser aside so as I can come down." The old empty metal drinking pot and plate clanged as Lloyd gathered them up.

"P-please tell his lordship I wish to have a word with him." The isolation and fear had worn Grace down. She would ask for her release—beg him if she had to!

"Not possible at this minute. His lordship has a visitor. Saw him arrive when I was polishing the banisters."

Grace snatched hold of Lloyd's arm. "Tell him of me! Tell him I'm down here. Please, Lloyd!"

"Oh no, milady! 'Tisn't worth me neck." Panic pitched Lloyd's whisper into a squeak. "Besides, there's no chance of me begging a private word with a captain."

"Captain?" The dank, sooty air caught in Grace's throat. "Did you get his name?"

"Fitz … Fitzsimmons or some such, I believe."

Grace grasped Lloyd's other arm, dragging the maid towards her. "Fitzwilliam? Is he tall? Blond?" An icy sheen of sweat broke out along Grace's hairline. Could it be?

"Y-yes." Lloyd's voice wavered uncertainly as she tried to peel Grace's fingers from her upper arms. "You're hurting me, milady."

"Lloyd! That's my fiancé! Please, you must tell him of me! Please, Lloyd, I beg you!"

Wrenching herself free, Lloyd staggered back. "I can't risk his lordship's wrath."

"Come with me!" urged Grace desperately, her voice reverberating loudly in the blackened vault. "My fiancé will protect us both."

"P-please, milady." Lloyd's voice quivered. "His lordship is pleasant enough if you do his bidding. Jenny was right, 'tisn't that bad." Lloyd's urgent whispers offered Grace little comfort. "You'll see. It'll all be right as rain once he lets you out of here."

Grace's stomach flipped, her opinion of the sweet woman souring. Oh, Lloyd! She had hoped they might be friends. How could she trust her now? Silverton was in her ear—and in other places!

Scrambling up the stairs, Lloyd glanced back briefly, whispering, "I'm sorry, milady, I must go. I've already said too much."

"No, Lloyd! Wait!" Grace stumbled forward to catch Lloyd's skirts but missed. "Seamus!" she shrieked, scrambling on all fours, the rough wooden steps spitting splinters into her scabbed palm. "Seamus! I'm down here! Help!"

Grace was swallowed whole by the dark as the cellar door thudded shut. Dickson's muted tones scolding Lloyd were drowned out by the dresser's dry scrape across the entrance.

Grace's hammering echoed mockingly in the cavernous coal cellar. Screaming herself hoarse, she ignored the jarring crunches of her shoulder as she repeatedly threw herself against the door.

For the next few days, it was Dickson who brought Grace her bread and water. One day, the cellar door opened, and Grace's blood coagulated in her veins, her sensitive ears instantly alerted by the heavier scuffle of a man's boots. She shot to her feet, her arm shielding her eyes.

"It has been two weeks. Have you repented, my sweet? Are you ready to accept your divine fate?" drawled Silverton.

Desperate to be free, Grace made a quivering noise of agreement and trailed him to her luxurious chambers. He turned outside her door, sniffing disdainfully and scowling at Grace's ruined dress. "I'll send your lady's maid to help you bathe. You'll dine with me this evening." Grace did not object, too relieved to be out of the hellhole.

Alone in her bedchamber, she dropped to her knees and peered beneath the chest of drawers. Whimpering with relief, she retrieved her bone knife. Unpinning her brooch from under her filthy shift, she shuffled over to the broad chest of drawers and wiggled open the sticky bottom drawer. She buried both items beneath several layers of scarves and shawls. Her tartan shawl lay in a neat clean square, and she ran her fingers over the red wool for comfort. Oh, Seamus.

Sidling over to the tall windows, she stood with her forehead pressed against the cool glass, admiring the bright day. There was only a scattering of clouds in the sky, and she longed to take a stroll through the manicured gardens and march right on past the gatehouse, down the dirt lane, and back to London. To Seamus!

After a soft knock, the chamber door opened, and a new maid scurried in with a large ceramic water jug.

"Who are you?"

"Wheeler, milady."

"Where's Lloyd?"

"I'm not at liberty to talk about that, milady." The maid's eyes flicked towards the door. Crossing the room with quick, light steps, Wheeler set down the water jug on the washstand. "His lordship sent me to ready you for supper, milady. I've brought some warm water for you to have a bit of a wash."

Grace dropped down onto the stool before the dressing table and leaned closer to the mirror to study her coal-stained face, startlingly reminiscent of the face that had peered back at her in Billy's room above the stables. She pulled the skin tight under her eyes, but the dark bags reappeared when she let go. She gingerly rolled the shoulder that had stiffened and bruised after she had used it as a battering ram against the cellar door.

"Would you like to choose a gown for this evening, milady?" sang out Wheeler, oblivious to Grace's discomfort.

Rising to the washbasin, Grace glanced casually into the dressing room. She spotted a plum-coloured dress, blissfully lace-free. She pointed it out. "That one will do."

Wheeler hesitated. "But milady, that's but a simple day dress. I'm sure his lordship's appreciation of fine things would include you in one of these lovely gowns." She held up a garment. The underdress was cream satin, and the overdress was silk net and pale lace embroidered with gold metal. The puffed sleeves ended with cuffs of more frilly pale lace. Its opulence stank of Silverton's influence, and the gown's exquisite craftsmanship did little to dispel Grace's loathing of it.

"Lord Silverton has no claim over me." Grace's heart ticked a beat faster. "I make my own choices."

Doubt flittered across Wheeler's face. "Oh, milady, I don't reckon his lordship'll take too kindly to that."

"I don't care what he thinks." Grace dipped her hands into the hot water, hissing at the heat of it stinging her icy fingertips. "I'll wear the plum dress." Her words were clipped short by the pain. "Please fetch a bucket of warm water. I wish to wash my hair."

"Yes, milady." The maid bobbed again and scurried away in a flash of skirts.

Removing her shift and the blackened tatters of the lemon dress, Grace cringed at the gaunt state of her body and the mottled yellowing bruising spilling over her shoulder and down her arm. By the time the maid returned with another bucket of boiled water, Grace had washed away the grime and indignity of the coal cellar and was once again dressed in a clean shift. Wheeler helped her wash her hair, and Grace sent Wheeler into a twittering flutter once more by refusing to don a corset, unable to face the tight laces biting into her thin waist. Once dressed in the plum gown, Grace pulled on her stockings and, spying little silk slippers, slipped them onto her feet. They fitted remarkably well —Silverton's obvious care in selecting them repulsed her. She perched before the dressing table as her lady's maid worked silently, her nimble fingers styling Grace's curls with clips.

"Not too tight. I've a headache coming on." Grace's skin pebbled at the prospect of the evening ahead with Silverton.

Silverton knocked on her door in the early evening. He eyed Grace's day dress dispassionately. "Couldn't you find a more suitable evening gown?"

Grace lifted her chin. "I'm perfectly comfortable, thank you."

Silverton tipped his head and hooked his thumbs into the inset front pockets of his grey waistcoat. "Very well. Just this once, since it's only the two of us for supper." He shook his head scornfully. "There are standards I expect you to adhere to as my wife—"

"I'm *not* your wife and never shall be." Grace tipped her chin up. "I'm set to become Mrs Seamus Alexander Fitzwilliam. But this you no doubt know since I know my fiancé was here."

"Ah, yes, Lloyd's slip of the tongue cost her dearly."

"What did you do to her?" Grace's skin turned icy with dread. "Will she turn up in a hedgerow too?"

Silverton's eyes narrowed. "My, my, that little trollop certainly had loose lips." Grace's stomach contracted at his grey stare. Then, as though shaking off his thoughts like a wet dog shaking its fur dry, he scoffed, and his jowls wobbled. "As for your so-called *fiancé*, he was only planning to wed you out of chivalry." He superciliously brushed an imaginary bit of dust off the sleeve of his coat with his chunky knuckles. "He offered you no true prospects."

"Think what you will, but I made him a promise and he me." Grace looked pointedly at the toady creature before her. "He's the only man who has ever touched me."

"That is an honour *I* should have claimed," leered Silverton.

Good! Let him think Seamus had taken her maidenhood. Revulsion juddered down the back of Grace's neck at the memory of Silverton's touch. "You're a foul beast! Always been set to force me against my will." Grace tensed, her bruised shoulder pulling excruciatingly. She gritted her teeth, not prepared to give Silverton the satisfaction of witnessing her pain.

"I was only trying to lay claim to what was rightfully mine. You forget, your father permitted our betrothal."

"I'm sure my father didn't permit you to steal into my chambers to have carnal knowledge of me." Tears of anger prickled her eyes. "Besides, my fiancé knows what you tried, but it matters not to him."

"Weak men like Fitzwilliam maintain a skewed sense of magnanimity—trying to right all the wrongs in this world." He squinted at her disdainfully. "I'm sure he feels vindicated by his actions, protecting your honour, and all such noble sentiments."

"He's anything but weak, and he loves me."

"Pah! Love!" Silverton flapped his hand. "Love is crushable, like a cockroach under a heel." His lips twisted as if he had a vinegary taste in his mouth. "Power, on the other hand, is the secret key to life. It dwells in most places—if you know where to look. Position and money the most obvious, of course." He leaned forward, his words as toxic as his breath. "I'm sure, after your rutting with Fitzwilliam, you now also comprehend a little of the power of the flesh."

Blast him to hell! Were her knife to hand, she would show him the power of a weapon! Grace bit the inside of her cheek to avoid shrieking aloud.

"Believe you can live happily ever after on love and the paltry pay of a sea captain?" wheedled Silverton.

"Yes, I do!" Grace's cheeks and neck prickled with angry splashes of heat.

Silverton's lips curved humourlessly. "You only *think* you can, my sweet. Love is a short season that fades quickly into obscurity. Wait until you possess the power of a title and this grand manor, not to mention enough money to buy anything your heart desires."

The arrogance! "The only thing my heart desires is to return to my fiancé. When he finds me—and he will—you'd better be as quick with your sword as you are with your insults."

Silverton sighed, his bulbous lips quivering gelatinously. "My only concern is the empty state of my stomach. Come." Silverton extended his arm to her. "Let's head down to supper."

Grace would have loved to tell him to shove his supper into the same orifice that O'Reilly insisted Jonas stick his head into during one of their arguments, but after her restricted diet in the cellar, Grace was dizzy with hunger. She hesitated.

Silverton's lizard tongue darted to the corner of his mouth, catching the yellow spume there. "Must you *always* be so difficult?"

Grace elongated her spine and slid her clenched fist in the crook of his elbow, fighting back a shudder as he patted her hand in approval.

The dining room housed a twelve-seat table set for two

nearest the door. Grace squirrelled away another potential escape route through the French doors leading into the garden. Oriental bamboo shoots adorned the sandy-coloured wallpaper, and a macabre, framed-mausoleum of dragonflies hung on the wall.

Grace dropped into her chair and scraped it forward before Silverton could push it in. He shook his head in silent displeasure, his thick lips pinched tersely, the globs of sputum bulging in the corners. Ignoring him, Grace turned to Dickson. "A glass of wine, if you please."

Dickson's eyes widened at her audaciousness, and he looked to Silverton for guidance. Grace did not care that wine was only supposed to be poured after the soup was served. Silverton reluctantly nodded.

Dickson poured Grace a glass of deep, blushing claret, which she picked up and swilled back in one large, unladylike mouthful. It was a good vintage. Silverton lowered his bulbous frame beside her at the head of the table, and Dickson poured him a glass too.

The butler clapped his hands sharply, and a string of footmen shuttled in a stream of aromatic dishes. Taking the tray with the soup tureen from the nearest man, Dickson ladled several servings into Grace's bowl. The rich, meaty smell of the pea-and-ham soup almost made Grace pass out with hunger. She immediately picked up her spoon and gulped blistering mouthfuls of the deliciously creamy, salty soup. Each swallow slid down her gullet, hitting her empty stomach with a satisfying curl of warmth. Without waiting for Silverton to finish his, she shoved her empty bowl aside and reached for the sautéed asparagus in breadcrumbs.

Silverton stared dispassionately. "If your deplorable manners are an attempt to dishearten me," he said in his slow, uppity drawl, "your actions are in vain. I'm not that easily discouraged." He smeared his napkin across his mouth, wiping away the mucus globules. "Don't prove too irksome, Miss Baxter. Husbandly discipline comes in *many* forms."

Grace pointed her knife at Silverton and speared him with a look of pure hatred, the muscles in her neck tensing. "What will you do? Finally force your way with me?" Oblivious to Dickson's presence, Silverton slowly laid his spoon down. At the treacherous glimmer in his eye, the pea-and-ham soup soured in Grace's stomach.

"Oh, Miss Baxter," intoned Silverton, "you own no notion of the *unimaginable* pleasures that await you." He dipped his jellified chin and narrowed his eyes. "Your time in my cellar has done little to dampen that temper of yours."

Swallowing the plum-sized lump in her throat, Grace nonchalantly picked up her wine and took another large mouthful to steady her nerves. Her aching shoulder twinged as though to remind her that she should not risk his rage again. Lowering her glass and feigning indifference, she twisted the conversation. "Do enlighten me, Lord Silverton, of the resourcefulness that enabled you to find me halfway across the world."

Silverton perked up at the unexpected turn in the conversation. Typical braggart! Could not resist the temptation to crow.

"Well, my sweet, you did leave a convenient trail of breadcrumbs in your wake." A smirk tugged at his fleshy lips. "Upon hearing of your disappearance, I went to your parents at Wallace House. Admiral Baxter was there too, naturally. The admiral explained how he and you had taken some air with that upstart, Fitzwilliam, before you retired early." Silverton shovelled in a large mouthful of roasted partridge and wilted cress. Barely chewing, he swallowed it down. "Lord Flint immediately ordered a search of Wallace House, including the stables. Your torn and bloodied gown was discovered under that rogue, Sykes's, bed, and a pile of your hair in his drawer. Naturally, he was arrested immediately."

"Billy was arrested!" spluttered Grace.

"Of course!" Silverton peered down his nose. "What would he be doing with your bloodied gown under his bed if he hadn't been up to some mischief?"

"*I* hid it there!" rankled Grace, twisting her fingers in her lap.

With a dismissive shrug, Silverton emptied his glass of claret and nodded at Dickson to top it up. "Needless to say, that ended your family's investigation into the matter. Once the papers had something of substance to sink their teeth into, they were easily persuaded to run with the story of your assault. Sykes was thrown into Newgate Prison to stand trial at the Old Bailey. He was sentenced to transportation for life with fifty strokes thrown in for good measure."

"How can that be?" Grace gripped the silver dessertspoon hard, her hand trembling at the notion of Billy crammed into the stinking hold of a prison bark.

"Why distress yourself over the wellbeing of such a lowly creature?"

"Because he's *my friend*!" Grace slammed her spoon down, flicking peaches and custard into the flower arrangement. It was worse than she imagined. What a selfish fool she had been!

Silverton sniffed, ignoring her distress. "Your family believed you had met with foul play and were satisfied that justice had been served by Sykes's arrest. I immediately posted a handsome and public reward to anyone who could bring you back safely from wherever it was you had run to. I had to be seen to be doing my bit as the concerned fiancé. Except, I initiated a private investigation. After enquiries at several alehouses, my man discovered that the Two Chairmen's publican was only too happy to sing for a few coins. He recalled a skinny, bald boy with polished manners trying to filch an ale before being rounded up by the recruitment gang of the *Discerning*. I called on my connections in and around Woolwich dockyard. My spy greased the palms of a Royal Artillery guard at the gate. He remembered laughing and joking with the *Discerning*'s clerk and a new recruit."

Silverton chuckled condescendingly. "Of course, it was pure supposition that said boy was you, but your hair in the drawer is what did it for me. It was apparent you were disguising yourself as a lad. Everyone else believed Sykes had hacked your hair off in a vicious attempt to spoil you for others and that he kept your hair as a keepsake—a sign of his obsession with you. A Rear Admiral, who shall remain nameless, unwittingly supplied the route and intended destinations of the *Discerning*'s mapping expedition at a dinner party, his tongue loosened by a port or three. It wasn't so hard to have my connections disseminate your route to those interested in pursuing the prize money."

"So, you essentially employed O'Reilly to hunt me down?"

"O—who?" Silverton smiled smugly. "Who my connections use and how their contacts deliver the required outcome is no concern of mine."

Grace's dinner roiled biliously in her stomach. She wanted to flee, but she was fixed in place by a morbid need to hear the end of his story.

"Imagine everyone's surprise at the arrival of a letter from the magnanimous Captain Fitzwilliam," chortled Silverton, his bulging belly jiggling.

"A letter?" A spark of doubt stabbed Grace's breastbone. "From Seamus?"

"Indeed! All the way from Montevideo." Silverton's voice was undulating in a sing-song tone like a nursery maid reading bedtime stories to a child.

"Seamus wrote *you* a letter?" Grace's breath quickened as her brain swirled with memories of conversations with Seamus in her sickbed in Montevideo.

"Not *me*, you silly girl."

Grace's nostrils flared. "But he *promised* me he wouldn't write to my parents."

"Tut tut, you little fool. He wrote to Admiral Baxter."

Grace frowned and blinked in disbelief.

"I bribed a postal functionary to intercept all mail to your father and uncle. That fool Fitzwilliam detailed that it was our little rendezvous that caused you to flee London. He noted that he had promised not to write to your parents about what had happened, but he believed it vital that Baxter be made aware you were under his protection. What a pity the packet was so travel worn, with just enough of the corner torn and smudged to eliminate the perpetrator's name." Silverton yawned at the warmth of the fire and the effect of his after-dinner brandy. "Naturally, your parents were horrified by the ruination of your reputation, not to mention the ruination of *theirs*." Silverton rubbed his swollen stomach and belched.

Curdled custard threatened to rush up Grace's throat, and she swallowed several times.

Silverton, obviously enjoying the sound of his own voice, continued. "Fitzwilliam explained to Baxter that he was required to press on with his exploration of Tierra del Fuego but assured your uncle he was leaving you behind in Montevideo with Lord Ponsonby, who would set you on the first British ship back to London."

Grace was utterly spent, but she waited, immobile, in the hard-backed chair, her elbows propped on the table for support.

"Of course, Baxter lobbied the Admiralty to fetch you, but since Fitzwilliam's letter clearly stated that Lord Ponsonby was planning to place you on the next British ship, they did not feel it necessary to waste the resource of sending a ship after you. Knowing how rarely British vessels dock in that part of the world, the chance of a prize hunter bringing you back before Ponsonby could secure you passage was favourable."

She glared at Silverton. "Do you have any idea of the conditions I endured on that evil hulk of sin?"

"What matters is that you're back." He stretched his legs out beneath the table, his eyes wandering dreamily over her bodice.

She folded her arms to block his roving gaze. "What's to stop me testifying that it was *you* who attacked me and not Billy?"

"Really, my sweet? A gentlewoman of your breeding enduring such a traumatic ordeal—your interpretation of events is bound to be muddled. Besides, it is my word—me, a prominent lord in London society—against that of a common apothecary's apprentice who had your soiled gown in his possession. Whose version of events do you think the papers will be persuaded to print, hmm?"

"And the scratches to your cheek roused no suspicion?"

Silverton stroked his cheek and shrugged. "But the handiwork of a carelessly controlled razor."

"My fiancé will kill you."

"Your fiancé is facing disgrace. His decision to abandon his expedition hasn't cast him in a favourable light."

"What do you mean he abandoned his expedition?"

"The fool resigned his commission to chase after you. A dishonoured naval captain will hold no sway in this town, certainly not against the likes of me."

An icy slide of guilt cramped her belly. The wake of destruction in her path was worse than she had ever imagined. Lord knew she had never intended for any of this. Grace clenched her teeth. "My father will—"

"Your *father*, scandalised that word of your ruined reputation had leaked out into society, threatened to disown you." Silverton leaned forward with a conspiratorial twinkle in his eye, his elbows thumping on the white tablecloth. "But I persuaded him I'd still take you as my wife and that neither my affection for you nor our financial dealings would be in any way altered." Silverton reclined, and the wooden frame of the chair groaned in objection.

Misery welled up in Grace like an over-boiling pot. Silverton's words disturbed her, and she wanted to lash out at him—deploy a few of the moves she had learned in the forecastle. She envisaged Silverton's blubbery lips bursting like ripe grapes as she headbutted him or his eyes wide with astonishment as she punched him in the throat—or better still, stabbed him with Darcy's knife. Despite her desperation to hurt him, the voice in her head reasoned at the improbability of her success. He had already proven that, despite his girth, he was a powerful man. Now that she knew he had no intention of releasing her, she had to figure a way back into town—back to Seamus.

Chapter Thirty-One

The next day, Silverton appeared to make amends for keeping Grace holed up in the cellar, and granted her permission to walk around the grounds. Glad of her freedom, Grace admired the immaculate shrubs and lawns being tended by several gardeners. Escape was impossible, with a high sandstone wall surrounding the property. She had already dismissed the idea of splicing her bedsheet into a rope to clamber out of the window. The only way out of the grounds was through the black iron gates and past the taciturn gate guard. Who knew what criminal background the man had or what his orders were should she attempt escape? If he was not a criminal, she dared not put him at risk as she had Lloyd.

That night, she waited with bated breath and listened for Silverton's inevitable visit. But it did not come. Perhaps the new girl, Wheeler, was keeping him satisfied for the moment.

The following morning, Silverton barged into Grace's chamber, his eyes bloodshot from his overindulgence the evening before at supper. His reflection leered at her in the dressing-table mirror. "We're taking a stroll through the woods."

Panic rose in Grace's chest, but she said politely, "Certainly. I'll ready myself for our excursion." She studied him for any signs of the simmering volcanic rage that scattered his staff from his path like gazelles fleeing a fire. When he did not make a move to leave, she forced a coy smile. "A moment of privacy, please, your lordship."

"Two minutes, my sweet. I'll await you out here." The door shut with a solid thud.

Grace eyed her reflection in the mirror. Her face was colourless and drawn, but her green eyes sparked with determination. This was her chance! *Be ready to run like the bloody wind*! Fussing with her frizzy, unkempt hair, she pinned the sides in place with two silver combs inlaid with a cluster of pearls. With an indelicate yank, she opened the sticky drawer and lifted out her clean tartan shawl. It was not particularly cold outside, but Seamus's red wool shawl was a comfort. She gripped the leather handle of the bone knife and tucked it into the top of her stocking. Once they were off the property, she would stick him with it!

She reflected on an opportunity when she might stab Silverton, discouraged by her uncertainty over whether the servants would come to his aid. Lloyd was gone—had she cost the maid her life? Wheeler's sullenness proved that her loyalties lay in her purse. Dickson would never risk the discovery of his dirty little side business by betraying Silverton.

Grace snatched up her Luckenbooth brooch and pinned it to the underside of the shawl over her heart. *Please, Lord,* she prayed. If there was any merit in her brooch bringing good luck, she could do with liberal doses of it right now. *Drive my knife straight and true.*

Dropping the skirts of her favourite plum-coloured day dress, she released a quivering breath as Silverton thrust the door open again. His fleshy lips widened into a smirk, revealing a remnant of parsley from the breakfast kippers stuck in between his teeth.

He clamped her arm against him, snaring her like a rabbit in a steel-jawed trap. Silverton dragged Grace through the gate, down the lane, and over the uneven mounds of a fallow field towards the woods on his land. Glad of her leather boots, she was surprised at how unfit she had become from her inactivity aboard O'Reilly's ship and in the coal cellar. Silverton, for all his size, kept up a punishing pace. She would never be able to outrun him.

She panted breathlessly. "Please, Lord Silverton, slow down. I can't walk any further." She licked the beaded perspiration from her top lip, her red shawl hanging limply over one arm. "May I rest?" Maybe she could sink her knife into his eye.

Silverton's scowl slid to the glistening slit of her cleavage, his eyes flashing hungrily. "You can rest at the pond." Despite his heartless attitude, he did slow his pace a little. Grace's calves burned fiercely, her breathing that of a blown horse.

After an eternity of weaving through masses of tree trunks, they emerged from the shaded forest at the edge of a large pond. The breeze stirred the pond's surface, and the slow-moving ripples washed back and forth over the pebbles. Despite her gown sticking to her sweaty legs and the air scraping through her dry throat, Grace was mesmerised by the beauty of this unexpected oasis.

"I'm hot. May I splash my face?"

Silverton begrudgingly dropped her arm. Grace abandoned her heavy shawl on the grassy bank and stepped out onto the pebbly bar, bending to her knees, her skirts billowing around her. Several swans resting among the reeds flapped their wings in objection and honked as they glided across the still water. Grace tracked the sleek wake behind the majestic white birds, jealous of their freedom to wander off as they pleased.

She plunged her hands into the icy water and wiggled her

hot, swollen fingers delightedly. She dabbed her dripping hands against her neck and cheeks. Refreshed, she rose and turned then froze. Silverton was sprawled on the grassy knoll, the soft red square of material laid out beside him. Grace held his lewd stare until he broke away first, glancing down at her shawl in unmistakable invitation. Grace's insides liquified, and fresh sweat prickled the back of her wet hands. Sitting that near to him, she would never be able to slip her knife from her stocking unnoticed.

"Join me, my sweet," he said, patting the tartan shawl. His sugary tone did little to hide the predatory longing in his gaze. Grace's eyes flicked uncertainly to the dark forest of ancient English oaks where dappled sunlight danced in the muted brown shadows.

"Uh, uh, uh!" Silverton waggled his stubby finger at her, the sun glinting off the gold-crested ring on his little finger. "No running."

Grace gave the thick undergrowth one last, regretful glance and flopped ungracefully onto the shawl. Silverton patted her knee as though praising an obedient dog.

"Such a lovely day. Are Highgate Ponds not the epitome of splendour in spring? And so private too."

"Oh, enough of your inane jabbering. Have your way and be done with it." Grace feared her shaky resolve would evaporate if he prolonged matters.

"My, my. Someone's had a change of heart," he simpered. "You know, I've had my eye on you for several years— enjoying you bloom from a bud of a child into the blossom you are today." His large hand stilled heavily on her knee, and Grace nearly jerked back. "Come now, my sweet, it would be more agreeable for you if you were not so uptight." Silverton trailed his fingers across her décolletage and dipped an engorged finger slowly into her sweaty cleavage. He buried his nose in her hair and inhaled. A rumble of desire made its way up his throat, and Grace squeezed her eyes shut as his searing, fish-tinged breath hit her cheek. His moist, fleshy lips sought hers, but Grace twisted her head and threw herself back on the shawl.

"Do what you wish to the rest of me, but you may not kiss me in such a manner." The muscles in her legs juddered.

"Very well, Miss Baxter." He skimmed his damp forefinger over her lips. "I've plenty of other activities in which to engage that pretty little mouth of yours." His finger forced her lips open, and he pushed it in slowly and deeply. It tasted of sweat and leather and kippers. Grace gagged as his finger slid over the back of her tongue.

Withdrawing his finger, he placed his moist lips against her ear. "See, my sweet, so much fun to be had." He barrelled over on top of her, forcing her thighs apart with his knees. He buried his face into her chest, his slimy tongue burrowed between her breasts as he groped up the hem of her dress.

Grace lifted her legs and wrapped them around Silverton's wide hips. *Now! Stab him now!* Silverton pulled up in astonishment, staring incredulously as she shuffled her hips under him, drawing her skirts up over her knees. Gripping the doughy sides of his head, she stuffed his face into her chest, whimpering in revulsion. Clearly mistaking it as a mewl of passion, Silverton wrenched the front of her gown down and clamped his mouth feverishly onto her exposed breast. Clutching his head firmly with one hand, Grace fumbled down her exposed leg and grasped the knife.

With the strength and fury of an animal fighting for its life, she plunged the bone blade into Silverton's back. Ben Blight's words shrieked in her head. *Below the ribs—into the kidney!*

At the first stab, Silverton tensed in astonishment. *AGAIN!* At the second stab, he roared in pain. *AGAIN!* At the third stab, he flung himself off her, the motion snapping the blade. Grace stared at the broken knife, recoiling at the smear of blood on her quivering fingers. Throwing the handle aside, she sprang to her feet, whirling around at Silverton's deep groaning.

His face, distorted in agony, was turning a deep shade of purple. He puffed in sharp bursts as though he was having trouble breathing. Growling at Grace, the whites of his beady eyes bulged. "Wh-what have you done? You've k-killed me!" He attempted to roll over and rise, but he fell back like a whale flailing in the shallows, panting and clutching his back. He drew his hand away, squalling at his blood-slicked fingers. A dark puddle pooled beside him, staining the green grass red. Silverton's eyes rolled back in his head, and his tongue protruded from his mouth like the globular stamen of a flower as his juddering jowls deflated with a long, quivering rasp that reminded Grace of Gilly's final breath.

She bolted. Twigs and branches mercilessly slapped and scratched Grace's face as she tore through the forest, skirts bunched, lungs on fire, muscles searing. Throwing herself over a low stone wall, Grace sobbed in relief at the sight of a little dirt lane. Catching her breath in great gulping blubs, she straightened her bodice while scouring the track. Enormous haystacks dotted the stubbled earth around her, but it was barren of people. She flicked a look back at the row of dense trees, half expecting to see Silverton lumbering after her. With her hands on her hips, Grace swayed from one exhausted leg to the other. The blood pounded in her ears, and she desperately sucked fresh air into her tortured lungs.

"Hold up!"

Grace whirled round. Her rasping breaths had masked the crunching of the approaching cart. A wizened man, not a day under eighty, was hunched over the reins on his lap. A gargantuan carthorse studied her calmly and patiently with its gentle brown eyes, not perturbed in the slightest by the obstacle she had created.

Grace patted the horse's flank, and its long-haired black coat juddered in pleasure. The leather reins were warm, and the low-sided cart was laden with baskets of fresh rhubarb, radishes, and turnips, the aroma of newly tilled earth still clinging to the vegetables.

"You all right there, lass?" The old man's rheumy eyes squinted for a better look at her, his toothless gums gnashing together and sucking his lips inwards.

"I'm quite well, thank you, sir." Grace swiped the perspiration from her brow. "However, I've foolishly wandered too far from town and become lost." A cool breeze tickled her damp nape.

"Where you headed?" He scratched his stubbly weatherworn cheek with nails that had a field's worth of dirt under them.

"Anywhere I can hail a hackney."

"Right you are. Hop up on my cart here, and I'll have you there in two shakes of a lamb's tail." The old farmer shuffled over, the weathered cart squeaking in protest at his movements.

Grace hesitated. He did not look too threatening. Moved like a sloth.

The farmer flicked the reins, and the carthorse set off at an unhurried clop down the lane. Grace wrinkled her nose at the tangy, stale smell of the farmer's sweat overlaid with the fumes of cheap alcohol.

"There hasn't been nearly enough rain this summer," he mumbled conversationally. "Me and the missus have had to water the crops by hand 'cause of the lack of pre … precip … rain." The wizened old man droned on about the predicted demand for his rhubarb and what price he hoped to fetch at market, enabling Grace to settle unobtrusively while he put some distance between her and Silverton. Grace's thoughts wandered. An oppressive chill settled in the pit of her stomach when she remembered the resistance of Silverton's flesh as she repeatedly jabbed the bone blade into him. His grunts of agony and surprise echoed in her ears. How long before someone found his body?

The elderly farmer was in no hurry, and neither was his carthorse. Jostling carts and horses, with wheels and hooves clattering noisily, passed in the opposite direction. The throng of people thickened. With a bone-chilling jolt, Grace gasped, *her brooch*! It was still on the shawl. Seamus's shawl!

She fought back the urge to scream and swallowed the press of tears. Despite her misery, she caught the farmer's phlegmy cough.

"I'm heading to Spitalfields Market, if 'tis all right by you, lass?" He wiped the back of his hand across his mouth.

The crush of devastation at her loss squeezed the breath from Grace, and she gulped back a sob. "That'll do, sir."

The disharmony of market smells wafted around her; the heady scent of freshly baked bread and the odour of rotting seafood were all blanketed by the smog hanging heavily over the chimney tops. The weary carthorse's hooves shuffled past livestock clustered in pens, the bleating sheep sounding only marginally happier than the mournfully bellowing cattle.

Familiar with its routine, the carthorse halted near the rows of trestle tables groaning with a colourful collage of fruits and vegetables. The horse, oblivious to the bewildering whistles of the drovers, the snarls of dogs, and squalls of hawkers, shook the flies from his eyes. A jolly woman with a mob cap plopped haphazardly on her nest of frizzy, greying hair clapped her hands in delight at the farmer's arrival.

"Alistair! We thought you'd never get 'ere, you old curmudgeon. 'Tis nearly noon!" The spider veins on her round cheeks flushed with pleasure.

The din of the market masked the protesting groan of the rickety cart as Grace alighted. "Thank you, kind sir," she called. At his muttered farewell, Grace hoisted her skirts and dissolved into the busy crowd.

Picking her way through the throngs of shoppers and marketers, Grace burst onto the bustling street front. She spied an empty hackney trotting towards her and waved enthusiastically. The black-cloaked coachman reined in his horse with a clatter of harness and creak of leather.

Where to? She refused to go home. But where? Uncle Farfar! The club or his naval quarters at Chatham? The club was nearer. Grace climbed aboard, "White's at St James's, please, driver."

Outside the club, the driver helped Grace to the pavement. The ruddy-faced man silently extended his hand in expectation, his palm calloused and stained dark by the oil of the leather reins.

"Apologies," Grace blustered. "I've no coin for the fare." The cab driver's whiskers tensed into a straight line. "But I do have these," Grace tugged at a pearl combs, wincing as they snagged several hairs.

The cab driver bristled as he eyed the trinkets. "Ha! You're lucky 'tis my missus's birthday soon. Those combs'll do nicely as a gift." He snatched them from her grimy fingers and hauled himself up to his seat.

The club's columned exterior was grand and imposing but not half as imposing as the smartly attired doorman Grace spied through the glass doors. She turned to scour the street. Across the way, a stylish lady, escorted by a dapper gentleman, was shading herself under a white lace parasol when a grubby street urchin tore around the corner, colliding into the unsuspecting couple. It was a violent impact, and all three yelped in surprise. The barefooted urchin resumed his sprint up the street, and the gentleman patted his pockets in a panic. Grace shook her head, turning it sharply at another cry of astonishment behind her.

"By Christ, and for the love of all that is holy! Miss Grace?"

Chapter Thirty-Two

G race whirled around in a flurry of skirts. The protruding ears and achingly familiar face of Jim Buchanan stared at her from beside a column at the top of the stone steps.

"Jim! Good Lord, you're a sight for sore eyes!"

With no regard for propriety, Jim bounded down the stairs, scooped her up and spun her around. He had grown—evidenced by his bear-sized hug and new deep voice. Grace squeaked, hugging him back.

"Crivens! Sorry, lass. I didn't mean to hurt you." Jim deposited her on her feet and scraped a hand through his thatch of black hair, sending it spiking in all directions. "I cannot believe yer standing here with your scraggly curls waving at me! How did ye manage it, lass? We thought ye done for when we heard ye were taken. Captain Fitzwilliam has been—*Captain Fitzwilliam!*" A configuration of horror and relief scuttled across Jim's round features. "I must let him know you're safe!" He gripped her uninjured shoulder firmly with the strength that comes when a boy steps across the threshold into manhood. Grace's heart dissolved into the soles of her filthy leather boots at Seamus's name. Jim spun around to head up the sandstone stairs, but Grace caught his hand.

"The captain's here too?" The tangled threads of her emotions wound so tightly it was impossible to decipher where each strand began.

"Aye, lass, he is. The captain's in yon gentleman's clubhouse with yer uncle. He's just given me this wee list of errands to run." Jim proffered the slip of paper.

Grace took in a sharp breath as she recognised the neat, slanted writing. "Gracious me! How did you get here, Jim? Did the *Discerning* not press on with the expedition?"

"No. 'Tis the crying shame of the whole matter. Not long after Captain Fitzwilliam resigned, Lieutenant Wadham received orders to return to England." Jim rubbed his temple, shaking his head. "Had the captain held on a wee while longer, he'd still have his post *and* be back here to search for ye."

"Oh, Jim! I've made such a mess of things."

"Ne'er mind about that now, lass. The captain'll skin me arse if he finds me prattling out here wi' you instead of summoning him. Come wi' me." Jim pulled her hand. They only made it as far as the top step before the doorman, decked in full dress coattails, including a shiny black hat, barrelled through the brass-handled glass doors.

"And where are you two going?"

"We're to see Captain Fitzwilliam immediately!" Jim demanded. Standing beside the slim doorman, Grace could see where Jim had thickened through the shoulders.

The immaculate doorman stared dispassionately down his bristly whiskers. "Certainly. May I see your membership, please?"

"Ye just saw the captain task me with errands upon this very step before entering yer establishment." Jim waggled the white paper before the doorman's nose, bridling at the wall of official-dom. "'Tis urgent I see him."

"Please!" Grace implored, "I'm his fiancée!"

The doorman's eyes scoured Grace's muck-caked skirts and torn bodice, his lips twitching. "These hallowed walls provide our members refuge from wifely foibles. No gentleman here wishes his tranquillity disturbed. Women are certainly not allowed." He turned his condescension on Jim. "And without membership, I can't grant *you* access either. Good day!" He spun round smartly on his well-polished heels, reaching for the brass door handle.

Jim seized his coattails. "Wait a minute, ye dozy galoot!"

"Unhand me this instant!"

"Aye," Jim spat. "I'll unhand you, but not before I skelp your arse if you don't scarper and fetch Captain Fitzwilliam right away!" The two men stood nose to nose, simmering at one another. "Do ye not realise it, man? This is Miss Baxter. Her reward's been splashed across the front pages o' the broad-sheets. 'Tis the missing daughter of Lord Flint. The one they believed attacked by the stablemaster's son, but turns out she escaped out to sea—rescued by the good Captain Fitzwilliam hi'self."

"Gentlemen, please." Grace placed a hand on each of their chests, their pounding hearts pulsing against her palms. "If you'd kindly announce me to Captain Fitzwilliam, we'll clear this whole mess up in an instant."

The doorman hesitated, and Grace elaborated. "I assure you, if the captain turns you away, you've permission to punch Mr Buchanan here squarely on the mouth for his insults."

Jim harrumphed in indignation. Grace knew the whippet stood no chance against her friend.

Smiling sweetly at the doorman, she added with polished diplomacy, "Let's examine this another way. If you do *not* announce me to the captain, and he finds out you're responsible for this negligence, what do you suppose will happen to your position here?"

The doorman's eyes flicked between Jim and Grace, his bravado evaporating. "Very well. Wait here, the both of you." The glass doors whooshed behind him, sucking the club's secrets back inside.

"Thank you, Jim, for defending me," she said, and Jim's spine lengthened at her compliment. "And I know you could trounce that man with one blow, if it came to it."

Through the glass doors, a rush of shadows burst into the sunlight. Seamus froze in all his towering glory. His blond head was bare, his hat forgotten in his haste. Uncle Farfar blustered through the doors a moment later. He halted beside Seamus, both like statues.

Grace stirred first, stepping forward to gently place her hand on the lapel of Seamus's jacket. At her touch, his rigid disbelief exploded in a rush of breath, and he crushed her to his chest. Grace, encased in the safety of his embrace, was unable to stem the prickle of tears she had valiantly kept in check. Her hot sobbing soaked his shirt front.

A gentle hand stroked her head. "Aah, my darling niece," said Uncle Farfar.

Grace buried her face into Seamus and inhaled the heady aromas of his freshly laundered shirt, spicy brandy, and that familiar scent of *him*—the bouquet she never tired of breathing in. Sniffing, she peered up. He looked worn out. Dark smudges and deep-set furrows marred his clear, blue eyes, but the fanning creases in the corners of his mouth deepened as he grinned in awe.

"Are you all right, Dulcinea?" he whispered, inspecting her. She knew she looked a mess, but she did not care.

"I am now," she breathed, tightening her grip on his forearms.

Grace caught a movement over Seamus's shoulder as the

dapper doorman waggled his frowning brow at Jim and hissed, "Why didn't you announce her as *Admiral Baxter's niece?*"

"Bugger off, ye dolt," growled Jim. "Go play in yer land of brandy sippers."

Exhaling loudly, the doorman doffed his hat and stepped into the safety of the club, no doubt off to gossip with the maître d' about the prodigal lady who had returned.

"Christ, Grace!" Seamus squeezed her tightly, his breath hot and urgent in her ear. "I've been going half-mad trying to find you. Where've you been?"

"Silverton had me prisoner." Grace winced as Seamus thrust her back, his eyes crazed with rage and bewilderment.

"But I went there asking for you!"

"I know you did. He had me locked in the cellar the day you came. The maid let slip you were there." Her voice trembled. "Oh, Seamus, I nearly died with despair having you so near but unable to reach you."

He crushed her to him again. "Christ alive! Had I known, I'd never have left. You must believe me. I'd have torn the place apart to find you."

"I know you would. I screamed myself hoarse and nearly broke my shoulder trying to barge my way out. But it was no use." The nerves that Grace had held in check loosened, and she began to tremble.

Seamus flagged down a passing carriage. With a fond farewell smile to Jim, Grace climbed in. She was glad to be seated and hidden from the stares of curious onlookers. Seamus twisted on the bench to face her, his knuckles gently brushing her cheek as though to check she was real.

"My heart. I employed a dozen men to search for you. There isn't a ship's hold, tavern or warehouse that has not been examined in the effort to find you."

"O'Reilly—the woman who took me—docked at a rotted

jetty further down the river. With no one about, I couldn't call for help."

"O'Reilly's a woman?" Seamus's blond brows shot up.

"You can't tell by looking at her, but yes, she's a woman. She's the master of that brigantine I saw the day Gilly was killed. The bald man who led the search party is her husband and"—Grace slid her hand over Seamus's to brace him for the next bit of news—"Tibbot is their son."

Seamus tipped his neck back, his eyes squeezed tight. Righting his head, he pressed his lips into a thin, white line. "Yes. I suspected he had something to do with your disappearance. And Holburton finally followed through on his threats to rid you. A bunch of bad apples, the lot of them. Though, Silverton's been careful to ensure he has no connection to them."

"You were right about showing Holburton leniency. I'm sorry for challenging you on the matter." A hot bloom of guilt and misery crept up Grace's décolletage. "And you resigned your commission because of me? Seamus, it's too great a sacrifice!"

Seamus ran a gentle finger along her jawline, a spark refreshing his tired eyes. "No, Dulcinea. It isn't."

"The *Discerning*'s crew were right. I've disrupted the course of nearly everyone I've crossed paths with."

Uncle Farfar cleared his throat. "Come now, my darling. If anyone's to blame, it's that bastard, Silverton."

At the mention of his name, Grace shuddered. She squeezed her thumb and forefinger tight against her eyelids, seeing sparkles when she released them. "There's something I must tell you," she whispered. "I've killed Silverton."

"Christ Almighty!" Seamus stiffened.

"Good God!" burst Uncle Farfar.

Grace searched Seamus's face for any trace of condemnation as he crushed her hand. "The right was yours, Dulcinea. If you hadn't done it, then I would!"

"Do you wish to tell us of it?" asked Uncle Farfar with a nod.

"Killing a man isn't easy. Sometimes this burden is eased by sharing it."

"He took me to a secluded glade beside Highgate Pond." She flicked her eyes at Seamus.

His nostrils flared at her unspoken implication.

"When he rolled upon me, I stuck him in the kidneys. An impressed man aboard O'Reilly's ship armed me with a bone knife." Grace took a breath, pinching the tip of her nose to quell the tears. "O'Reilly killed Travis Hopwood and Jack Blight. And I believe Silverton disposed of his maid who told me about you. You can't imagine how awful I feel having the deaths of more innocents on my conscience."

Seamus held her gaze in an unblinking look of admiration. "You took what measures were needed to protect yourself when you could."

"Silverton tried to get up, but he collapsed. There was so much blood." Grace curled her fingers closed to hide the dried brown smears on her palm. "I heard his last breath. It sounded just like … like Gilly when he—" A swelling sob cut off her words, and Seamus rubbed a hand across her back.

"I'll send a couple of men over to the pond to clean up." Seamus sounded so sure and so unworried that some of the tension in Grace's shoulders eased.

"Won't the authorities question Silverton's servants about his disappearance? What if I'm implicated?" Grace unclenched her fingers and curled them around Seamus's long, clean ones. He squeezed back reassuringly.

"Silverton isn't the only one with connections in this town." Seamus's warm voice was a balm to Grace's fraught nerves. "It's London's worst-kept secret that Silverton's staff all began their employ with him under less than illustrious circumstances. Dickson might be clever enough to have side-stepped the law—for now—but the man's an out-and-out smuggler. With enough coin in the right hands, I could extract the sort of information that would persuade Dickson and those other rogues to hold their tongues. Besides, it shan't be hard to make Silverton's death look like a crooked deal gone wrong." He lightly brushed her cheek with his thumb. "Don't trouble yourself about it."

Grace sniffed. "What about the Admiralty? Silverton's convinced you'll be disgraced."

"Ah, you leave that worry to me," said Uncle Farfar. "I'll do my utmost to remind my counterparts how Fitzwilliam saved the lives of over a dozen men. God knows what would've happened to Burns's crew. With a more affirming tale circulating, I hazard it won't be long before another commission comes his way. Plus, the charts Wadham delivered have expounded Fitzwilliam's excellence. He's not a commodity to be so easily dismissed."

Grace glanced back and forth between the blue eyes and the pink face of the two men who loved her unconditionally. Drawing strength from their offers of support, Grace took an invigorating breath and glanced out of the carriage window. The air lodged in her throat, and she frowned, turning to Uncle Farfar. "Where are we going?"

"We must advise your parents of your return," said Uncle Farfar softly.

"I don't wish to see them."

Uncle Farfar gave her knee an avuncular pat. "Now, poppet, surely you don't wish them to be broadsided by the news through the rumour mill?"

Seamus nodded at Uncle Farfar, his voice dry with seriousness. "The admiral is correct. Delicate matters such as these need to be approached head on."

Uncle Farfar's eyes softened. "I'll introduce Captain Fitzwilliam to your parents. Their relief at seeing you safely returned will no doubt earn him their undying gratitude. I'll do my utmost to convince them of the suitability of your marriage to him."

Anticipating her parents' inevitable antipathy, Grace crossed her arms, doubtful of her uncle's success.

"Your parents might be prickly and rigid in their ways, but trust that they've your best interests at heart," offered Uncle Farfar gently. "Let's do things in proper order. Keep the peace, hmm?"

The black carriage pulled up outside Wallace House, and Grace gathered her skirts for the dismount.

The incessant ticking of the grandfather clock in the hall punctuated the obstinate silence in the parlour. Mother coughed pointedly, and Grace swivelled her eyes towards her purse-lipped face.

"Well, young lady." Mother's clipped tones were as tight as the bun into which her hair was drawn. "What have you to say for yourself?"

Grace noticed with satisfaction that her scum-coated boots had left a smear on Mother's prized woollen rug. She raised her chin, meeting Mother's glare head on. "What would you have me say?"

"Explain the downfall of your virtue, for starters." Two red spots of agitation irritated Mother's usually creamy complexion.

"You mean how Lord Silverton attempted to force himself on me after informing me of our betrothal? A fact you neglected to advise me!" Grace bristled.

"Advise you!" Father exploded from his seat, his salt-and-pepper head shaking. "As your father, it is my right and duty to match you with a suitable husband. Such frivolities as your opinion don't enter into the equation." His indignant snort reminded Grace of a bull she had seen at the market earlier.

Mother interjected. "How dare you besmirch Lord Silverton!" Her voice rose an octave. "You opened your legs for that filthy stable boy but accuse a gentleman of being the perpetrator?"

Seamus launched to his feet. "Lady Flint!" His dry authority cut Mother short. "I insist you refrain from issuing such vulgar accusations against my fiancée." Seamus's face was deadly calm. Grace knew the look well.

"Your fiancée?" The tip of Mother's sharp nose reddened. "You would ruin your name by admitting to having relations with her?"

Seamus's icy blue glare chilled the room by several degrees. "Lord Flint, caution your wife to tread softly with my wife-to-be."

Grace blinked in confusion as Father meekly settled back down. *By the bells of Old Bailey!* Her Father had no stomach for confrontation. He had dominated her all her life and yet cowered at the slightest challenge from another man.

Uncle Farfar snapped. "Yvette! Muzzle your mouth, you poisonous asp! Grant the child a chance to explain herself!"

Seamus edged over to Grace and placed a hand on her shoulder, a dependable lifeline. "Please, Miss Baxter, tell your parents the truth of the matter." Seamus glared at Mother, and Grace saw her defiance waver.

Grace elucidated the series of events that began on the night of the dinner party, and concluded with her stabbing Silverton. The incendiary pit of fury burning within enabled her to complete the whole story with stoic bravery. Seamus's fingers gripped her shoulder during the retelling of her time aboard O'Reilly's barbaric ship. At the mention of Silverton's second attempted assault upon her arrival at Clovervale Manor, Seamus's hand vibrated on her shoulder.

When she was done, Uncle Farfar coughed thickly. "Good God, girl! You would've made a worthy Royal Marine with that spirit and bravery."

Father made a derisive noise. "Gets that from her father, no doubt."

Mother rallied on the sofa, frowning. "Now husband, you

need not dredge up that business again. Especially before *guests*." The agitated spots reappeared.

Uncle Farfar's voice held a cautionary note. "Cornelius. Enough."

Father paled, stepped over to the drinks cart, and downed a sizeable brandy. Clanging the crystal tumbler on the silver tray, he turned and spoke from the relative safety of the other side of the room. "Damned right it's enough! Mother and daughter alike. Both intent on ruining my family's name. Not even a decent upbringing was enough to prevent either of you from opening your legs to all and sundry."

Seamus stepped threateningly towards Father. "I caution you, sir. One more caustic word against Miss Baxter, and you'll leave me no option but to defend her honour."

Father puffed out his chest. "Perhaps avail yourself of the full truth of the matter, Captain, before issuing any challenge."

"Of what truth do you speak, sir?" demanded Seamus.

What truth indeed? Grace wondered.

Seamus continued, "This is a perplexing and insidious conversation in light of the tragic events surrounding your daughter. I demand you explain yourself."

Father barked abrasively, pouring another brandy. "I'm not the one who should be explaining, Captain You should ask Grace's father—the high and mighty Admiral Baxter." The empty brandy glass clanged again.

Mother let out a squeal. "Cornelius! Shut your mouth, damn you."

Grace flinched at Mother's colourful choice of words. Uncle Farfar glanced at Grace, his eyes filled with resignation, a tender smile tugging at his lips.

"My brother speaks the truth, Grace. I'm your natural father."

Grace flinched again. "Pard— How?"

"When your mother and father were courting, your mother

and I entered a foolish dalliance after an overindulgence of wine."

Grace barely heard the derisory grunt from the man near the drinks cart.

Uncle Farfar's face tensed. "It was a mistake I swore never to repeat. However, when your mother discovered she was with child, we had to confess our digression to your fath—to Lord Flint." A mixture of pity and guilt mingled on Uncle Farfar's face as he glanced over at his brother, who was staring sullenly into another glass of amber liquid. "Despite our betrayal, he knew your mother couldn't endure being a navy wife and upheld his offer to have her hand in marriage."

Stiff and pale, Mother tutted. "It was my father's money that lured him into the marriage, not the opportunity to rescue my virtue."

"Just as it was Father's money that lured Silverton into wanting to marry me," spat Grace.

Mother sagged back in her chair with an indignant squeak.

Uncle Farfar fixed his gaze on Grace. "Despite everything, Lord and Lady Flint civilly allowed me to be a part of your life." His mouth softened in a smile. "I must confess, poppet, you've brought me unimaginable joy."

Grace frowned at Uncle Farfar, waves of dismay and uncertainty rippling through her. "Don't *poppet* me! If I meant so much to you, why didn't you object to my betrothal to Lord Silverton? You admitted knowing of his reputation!" Angry tears simmered on the edges of her eyelashes.

Uncle Farfar's gaze flicked guiltily to the carpet. "The arrangement was that I didn't interfere." He looked up, his soft, grey eyes full of remorse. "I couldn't bear not being a part of your life. I kept quiet to keep the peace. But I assure you, had you come to me to plead the end of your betrothal, I would have addressed the issue with my brother." He swivelled a hard gaze between Mother and Father. "Though God knows what you two are like once a decision is strengthened by your unification on the matter."

The ticking grandfather clock filled the silence again, its slow pace clashing with Grace's thumping heart. "Is that why you hate me, Father?" Four heads swung in her direction. She fixed her eyes on Lord Flint, who was glowering at his brother with contempt, an expression that did not diminish as he turned to look sullenly out of the window.

Lord Flint's right cheek twitched—his silence answer enough.

Grace regarded Mother, her chest brimming with pain. "And you, Mother? Is that why *you* hate me so?"

Mother's sharp features frowned in puzzlement. "I don't hate you, Grace. Whatever gave you that notion?"

"You never showed me any warmth or compassion."

Mother looked even more perplexed. "What have warmth and compassion to do with mothering? You had the best nannies and governesses. Not to mention the finest clothes and excellent food."

Grace blinked back burning tears. "But what about love?"

Mother sniffed dismissively. "You've been reading too many works of fiction. Motherhood has nothing to do with love. A mother's duty is to make the best provision for her offspring. You certainly weren't left wanting."

A wail of despair erupted from deep inside Grace. "I wanted you to love me—*both* of you. No matter how good or polite I was, it was never enough for you. It's why I stopped bothering."

"Well, Grace, I did my best." Mother's voice held little warmth or conviction. "I did for you as my mother did for me. It did me no harm. It can't be helped if you filled your head with silly notions of idyllic childhoods. God knows Arthur's sentimental attachment to you was taxing enough. He spoiled you rotten."

"He showed me love!" Grace's voice rose, and Seamus's warm hand glided across her nape.

"Perhaps you're right." Mother's grim features hardened. "If I'd been a more attentive mother, you'd not have had the liberty of fraternising with the servants' children, and we wouldn't be in this mess."

"What are you implying, Mother?"

"If you weren't so familiar with the servants, you'd not have rushed to that boy in the stables at the first sign of trouble. It was a private matter and should have stayed within the family." Mother's half-finished cup rattled on the saucer as she slid it onto the side table. "We could have covered it up without any fuss, but your sneaking to that boy caused a public scandal, discrediting our family name."

Grace darted from her chair like a hornet smoked from its nest. Seamus caught her arm as she flailed angrily. Summoning a filthy insult to mind, Grace shrieked, "You beard splitter! You would happily marry me off to that despicable bastard and turn a blind eye to his abuse." Mother inhaled sharply. "I hate you!" squalled Grace.

"Pah!" Lord Flint swayed before the significantly emptier brandy decanter. "I've had enough of this foul-mouthed drivel. I'm leaving for the club." He tottered off unsteadily without a backward glance.

Mother raised her upturned nose. "With language like that, it's no wonder you fitted in with a crew of filthy sailors." She stood, unapologetically ignoring Grace's boiling tears of anger. "I too grow weary of these histrionics." With stiff-backed dignity, Mother glided across the parlour and turned at the door. "You needn't worry, Grace. We shan't breathe a word about what you did to Lord Silverton. God knows you've already inflicted enough shame on this family. I'm not sure we could ever redeem ourselves in society if word got out that you were instrumental in his death." She gripped the door handle tightly, squaring her shoulders. "Take your little sailor boy and see yourselves out. Oh, and Grace dear, since you've clearly chosen the unhappy alternative of being a stranger to us, you need not trouble yourself to return to this house." Lady Flint strutted out after her husband.

Grace dropped to the sofa, thumping her fists against her knees. "Cursed rats' tails and stinking bloody seaweed! What a fool I am! Believing all these years that I could win my parents' love." She wiped the back of her hand across her runny nose. "Perhaps that shrew is right. I foolishly accepted that rubbish in literature about finding happiness."

Seamus brushed away a strand of damp hair plastered to her cheek and tucked it behind her ear, his voice deep and reassuring. "No, Dulcinea, don't be discouraged about finding happiness. You've the heart of a lioness. You're fierce and brave and capable of delivering and receiving abundant love."

Uncle Farfar rubbed comforting circles on her back. "He's right. I don't regret what happened, because I created you. You're my greatest achievement, my darling Grace. Nothing compares to the fatherly love burning in my heart."

Seamus coughed politely, his mouth twitching as he peered at Uncle Farfar. "Begging your pardon, sir. I challenge that statement. Does the love of a future husband not transcend that of a father?"

Uncle Farfar's stern face softened, and both men respectfully dipped their heads at one another. The shards of Grace's shattered heart drew into place, magnetised by the strength of the two men beside her.

"Rightio then." Uncle Farfar slapped his thigh. "Let's get you out of this miserable ice palace." He caught Seamus's eye. "There's the urgent matter of having Billy Sykes's conviction overturned. The boy is innocent, and it's immoral for us to keep new information that can prove his innocence."

"Billy?" sniffed Grace. "Can you bring him back from Port Jackson?"

"Port Jackson? Good God, no," blustered Uncle Farfar. "Sykes is in Newgate Prison still awaiting transportation."

Grace inhaled sharply. "He's here? Billy's in London?" Rubbed her nose across the back of her sleeve again, she turned to her uncle. "Uncle, will you really have Billy freed?"

"Of course, poppet." Uncle Farfar reached into his breast pocket and handed her his handkerchief. "It's my civic duty to see that an innocent boy isn't sent to the colonies. The fact that the boy is your friend weighs heavily in his favour. Don't worry. I'll use absolute discretion. The magistrate owes me a favour." Grace threw her arms around Uncle Farfar's wide neck, ignoring the prickles of his afternoon stubble as she peppered him with kisses.

Seamus stood, offering Grace his hand. She slid her fingers into his warm palm, and he bent, his soft lips brushing her knuckles. "Come, Dulcinea. It's time to go home."

Chapter Thirty-Three

S eamus strode briskly along the oak-panelled hall in the south wing of the Admiralty, his footsteps upon the summer-sky-blue carpet muted like the stealthy steps of a cat. Somewhere down the thickly carpeted corridor, the low-key chimes of a clock measured midday. Stopping before a glossy varnished door, he rapped on the wood.

"Enter!"

Seamus stepped into Admiral Samuel Courtney's office, the sunny yellow wallpaper doing little to revive his spirits. Passing the Chesterfield lounge, he stopped smartly before his former superior officer's wide desk inlaid with maroon leather that matched the bold carpet. The walls were surrounded with various naval scenes, and Seamus wondered whether any were of the action Courtney had seen. Standing at attention, Seamus found himself under the stern scrutiny of Courtney's intelligent eyes.

Alongside Fincham and Baxter, Courtney had taught Seamus most of what he knew about being an officer.

"Ah, Fitzwilliam." The familiar, pleasant waft of mint and brandy emanated from the man behind the desk. His mentor's once dark brown hair was ashen with age. "Please sit. I'd be glad to see you, were it under more pleasant circumstances."

"Yes, sir." The leather seat squeaked as Seamus sat.

Courtney pushed his brandy glass away and leaned back into his chair, his fingers steepled against his lips. "Fitzwilliam, I've liked you from the minute I met you as a fresh-faced lad all those years ago on the deck of the *Windfall*. I had thought you a sharp sort with a straight head on your shoulders." Courtney dropped his hands to the tabletop. "But Christ, man! What were you thinking? Throwing in your career to chase after a woman like a lovesick pup?"

Courtney's quick brown eyes regarded him a beat longer than was comfortable, and Seamus fixed his eyes to the panelling behind Courtney's head. His heart pounded loudly in his ears, and his intestines shrank in humiliation. Heavens above! The last time he had felt like this, he was a five-year-old standing in his father's library. He knew that delivering up his commission had potentially corrupted his status and reputation, but there had been no other choice. Not as far as he was concerned.

Seamus stiffened. "Pardon me, sir, but that's of a delicate and personal nature that involves my fiancée." He stared at the wooden panels again.

Courtney inhaled sharply. "God knows I've no right to force you to answer." He rose and poured a second generous brandy at the drinks cart, handing it to Seamus. "But indulge me. Just how did you discover her?"

Seamus flexed the wrist of his right hand, the tension in his old knife injury clicking with release. The long-faced man before him had been invaluable to Seamus during his years of study, but he was also deeply entrenched in the system. Seamus continued cautiously, "We'd just crossed the equator when Miss Baxter's presence aboard the *Discerning* came to light. She was stripped to be flogged for insubordination."

"Good God. What an interesting turn that must have been. What was she doing aboard the *Discerning* in the first place?" asked Courtney.

"An attack on her person caused her to flee London for her safety. She fled under obscurity, disguised in men's clothing. The late Mr McGilney mistook her for a new joiner and signed her up."

"Ah, yes. Her disappearance caused quite a scandal around here, especially when they found her belongings in those stables. It's a jolly good thing they have the scoundrel locked up."

Seamus clenched his jaw. He was loathed to correct him and tell him that it was not Billy Sykes who had attacked Grace but rather Silverton. The risk that Courtney would be one of those who took Silverton's side on societal principle was not one he was willing to take. He took a large swill of brandy, appreciating the distraction of the burn of alcohol down his throat.

"Indeed, sir." Seamus waited a beat before continuing, "Captain Fincham, God rest his soul, was most disconcerted with having Admiral Baxter's niece aboard. So I offered to take her under my protection, as well as pay all her expenses. After Captain Fincham died, we were too far south to warrant turning back to Montevideo to drop Miss Baxter ashore. As commander of the *Discerning*, I decided it prudent to continue with our orders until such time as I was instructed otherwise."

"Not before you tried to marry her first, I heard?" said Courtney.

"That's correct, sir. I wanted to shield her honour and give her the protection of my name."

"Good God, what is it with you naval commanders and marrying your women in secret? Cochrane did it too." Courtney shook his head. "Sentimental codswallop is what it is."

Seamus stiffened at the slight. "Alas, the ceremony was interrupted when the locals stole a cutter."

"Did you retrieve His Majesty's property?" Courtney dipped his chin, peering at Seamus through his lashes. The early afternoon sun painted the walls of Courtney's office a deeper sunflower gold.

"No, sir. It cost me the life of one of my men. I didn't dare risk another."

Courtney shook his head minutely. "What then?"

"We eventually returned to Montevideo to restock. I arranged for Miss Baxter to remain with Lord Ponsonby. He was to place her on the next ship back to England."

"But this didn't transpire?"

"No, sir. I found out that there were merchantmen after her for a reward offered by Lord Silverton. She'd been betrothed to him before she left London."

"Surely this was the most expedient solution for her to be returned to England?"

"Yes, sir, but not under those circumstances."

"What circumstances? Silverton's betrothal? Would a letter to his lordship accompanying your fiancée's return not have cleared up any misgivings?"

"I didn't wish my fiancée to have to face him," bristled Seamus, leaning forward. Resting his elbows on his knees, he fiddled with his scarred wrist.

"So, it was selfish indulgence and jealousy of a rival that saw you keep her aboard?" Courtney did not sound impressed.

Seamus bit the inside of his cheek, and the warm tang of blood coated his tongue. *Keep your head.* Fixing his eyes on Courtney's stony face, he wore the accusations with good grace. "Yes, sir."

"What happened then?"

"I was ashore, surveying the lay of the land, when Miss Baxter was taken from the *Discerning* by a prize hunter."

"What did that little lark cost the *Discerning?*"

A twinge of regret tightened the muscles between Seamus's shoulder blades. "We lost four men, sir. Two were killed in the ensuing kidnapping, and two fled with the kidnappers."

"Tell me you at least laid chase?"

"Yes, sir. We were attacked. I couldn't let them go without a fight. We damaged her main yardarm, but we lost her when we stopped for Captain Burns and his frostbitten lot."

"That's the only redemptive bit of this tale!" grunted Courtney. "Your illogical resignation to chase a skirt all the way back to London is what I find the most disagreeable." He snorted. "I don't suppose Silverton envisaged Miss Baxter having the gall to run off to sea?"

"No, sir." Seamus levelled his eyes with Courtney's. "About Lord Silverton, sir. Have you news of his whereabouts?" Seamus's question jammed in his throat like a cherry pit.

After Grace had stabbed Silverton beside Highgate Pond, believing him killed, Seamus had taken Buchanan and Hicks with him to discreetly clear the murder scene. They were greeted by a blackened stain of blood, her rumpled red shawl, and the leather-bound handle of the bone knife Grace had used. But no body.

Courtney frowned. "Slunk off to Paris, last I heard. Declared London no longer safe after being set upon by highwaymen and stabbed."

Seamus's breath juddered out of him. *Christ Almighty! He's alive!* His surge of fury collided with relief. Fury because he wanted Silverton dead for his callous disregard of Grace's well-being that had left her soul scarred; and relief that he might get to see Silverton's bulbous face when he killed him himself.

Twisting his lips wryly, Courtney added, "No doubt to also lick his wounds after having his betrothed swiped from under his nose."

"No doubt, sir," said Seamus. Heavens! Silverton's lie about being attacked was far more heroic than admitting he had been overpowered by a woman. Fat bastard's ego could not bear such shame. Seamus would not—could not—tell Grace he was still alive. Believing Silverton dead had freed her from perpetually looking over her shoulder. She had confessed that even her nightmares had lessened. Seamus was loathed to destroy the new peace that had settled over her. As long as the lecherous toad stayed in Paris, Grace was safe enough in London.

Seamus's wandering mind snapped to attention as Courtney rose and stepped around his desk. "The Admiralty isn't so lenient when it comes to matters of the heart. Your duty is first and foremost to King and Country." The silhouetted man wore a glowing halo from the window behind him, and Seamus was pleased not to be able to see his expressions clearly.

With his gut swooping as though he were dropping over a thirty-foot wave, he rose stiffly, drawing his shoulders back. "Yes, sir. I accept my naval career is done."

"Never say never." Courtney took a deep breath, his tongue toying with the corner of his mouth. "You were one of my most promising recruits, but you've well and truly tarnished your name, Fitzwilliam. Best keep your head low and your nose clean for now."

Seamus's irritation prickled at Courtney's scolding. It had been a long day, and he wanted to go home. "I understand your disappointment, sir, and I'm sorry for my part in it."

Courtney rubbed one eyebrow, regret heavy in his words. "Me too, my boy. Me too." He nodded in dismissal.

Spinning stiff-backed, Seamus marched swiftly from the room, the prickle of sweat at his hairline cooling. Shaking off the swell of disappointment at having upset Courtney, Seamus weighed up what really mattered—having Grace back, and his life intact to remain by her side.

Back at Abertarff House, Seamus froze in the hallway as Grace swept down the stairs cloaked in her red shawl. After he had retrieved it from the pond, he had scrubbed the stains of mud and blood out with his own hands. Grace had wept with relief and joy when he presented it to her, wrapping it tenderly about her and pinning it in place with the Luckenbooth brooch.

With nowhere else for Grace to go since being expelled from her parent's house, she was staying at his townhouse on the guest floor. With only his naval accommodation and his room at the club, Admiral Baxter was unable to put her up. What did it matter to have her share his roof and add to the black marks society had already drawn against them? People already assumed the worst, and there was no undoing that now.

"You're back." Her smile of welcome was one he relished, and her spirited greeting penetrated his gloom like a shaft of sunlight slicing through thundery clouds.

Seamus turned his back to her to hang his coat and hat. He dipped his chin and shivered as she ran her small hand up the middle of his back, her gentleness erasing the weight of Courtney's reproach. Taking a deep breath, he turned and caught her hands in his. Meeting her green gaze, he braced for judgment but found only tenderness.

"Was it as bad as you imagined?" she whispered.

He nodded stiffly. "I'm glad it's over." He drew her to him, burying his face in her lavender-powdered curls. "It's been a long day." He pulled back, tipping up her chin with one finger. Her aquamarine eyes were filled with a mix of relief and empathy. "Know that were I given the choice, I'd make the same decision again. To come and find you," he whispered. "Nothing will *ever* stop me finding you, Dulcinea."

"You're quite the poetic Don Quixote. Am I still an object of hopeless devotion and unrequited love?" she quipped. The amusement in her voice trailed as he dipped his head lower.

He gently kissed her soft, pink lips and breathed in her fragrance. The bewitching tang and salty lure of the ocean was nothing compared to the magnificent mingling of lavender and soap and—*her*. The smell of home. "Unrequited no more."

"Do you suffer for it?" she whispered.

His heart lurched at the intensity of her gaze. "I love you without understanding where it began because, Christ knows, I wasn't searching for it."

The smile on her lips widened. "Love? What happened to admiration?"

Chuckling, he said, "My love for you is shaped by many things. I'm so glad I found it. Found *you*."

A look of wonder danced across her face. "Gilly was a wise man. He always said you can build on the deeds that have happened or put the catastrophes behind you and begin again."

Laying his hands on the swell of Grace's hips, Seamus rested his forehead against hers. "I can't imagine anything finer than starting again with you by my side, Dulcinea."

ALSO BY EMMA LOMBARD

Bonus Scene

You're invited to Seamus and Grace's wedding! Read a bonus scene before continuing the adventure in *Grace on the Horizon* (The White Sail Series, Book Two).

https://www.emmalombardauthor.com/bonus-wedding-scene

If you enjoyed *Discerning Grace*, come join my crew! Subscribe to my newsletter at www.EmmaLombardAuthor.com for behind the scenes shenanigans, fun giveaways, and a first look at future book releases.

OTHER BOOKS FROM EMMA LOMBARD

Grace on the Horizon

The White Sails Series, Book Two

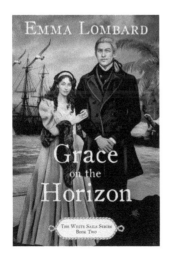

Cast adrift on a raft of shame in 1830s London society, Grace once again seeks sanctuary at sea. But someone aboard the *Clover* keeps sabotaging the life she is attempting to build with Seamus. Will Grace discover who it is before he destroys her completely?

Grace Arising

Book Three of The White Sails Series

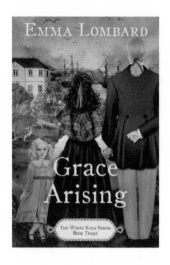

A new clipper ship means a new adventure. With Seamus gravely injured, and the First Mate an incompetent risk-taker, it's up to Grace to see the crew and her family to safety. Can she reach the New Holland wool market ahead of their competitors, and in time to save Seamus's life?

9 780645 105803